Black Light

Christian Tremain

Local Legend Publishing UK

ISBN 978-1-907203-02-2

Local Legend Publishing
Park Issa
St Martin's Road
Gobowen, Shropshire
SY11 3NP, UK
www.local-legend.co.uk

Cover Design by Titanium Design
www.titaniumdesign.co.uk

Cover illustration courtesy of
HAAP Media   All rights reserved

For my parents

Thanks to Leslie, at Artellus, for her valuable advice regarding the early draft of this book.
And special thanks to the nine friends who kept me smiling.

Table of Contents

Prologue

The pavement underfoot felt real enough, but of course she knew better. As she patrolled through the downtown avenue of skyscrapers the lingering heat from the dying sun caressed the back of her neck, the sun-warmed asphalt beneath her bare soles soothing but forewarning her to remain on guard. *Wall Street at the end of time.* At least it looked like Wall Street. Having never been to New York she couldn't be sure, but thought she recognised the impressive canyon of concrete towers stretching for the heavens as those that constituted the nation's financial heart.

After careful scrutiny of her surroundings she concluded it was vacant of life, long departed before her arrival in the wake of those that preceded her to the desolate cityscape. She had been in this place many times before, and though these particular streets were alien and unknown to her, this new world of which it was a part had become her home. Except this time things were different. Aware that the rules had changed she quickened her pace towards whatever had summoned her there. Since accepting the key all those years before she suddenly felt as though she walked blindfolded for the first time.

The only companion in the barren void was the spectral reflection that mirrored her procession in the glass frontage of the deserted buildings which funnelled her along with the low, molten sunlight. Her dress was the same. It was always the same. The long ethereal gown in flawless white, complimented by bobbed blonde hair and childhood notions of divinity. On those streets however it only reinforced her fear she was now a stranger in a strange place.

With every step her elongated shadow seemingly mocked her with its mechanical march on the asphalt before her, but soon its solitary parade must end. *They* had brought her here, their motives unknown but tempting her ever onwards as she searched for the courage she imagined she would possess in such an encounter. Ignoring her growing trepidation she evoked the otherworldly power that animated her current form. It would give her the strength she needed to face her demons, or so she prayed.

The end of the street converged with four other identical avenues at an intersection. Reaching the end of the journey she strode to its centre, an open invitation to who ever had summoned her there.

"Show yourself!" she yelled. Her voice echoed for miles as it faded into the abandoned streets, but silence was her answer. "I am here! Answer me!" she petitioned again. The demand felt hollow in the vast arena, but she knew They listened. "Don't tell me you are afraid." The taunt was brave, though it betrayed her own brooding sense of doom. *Surely there is a reason why I am here.* Instinct urged her to turn and look up to the large electronic bill boards perched on the outer walls of the giant citadels overshadowing the intersection. *I know you're here.* The centre screen was suddenly brought to life by the large neon words that crawled across it.

Do you know who this is?

The cryptic question appeared for a second then was gone. The young woman, confused, chose her reply carefully.

"You are nothing!" she yelled in response, the venom with which she spoke surprising herself. The blonde visitor refused to take the bait. "Why have you summoned me here? Is this the extent of your power; to play games?" For a second it appeared there would be no reply, until the anonymous words reappeared.

Angelica, we know you.

Again the words disappeared before delivering the following threat.

Beware the shadows of dusk Angelica.

The repeated use of her name was like a twisting of the knife. *They know my name. The time has come to end this,* she thought, before the screen continued.

For we are nowhere, it declared then paused, *but we are everywhere!* Angelica felt the veil of reality stir around her. Something was coming. Turning from the electronic discourse she gazed around to see the once cold, dead surroundings were no longer void of life, but were seething with it.

As the molten sun finally set below the horizon it left behind a void of living shadows. All around her, human shapes were now forcing their conspiring limbs towards their prey through the intangible fabric of the counterfeit surroundings, taking form from the very walls and the streets that were now a writhing cabal of arms, legs and wretched faces. She stepped back, realising she was surrounded. The twisted forms of living asphalt were consolidating their strength and now slithered toward her like an army of malicious serpents. *It's a trap.*

Underfoot she felt the street move. She stared down at the fingers of tar clawing at the milk white skin of her unprotected feet. There was nowhere to run. Fear paralysing her sacrosanct form Angelica looked up to see the screen reveal its final mockery.

Have a nice day.

Chapter 1

The light rain was warm as it fell onto the young man's face. It was the first time that he had been in this garden but the scent of the freshly cut lawn reminded him of those innocent, long gone days of his youth. He couldn't remember the last time the world had felt so real though risked its loss by slowly opening his eyes to invite them to join in the revelation. It *was* possible to feel happiness again. The night sky above drew his gaze as the clouds parted to reveal a stellar canvas that stretched from horizon to horizon. At that point the awe struck voyeur wondered how had it been so easy to forget the world, even in its simplicity, could be so beautiful. Though not ready to shut out this vision, he let himself be drawn back under, back into the womb of his mind as he resealed his eyes and etched the vision upon his memory.

"So Cantonese or Thai?" a woman's voice asked, its familiarity now making him glance to his left. She was smiling, that mischievous smile that came from the pleasure of catching him red handed again. "What's it to be Smokey? You're shouting a meal tonight remember?" Her hazel eyes sparkled with the secret enjoyment of his struggle to give up the filthy vice for the third time.

"You're holding me to ransom over one lousy puff, and I gotta decide as well!" he exclaimed jokingly. He had never gotten used to her driving him around; his Conservative mid west upbringing had imparted an old fashioned code of masculine/feminine roles that meant living by some prehistoric ideal. But that was what he loved about Sarah, she freed him from his past, a past he felt he no longer needed. But it was all to be stolen from him again.

"Look out!" The warning shot fired from his mouth but the danger was already upon them. He had seen the brown sedan drive up to the intersection but, turning away to answer his wife's tease; he hadn't seen its lack of intention to stop.

"Josh!" Her last word was cut short as the impact of the stolen car crushed her to death. In a split second the darkness returned and Josh woke with a start.

The electronic bleeping of the bedside alarm clock did its job hideously well. Dragging a limp arm out from under the damp sheets Josh brought it down hard onto the snooze button, inadvertently knocking over a plastic container in the vicinity before he rolled onto his back. It was seven thirty AM, Monday and another utopian Los Angeles morning.

The stinging sensation in his eyes caused him to blink several times before he realised he had been crying again in his sleep. In the past two years the words morning and mourning had become synonymous, though instead of the usual melancholy he felt after reliving the dream he just felt numb. This morning there was another reason to push the past to the back of his mind and face the day.

Blearily, Josh stared up at the ceiling. Relaxing his vision he allowed his mind to create faces and pictures from the imperfections in the paint, brought to life by the early rays that sneaked in through the bedroom blinds. The distraction was a voluntary one; he knew all too well just how inescapable time and fate were. Turning his head to check the green digits on the bedside clock he recalled what cruel companions each had been in the past two years. Several minutes were lost in this abyss of squandered existence before reluctantly he tossed the covers aside and swung his legs onto the floor, minutes away from being late for the rescheduled appointment downtown. For a second he was tempted to stay, just a few seconds more, but reminding himself of what lay ahead he found the motivation he needed to shake the nightmares from his hair and leave both the bed and the dark cloud of depression behind.

The approaching anniversary of his first year of unemployment was incentive enough to claw back what was left of his life. The memories of the promising architectural career at Cohen and Pierce were now a distant dream, seemingly implanted to ridicule his obvious demise onto the breadline. Two years previous the real life car crash had destroyed his will to live in a flash of crumpled steel and crushed organs. *Five months suspended sentence, son of a bitch should have fried.* From that hot July morning onwards the gradual fall from grace had slowly poisoned his prestigious career, until it too had withered alongside his soul. *Why Sarah? Why not me?* he'd asked.

The depth of this fall from grace was no more apparent than in the previous week's walk into the Glendale branch of Eat-A-Lot, where he'd enquired about the staff vacancy in the window. To his surprise the squat-faced manager had offered him the job on the spot. With a growing pile of unpaid bills testament to the breadline becoming a deadline, any injection of hard cash was a welcome appeasement. It was from amongst this mixed blessing Josh had begun to find strength from his dream. Reliving its tragic conclusion most nights would eat away a little bit more of what was left of his former self, but the few seconds that preceded it, the brief glimpse of the hazel eyes and that mischievous, luscious smile, had recently started to give him back his soul, even if only piece by piece.

Josh gazed at the pristine low gorge tapered fit, athletic cut, bouttonnaired business suit hanging in the bedroom doorway. Before retiring to bed to face another potentially sleepless night he had hung it from the frame, both enticement and reminder why this morning was going to be different. He then looked to the hand stitched Italian leather shoes sat prominently on the ornate bedroom chair. Both items had been pampered into becoming the cherry on the proverbial iced cake that was the rejuvenated Josh Brenin. Instilled with an architect's psyche through years of study and apprenticeship, he appreciated the value of outward appearance as a necessary evil.

The phone call he had been waiting for had come late on Friday afternoon. His recent application for a more prestigious vacancy at a surveyors company had resulted in a request to attend an interview eleven thirty AM Monday. Josh had taken it as a sign positive thinking and affirmative action were the only way to resurrect his life from the living hell that was depression; except it had conflicted with his first shift at the North Glendale diner. The secretary had phoned back five minutes later to confirm the compromised time of nine thirty was acceptable. With a little luck he would only have to suffer a few days at the diner until he started the consultancy position. Fate could not be so cruel, he decided, as to imprison him in any further degradation, for there was little left of his pride to take.

Gazing at the hanging effigy Josh remembered the last occasion that had required him to wear that suit. He recalled how unseasonably it had rained on that day and that the same leather shoes now placed regally on the chair had been muddied in the newly disturbed earth of the cemetery. He shook the memory from his mind. *Not now.* He checked the clock face again. *7:39. Time to rebuild my life.*

Righting the toppled prescription container on the bedside cabinet Josh got up, unhooked the suit from the doorframe and left to make the first coffee of the morning. Preceding the godsend of deep healthy sleep he had popped its lid and swallowed one of the small blue pills it contained with a little of the foul tasting water, the same water with which he had started the trial prescription of sleeping pills a week earlier. Never one to experiment with illicit drugs in his youth Josh had maintained an inherent reserve towards the specialist's claim of the drug's miraculous powers. *Your case is rare but not unique, within a month you'll be sleeping unaided like a baby at his mother's teat.* He didn't care if his favourite blend of fresh ground coffee aided the enemy that was insomnia, that morning he would need all the help he could get.

*****

Sat in a chrome-framed chair Josh struggled to find a comfortable posture. He knew his wriggling simply covered up an urge to fidget and his hands felt clammy as he finally interlocked them on his lap. Being blessed with a thick covering of short black hair that had an elastic ability to remain *just so*, he still mentally chastised himself for forgetting to run a comb through it before leaving the house. As he faced the bald, middle-aged man across the desk in the tired looking office, he thanked the gods of fate he still had hair to groom.

The surveyor's company headquarters was not as impressive as Josh had hoped. He disguised a disappointment with a forced smile he hoped also concealed his anxiety. During a ten minute hiatus in the quiet lobby he had stared at the receptionist behind the worn and dated desk, intrigued by how long it had taken her to craft the sculptural hairstyle that emanated from her scalp like a modern art piece. After a nervous wait she had eventually waved him through to the manager's office with a plastic smile, and he had greeted his heavy set inquisitor with an over zealous handshake.

"Well thank you for coming in Mr Brenin we appreciate you are a busy man," the manager began. "Hopefully this won't take up too much of your time." He reeled off the formalities while his beady brown eyes scrutinised the résumé at his fingertips.

"No, thank you for seeing me," Josh returned the formality, cringing at the hint of desperation in his scratchy voice. His gaze wandered to the large plant in the corner behind his inquisitor. It had obviously been purchased as an attempt to liven the dull, tired room with a touch of the exotic, but failed miserably as its long brown leaves suggested its dismal surroundings were killing it.

"Can I offer you anything? Coffee? Evian?" The manager's intense gaze bored into Josh from behind the rimless glasses perched on the greasy nose. The offer of the caffeine injection was a welcome one but his nervousness forced him to decline.

"I'm fine."

"Okay, Josh, first of all let me say that we were impressed with your résumé. It's a rare day when we see such high standards interested in a position here let me tell you." Josh sucked up the compliment with an appreciative smile. "But to be blunt, Mr Brenin," he paused to remove his glasses and lock gazes with the nervy interviewee, "it doesn't wash with me." Josh swallowed, giving him precious seconds to construct a respectful reply. His inquisitor continued brazenly.

"The way I see it you can train monkeys to fly planes, but that doesn't make them fighter pilots, does it?" Again he continued before Josh could construct a reply. "Do you consider yourself a fighter Josh?" A bead of sweat rolled out from under Josh's armpit and was soaked up by the immaculate shirt.

"I'd fight to secure this job," Josh replied hastily, instantly realising how desperate he sounded. His inquisitor took in a deep breath, replaced his glasses and lowered his gaze.

"Perhaps that might extend to being more punctual Mr Brenin." The offhanded comment further stumped Josh. *What the hell!* He cast a sly glance to the fake Rolex poking out of his sleeve, then to the wall clock to his right. His watch was a whole seventeen minutes behind. *Crap.* The cheap trinket brought back from a trip to Hong Kong had been saved from the refuse because it looked the part, though after its long exile in the drawer its wearer had forgotten about its terrible time keeping. He felt his heartbeat thundering at his temples. Fight or flight responses were working overtime and Josh recognised that the months of morbid solitude had left his self esteem in tatters. *What's wrong with you? speak!*

"What caught my eye was your recent work history, or to be more exact, lack of." The beady eyes were scrutinising his résumé once more, allowing Josh a brief chance to recite the secret mantra, *Relax, RELAX.*

"Straight from Berkley to Cohen & Pierce to complete your architectural diploma, very nice, but followed by a string of unrelated, less prestigious employers which ended almost a year ago." Josh had hoped the quality of his academic history would camouflage this particular glitch in his career, but now he realised he had just been kidding himself. It had been over two years since he'd completed his apprenticeship at the prestigious architect and surveyor's company, within a month Sarah had been killed. In the remainder of his time there he had done little else but allow himself to become a slave to his despair.

For the first few months after the accident Josh had managed to hold onto some sense of purpose by burying himself in what was expected to be a promising career. But papering over the cracks was no solution for the rookie Architect. After admitting that an all too important part of himself had also died on that sun-kissed morning, he couldn't continue with the vain attempt at normality. The string of *lesser* employers his inquisitor now drew attention to had simply been attempts to re-address a lack of funding, to enable him to hang onto their Edendale home. Sarah and he had fallen in love with the neglected property but without his aspirations and its accompanying wage he had continuingly struggled to keep up with the monthly instalments. It had been their dream, but now its continuing deterioration paralleled the nightmare that was his life.

"Now what sort of message do you think that sends to a potential employer like me Mr Brenin?" the manager sniped once more, shaking Josh out of his self pity. *Why did this bastard ask me to come here?* The bead of sweat was now a torrent under both arms, soaking the snow white shirt he had so piously ironed. After resigning there was no escaping the past twelve months of depression and indifference, he gave the inquisitor his answer.

"I'm sorry to have wasted your time." The unexpected reply made the beady eyes widen disdainfully.

"Excuse me?" the bewildered manager queried, but Josh's tattered pride saw no reason to stay and continue the charade. Without the professional etiquette of a goodbye handshake Josh stood and walked out of the dank office, purposely avoiding the manager's startled gaze in case they held him to the spot like a charmer might a snake.

Outside the smeared glass doors of the surveyor's lobby the early morning sun hit Josh full in the face. His shirt was drenched with perspiration and clung to his chest like a second skin. Cringing at the adverse sensation he rooted in his trousers for his car keys and paced across the car lot to his car. His interrogator had made no exclamation of encouragement to stay and Josh Brenin had accepted defeat by walking quickly back through the lobby, aware that the receptionist's disapproving gaze had tracked his reprehensible exit with a raised eyebrow.

Several suited employees now passed him with a polite *Good Morning* after mistaking him for a fellow executive. For a second he imagined what it might have been like to join their ranks but the fantasy was pointless vanity. The silver coupe beeped its welcome and he wondered how such cheery people worked in such a dull environment. The exotic flora obviously made all the difference.

The decision to drive straight home was a last minute choice. Josh had originally wanted to travel directly from the Surveyors to the Eat-A-Lot in North Glendale to make sure he arrived in plenty of time. He would have been way too early but had planned to park up outside, switch clothes and stakeout the diner for a better idea of what he was letting himself in for. He had wanted to arrive on a high knowing that the interview had gone well and that he wouldn't have to belittle himself by working in the fast food joint for longer than was necessary. Now he was resigned to the fact that the diner was all he had.

Stopping at a red light he glanced over at a ragged man pushing a stolen shopping trolley full of bulging trash bags. His soiled trench-coat looked out of place in the hot summer sun and Josh realised it was likely that the bags of garbage were in fact the entirety of the hobo's possessions.

Though he knew it was unfair to regard unfortunates with contempt, he was glad to be locked in behind the panels of steel and reinforced glass. The reoccurring thought that whatever had driven the poor creature to destitution might also lie in his own future was a constant reminder of his own inadequacies. The lights turned to green and he left the dismal thoughts behind.

Surviving the mid morning traffic Josh pulled into his drive in good time. *Home sweet home.* A lighter than usual torrent of downtown commuters had prevented him from being roasted alive behind the wheel. The car's air-con hadn't worked in weeks, much like its unpredictable starter motor it would demand a hefty libation from his first pay-cheque. Yanking up the slack handbrake he relived the manager's tragic condemnation in his mind. *A monkey? That's a new one.* As Josh had manoeuvred negligently between the fastest lanes of the shimmering sun baked freeway the inquisitor's brazen attitude had tormented his shaky pride, but now he was home the notion he'd at least won some small battle against apathy went someway to appease his despondent walk through the long grass to his front door.

The property's small front garden was hopelessly neglected. Gardening had always been Sarah's love; his had been enjoying her love transform the small piece of scrubland into something resembling perfection. As a result the lawnmower had only seen the light of day a couple of times in the past two years and even the polite reminders from his neighbours had failed to persuade Josh to devout more time to maintaining the once more neglected plot.

The house itself was a small single floor building that sat between two much larger residences. Unique amongst its Edendale caste, the wood panelled exterior gave it the potential of being labelled quaint though unfortunately prone to a more dramatic look of dilapidation. It wasn't until the casual viewer walked up the grass smothered path to the open porch that the years of neglect became visible. White paint flaked from rotting wood trims while subsidence had caused a fissure on the western wall, making the property less desirable as well as un-sellable. Surprisingly this unsavoury fact didn't faze Josh. He couldn't abandon it even if he wanted. Somewhere amongst its unused rooms he imagined Sarah's essence still clung to walls and hidden timbers. As her surrogate body it caged their loving bond in reality until he was ready to join her. Josh didn't believe in God, but he refused to accept Sarah's complete departure from existence. After the doctors had pronounced her on arrival, their home had conferred more comfort than any church or priest could ever do. Tossing his jacket over his shoulder to aerate his damp body a familiar face walked up to greet him on the flaking porch.

The cat's big eyes had clinched his purchase when they had first moved into the street; aptly named Samson he was a Rag-doll cat of enormous proportions that seemingly ate his own weight in food each day. As the faithful companion welcomed the master of the house with a loving caress of the leg and a cordial purr he remembered how visitors would comment about its incredible volume. But these days there were few to impress. Usually Josh refrained from talking to his pet in public, though today frustration outweighed vanity. The big cat's eyes looked up and Josh recognised the pleading look.

"You hungry again big guy?" Thrusting the door key into the stiff lock he shoved the front door open and watched Samson run inside with an obvious destination in mind. "Maybe you should consider that diet we talked about!" He then unplugged the wad of morning post from the mailbox and followed the hefty feline to the kitchen, then remembered he had little to feed his dependant. The milk from the fridge was beginning to curdle but the hungry cat never seemed to mind. Content with the sound of the Samson's eager tongue lapping the makeshift brunch, Josh went to prepare for the day's second tribulation, assuring himself life would get better, if he could bare to give it a chance.

*****

Situated below street level the drinking den catered for those wanting round-the-clock access to topless girls. Clientele were led down from the sidewalk into a nocturnal underworld of lust and over priced drinks via a steep, red neon lit staircase, garishly designated by the sign above its entrance which spelled *The Zoom* in an old-world western font. At ten in the morning, only a scattering of hardened drinkers and depraved insomniacs who inhabited such places as a way of life, currently patronised the establishment. One such regular, sat at the bar in a pair of jeans and a faded Lakers t-shirt, was already sipping at his second beer of the day when the tall stranger's face caught his attention.

The stranger's entry into the secret world was a hasty affair. After distracting the muscular doorman at the base of the stairwell from his listless ogling with a collision of elbows, he rashly skirted his way around the small circular tables on the main floor in search of anonymity. From the anxious wide eyed expression on his broad features it was obvious to the regular it was the stranger's first time in the Zoom, the nonchalant way he rested an elbow on the glistening bar failing to impress him. From behind it a slim brunette made her way over with her best smile and asked for his order. Momentarily distracted by the sight of the girl's nymphet beauty the stocky stranger simply replied with a shake of the head. The regular smiled to himself and called her back over.

"Here, get me another beer," he instructed, holding out the ten dollar note before looking back at the nervous newcomer. The brunette removed a fresh one from the cooler, popped the bottle's lid under the bar and handed it over with the change.

"Go steady Jonny it's still early," she warned, shouting over the hypnotic dance music that coordinated the dancers sensual writhing on the club's many podiums.

"Don't worry sweet-cheeks, this is for our first-timer over here," he explained picking up the bottle. Drying his mouth on the back of his hand he walked over to the Zoom virgin.

"Hey buddy, you look like you could do with this." Jonny placed the second drink on the bar and relished the thought of inducting the new face into the merits of his world. The stranger's wild eyes turned to greet his with a look of mistrust, immediately adopting a defensive pose. "Go ahead it's on the house, it's your first time in the Zoom right?" he continued brashly. It was then he noticed the scarred flesh that snaked down the side of the stranger's head and behind his shrivelled ear. He wasn't pretty, but then pretty men didn't need to pay for female attention.

The stranger shrunk his eyes in an attempt to fathom the regular's intentions, then turned away to scour the dim lit floor of mostly empty tables.

"Don't worry," he assured the stranger, mistaking his silence for reserve, "I ain't no fruit or nothing, you just look like you could do with a drink. Take it." The regular pushed the bottle towards him but the surly stranger wasn't listening. Instead he preferred to gaze around while resting a hand awkwardly near the base of his back. "Hey buddy you got shit in your ears? Loosen up, it's all good." The stranger turned again to meet his advance, only to gaze wildly beyond the jovial regular and catch sight of the bald man at the far end of the bar. Instinctively the stranger stiffened and clasped at the hidden object tucked into the back of his pants.

"Jerk!" the regular cursed. Angrily he snatched back the second bottle and returned in disgust to his favourite stool. The stranger's gaze temporarily diverted away to the retreating regular though quickly darted back to the end of the bar, only to find his bald headed stalker was no longer there. *He's found me!*

*****

Josh let the hot downpour wash away the bad start to the day. He hadn't planned to take a shower in between the morning's appointments, only after what he knew would be a long first day at the diner. But feeling soiled, both physically and mentally, it was a reluctant necessity. Under the hot water he relived the antagonising comments that had pierced through the eggshell of confidence with an unexpected ease. *Who was I kidding?* He rebuked his weakness with a hard punch to the tiled wall, and then cringed from the self inflicted pain. The bundle of morning post that day had been a mixture of cash prize notifications and outstanding bills, none of which particularly benefited his current state of mind. Glumly he had tossed them onto the glass top coffee table with the rest of the unopened mail then sneered as the pile had spilled over onto the carpet.

The phone rang, Josh cursed. He had already started to lather the cheap shower gel he had rooted out of a bargain bin onto his slim body and so left the answer machine to take the untimely call. After five rings there was the familiar beep, followed by the sarcastic greeting he had forgotten to erase.

"Josh Brenin has left the building! So if that's you my darling, it means I'm out looking for a job so you can hang up!" He cringed again. The message had been recorded without premeditation after finishing a previous call. Even though he had relished the idea of his tedious girlfriend's call being answered by the pre-recorded taunt, right then he wished otherwise.

"If you're fortunate enough not *to be Sharon then leave a message and I'll decide whether or not you're important enough to call back."* The sarcastic greeting was followed by the familiar pause where the caller decided how to respond. Josh's heart cramped and then relaxed when a familiar male voice resonated from the speaker.

"Nice message Asshole I'm sure that'll have her crawling back." It was Matty, the closest thing he had to a best friend and he was his usual cheery self. Josh turned off the shower and cocked his head out for a better chance at hearing. "Well I obviously fall into that large bracket of people who are not worth speaking to because I know you're there, you're always there, but here's the bulletin, deadbeat. I've got some good news and some bad news. Good news is I got the tickets, at great expense I might add, so right now a little appreciation of my God-like status would be greatly advised."

The tickets the grainy voice referred to were for a gig Matty had been itching to see for months. Josh had initially been reluctant to go, but after his friend had offered to pay for them both Josh had put aside his reservations and taken up the generous offer. The daunting alternative had meant facing Matty's tenacious gnawing of his right to say no, the same tenacity which had kept their eight year friendship intact throughout the duration of Josh's tribulations.

"The bad news is the venue has been changed because of a bomb threat," his disembodied voice continued. "Or due to some bull that went down at the last show. So I know you're going to love this when I tell you it's been relocated to the Helter Skelter," Josh cringed again. He knew the hype around the band was pretty controversial but hadn't expected the bolt from the blue. The Helter Skelter was a junkie infested flea pit on the Hollywood Strip, a flea pit Josh had vowed never to set foot in ever again after closely avoiding a stabbing from a psychotic coke dealer who'd mistaken him as a rival. Times were desperate. What had seemed like a unique way to take a break from the monotony of his lack-lustre life now seemed like it was going to be a chore.

"Anyhow, when you've finished doing whatever it is you do with yourself all day, call me. I'll be at work!" Matty hung up and Josh stepped out of the shower to dry himself off, mulling over the bad news and his subsequent exit strategy from the inconvenience.

The two friends had met at Berkeley after following up on flyers touting for members of the *Headbanger's Society*. Josh had simply joined as an excuse to make new friends while for Matty it had been about a life long love of hard rock and metal music, and as he saw it, a great way to meet easy girls. Both had finished top of their classes, albeit in two separate fields, Josh in Architecture and Matty in Corporate Law. The latter now worked in mergers and acquisitions for a high profile law firm downtown, a job, Josh believed he managed to carry out with the least amount of effort whilst retaining an envious salary and bonus each year.

As he dried his hair Josh looked out from under the towel and stared at his steam smeared reflection in the mirror. Gazing into his green eyes he searched for the lost fire that had made him the charismatic young man he had once been. The past it seemed was the only thread that maintained the bond between him and his college buddy, a past he still wished to rekindle if only he could fan the flames of the old him once more. For Josh it was the number one reason for not burning bridges with a person he no longer felt akin to. It was Matty's assertive personality that helped him retain the part of his own soul he feared lost forever.

Along with the best years of their lives the two under graduates had once shared similar vivacious aspirations. Except now it seemed tragedy and time had dragged their worlds apart, leaving Josh to wonder why his prosperous friend still wanted to associate with such an accomplished loser. Josh missed the past. Unfortunately the future was all he had left. Placing his hand strategically over the goatee beard he decided it was time for the tired reflection to join in the progression. *Sarah had never liked it anyhow.* He had wanted to shave it off for sometime but its association with the past had prevented an easy decision.

Deciding he no longer wanted to look as old as he felt he knew it had to go. Josh squeezed the remnants of the shaving gel from a near empty bottle and lathered it over his jaw. The phone rang again but an apathetic mood meant he would finish what he had started. Deciding it was Matty testing his resolve Josh poised the razor to his chin. The recorded message resonated through the house for a second time before an irate young women answered.

"Josh you pig!" He dropped the razor. "Lucky for you, Mr Deadbeat, I can understand your sarcasm is a reflection of your frustrations, but that doesn't give you the right to humiliate me every time someone else calls!" Sharon's usual hypersensitivity had been amplified by the act of defiance. Abandoning his shave he stormed from the bathroom, foam dripping onto the front room carpet as her incensed voice grew louder. "You know some people get a job to pay their rent!"

The last comment was purposely vengeful. His last social security instalment had been used to pay off a back-log of utility bills, leaving him without the necessary funds to pay off his monthly obligation. Reluctantly he had accepted Sharon's offer of help, knowing full well acceptance meant being indebted in more ways than one. Josh swallowed his temper and snatched up the handset, dousing it in foam.

"For your information…" he retorted but was met with the dial tone. *She hung up.* Biting his tongue he smeared away the foam to redial.

"Who is this?" Sharon answered coyly after several rings.

"For your information I start a new job today," Josh snapped, "So you'll get your precious money back as soon as I get paid, okay?" A future of drudgery awaited him and he was going to be late.

"Where is it?" Her voice was cold; she didn't like being shouted at.

"What, the money?"

"No the job you idiot," Josh felt like an idiot. He also felt as though he was always trying to prove himself to a woman he hardly knew. *Why do I bother with her?*

"It's a new outfit up in Glendale, you won't have heard of it," he replied dismissively. Everyone had heard of Eat-A-Lot diners but he didn't want her to know that was where he had grudgingly found employment. As far as she was concerned Josh Brenin was finding his way back into the white-collar world. "It's a job Sharon." Being purposely vague he counted on her reluctance to reveal her own ignorance.

"Glad to hear it, so am I seeing you this weekend?" Josh guessed this was this was the real reason behind the call. "We can celebrate this great achievement of yours, who knows you might get lucky." The last comment reminded him why he bothered with her, though he reverted to the truth knowing she wouldn't like it.

"I can't make this Saturday."

"What!"

"It's just some gig, it's been planned for months. Look I've got to go I'm soaking my carpet over here. I'll call you," with the truth delivered he simply hung up the phone.

The gel on his chin began to make it itch. Marching back to the bathroom to complete the delicate shave he ignored the unwanted pang of guilt. *What the hell does she want from me?* Sometimes it was hard to admit it but he liked Sharon, the neurotic beauty could be a lot of fun. Being the closest thing to representing any real future, she also reminded him that in some ways he was still a man.

When the past was eradicated from his smooth skin, he admired the naked rediscovered chin it had revealed. Unsure of the new look he left the smart shirt and pants on the bathroom floor like a discarded skin and paced out to get redressed, opting for a pair of jeans that had fallen behind the bedroom chair and a clean t-shirt from the drawer. He didn't expect burger flipping and selling fries required much of a dress code, and if he was honest with himself, he didn't care if it did.

Josh spotted the closet door was ajar. Out of sight it had an annoying habit of creeping open of its own accord. Though he was becoming pressed for time the white shoebox inside stole his weary attention. *Just this once won't hurt.* Facing an emotional low he knelt down to the Nike box in a hasty confession of weakness and lifted off its ill-fitting lid. As he removed the selection of bittersweet memories on top and put them to one side it revealed the small plastic bag of white powder he'd secreted underneath.

He knew the rush of euphoria the cocaine could induce would be fleeting and synthetic but the memory of instant heaven made it hard to resist. Flipping over one of the photos he poured a sparing amount of the fine powder onto its glossy surface, then deciding the situation warranted a sufficient dose, poured a little more. Another photo served to chop and align the two generous lines while a rolled one dollar bill from his back pocket became an adequate snorting pipe. Inhaling the two lines one after the other was like consuming powered heaven.

Josh Brenin's white powder slavery had begun after accompanying Matty to one of the many sordid nightspots the Strip had to offer. In the men's room cubicle the flood of dopamine into his neural network had filled the void in his soul with instant bliss and he had denied his conscience ever since. *Sarah would have killed me.* His nasal membranes began to sting. He rubbed the sensation away with the back of his hand, pinched away the residue and packed away his box of secrets. Dusting the wayward evidence from the photo he noticed it was the one of the bright eyed couple celebrating the end of their first year.

Sarah was wearing the tight denim jacket that emphasised her petite beauty and a low cut white top that revealed her flawless buttermilk skin. They had gotten so drunk on that day that he had found the misplaced courage to ask her to marry him. Little had he known he would ask the same question again for real several years later. Josh felt a well of emotion jump into his throat. *No not now!* He put the memory back into the box where it belonged, replaced the lid and re-hid it deep in the closet.

Samson wailed. He had been watching the curious behaviour from the bedroom doorway with a cat's natural curiosity, his large invasive eyes seemingly reminding Josh of the hell the magic white powder could create. Replacing the loss of heaven with a chemically induced one would ultimately drain his body of its limited supply of dopamine, leaving a new void of depression in its place that would subsequently worsen his chronic insomnia. Aware of the dilemma Josh shamefully patted the cat goodbye before grabbing his keys. As he left the house enjoying the illegal rejuvenation he assured himself he would not relive his addiction. He couldn't, not if he wanted to sleep.

*****

It had taken the threat of force-feeding the pervert his empty bottle before he'd conceded the pay phone's existence. Fearing the stranger's fearsome conviction, the Zoom regular had directed him towards the men's room door across the dingy club. The pervert's alarmed eyes had darted from his to the scar tissue on his head. The war wound received in the line of duty had a way bolstering his fearsome presence; sometimes revulsion had its uses. Now inside the damp four walls of graffiti stained tiles the stranger found he'd told the truth, but forgotten to impart one important fact; the handset was no longer attached to the wall mounted phone box.

After staring at the frayed cable end the stranger threw the severed handset to the slippery floor. The subterranean club had made his own cell phone redundant and as he spun around to search in vain for some other way through to the outside world he quickly realised he was a rat in an underground trap. *Who the hell am I going to call? No one's gonna believe me.* The cubicle doors had been kicked in. One hung on by a bent hinge while the other was propped against the wall. There was nowhere to hide.

Turning back to the entrance the stranger flinched at the sight of the man in the mirror. *Is that me?* His perspiring skin reflected the harsh fluorescent light with a ghoulish pallor. For a moment he acknowledged the past few days had taken their toll his weary features, then cuffed the sweat from his brow and decided to get the hell out of there, out from the underground pit and back amongst people and the sunlight. A sudden chill halted the urge.

"Going somewhere Ben?" a voice from behind suddenly asked. He had been the only one in that room, now It was there. Frozen with fear, Ben dared not to turn and look at the creature that had stalked him relentlessly for the past two weeks.

"You're not really there, you don't exist!" Ben condemned the speaker, eager to convince himself he still maintained a firm grip on reality. *But this can't be a dream.* A snort of amusement from behind discredited his denial.

"Turn around. It is time," the voice stated ominously. Reluctantly Ben did what was commanded but kept his eyes closed, his only consolation the press of the revolver hidden against the base of his spine. "Open your eyes Ben, or should I say, Alpha." Again there was no option but to obey. Doing so, the bald headed man appeared just as before, a figure in black that had forced him to abandon his work, his home, his sanity, and now seemingly a real and present danger.

"How do you know that name?"

"It's partly the reason why I am here," the spectre explained. Face to face with the black clad stalker Ben found him less intimidating. Smaller than him in height and build he was dressed in a style Ben normally would have found amusing, had the circumstances been less threatening. "Now tell me, have you walked amongst them?" *The same question.* This time round Ben knew there was no avoiding its answer. With a well tuned reflex he freed the Glock 9mm revolver from the back of his jeans and pointed it at the stalker's austere face.

"Who the hell are you?" he demanded, the question blurting out of his mouth with a reassurance that came from finally having the spectre at the wrong end of a gun. "Who do you work for?" The bald figure removed his sunglasses and grinned.

"I am a servant of the light."

"Oh yeah? And what *light* is that?" Ben thumbed back the gun's hammer.

"The light of truth." The spectre stepped forward. "The truth that you're life is not your own. So now for the last time, have you walked amongst them!" The gun trembled in Ben's hand. His defensive instincts had been drilled into him through years of elite military training, yet right then he knew they were obsolete. Still he decided to discharge a round into the stalker, but this last resort was stolen from him as the men's room door suddenly burst open and collided with his shoulder. The brute force behind it knocked Ben to the floor and sent the Glock sliding under a cubicle. In the entrance stood the muscular doorman wielding a shabby baseball bat.

"You!" the doorman yelled down to Ben, "You got three seconds to get the hell up and out of my bar before I bust your head wide open." He enforced his over reaction by raising the bat as proof of his conviction, before it was abruptly whipped out of his hand by an unseen force.

Ben stared up from the floor as the doorman was then seized by the same invisible hand and sent crashing up to the ceiling, where knocked out by the collision he became pinned up against the strip lighting like a stray helium balloon. Ben couldn't believe his eyes. He blinked but the sight remained. Mesmerised by the unconscious doorman suspended above his head he staggered to his feet. Looking back to the stalker he saw the upturned hand relayed the source of the invisible force that defied gravity and belief.

"I think it's time you came with me Alpha," the spectre stated calmly. With a gentle movement of his hand the spectre guided the doorman's limp body down into a cubicle. Its one hinged door then slammed shut as the invisible hands concealed it from view.

"Are you going to kill me?" Ben asked, realising this man or spectre was in control of forces beyond his comprehension. The stalker's otherworldly power was then ghoulishly conveyed as his eyes transformed into two mirrored orbs. Ben's spine froze in terror.

Somehow his dreams had crossed the boundaries of insanity into real life. With his military alias compromised and his sense of reality shattered by the demonstration of unnatural powers, he knew running was as futile as denial. As the stalker returned the sunglasses to the bridge of his nose he flashed an impish grin.

"My name is Monk, and you're no use to us dead."

Chapter 2

Josh hated public transport, the bus he currently travelled on a prime example why. He never relished being in close proximity to so many strangers packed into one vehicle, sharing their air and avoiding their eyes, but that morning it was a necessary evil. An unhealthy odour of stale urine hovered close and even with the fresh draft from the open window nearby he could still smell the vomit he had spotted on the vagrant's jacket three seats in front. Not only was it turning out to be one of the worst days of the year, the bus was also one of the worst he had ever travelled on. *God-damn car!*

He had left his house not fifteen minutes before, still buzzing from the affect of the lines of the Bolivian powder, only to have his car stall and die in the middle of the street. The queue of suburban off-roaders and hatchbacks had built up quickly in the few minutes he had been stranded. After a middle aged woman at the front of the tailback had surprised him with her colourful use of curse words he had resorted to getting out and pushing his dead car back into the drive. By chance he had recalled the bus route at the end of his street went as far as North Glendale and so had tagged onto the end of the queue just as the city bus pulled up.

Scowling as the bus now came to a stop outside his favourite Taco Bell restaurant, Josh stewed over the day's events so far. A well dressed woman in her forties got on and took the vacant seat in front of him. While he imagined the unwelcome cost of the car's repair the woman's sickly perfume caught his attention, instantly reminding him of the bug spray his grandmother had used when he was a kid. It had been a long time since memories of his grandparent's house had crossed his mind and the scent's familiarity brought with it a wistful distraction from his woes. As the bus pulled out again Josh looked up to a route schematic plastered on the interior above his head. He calculated that the closest stop, located where the Golden State Freeway met North Glendale, was a good ten minute walk from the Eat-A-Lot diner and became unsure he could make the rendezvous in time. However after some mental projections he decided it was an easy trek and looked back out of the window for familiar haunts.

"Clarence?" a voice in front suddenly asked. The woman had turned around and was looking at Josh with a doting glance. He took several seconds to absorb the curious question.

"Are you talking to me?" he asked, doing his best to sound polite.

"Are you my Clarence?" she repeated the question with greater clarity.

Christian Tremain

"I'm sorry lady I think you're mistaken," Josh smiled and turned away hoping she would reciprocate, but her stare remained on his face. Something suddenly short circuited in the woman's mind.

"Where have you been?" The new question was shrieked through the bus and Josh flinched before staring back at his accuser. "Why did you leave me?" she shrieked once more. He looked around for assistance but was met only with apathy. To his horror the woman then produced a long, thin kitchen knife that she rested threateningly on the back of her seat. The curious glances of fellow passengers turned away and Josh panicked.

"Lady, what's with the knife?" he pleaded, stress levels optimising.

"If you come near me again I'll kill you!" she yelled into his face, her glazed eyes wide but not really seeing. Josh was equally baffled why no one was coming to his aid. Such was city life.

"Believe me lady, if you put away that knife I'll never come near you again." The plea was sincere. He had no intention of finding out if the shiny blade was as sharp as it appeared. Then just as quickly as the woman had exploded into her unwarranted psychosis she returned to her original state of serenity.

"You're not my Clarence," the woman admitted, her voice weak and passive, as she retracted the knife and stood up. Indifferent to Josh's trauma she shuffled down the aisle and into a seat nearer the front. Likewise he took the opportunity to escape to an empty seat at the rear.

"Did you see that? She pulled a knife on me!" Josh blurted, eyes glued to the muttering schizophrenic who made herself comfortable up front. His exclamation had not been aimed at any one particular though as he watched the unstable woman groom her hair with a lethargic hand, another passenger seemingly empathised with his predicament. Josh was unable to tell whether the man was smiling or grinning at him from behind the sunglasses, who then nodded in silent acknowledgement and turned away. Sensing something equally unnerving Josh quickly reciprocated as his DVD store zipped by. Taking a deep breath he calmed his nerves with thoughts of his grandparent's house in Maryland.

Josh's stop came into view up ahead. He had guessed the walk to the diner would take him between five and ten minutes, and as he gladly alighted the bus he checked his watch. Taking into consideration the seventeen minute lag of the counterfeit Rolex he decided he had plenty of time if he walked quickly. He also made a mental note to throw out the trinket when he got home. He had only been to this part of Glendale once or twice before. With good reason he believed for the current bland streets were the soulless concrete labyrinths of backyard LA that offered nothing more to the casual visitor than a sun kissed eyesore.

26

Where he was heading was known locally as the Fast Mile. Though not literally a mile in length the busy street was packed with every kind of fast food outlet and convenience store known to man, a veritable oasis to the local workforce stranded amongst the warehouses and factories that dominated the area. As he turned into the Mile an attractive young woman on the opposite side of the street, in her twenties, caught his eye as she puffed on a cigarette. Hiding from the sun in a shop doorway she returned his glance with a smile before tossing the smoking butt away. *Still* got *it.*

Fifty yards further down the Eat-A-Lot came into view, just as he had found it the previous week after another failed interview in the area. Tentatively walking the last few steps he braced himself mentally for what he would face inside. A bead of sweat emerged from his armpit and ran down his ribs, this time due to the brisk walk in the midday sun rather than to undue stress. Taking a deep breath he pushed the glass door open. As he did its corner caught the heel of the last man in a long queue. He apologised and took a quick glance around the interior to see all booths and tables were occupied with more of the local work force. *Busy.*

Josh swallowed but found his throat dry. A quick dose of light headedness then trampled over his brain, though breathing in the savoury air gave him strength. *Keep it together.* He refreshed his memory with the instructions from the brief interview and cautiously made his way down the line of hungry workers. Ignoring a maliciously placed leg that obstructed him from the counter he stepped over it to where the maroon uniformed teenagers rushed to serve the influx of custom. One of the adolescent employees, a tall and unhealthily thin youngster, had watched Josh force his way to the front and now looked amazed by the daring advance through the impatient crowd.

"I'm sorry sir you'll have to go back and wait in line." The young beanpole's instruction was backed by a jeer from a short, heavy set Hispanic man in blue overalls. Josh knew better than to look around.

"No wait I don't want any food, I'm here about the job." As the gangly youngster looked vacantly at Josh, he started to feel his anxiety boil into frustration. "The staff vacancy? Is there a Carlos back there? I was told to ask for him.

"Why didn't you say? He's through there." The youngster gestured to a side door marked *Staff Only.* "Step aside and let me serve this gentleman." The Hispanic man pushed forward and reeled off his order while Josh ducked through the staff door into a storage area. Amongst the boxes of flat-packed Eat-A-Lot containers and vats of cooking oil Josh came across another young employee rolling a cigarette who, after shooting him a dismissive glance, pulled the maroon baseball cap over his bird's nest of peroxide blonde hair.

"I'm looking for Carlos," Josh stated. The teenager jerked his head towards another door that led into the kitchen.

"There. You the new boy?" Josh didn't feel comfortable with being called a boy by someone who looked ten years younger than himself.

"You could say that."

"I'm Dink." There was a pause while Josh wondered whether he'd heard him correctly. "You'll find Carlos in there driving the rest of his slaves. If he asks for me tell him to stick his head up his ass!"

"Will do," Josh offered amiably, amused at the young man's rebellion. Smiling his thanks he watched Dink leave through a fire exit onto a loading bay. No sooner did Josh enter the bustling kitchen he slipped in a patch of spilt grease and grabbed a prepping table to correct himself, inadvertently pulling over a container of utensils that clattered embarrassingly onto the floor. Before Josh had time to apologise an imposing middle-aged man with matching spread marched over.

"Who the hell is this?" he demanded to know aggressively. He eyed the intruder up and down with yellowing eyeballs.

"Carlos?"

"That's what it says on the nametag numb nuts!" he replied crudely. The diner manager was obviously a man of little patience and Josh's clumsiness had just made a bad mood worse.

"Josh Brenin," he reaffirmed. Carlos looked at his watch. "We spoke…"

"Branning, you're six minutes late! Never mind, I take it you know how to use one of these?" The manager grabbed a mop handle that was stood in a soapy bucket. "You see a mess you clean it up, starting with this mess right here, understood?" Josh had reached an all time low. "Back in there you'll find a locker with a spare uniform about your size, put it on. No smoking, no jerking around and you break at two-thirty."

"Is the floor always this greasy?" Josh blurted out. Carlos's face twitched.

"If it wasn't you'd be out of a job, now get to it!" The brief induction was concluded when Carlos walked out to the counter to check on business. Josh glimpsed around the cramped kitchen expecting a wall of curious faces but found none had seemingly dared. The workforce of hushed teenagers was obviously scared of their pot bellied boss and in like minded obedience Josh went to get changed. Inspired by Dink's rebellious tenacity however he decided to sneak in a personal call first.

Across town in the city's financial district it was a contrasting existence for Josh's best friend. Matty was reclined in a recently purchased executive leather chair. Its protective wrap still lay on the floor next to the custom order mahogany desk that propped up his feet, the panoramic view of downtown's cityscape through his office's tinted glass an impressive backdrop to admire his hand made Italian shoes. Though wooing his latest conquest on hands-free he welcomed the incoming call on his cell, which rang from inside his elegant hand stitched briefcase.

"Listen that's my cell, important client calling from DC. I promise we'll go out this Saturday, Ciao." Hanging up the desk phone he saw Josh's ID on his cell.

"So I'm *worthy* now am I?" he answered the call.

"Let's just say I'm feeling desperate," Josh replied slyly, struggling to pull on his maroon uniform with one hand. "So you got them?"

"Right here buddy boy." Matty reached inside the brief case and plucked out the two tickets to admire the bold black letters that spelt *Devilwhore*. "You won't believe how many kidneys I had to sell to get them, but yeah, we're going!" Josh had managed to pull on the pants but found they were a couple of sizes too big. "So has the basket-case called?"

"Sharon wants to go out this weekend but I told her I was too busy wasting my life with you" He picked up the matching shirt from the bottom of the locker. "The frigging Helter Skelter Club!"

"Relax, I'm sure that guy's making car plates in Chino by now, you'll be safe. Trust me." The locker room entrance swung open as an employee came to restock on Big Eat containers. "Where the hell are you?" he asked suspiciously. "It sounds like you're in a clinic." Josh made a split second decision about telling the truth or not.

"I'm at work." Then decided he couldn't. "I mean in the diner on the way to work, you know the Eat-A-Lot in North Glendale?" The employee gave Josh a confused glare then exited.

"Work? Glendale? Jeez what new world are you living in?" Matty decided he preferred to keep the tickets in his shirt pocket. "What's the job, factory rat?" he joked inappropriately before his desk phone rang again. While an unsuspecting Matty picked up the handset and immediately hung up, Josh forced an arm into the musty shirt and contorted his body to insert a second.

"As if! It's a new outfit up here that…" Josh stopped mid sentence and looked at the shirt cuffs as they rode up his arms; the shirt was two sizes too small. "You gotta be kidding me! I'll see you Saturday. I gotta go." Josh hung up to stare at his exposed forearms. As Carlos entered unexpectedly from the kitchen his boss's stern features quickly stretched into an unappreciated snigger.

"Nice outfit Brannigan, you look the part," he teased then tossed the mop he was carrying at Josh. Fumbling the catch Josh instinctively wanted to hurl it back, but swallowing his pride he walked subserviently past his boss's protruding gut into the kitchen. Matty wouldn't be impressed, he knew that for sure. But what he didn't know was why life had thrown him the wooden spoon when he had been destined to hold a silver one.

Eyes down he bent to collect the fallen utensils as he questioned his better judgment. Was the aversion to poverty really worth the humiliation? It felt wrong. It all felt wrong. His life had never meant to turn out this way. Never more so than right then did Josh realise he was the product of his own weakness. Matty was strong willed and ruthless, just as he had been, that was why fate hadn't abandoned his high flying friend to a life of slavery. A first class degree in a professional trade and here he was a simple grease monkey. That was why he couldn't dismiss Matty from his life; ironically he needed his arrogance and vigour to regenerate his own.

He knew that now. But until fate designated otherwise, cleaning spilt grease from the diner floor tiles was the best he could hope for.

*****

The loading bay at the diner's rear offered temporary refuge from the mayhem unfurling inside, but Josh's emotions were far from those of relief. Sitting on its sun-baked concrete ledge, legs dangling above several bloated garbage bags, he drained the unknown brand of soda produced by the battered vending machine inside. Frustration threatened to coerce him into acting against his normal reserve, though he managed to swallow it along with the ultra sweet beverage. The humid environment of the Eat-a-Lot kitchen was not proving an easy ordeal. He had spent the last three hours being sheparded from one soul destroying task to another as the laborious work demanded. As a jack-of-all-trades it seemed he was to be master of none.

"Hate to say it but it comes with the territory," Dink explained casually. He drew the last few puffs from the roach in his mouth. Upon his eager escape from the veritable slave ship, Josh had found his young rebellious colleague sat smoking another of his roll ups. After some small talk Josh was surprised to find the young man both intelligent and jovial.

"You just gotta grin and bare it like the rest of us," he then instructed as he reached into a back pocket.

The casual advice referred to the stand off between Josh and a disgruntled customer. Facing his unwanted public amongst the main seating area with mop in hand, a squat faced Hispanic wearing blue overalls had seen fit to taunt Josh's subservience by continuingly flicking fries into his path. Josh had faced the blatant antagonism with a professional courtesy, though simply received a mouthful of homophobic abuse in return. No one had ever threatened to insert a mop handle inside him before, and outside in the garbage tainted air of the diner's rear, he hoped never would again.

"There's only so much a man can grin and bare!" Josh exclaimed, hoping his new colleague exaggerated. "Territory or not, I just don't need another reason to quit this job right now." Helpless to act in any other manner than that of the humble servant, Josh had let the insult slide and cursed his miserable retreat back to the locker room. The Hispanic's blood shot eyes remained imprinted on his mind's eye. As Dink opened the battered tin he freed from his jeans and began to roll a fresh one, Josh thought of Dolly Parton's famed song, and decided surely it was harder to be a man than a woman, expectations were traditionally always higher. And that was why the Hispanic had chosen his prey; Josh Brenin's face just didn't fit. He was a stranger in a strange land, an easy target for those that persecuted the weak for kicks.

"Josh my man it's your first day and already you're sweating bullets, you smoke?" Josh looked tempted. The smell of the fresh tobacco had been reviving past pleasures.

"Not anymore," he admitted. He drained the last few drops from the can before throwing it into a nearby dumpster.

"If you want my opinion, you'll take up some new vice," Dink explained ominously, sealing the roll up with an experienced lick. "You'll need one if you wanna survive in this place. Trust me. You sure?" he offered again with a grin. The buzz from the cocaine a distant memory, another pick me up was just what Josh needed. He had managed five long months without a single cigarette, but decided there and then it had been long enough.

"I suppose one won't hurt," Dink grinned a self appraisal and handed over the fresh roll up and lighter before re-opening the tin.

"So how old are you?" Josh looked disapprovingly at the question. "Come on, how many rings on your tree trunk?" Josh knew he was no longer the teenager he still felt like inside, but he felt even older conversing with a real one.

"Well how old do I look?"

"Too old and too white collar to be mopping goddamn floors that's for sure," Dink replied as he sealed the second roll up with another lick of the tongue.

"Well let's just say a year of bad luck forced me to dye my white collars blue until I get back on my feet." Sparking up, he took a big drag and savoured the warm smoke that filled his lungs. *Damn that feels good.*

"Let me guess, there's a woman somewhere in the mix," Dink persisted. "I don't care what you say; universally there are only two things that bring men down, money and women, or the pursuit of!" The youngster took a huge drag on his own before continuing brazenly. "Obviously money is a problem; you wouldn't be in this dump if it wasn't. But betting my bottom dollar, behind every money problem you find a woman." For Josh's reserved manner he was digging too deep too soon. "Am I right?" The youngster grinned with a misplaced recognition of his straight cut wisdom.

"You're very perceptive," Josh humoured him and flicked away the half finished roll up. "But it's not what you think." He got up to stretch his legs, deciding the lingering aromas of garbage and exhaust fumes were preferable to the inquest.

"So what did she do?" Josh had hoped Dink would get the hint if he looked away to survey the concrete walls and over flowing dumpsters, but the vigorous curiosity of youth wouldn't let go. "Leave you for the mail man?"

"She died," Josh replied bluntly. Dink's grin fell from his face. For the first time the teenager's brazen attitude faltered.

"Damn I've got a big mouth. I'm sorry man, forget I asked." A little amused by the humbled posture, Josh leaned onto the safety rail.

"We married when we were twenty, in hindsight too young, but love is blind to reality."

"What happened?"

"The usual, a tragic accident, died before her time." Josh looked away and wondered why he was telling his life story to a complete stranger. "The past isn't always a friend to the present, but life goes on, even if it sucks." Dink looked uncomfortable, took another deep drag and exhaled a thick plume of smoke as the exit door suddenly burst open behind them.

"Well if it ain't Eddie Munster and Joe College!" Carlos blurted candidly, his bulky frame filling the fire exit. "Break's over slackers, time to earn every cent I'm paying you." Their irate boss whipped off his maroon cap and wiped the sweat from his brow with a thick hairy forearm. Dink looked behind in disgust.

"Yeah whatever Chief, when we've finished our smokes." There was no love lost between middle-aged employer and his *Eddie*.

"Now Reinhold!" Carlos yelled impatiently. "Second wave's come in and they're hungry." Josh got up and dusted off his backside ready for his return to the galley. "And I presume you two smart asses can read?" He enforced the comment by tapping the small *No Smoking* sign with a large, hairy finger before shooting back inside.

"Yeah, read this Jerk," Dink sniped, flipping the bird before flicking his roll up with precision at the sign. Josh was beginning to like Dink's style. After a week of working at Eat-A-Lot Josh imagined he too might enjoy similar liberties.

"Second wave?" Josh asked concerned.

"Mid afternoon burger and fries fiends from the warehouses." The youngster got up and scratched his groin. "Border jumpers and retards mostly." Josh smiled at Dink's lack of shame. "Word of advice though, don't clear the tables until you're sure they've finished, it can get pretty ugly otherwise." He finished his spiel with a guttural noise, brought up some phlegm then launched it into the air. Josh held the fire escape open and watched the slimy projectile land behind a dumpster.

"You're alright Reinhold." Dink turned and scowled.

"Don't call me that, old man!" Leading the way back inside, Josh found his mop and bucket were just as he'd left them in front of his dented locker. Steering it back to the kitchen by its wayward wheels he prayed the *second wave* would be trouble free.

A claustrophobic wall of heat and stale sweat greeted Josh as he ascended the bus steps. The city transport was closer to capacity than the one he'd travelled into Glendale, but spying a spare seat at its rear, he tapped his latest purchase in his jeans pocket and slumped wearily into a hard seat. The hellish shift was over. The last few hours had seemed to bypass his misery. After cleaning duty the promotion to monitoring the deep fat fryer had meant maintaining the steady input of freshly cut fries into the insatiable vat of boiling oil. Replacing a scrawny young girl, who he sussed owed her drawn, haggard look to the track marks on her arm, he had simply stirred and stared, allowing the hypnotic bubbling of the steaming hot cooking oil to distract him from reality. The relapse of vices revisited had made his first day just that little bit more bearable, though compared little to the elation of finishing his first day.

Walking the return leg down the Fast Mile, the faded Marlboro sticker in the convenience store window had been a beacon of hope in a sea of concrete drudgery. There were still some good in the world he thought. With a pocket full of small change he had bought the pack of twenty cigarettes from the suspicious Korean guarding the shop counter, then left with the satisfaction of having twenty more reasons to feel good about something. By the time he reached the entrance to the Mile he had already puffed away his first, and with a spring in his step made the bus stop in time to catch his ride out of the inhospitable precinct and back home sweet home to Edendale.

As the bus lumbered along Josh used his spare time to study the back of the many heads in front of him. He tried to imagine what circumstances had led each of them to be there, at that time and on that bus. As he studied the faceless heads he found them an inspiration for countless fantasies, about who they were, the lives they lived, and primarily for Josh, why they weren't driving themselves to their destination. Turning off the Golden State freeway they passed his favourite Mexican fast food joint again. Recalling the last time he had sampled the mouth watering sensation of spicy takeaway made his stomach growl loudly; reminding him he'd been around food all day but had consumed none.

He was suddenly distracted from fantasy by a pale face staring intently back at him. The man was dressed entirely in black, his raven black hair immaculately combed back away from his broad forehead. His eyes remained hidden behind dark sunglasses and he appeared to be grinning, not essentially at Josh, but at some personal amusement he was getting from him. Josh recognised the man as the same who had acknowledged his discomfort that morning, and was surprised not to have noted the peculiar presence when making the pseudo social study of his fellow passengers. The man continued to look directly at Josh for what seemed minutes, the grin subtle but always there, the awkward confrontation causing a sense of the unreal to creep down his spine like a stream of ice water. Before Josh scowled his disapproval the man turned to face the front, leaving him with a sense of relief. *Frigging Weirdo.*

Josh gazed out at the buildings and people that zipped by as the bus travelled on closer to home. Finding he couldn't beat the urge, he looked back at the intrusive passenger. He had half expected to find the pallid features glaring back his way, but the thick, perfectly groomed black hairs covering the back of his head remained in their place. *How did I miss you a second ago?* Josh recalled it had been a hell of a day. A long day full of new challenges and traumas he was unaccustomed to after hiding away from the world for the past year. He was tired, hungry and just wanted to get home and pass out on the couch.

As the bus slowed down the man slithered into the aisle. His long black coat flapped about his legs as he casually strode up to the front of the bus. The choice of all black in a Californian summer was not the wisest choice and Josh noticed the matching shoes were impeccably polished, the overall look betraying the eccentric persona behind the unconventional choice of attire.

In ways not to dissimilar to the knife wielding female psychotic, the man's interest unnerved him. As Josh watched him stride effortlessly into the early evening sun he released a captive breath. Like a sentinel dropped at some solitary outpost, the man turned slowly to watch the bus pull away as it abandoned him on the sidewalk, his shielded eyes never leaving Josh's curious gaze. Safely away Josh concluded that there were far too many cranks using public transport. The sooner he had his car back on the road then the safer he would be again.

*****

The young blonde was forced to protect her eyes as she looked upon the real world once more. *Awake again.* She knew she was free of the legion of macabre grasping forms that had endeavoured to overpower her luminous form on the other side of reality, but as her blurry eyes adjusted to the strong white light that surrounded her in the sanctuary of mirrors, she was also aware that she had escaped with her life. By precedent she would never normally heed the call of the black light, though something had made it too irresistible to resist this time; the chance to finally look upon the face of the enemy.

"Rise and shine Angelica." The man's voice drew her away from the memories of her nightmare. She turned to see he had returned to watch over her. "Pleasant trip, I hope." The voice belonged to a man she knew simply as Monk, its calm tone paternal and soothing.

"Not exactly," Angelica corrected. She leaned forward and swung her legs over the edge of the low mattress so that they joined the ground once more. "But, informative." She abhorred the intrinsic sense of fatigue that followed the projection of her living form into the higher plains, but the sacrifice was trivial in the face of the greater battle that was raging about them, and the rest of mankind. Monk, normally retaining the reserve of his ecclesiastical namesake, lurched forward from the wicker chair with uncommon impatience. In the room of infinite reflections he crouched in front of his weary comrade.

"What did you find?" he asked, looking up into her bowed features. She drew a revitalising breath then relayed the truth.

"They are stronger than we feared."

"And the great traitor?" he asked with uncommon zeal.

"The dark architect was there," Angelica revealed ominously. "And he has built his temple of betrayal on a foundation of thousands. The lost are many; we cannot afford to lose another single one to Him now." Monk's familiar reserve returned as he weighed up the significance of Angelica's cold certainty.

"You forget the inherent light in us all is far greater than whatever darkness He can manipulate. That is why we must not lose heart." Angelica looked into the stern features that echoed the assurance and knew he was right. "There are still those who are ready to be brought into the fold."

"So you've caught another?" she asked playfully, sensing some good had come of the day's developments.

"The soldier is strong and he follows my call as we speak. We'll know before long if we caught him soon enough, then he will lead us to others. Then we will be strong enough to end this for all time."

"Time is a luxury we don't have," Angelica stated, matching her comrade's certainty with her own. She stared at her infinite reflections created by the protective prism around them and wished the reflected doubles were an army of flesh and blood. "This is their war, played by their rules. They find the Low Grades before we even know of their existence. We cannot end a war that over runs us with disposable pawns and secret enemies."

"Then the pawns are to be sacrificed one by one until we do," he replied coldly. The use of allegory did nothing to lighten the protocol that meant destroying human lives, lives that were hijacked and enslaved without free will, but she knew the morbid logic was the only path to victory. Save or destroy, ignorance was no defence in the face of the imminent battle of ages, and there would be no rest until their secret enemies had been destroyed.

*****

Samson came running over from the couch greet his master. Josh Had slammed the front door shut behind him with a last spurt of energy and tip toed around the friendly feline encircling his ankles. He wondered how such a fat cat who spent most of its time lazing in the sun had the motivation to appreciate his company with such endearing vigour, but the cat was obviously hard up for friends. As Josh tugged open the heavy door of the fridge in search of food it wasn't hard to fathom his companion's interest. Unfortunately only several mouthfuls of the full fat pasteurised milk Samson so loved remained, and in an act of worn frustration, Josh drank it greedily.

"Sorry buddy, we're all out," he announced before crushing the empty carton. Samson trotted off in disgust. "User!" Josh was suddenly alerted to the negativity brooding inside him. Aware he could be cruel when moody, and moody when he was tired, he decided to do something about it. Walking into the lounge the flashing light on the answer machine relayed there were four new messages. Pressing play he then continued to the bedroom to dig out another pick-me-up from inside the closet. As he dropped to his knees in homage for what he was about to receive the familiar electronic voice could be heard making its announcement in the distance. *"You have four new messages: first message…"*

"Hi it's me. Why is your cell switched off?" Sharon's voice crackled from the speaker, her words slurred from the effects of alcohol. *"Just checking to see if you are home yet and how the new job's going. Call me when you get in Lover, oh and change the message you jerk!"* Josh slid the shoebox out and removed its lid, ignoring the usual inquisitive message his girlfriend left after drinking alone in the daytime. He would receive several of them a day when Sharon was on a day off, and he sometimes wondered whether she was really a resident rather than an employee at the care home where she worked. *Message two…*

"Hi, it's me again!" her voice declared. Josh sighed and cut himself two fresh lines. *"You still aren't home, what time is it? Oh, still early I guess. Oh well…call me. I hope no one else is hearing that message!"* He sliced and diced the fine powder with an old credit card he'd found in the box. Recanting his earlier vow of abstinence he rolled a fresh note into a pipe. He knew Cocaine was an empty promise of heaven, but what the hell he thought; the day had sapped what remaining will power he had possessed and the brief rush of euphoria was preferable to the usual numbness that accompanied his insomnia. *Message three…* Josh braced himself. A man laughed.

"Has she called yet?" Matty's voice asked, Josh paused. *"Listen; what do you think to a foursome next week?"* Josh was intrigued. For all he knew Matty was suggesting another night of sexual depravity. *"My latest concubine wants to meet my friends so I can prove to her I don't just hang around in bars picking up women, plus it would give you a chance to check out her stats for yourself, what do you say?"* Josh remembered the last double date with his college friend. The bleach-blonde, silicone-breasted swimwear model he'd introduced as his latest conquest had been a real stunner, but had lacked any finesse. He bent down and snorted the first line. Matty sounded desperate.

"Anyway just tell that nut job girlfriend of yours it's a corporate dinner or something and to make an effort this time. No gum and no ratting me out in the lady's." Josh reeled back from the heavenly effect of the narcotic causing his brain to flood with Dopamine, before quickly bowing forward again to

inhale the second line. *"Oh and her name's Serina NOT Sabrina, that was that bikini model with the fake breasts. This one's nice. Ciao."*

Josh pinched the end of his nose. The drug's potency was greater than he'd anticipated. He winced before sneezing over the powdered photo. *Message Four...*

"Christ's sake Josh, call me!" Sharon's angry voice made his head hurt. *"You'd better not be ignoring me, are you? Look, do you have to go out with that Imbecile you call a friend this Saturday? I'm supposed to be your other half, not him!"* Josh was staring with blurred eyes at the photo of Sarah and himself celebrating; happy. He didn't know why he continued to use the sacred memory for the abominable vice, but somehow he thought that in his grief the loss justified his decline into self abuse, the all too familiar well of emotion now beginning to flow from staring at the soiled memory.

"Saturday nights should be OUR time. Tell that prick to take a hike or something, and call me as soon as you get this. Erase that frigging message to!" Sharon's threats were merely static in the back of his mind. He picked up the photo and brushed away the white residue on his jeans. *I miss you so much.* After smoothing out the creases that had appeared from the years of neglect he then slid the photo under the mattress where it would be safe and free from further abuse. *This isn't how it was supposed to be.* His cell phone vibrated suddenly in his pocket. He cuffed away the stray tear from his cheek before answering.

"Don't you ever take a break?" Josh answered venomously.

"Oh so you're answering now, how nice!" She sounded sober. "How did it go?" At first Josh wanted to hang up, but he sensed a naïve sensibility in the question. When she wasn't under the toxic effects of alcohol there was a sweet side to Sharon he could only liken to a disobedient puppy, making it hard to be cruel when he imagined she knew no better.

"As well as could be expected," he replied nonchalantly. Quickly remembering he was to bolster the falsehood of finding his feet again in an executive environment, he committed to a future relieving of curiosity. "I'll tell you about it later I'm beat."

"I'm coming over," she replied abruptly and hung up before he could talk her out of it. The eager knock on his front door made him jump. *It couldn't be.* On getting up to answer the loud thuds he found Sharon was already standing on his porch, a four pack of his favourite beer hanging from the tip of an index finger.

"Sharon!" he said stunned.

"That's what my Mom called me. Samson!" Spotting the inquisitive cat behind him she walked past to crouch down and stroke the purring feline. For some reason the cat was fond of her to the point of making Josh a little jealous. Samson sniffed at the cold cans with interest.

"No these are not for you," she explained, before standing up to look seductively at Josh with her pretty eyes framed in thick, black mascara. "For my handsome man." She held out the bribe and Josh took the cans and shut the door. "What, no thank you kiss?"

"I'm sure Samson will oblige if you ask him nicely." He walked away into the lounge, dumped the cans onto the couch and picked up the television remote. Sharon followed a little uneasily in her garish pink stilettos.

"It's not my fault I have to turn up unannounced." Her tawdry matching jewellery clunked and rattled as she made the short trot. "Since last month's morbid anniversary it's the only way I could get a look in." The twentieth of July had been the second year marker for the fatal car crash. Josh had shared the moment at home with Sharon, knowing she sensed the deep longing he still clung to. She had felt an outsider, and he had denied her his thoughts.

"It's going to be one of those nights is it?" Josh asked his unwanted guest sarcastically. Her dress sense like her temperament was manic bordering on eccentric, but with a quick glance he noted how it revealed her tight form.

"Didn't the deadbeat have a good first day at the new job?"

"I'm not in the mood for any of your crap Shaz, just go make a coffee or something and put your feet up." Biting his tongue he walked back into the bedroom. Sharon looked around the untidy front room and wondered whether to stay or go. She decided to give the night a chance.

"When are you ever in the mood Josh?" she hollered over her shoulder. Dropping her handbag onto the couch she hooked the four pack and yanked a can free. "First you want me then you don't, then you call me then you blank me, you commit to me then you want space." Sharon took a big swig of cold beer and winced at the taste. "You screw me then you won't. What is it with you? I am the only women in your life right?" Josh remembered the photo under the mattress. Unlikely as it was, he imagined Sharon stumbling across the hidden memory and so decided to remove it. Ironically his timing was unfortunate; she was already standing in the bedroom doorway.

"Right?" she insisted. He fumbled the photo into his back pocket. "What was that?" Josh's heart sank. *I don't need this shit now.* She walked over, can in hand. "What are you hiding?" Before he knew it her hand had manoeuvred to his backside. He froze. Knowing he couldn't react without increasing suspicion, he succumbed to the face to face search of his back pocket. He willed her to stop, but she plucked the creased photo from his jeans and stared at the image.

"You're kidding me!"

"It's not what you think," he explained, but the pretty eyes projected their hurt. He braced himself for the obligatory slap across the face. To his surprise she capped the urge and rushed out of the room, the heavy thump on the carpet signifying the beer was now spilling onto his carpet. Only days before he had promised he would try and leave the past in the past, give their future a chance. Unsure if he truly meant it at the time, he understood playing second best was not something a tempestuous woman like Sharon would endure. He ran after her.

"She was my wife, you don't just forget about people you get married to!" he petitioned to her backside as she stretched over the back of the couch to grab her synthetic fur handbag. "I was just going through my things. I've moved on." Sharon turned to face to him.

"Yeah you were married. Yeah she died in a tragic accident, but it's the past Josh." He bit his tongue again. "This is the present. This is what counts, you said that yourself." Josh realised her casual manner had hidden the depth of her feelings. "And I go in there and find you doting over an old photo. What am I supposed to think?"

"Nothing, you're supposed to think nothing, because there's nothing to worry about. Come here." He lifted his arms to wrap them around her, but found she was unrelenting. "I do care about you. Okay I have a funny way of showing it sometimes but that's just me and my *issues*." Suddenly he felt exhausted. His words sounded hollow, though understood they reflected a truth he was simply too tired to tap into.

"Is this Josh admitting he's been a jerk?" She wanted to believe him. She studied his face for signs of sincerity.

"Well everyone's entitled to an opinion, but yes I've been a jerk." Her eyes warmed to him; instinctively he leaned in for the kiss. She was a good foot shorter than him, making her seem all the more vulnerable. Her favourite scent, an ethereal scent aptly named *Angel* filled his nostrils as they parted lips.

"So would I be right in thinking that now would be a good time for a dash of make up sex?" she asked softly. Her hands slid up his chest. The mischievous look of seduction returned, the same that had softened his heart and encouraged his latent desire the first night they had met in the wine bar four months previous.

"Is that your only answer to our problems?" he asked but didn't care as he was aware of his body's discovery of hidden energy reserves. She smiled her perfect smile and slid a hand down to his crotch.

"No, but it'll do for starters." Her hand was already undoing his belt buckle, and Josh hoped to be sleeping soundly after the evening's exertions without the aid of his prescription.

*****

The house was in darkness. In the weak exterior light that illuminated his furnishings in an eerie glow, Josh realised he was meandering wantonly from room to room. As his bare feet left the cold kitchen tiles for the soft carpet of the front room, the contrast converted disorientation into alertness. *Why am I awake?* Entering the hallway he saw a man's silhouette walking towards him. At closer inspection he recognised his own reflection in the regency style wall mirror inherited from his grand mother. *Why am I walking around?* His ghostly features stared back at him as he passed. Eyes vacant and with no detection of purpose he kept on walking.

The bedroom door was wide open as usual. He entered and saw the outline of his bed bathed in the dull electric light supplied through the blinds by a streetlight. Sharon slumbered on the side closest to the door, but from the lie of the duvet he recognised a second body beneath it. Josh walked around the bed to where the room received the most light and saw the other man lying next to her. *Who is that?* He leaned over the sleeping man. Even without ample lighting he recognised the face well enough. It was his own.

Before he could fathom the revelation his body acted without premeditation. He positioned a hand over the doppelganger's face, only to find their places immediately switched. As Josh now lay on his back the stranger hushed his protest with the hand upon his mouth. In his shock he asked himself again, *am I awake?* The leering intruder lowered his shadow veiled face and hissed six words into his ear.

"We are running out of time." Josh convulsed as he tried to swipe the intruder's hand away, but found the best he could manage was to make his torso spasm like an electrocuted eel while his limbs remained dead weight, numb and useless. His chest ached as his heart cramped with terror. In seconds it was over.

Josh opened his eyes with a start. He was lying in bed. Except for the streetlight that crept in through the blinds he was in darkness, his bedroom exactly as it had been just seconds before. *There's somebody here!* Josh panicked and scrambled for the bed-side lamp, managing to flick the switch before it toppled onto the floor to project a myriad of deformed shadows across the room. He stared towards the open door, then to

Sharon who still slept as his side. In the silence of the night he quickly recognised his own stupidity. Slowly he laid back down into the damp sheets and breathed a sigh of relief. *No more drugs!*

It was a dream, just a vivid dream. They were rare occurrences but not uncommon. The recent re-ingestion of class A narcotics had no doubt shorted a few brain cells he decided. For a brief period he had suffered with sleep paralysis as a teenager. Though he had managed to control the worrying episodes by learning to recognise the sensation of his mind waking before his body, he couldn't recall any past experience being so dramatic. He glanced back at Sharon, instantly soothed by her presence though his heart raced in his chest. After reaching down to replace the fallen lamp he popped the lid of the prescription container. Another one of the wonder pills would do the trick he decided. The stagnant water made him grimace as he swallowed one. Lights out.

The transport was familiar, and so was the journey it was taking. Josh was back on the city bus as it made its way north to Glendale. Few travelled with him that morning and from his seat at the rear he could see them all, including his schizophrenic attacker. He looked outside and saw his favourite takeaway pass by and decided he would visit it again sometime soon. But something was different that morning. It took a few moments of careful scrutiny before he realised there were no repulsive odours lingering in air. Suddenly he became disorientated when he recognised his surroundings. *This is my street!* The journey was back to front. The bus began to slow before pulling over to stop; as it did a familiar face came on board.

Josh instantly recognised the T-shirt and the jeans as his own. Frozen with bewilderment he found he was looking at a mirror image of himself walk up the aisle to sit next to the crazy woman. Josh's senses were paralysed as he struggled to comprehend what he was seeing. He watched himself look around before turning to chat with the lunatic sitting behind. Josh wanted to shout a warning, but found his mouth refused to issue the words to attract the attention of his other self.

A morbid notion then sprung into his head. *Am I dead?* Watching the rerun of the previous morning's twisted episode from the disembodied perspective caused a shiver. He simply stared on as the agitated woman produced the thin knife over the edge of the seat and tried to lunge the shiny blade at his throat. His double looked around for help, but no one was taking a blind notice as the woman tried desperately to slash at his vulnerable anatomy. Josh gathered his senses. He watched his double grab her wrist and escape his seat to flee to the rear of the bus.

"Did you see that?" his double asked him, brow shining with sweat as he slumped into a nearby seat. "That crazy bitch just tried to kill me!" His double acted without any recognition and Josh could only respond with an unnatural calmness.

"Yeah." The single word reply was all he could muster. His brain functions were too busy taking in the uncanny details of his double's features. The small white scar on the forehead caused by gauging his skin against the corner of a cabinet door could be seen clearly amongst the few freckles he had carried into adulthood. Josh looked down at his own hands. They were his hands, but for some incomprehensible reason he couldn't be sure if they really belonged to his body.

"Look at her," his double urged him, still agitated and unable to look away from the now subdued lunatic. *Has he even looked at my face?* "She's frigging crazy!" Josh was just as unable to tear his eyes from the familiar face. "Look at her!" the double now insisted. Finally he turned to Josh and pointed down the bus. *Are we still moving?* He lost all sense of reality as his senses reeled into a feeling of intoxication.

His eyes followed the end of his double's arm to where the index finger pointed to his attacker. But he could no longer see the crazed woman. Instead in her place were the warm features of a young, attractive dark haired woman who gazed back at them through hazel eyes. Without thinking Josh stood and walked down the aisle to sit next to her, overwhelmed to find it to be who he hoped it was.

Sarah held out her hand, gesturing for Josh to take it so she could draw him down into the seat beside her. Like an obedient puppy he complied and gazed into the face of his dead wife.

"Sarah?" he asked in total disbelief. "Is this real?" As he lifted his hand to touch her face she looked down into her denim handbag, the handbag she had bought on the anniversary of their first month together. She reached inside and to his astonishment produced a large golden key that she then handed over. He felt the very real weight of the medieval-styled key in the palm of his hand and studied it with bemusement.

"This is what you are looking for Josh," she declared softly but resolutely. "I found it for you and now it's yours." She closed his fingers over the shiny object with her own hands, warm and soft, just as he remembered them.

"This isn't mine," he replied. Confused by the gift that meant nothing to him he let the key drop to grasp her hands, "I've missed you so much." He gently tightened his grip of her warm flesh. He knew it was all somehow too perfect to be true.

"I've missed you to Josh." She freed her small hands from his and placed them over his face. "But I'm here now." For a moment he was in a state of utopian bliss. It all felt so real, but he knew he had to be dreaming. Josh closed his eyes. *I want to stay in this place, don't let me wake.*

He opened them again to see her hands were no longer on his face, but clasping the brown synthetic leather of a steering wheel. Gazing around he discovered he was also no longer on the public bus. Sarah was next to him in the driving seat of their old car; it was the morning of the crash. She turned to smile as she had done on that fateful day, the sedan appearing in the corner of Josh's eye as his dead wife made her melancholy farewell.

"I love you Josh." He reached out for the wheel to avoid the approaching calamity, but found it locked into the doomed trajectory. He wrenched frantically again, still the wheel refused to budge. Fate could not be thwarted, and now paralysed with terror he faced his inability to prevent the fatal crash from recurring. The sedan impacted with the force of a Scud missile and the last thing he heard was her screaming his name.

A flash of pain woke the sleeper. The impact of his head colliding with the bedroom floor startled Josh back to reality. For a moment the rude awakening completely disorientated him, though the sharp pain in his neck caused by the awkward landing quickly recalibrated his senses. The car was gone and he was face down on the bedroom carpet. Glad he'd survived without breaking his neck; Josh let his legs topple out from under the duvet and rolled onto the floor. The crick in his neck caused a grimace of agony but he was right again. On his back he retrieved his senses from the dream world and decided he was now truly and finally awake. The coarse fibre against his naked back endorsed this decision, and so too did the pain that shot between his shoulders. He had never thought he would ever be so glad to be awake, and that the calamity he'd just relived just a brainstorm. *Frigging dreams.*

Back in the very real world the approaching thud of footsteps made him turn to see Sharon's lithe form appear in the bedroom doorway. Wrapped in a towel she was fresh from the shower.

"Why are you on the floor?" she asked, then nullified the question, "I don't want to know." She turned and walked back to the bathroom. "Get dressed!" Her instruction echoed off the tiled walls. "You'll be late for work." Acknowledging a new day of challenges waited to greet him, he sat against the bed and massaged the ache in his neck, then looked for the jeans he knew had been slung across the room in the pre-coital ritual of undressing. Lurching to his feet he found them behind the chair where Sharon had thrown them.

"And you were talking in your sleep again," Sharon called out.

"Was I?" he asked, feigning innocence. Josh hoped she would elaborate on the open comment, but the only response he received was the slam of the bathroom door. As he zipped up he spotted his T-shirt under the window. *We've got to fall out more often.* It had been a hell of a night. Perhaps he *could* put the past behind him and start afresh with Sharon, he thought. He pulled the musty t-shirt over his head. Images of Sarah and the dreamscape bus were flashing before his mind's eye, leaving him in doubt it would that easy.

He knew the mind buried its frustrations deep within the unconscious. Past regrets festered and projected into dreams to taunt and test the dreamer by forcing them to face their weaknesses. However the psychological symbolism posed by his dead wife's present of the novelty key was something of a mystery. During high school Josh had befriended an art student obsessed with the creative potential of dreams and been introduced to the bible of the unconscious, a dream dictionary. He remembered the hours spent researching the hidden meanings of specific objects within dreams, trying to relate the prophetic new age symbolism to some form of higher foresight. However, bored of trying to decipher the riddles posed by his mindscape he had eventually swapped the book for a marijuana plant.

As old concepts returned, the niggling feeling he had experienced a lucid dream became more certain; a seemingly vivid dream in which his conscious mind had awoken within it and enabled him to interact freely within a virtual dreamscape reality.

"Tell me you are not wearing those clothes for work!" Sharon had returned to eye him with a look of distaste. He knew the day's worth of sweat meant the t-shirt and jeans were verging on ripe, but took satisfaction from the fact he was making a statement about the contempt in which he held his job. But Josh had forgotten his masquerade. As Sharon searched the room for her furry handbag, he realised he should have chosen a shirt and tie; instead he looked like the bum he was.

"I think you'll find that thing you call a handbag is on the couch where you left it."

"That *thing* cost me fifty dollars! You've got ten minutes mister," she declared before rushing into the lounge. Out of sight Josh grabbed his rucksack from the closet, stripped and stuffed the casuals inside then went to get showered. The shave was a rushed affair but it didn't matter, so long as he looked and smelt suave enough in the fresh shirt and tie he now sported, it was all he needed to perpetuate the myth of success.

Pleasantly surprised with the transformation, Sharon gave him an appreciative kiss before returning to the reapplication of her ample mascara. While he waited for her to complete the cosmetic wizardry, Josh went out front to admire the growing patches of rust on the dull silver paintwork of his deceased vehicle. A quick call to the garage on his cell revealed a three day backlog was holding up its repair. Hanging up, he turned his attention to Sharon's car.

Though belonging to her mother she hardly used it, hence the little city car was littered with discarded items from her daughter's life. The collection of out of date celebrity magazines and fast food containers cluttering the foot-wells were a constant eyesore for Josh, but as he made his examination there was something new to incite his irritation.

"Unless you're planning to hot wire it, big boy, you'll need these." Sharon slammed the front door behind her, jingling her keys as she then waded through the tall grass of the lawn towards him.

"You've changed your seat covers, again!" he exclaimed. He caught her as a high heel buckled in the uneven ground.

"Jesus!" She straightened and disabled the central locking. "Well a girl's gotta have her accessories." Josh got in, looking bemused with the latest choice of interior car design.

"Zebra skin!" He couldn't believe the funeral pyre of taste he was sitting on.

"Do you want a lift or not?"

"Well as my usual ride is out of service you can drop me at the bus stand bottom of the street." Sharon was checking her makeup in the rear view mirror, but then turned with a look of suspicion. "If that's not too much trouble my love," he added warily.

"I thought I was taking you to your new job?"

"I'm sure you've got better things to do Sweetheart, like get to work yourself." She continued to glare, knowing her curiosity would be thwarted by the change of plan.

"I've been trying to work it out all morning but I'll be damned if I can tell what it is." Josh prepared for the worst.

"What have I done now?"

"What the hell have you done to your face?" It took a couple of seconds for Josh to realise what had gotten her so riled. He put her mind at rest by covering his top lip and chin with his hand.

"New me, new us," he offered.

"Whatever," she replied dryly, embarrassed by a lack of perception over the missing facial hair.

The short drive to the bottom of the street escalated into a lifetime. In the few minutes it took to drive to his stop, Josh cunningly avoided Sharon's curiosity with vague explanations that could be denied or elaborated. Reaching the stand he was forced to bolt from the small car to join the motley crew of strangers forming the queue. The words *screw* and *you* followed him out, relaying Sharon's renewed discontent. The car growled dangerously off into the street and he knew it was impossible to keep everyone happy, least of all himself. Sarah and he had rarely argued, but he had to let that dream go if he was to get on with his life. He knew that, but the lucid dream still fresh in his mind only seemed to re-ignite the past in glorious Technicolor. The touch of her flesh against his lingered in his soul, leaving him wanting more as he watched the Glendale bus approach. But there would be an emotional price to pay for his futility, whether his or Sharon's it was too early to say.

Chapter 3

Ben had been trained to endure any hardship that could arise in the battlefield. Extreme environments, personal injury, hunger, hand to hand combat and even torture at the hands of the enemy. These were the very real things he had been trained to countermand. But the months of elite training at a covert Delta Force training camp in the Everglades could not have prepared him for the psychological ordeals the past few weeks had thrown his way. His final tour of duty with the elite squad of killers had ended abruptly just six months previous. Honorary discharge from military service due to medical grounds had ejected him back into the civilian world. The head injury he'd received in the desolate corner of the Middle East had left him partially deaf in one ear, scarred down the one side of his face and his psychological stability in tatters.

Dubbed *Alpha* by his blood brothers in Red Four squad due to his roguish *Jock* looks and unrelenting courage, his superiors had adopted the call sign when assigning their pride and joy the delicate but lethal special operations in the particularly hostile theatre of war. The hidden explosive that had stolen his perfection however had severely shaken the once proud fighting machine's sense of immortality. But more recently he had become a slave to the torments he endured every night at the hands of his dreams.

The flashback would begin with the same deployment outside a remote dwelling in the barren landscape. He would rush into the same ramshackle building, find the same young Arab boy hiding the device behind his back, screaming the same fanatical prophecies in the desert tongue, and the same explosion which would steal his senses. Even when the prescription of blue sleeping pills would allow him to indulge in healthy sleep, they couldn't drown out the vivid realism he now faced in arena of his unconscious.

The nightmares had been traded for new ones. The Arab boy in the shack had been replaced by the ghoulish figure who called himself Monk. Instead of the fanatical ramblings there was perfect English, and the same testing of strength and will night after night, leaving both mind and body drained by the time he awoke in a cold sweat. He'd thought his sanity had finally fled from the terrors witnessed in the desert hell holes, but the bald headed intruder had forced him to relive them, to reason that he was not merely a projection of his own dementia, but an entity with power over his mind and soul.

"Welcome Alpha," Monk's now familiar voice intoned out from the darkness. "It's so good of you to join us." Ben struggled to see the figures standing amongst the collection of furnishings that were hidden in the near dark of the large room he'd been summoned to. What little light there was had to force its way through shuttered windows. "Please take a seat; it's going to be a long day."

After witnessing Monk's apparition in the strip club rest room Ben had been given clear instructions, which he had followed to the letter. He had quickly vacated the scene of the incredible display of power, headed straight past the bar and the topless girls then climbed the steep stairs back into the LA sun. The rendezvous point had only been a couple of blocks away and he had made the walk as if still in the grip of one of his vivid nocturnal visions. He had been on the run for almost two weeks, avoiding the trappings of sleep with the help of an over prescribed dosage of caffeine tablets. It had been several hours since his last measure, but with the current high of adrenaline he needed no booster.

"Who are you people?" Ben asked, ignoring the offer that resonated from the shadows around him. Fear and anticipation had combined into an indistinguishable sense of dread. His shattered sense of reality had left him a desperate man on the run with a Glock 9mm revolver. Though proving fruitless at the crucial moment, he still wished he had possessed the weapon as he'd entered the warehouse building via a fire escape in the adjoining alley. Moving with military stealth to the current main room, the same military cunning now told him a welcome party of several people waited in the darkness.

"Take a seat!" Monk's voice commanded. "I wouldn't want to pin you to such a high ceiling like our friend in the club. You might fall and hurt yourself."

Ben's eyes were adjusting to the low light, but still he couldn't make out his persecutor's form across the large, unlit interior. Though the threat was veiled in sarcasm it rang with an enmity that made him feel suddenly cold. He stepped forward to where he could just make out an ornate chair situated in a clearing amongst the collection of oddities. Ben did what was demanded. He had no intention of being thrown around like a broken doll. As he sat a single light spotlighted him from above and three figures emerged to surround him.

"Now Alpha, we need that answer." The man called Monk was now standing in front of him. From a quick glance around Ben saw two women accompanied him, but confusion locked his attention back onto his host. The voice was the same but the appearance had changed, the ghoul now appeared to be a man. The uncovered eyes were blue, the clean-shaven chin now sported a pharaoh-styled platted beard and to Ben's surprise, the baldhead was now covered in a thick covering of black hair that was pulled back into a long shiny ponytail. Monk sensed his confusion.

"You recognise the voice, then you know the man," Monk confirmed. He reached behind and dragged a heavy ornate seat forward. As he sat down opposite, Ben recognised the face now the harsh overhead light shone fully onto his stalker's stern features, while the two women, one blonde and athletic, the other petite with long auburn hair, remained standing out of his peripheral vision.

"I want to know who you people are," Ben petitioned Monk. "What agency are you with? And how the hell did you do all that stuff at the Zoom?" Faced with his tormentor on more common ground, the weeks of frustrated rage were now easily vented. But the answer was not what he had expected.

Monk's face tensed into a spasm of rage. Suddenly the invisible force that had disabled the Zoom's doorman now took hold of Ben's body, seizing his unsuspecting body like a cold steel vice that forced the air from his lungs in an instant. His arms were crushing his own chest, his oesophagus was contracting, he felt his ribs bending inwards and the crushing pressure encasing his head felt as though it would burst it like a boil.

"The questions are mine to ask!" Monk snarled at him. He tried to speak but the ability had vanished. He could only widen his eyes and squirm in a pathetic gesture that pleaded for mercy. "You give the answers here!" For a second Monk seemed to be enjoying the reprimand. Ben felt he was going to pass out.

"That's enough!" a woman's voice commanded. Equally as swift, the crushing force relented. With the lethal grip relinquished Ben heaved forward instinctively to refill his burning lungs. As the agony left his body he coughed and spluttered mercilessly, his traumatised brain reeling as it tried to recalibrate and recover from the hands of death. Opening his eyes he saw a second set of feet in front of him. He looked up to through blurry eyes to see the blonde was now standing over him, her face in shadow as the light shone from above her head.

"We are not the monsters here," she stated, "but you will answer our questions." Her blue eyes pierced the shadows with an energy that made his feebleness seem all the more absolute.

"Just tell me who you are," he pleaded. He was depleted of any energy to fight. She answered his question with a soothing tone.

"My name is Angelica." She touched his face. "And we are servants of the light." He sat back in the high back ornate chair to stare up and see the alluring young woman was every much the epitome of her name. Her answer stumped him, but he knew the peculiar explanation only heralded something profound rather than insane. Stepping aside she allowed the long-haired Monk to continue the interrogation, who then ominously stood over the stocky captive.

"Now Alpha, the answer to my question if you please."

*****

Josh rooted in his pocket for the packet of cigarettes. He had managed to sneak the packet into his pocket prior to leaving the house, but to his dismay found he had forgotten the lighter. The fast mile was busier that morning, gangs of factory workers walked into work together with an uncanny cheer that Josh couldn't comprehend, especially as his shift started early that morning. So impressed with Josh's keen instinct for the job, Carlos had insisted he came in for nine. Even though Josh found both the man and the job repulsive, it polished his dented ego to know he was still good for something, even if it was as a dog's body.

Reaching the convenience store he went back inside to make his purchase from the less than friendly Korean who looked concerned by the constant itching of his smooth chin. Back outside he tossed a cigarette between his lips, ignited it with the new disposable and took the first big drag of the day before striding off down the Mile, head bowed from the waxing sun.

Quickening his pace his unconscious decided to inject a flashback of the night's vivid adventures into his thoughts. *Sarah.* He was confused why his past was haunting him so avidly, and the clarity of walking through his house, of being in control of his senses but not of his actions, both intrigued and worried him at the same time. Something different was happening he concluded, and such experiences couldn't be healthy. He recalled how his aunt had suffered with delusions and eventually taken her own life. Paranoid tendencies that appeared in times of turmoil were igniting old fears that maybe he could be suffering a hereditary condition. *Bull.*

Josh believed he was probably the sanest person he knew. Digging out his cell he decided to prove it by dialling the number he hadn't planned to call again. As he waited for an answer he passed the store entrance occupied by the attractive women the morning previous, unfortunately she was nowhere to be seen. A woman with a thick southern drawl finally answered his call with a slow apathetic tone.

"Hi my name is Josh Brenin; I wonder if you could put me through to doctor Halberstram, I'm a patient of his." The southern voice seemed reluctant to help. "I understand, but it won't take but a few minutes of his time." He looked up and realised he wasn't far from the diner. "Regarding? Well he prescribed me these pills. He's been treating me since er, well they're having a - shall we say - an adverse affect on me and I…" His mind was a jumble of babble as he imagined the woman yawning in her chair whilst filing her nails. "Sorry? No I can't hold, I…Hello?" She put him on hold. Josh knew he was swimming against the tide and decided to postpone the medical dilemma.

He hung up and entered the diner to find the main floor already heaving with hungry workers. The first part of their shifts completed, the local work teams had escaped for the first food run of the day and Josh was forced to carefully make his way past the eager clientele, feeling quite out of place in the formal shirt and trousers he still wore. Carlos did a double take as he spotted the well-dressed queue jumper creeping towards the counter.

"Branny!" he yelled, embarrassing Josh. "The front door's for paying customers, you use the back in the future." Josh nodded, avoiding the faces the comment caused to turn his way. Making it to the staff door Carlos looked bewildered at the unconventional way he was dressed. "You been to court? Where's your uniform?" Josh stopped short and looked bewildered.

"I guess I left it at home," he explained. *Was I supposed to take that clown suit back home?*

"In the back now! Reinhold make sure there's enough Big Eats to go around while I sort your boyfriend out." Dink had been assigned burger flipping duty on the main grill, though flipped Carlos the bird as he walked out of the kitchen to meet Josh in the locker room.

"A uniforms no good if it's at home is it college boy?" Carlos looking him over curiously for a second time then waddled over to the lockers. Josh was in no mood for the barrage of abuse he knew this man was quite capable of.

"No Carlos it isn't", he replied dryly. He watched his boss reach up for a box perched on top.

"As you're new I'll cut you some slack, just this once." Josh ignored the reprimand. Instead he noted the grease marks on the maroon baseball cap that Carlos wore to cover up an on-setting bald patch. "Use that for today but leave it when you're done, it's useful for catching rats." He gave Josh a sly grin, implying the comment may or may not be the truth, "And your buckets where you left it" he added belligerently. Lecture over he waddled back into the kitchen. Josh held up the maroon shirt between two fingertips and caught a waft of stale body odour. He was unsure what part he hated the most, having to risk biological contamination from wearing the tattered shirt, or finding out the bucket was now *his*, his own personal ball and chain. The locker that had housed the previous day's uniform was now empty except for an empty soda can. There was no choice but to play ball. He pulled out the change of clothes from his rucksack and tried to convince himself things could be a lot worse, though struggled to imagine how.

The first hours of the hectic shift dragged like a broken leg. Knowing what to expect from his new vocation, Josh found it hard to silence the voice in his head telling him to down tools and walk out. He tried to empty his mind by focusing on the menial and endless task of mopping the kitchen floor, hoping he would forget about the relevance of time and try to develop the mindset of a dedicated Eat-A-Lot employee. Only twenty three minutes had passed before he realised it was futile. By midday the only thing that gave him solace was the idea of a smoke break on the loading bay.

"What?" Josh exclaimed as he noted Dink's smirking features. No sooner had the budding friends stepped outside and sat down on the warm concrete platform; the teenager had taken one look at the borrowed shirt and burst into a fit of laughter. "Am I missing something here?" Dink forced a straight face.

"A sense of decency, perhaps," he replied. The two had been working side by side for the past hour. Carlos had upgraded his newest wage slave from mop monkey to the grills under the adolescent's tutelage. Far from being a chore, Josh's wandering mind had been entertained by Dink's misadventures regarding two high school girls. Dink cocked his nose to the air feigning a bad smell, "Can you smell rat piss?" Josh's heart sank.

"Don't tell me that fat Grease-ball wasn't kidding."

"You got it! In more ways than one!" Josh jumped to his feet. "Wow keep your distance man I haven't had my shots for the plague yet."

"Right that's it, screw that guy," Josh cursed as he pulled his arm back through into the uniform, "And screw this shirt!" He whisked it over his head and completed the movement by slinging the shirt into the nearest dumpster.

"It's a bit late for that hombre. Smoke?" Dink held out a roll up. Josh wiped his bare arms down in vain, checked his t-shirt for lingering odour and then pulled out the packet of cigarettes he had bought.

"Here take one of mine, I took your advice." He sat back down, offering the packet. "What's life for if it ain't for living?" Dink snatched it and helped himself to two sticks.

"So how much longer is mister white collar willing to stick it out in this wonderful new career of his? I'll give it a week, tops." Josh wasn't listening to the question. He was looking at the tainted shirt sleeve sticking up between two simmering garbage bags and wondered whether he should go home, get showered and come back tomorrow to urinate on Carlos's cap. "Yeah in fact here, I bet you the rest of today's cancer stock you won't be sitting here on this bay a week from today." Dink offered Josh the battered tin of rolling tobacco. Josh turned to look at the scratched Cannabis emblem barely visible on its lid.

"I wouldn't want to deprive you of one of life's necessities."

"It's your call White Collar Man," Dink replied, a smouldering rollup sagging from his lip James Dean fashion.

"I'll take that bet, and raise you that rat rag Carlos calls a uniform in there. If I'm still here in a week so will you, wearing that biohazard!" Dink surprised him with a throaty laugh and held out his hand.

"You got yourself a deal old man." Again the fire escape door behind burst open. Carlos stood over them with a carton of half eaten fries in hand.

"What the hell are you two doing here? I got a floor packed with paying customers and you're sitting out here on your butts jerking around." He looked Josh up and down and stuffed the last of the fries into his ample mouth. "Brannigan where's that uniform I gave you?" Josh looked guiltily towards the dumpster. "Whatever, both of you get back in now!" Carlos spotted another victim in the locker room and left to expel some more abuse, leaving Dink to grin at Josh's attempt to rescue the Eat-A-Lot shirt from the overflowing dumpster.

The new wave of customers reminded Josh of an army of barbarians engaged on a mission of plunder. He had returned to the grill with Dink to listen to the ongoing saga of his extra curricular sex life, hoping to avoid the draft back onto the main floor. But taking him by the elbow, Carlos pointed him back to his ball and chain.

Reluctantly Josh steered the wheeled bucket out onto the main floor and began the arduous wiping of floor tiles around shuffling feet. If a table was vacated he was also instructed to clear it quickly. *Surely this can wait.* Due to a nervous over compensation Josh found his motor skills becoming jittery in such close proximity to his belligerent public. *No one is looking at me.* He recited the mantra in his head, while sneaky glimpses upwards proved that he might just be right. *Nothing to worry about here, all is good.* The boisterous crowd were taking their seats, filing the few free booths and enjoying their brunch without issue. Josh found his jittery nerves all but calmed themselves as a result. *See, nothing to worry about.*

Spotting a shake lid hidden near the wall he bent under the table to retrieve it, but as he backed out and straightened, his head collided with something hard.

The customer had tried to back away, but the tray, loaded with Big Eat burgers, Big Eat fries and Big Eat Soda was knocked clean out of the his hands. As his order fell to the clean floor tiles it showered Josh with sticky, sweet beverage.

"My food!" the customer growled furiously. The diner went deadly silent, the sudden agitated roar heralding the start of a tumultuous situation. Josh flayed his arms to shake off the liquid but it was too late, the musty Eat-A-Lot shirt rescued from the dumpster had received a much needed soaking. Fuming, he looked up to meet the customer's gaze, but found he had to look a good foot and a half above his own eye-line before he saw the man's enraged, deep set eyes. The giant standing in front of him looked fit to explode with rage.

"I'm so sorry sir I didn't see you there," Josh yielded. Immediately he bent down to pick up the scattered remains of the man's vast order.

"Leave it!" the man growled, eyes bulging with anger.

"I'll get you a replacement right away sir. I'm so sorry." Josh stacked the scattered food as best as he could into one of the splayed cartons, but the act of redemption was in vain.

"I said leave it you skinny faggot, that's my food!" Josh stared up at the giant standing over him, his heart pounding like a death knell. "Get up!" Josh did what was commanded, realising he shared the floor's sticky predicament.

"Leo forget it, it was an accident," the giant's friend intervened. "The kid said he was sorry." From the nervy intervention Josh guessed his fiery colleague was no stranger to hostility.

"That's easy for you to say it's not your goddamn food on the floor!" Leo swung his empty tray into his friend's chest, expecting him to hold it while he squared up to the new boy. His friend shrugged and backed off, knowing better than to agitate the big man when he was fired up.

"Sir please," Josh implored, trying to retain a formal hold on the situation. He noted Leo's jaw was disproportionately large to his grisly face, reminding him of a caricature brute. Josh was sorry, he was real sorry. "If you'd like to take a seat I'll retake your order and we can all calm down." A familiar figure then caught Josh's eye. His friend the Hispanic was leaning against a brick pillar with a grin that stretched across his chubby face. *Is this your doing?* Leo suddenly grabbed and twisted a grubby lapel of Josh's shirt, lifting him onto his toes. The man had more strength in one arm than Josh did in two.

"What are you, some kind of retard?"

"Sir I'm going to ask you to let go of me and take a step back," Josh advised. To a man of Leo's mindset the words only fanned the flames. He twisted the shirt tighter in his iron grip.

"Or what faggot?" Leo growled dangerously into Josh's face. The hole Josh had dug was as deep as it could go, another misconstrued word was all his assailant required. "I bust my balls all day for the money that paid for that," he continued angrily. "And for what? So you can knock it out of my fucking hands!"

"Leo for Christ's sake calm down, he said he'll get you another order," his colleague pleaded again, but Leo's brutish features further grimaced at his prey. Josh saw his enraged corneas constrict and knew what was coming. Frozen like a rabbit trapped in the headlights of a car, Josh could do nothing as the giant brought a fist crashing down into the bone and cartilage of his face. The impact sent him reeling backwards over a table. As he was splayed onto his back the flash of intense light was instantly replaced by the sanctuary of darkness. Before Leo could enjoy the aftermath of his actions however, a hero jumped into the scene.

Josh started to come around on the table. Through the blur of delirium he could hear the repeated thud of what sounded like someone punching packed meat.

"That's enough!" someone shouted, but the demand for calm was ignored as Dink continued to thrash out his limbs like a crazed animal. A stray leg kicked Josh painfully in the knee. He blinked at the ceiling, Dink's threats roaring out of sight and welcoming him back to reality. Whatever he was lying on felt hard and flat and quickly Josh concluded he wasn't at home in bed. Carlos then appeared over him.

"Brannigan! Get the hell up!" he ordered, and then slapped Josh's bewildered face. The Eat-A-Lot manager hauled his dazed employee upright until he sat on the edge of the table like a broken doll. The pang of pain soon brought him back to his senses and he watched the dazed giant drag himself up into a wavering stance, an open gash on his forehead oozing blood into one eye. Dink had jumped the giant with a reckless courage that had toppled his attacker to the floor, where he had repeatedly hammered his large skull against the clean tiles.

A howl of pain then announced Dink's escape from restraint via a hard stamp down the shin of Leo's friend. Once free he shot over to Josh and braced for a second bout. Uncomfortably, Carlos took one look around at the small army of gawking customers and acted accordingly.

"Both of you, you're fired!" Josh noted the dim-witted look on Leo's face as he tried to fathom which truck had run him over.

"What! You can't be serious?" Dink blurted out. "That asshole attacked him first!"

"I mean it Reinhold get the hell out of my diner, you to Brannigan. You're out!" Josh wasn't listening. He was glaring at the grinning Hispanic who sent him a mocking wink.

"Josh can you get up?" he heard Dink ask. His tone had dropped from manic to calm. The youngster knew there was little point appealing to righteousness where there was none.

"If you're both not out of here in five minutes I'm calling the cops!" Carlos threatened, empowering his decision. Dink aided Josh onto his feet.

"I'm okay!" Josh insisted, his world subsiding as he stumbled towards a sedated Leo, who attempted to adopt an intimidating pose though failed due to an on setting concussion. "Mister you did me a favour," he said to the dishevelled giant then pulled off the damp shirt and threw it into Carlos's face. "This *new boy* quits anyhow."

"You can't quit you're fired!" Carlos retaliated as he threw the shirt to the ground. "And you can forget about any wages you little prick," he blurted back, but Josh was already out the door. As the glass entrance sealed him and his avenging hero out of their place of work he felt nauseous and lurched to a nearby parking meter for support. Behind him he heard Dink running his mouth at the diner glass, but the warm taste of iron in Josh's own only made him want to spit the rush of blood onto the sidewalk. A couple of would-be diners approached, saw the two troublemakers and decided to go elsewhere.

"Yeah, where d'you buy your green card, jerk!" Dink muttered at the posturing men still inside. He turned to Josh with an amiable pat on the back. "Best get the hell out of here Bro before they really do call the cops."

"I can't believe that animal attacked me!" Josh spat another glob of crimson saliva onto the sidewalk. The draft of fresh air helped him to appreciate the gravity of the past few minutes. Resurrecting himself he held his head high and began the long despairing walk back down the sun kissed Mile.

"There goes another job down the pan," Dink mused after checking they weren't being followed. "Screw that guy, let's go get a beer." Josh's companion was on a sprightly, post-battle high, but all Josh wanted to do was recover in the solitude of his own company.

"I think I'll pass," Josh mumbled, "My head's already spinning." He appreciated Dink's intervention, but there wasn't anything worth celebrating in being attacked and losing a job. A fleck of blood on his jeans caught his eye. "Damn it! My stuff's still in my locker."

"You fancy strolling on back in there and getting it? 'Cause if you do you're on your own." Dink stopped and pulled out his tin of smokes. "Here, have a smoke instead."

"Something tells me I should probably quit while I'm ahead." The loss of clothing was frustrating, but he would have to write them off as casualties of war. Besides with Matty's help, he knew it was extra ammo for the lawsuit he was going to slap on the Eat-A-Lot franchise for unfair dismissal. *Easy money.* "Thanks for your help back there, I owe you." The taste of blood suddenly renewed his nausea.

"What are friends for?" His young saviour grinned and lit up. "Besides I was gonna blow that joint in a week or two anyhow. I'm better than that shit hole, and so are you." Josh held out his hand.

"I mean it," he insisted. They shook hands and Dink looked amused by the formality. "You drink one for me," Josh continued off down the Mile alone.

The strength of the midday sun began to sear his senses. For the first time Josh also felt as though the summer heat was actually cooking his skin. The TV weather girl had promised that year would see the hottest temperatures recorded in L.A. for the past ten years, and right then it felt as though she was going to be right. His eyes began to water from the intensity of the sun, but not so much he couldn't make out the man standing in plain view in the shade of a building on the opposite side of the busy North Glendale street.

Diverted from his woes Josh studied the black attired loner perched on the street corner and envied the shades he was wearing. Suddenly he clicked the straggler and the curious weirdo from the bus was one and the same. *You again?* The loner simply stood and stared back through the traffic stream, a composed voyeur of the concrete wonders of the Fast Mile, but Josh couldn't be sure of the point of interest due to the protective eyewear. *You looking at me?* Temporarily blocked by an overhang, the sun suddenly burst back into Josh's eyes. He raised his hand to block the harmful rays just as a passing security van interrupted his line of sight. As it hurtled by Josh looked back to see the loner had moved on. He stopped and double checked. The inappropriate dress code meant there was little room for doubt. *Got nothing else better to do Freak?* Fearing the unwanted attentions of another of the city's wandering lunatics, Josh decided to make haste.

*****

The cruel reputation of the Californian desert lands east of the Sierra Nevada was well deserved. As one of the hottest places on Earth the summer temperatures soared past ninety degrees Fahrenheit as a rule of thumb. Local landmarks such as Dead Man's Pass and Hell's Gate bore testimony to the God forsaken landscape endured by pioneers and travellers unlucky enough to have lived and worked the barren landscape over the centuries. But for the black book agencies that had made it their home from home since the early fifties, the infernal mystique of the secluded parched plains and rocky terrain had offered the perfect residence away from the eyes of the world.

Route two three seven was a neglected track that twisted and turned its way from the main road like the trail of some prehistoric serpent. It meandered through the steep canyon known as Devil's Creek, a former waterway that had dried up centuries before, and terminated at the foot of a steep precipice. The man made entrance at its end, reinforced with concrete and steel, was covered with intimidating, rusted signs that warned unauthorised persons not to enter the large hangar area inside. To the casual trespasser it was a dark and abandoned structure, a remnant of cold war security and long forgotten. However several stories below a labyrinth of corridors and technology remained hidden from the world, a clandestine place where unofficial agencies continued to manipulate the world from the scorched valley as they had done for the past five decades.

The corridor on level six looked the same as any other of the thirty-three levels that were illuminated by the cold neon light that reflected on its clinical walls and metal doors that ran along its length. The room behind door *K* was small and lit by a single source at the centre of the ceiling. Under the pillar of light a government agent studied the disembodied visual display unit that was a holographic projection from the steel table in front of him. Wearing a plain black suit that matched his collarless shirt and pants, his pale face seemed a ghoulish apparition suspended in a world of shadows. The applications from the ethereal VDU reflected in the sunglasses wrapped with ergonomic precision around his spectral face, protecting the sensitive eyes that lay behind as he scrolled through them with a keen gaze.

The door facing the solitary agent slid open, allowing another similarly attired agent to enter. The subordinate walked to the table as it slid silently shut and took the vacant seat opposite his sombre colleague.

"Report," the seated agent prompted. He was older and heavier set than the subordinate, who was careful to exude subservience as he watched his master scroll through the wealth of disembodied data emanating from the burnished metal tabletop. The subordinate shared the same milky, pallid skin, but not his superior's broad, squared jaw that conveyed his prominent status. His high cheekbones were oddly accentuated by thin dark eyebrows that peeked well above the sunglasses, creating an androgynous and macabre mystique.

"I am passed the primary protocols of engagement and have walked with the Nothos amongst the herd," the agent replied in formal monotone. "He has also responded well to second level engagement using his closest familiar." Fresh from the field amongst the cattle of the ignorant masses and supervising the progress of his befuddled charge, the subordinate agent hadn't been prepared for the encounter. The summons was against their organisation's strict modus operandi.

"Dead?" the senior agent enquired.

"Yes. I have begun the hyper blueprint," he replied, hiding his anxiety with calm resolve. "His awareness is already regulating without Ketron. May I?" His question was acknowledged with the superior's stern nod and he touched the table to generate a separate holographic display that appeared alongside the primary. The senior agent looked impressed by the flashing stats that were relayed. As he studied the illuminated information, the senior agent's pale features revealed an extension of interest. "I shall continue?" the subordinate asked hesitantly. His superior studied the array of graphical intrigue for a moment longer.

"Perhaps I should complete the blueprint myself," he replied bluntly. "Only the finest of seeds should be sown in such fertile mindscapes as this, Brenin Low Grade." The boastful intervention rattled the younger agent, but he accepted the instruction with mindful complicity.

"As you wish, though no doubt such a *fertile* mind will be highly sort by both sides of the divide," the younger agent added ominously. Sensing his superior's silent disassociation, he turned to leave. It was unheard of for the Principal to take personal interest in the recruitment of Low Grades, and proved the young agent's belief that his lowly charge's competence was of greater value than first anticipated. He had progressed quickly, too quickly perhaps, but now a fate had been sealed, it was no longer the agent's concern. It was now in the hands of his master.

*****

The newly renovated downtown offices of Zalman & Merchant were experiencing another busy day. In the high rolling world of commercial lending and mergers & acquisitions, Personal Assistants sat behind desks as guardians of the honeybees who brokered the multi million dollar contracts that made their Corporation one of the most prestigious financial firms in Los Angeles. Though one such *Honeybee;* Matthew Nugent, had achieved his position on the company's executive career ladder with honours, he was at heart a man of leisure who enjoyed the fruits of success, along with an uncanny luck with the opposite sex afforded him by his Californian good looks.

His thick brown hair and unblemished clean-shaven face were pampered with a range of cosmetic products that would make the average American woman green with envy, and thanks to the private gym reserved for the company's lucrative elite, maintained an athletic physique with regular workouts.

Matty purposely told his personal assistant, who he disappointedly found to be dowdy and uninteresting, that he preferred to leave the door to his office open while he worked. Compacting the request, by feigning he suffered with minor bouts of claustrophobia, the real blonde object of his desire could then be spotted across the acquisitions suite as she entered to Xerox hard copies.

With a well-homed instinct he spotted the leggy assistant enter the secluded room on its opposite side. *Right on time.* Usually he made haste hoping to find the sleek skirt riding up the PA's long, tanned legs as she leaned over to check the paper tray, but that day he had been uncommonly distracted by a notion he concluded was sympathy. Not for the integrity of the office eye candy, but for his humbled friend.

From amongst the gallery of framed pictures that adorned his office wall between a potted palm shrub and his panoramic view of the city's impressive corporate skyline, Josh's beaming face haunted the present as a cruel reminder of better times. Graduation day. Josh, Sarah and himself; faces revealing a picture of thwarted happiness. He had liked Sarah, and against the grain she had seemed to like him also, humouring his candid humour and open book policy on relationships with admirable liberalism. From the mounted snapshot of their shared history he could see how she had been the linchpin that held Josh together and inadvertently been the rock on which his friend's aspirations had been rooted. She had been everything his friend had wanted, everything that had been taken away by the envy and cruelty of fate.

The soft electronic tone of his desk phone broke his thoughts. His drab assistant was trying to patch through a call.

"Hold my calls," he instructed across its intercom, before removing his finger to press the remote that screened the partition window between his and her small adjoining office. It was unlike him to take the woes of the world onto his shoulders, but his friend, in fact his only true friend he confirmed to himself, was continuing to destroy himself and everything he had once dreamt of being. Prosperity, ambition and most of all happiness, these were things they no longer shared in common. He wanted to help his friend, but was increasingly frustrated by a lack of ideas how to approach so hypersensitive, and as he saw it, tiresome subject. His friend was a free man, but was enslaved to an unspoken depression Matty had no idea how to unlock. A knock on the open door snatched him from his thoughts.

"Yes Georgina," he acknowledged though a fake smile.

"I have the CEO from the Buckland Corporation on line one. He says the call requires your immediate attention," she said eagerly in the doorway, wary of her boss's temperamental manner. Matty glared at his PA as though she were the personification of chaos.

"Doesn't it always?" he replied bluntly. "Patch it through." Matty rose from his luxurious chair, plucking the phone from its cradle as he walked towards her.

"Can I get you a coffee?" Georgina whispered anxiously while the call remained unattended. Her boss nodded sternly then heeled the heavy door shut in her face. A glance to his platinum Rolex revealed the working day still had some way to go, though only a matter hours now sat between him and the much anticipated gig on the Strip. Though planned for some weeks, Matty feared his friend would still bail on the night.

The secretary on the other end of the call asked to him to hold and he mulled over his friend's suspicious call from the day before. *North Glendale?* Whatever was going on in Josh's life it was nothing a good kick in the ass could solve he decided. As he greeted the CEO's voice he reached for his cell. Tonight was going to rock both their worlds; that he would be sure of.

Josh's cell beeped the arrival of a SMS message. Covering the screen from the sun's prowess as it beamed through the bus window, he read the digital shorthand from Matty. *C U AT 8, YER HOUS.* In the midst of all that had happened in the past twenty fours hours Josh had quite forgotten about the exceptional gig. At least it would be a welcome diversion, he thought, from watching MTV or Discovery Channel into the early hours while he mulled over his disastrous day.

The dull ache from the impact of Leo's punch to his cheek had converted into a swollen feeling that persuaded Josh his face had inflated to Elephant Man proportions. A tender prod to the afflicted area confirmed his body was reacting to the collision of bone against bone. *Asshole.*

The glossy cover of the softback book on his lap felt hot and reminded him he still had a shot at being a member of the city's workforce.

An irresistible odour of Lavender still hung to his clothes and as the bus picked up speed joining the Golden State Freeway he wondered what new strange twist of fate had been handed him. He slid the book between the side of the bus and his thigh so that no one could see its mysterious cover. He had left the Eat-A-Lot with a headache and the lingering failure of unemployment, but had seemingly cured both ailments by his excursion into the bookstore he had stumbled across by lure of a beautiful smile.

The Mile was a concrete strip of warehouses and sun baked asphalt. Josh had been surprised to find it was also home to a hidden oasis amongst its soulless buildings. *Mind Matters*. The store name had been like a mysterious beacon that both intrigued and confused. Its interior; a tranquil haven of books upon books that had somehow felt familiar. Incense always brought back fond memories of Sarah's domestic charms and he had followed his nose into the unexplored store with the promise of a second chance at redemption.

Even in his woeful state as he had walked back down the busy Mile, eyes lowered from the sun and hand nursing the side of his wounded face, he had gazed to the doorway across the street and to the slim attractive woman finishing her cigarette in the shade of the familiar doorway. With a look of recognition she had smiled amiably before flicking the butt onto the sidewalk and then disappearing inside.

Though he considered himself reserved by nature Josh was also prone to impatience. From a frustrated glance to his counterfeit watch he had guesstimated he still had a half hour wait for the next bus back to Edendale and had decided to take a chance. Before yesterday he hadn't caught a bus in almost ten years. As a teenager his deceased father had threatened to throw him out of house and home unless he learnt to drive before hitting twenty years old. As a result he had been mobile and independent for so long he had forgotten what it was like to be dependant on others, government benefits aside, and it pissed him off.

The store's frontage had been composed of the same dull concrete and reinforced glass, though unlike its contemporaries the view into the store's interior had been screened off with heavily tinted windows. Josh thought he had been loitering outside one of the many sex shops the city had to offer, but then swallowed the little spark of excitement before looking for evidence he had not been trailing a woman who sold vibrating rubber penises and butt plugs for a living. The shop's name had been embossed above the door, directly below it was the eye of Ra, an ancient Egyptian symbol Josh recognised from watching reruns of Stargate SG.

For a moment the sense of foreboding exuded by the mysterious frontage had made Josh realise he was acting some-what out of nature. The thrill of the chase aside, he wasn't inclined to being so impulsive. He had pondered whether a primal male ego had overwritten his good judgment, or perhaps experienced a glitch in his fight or flight response was to blame. Which ever it was, he hadn't cared as he had fallen prey to the timeless mystique of the unknown. Bowing his weary head to check the Rolex once more his attention had been caught by the discreet handwritten card taped to the inside of the shielded glass. The flowery blue writing had read:

FULL TIME SALES CLERK REQUIRED
MUST BE OPEN MINDED, APPLY WITHIN

The popular proverb of one door closing and another opening had popped into his head. Smiling to himself at the far reaching hand of destiny, he had grabbed the door handle, pushed open the wooden door and walked in.

Inside the dimly lit store his nostrils had been instantly teased by the bittersweet aroma of Lavender, helping to impart a sense of providence. Preconceived visions of a pervert's paradise had gone out the window as he had stared into the secret labyrinth of bookcases and wall to wall shelving that had filled the store interior with a veritable library. *I can do this.*

The only sunlight infiltrating the store had come via a skylight from above. Again the fervent sun had touched his face as he walked through the pillar of sunlight that had pierced the heart of the store, then back into the coolness of the shade as he reached the counter. A shuffling of heavy boxes from behind it had revealed it was not unattended. As he had peered over the piles of unsorted books under his nose, he'd caught the sight of a tribal tattoo peeking out at the base of the woman's spine as she bent over to root through a box. Sensing she had company, the store clerk had quickly stood up to find the awkward man waiting on her.

Up close the young woman had been more attractive than he thought. Early twenties, naturally wavy black hair that hung loose about the perfect skin of her face. He had imagined her emerald green eyes to be some of the most striking he had ever seen, though unfortunately not the most friendly.

"*Yes, can I help you?*" she had asked with a petulant tone that suggested his appearance was on par with that of a cockroach. A failed attempt at civility had meant he had cut to the chase and enquired about the job. "*You got any experience?*" she had asked without masking a continued antagonism. Okay books were not his expertise, but how hard could it be? he'd thought, recalling Sarah's offers to explain the difference between

Hippies and Pagans as she had massaged Lavender oil into his back one blissful evening.

"So don't worry," Josh had confirmed. *"I won't be putting the Wiccan books in the arts and crafts section."* The quip hadn't been appreciated and the green, mistrustful eyes had made their thoughts perfectly clear. But Josh's sense of providence had somehow secured him a reprieve. She had instructed him to return the next morning to take it up with her boss. It was then, insight of victory that the book on the counter had caught his attention.

The Cosmic Explorer: Lucid Dreaming and Roving the Astral Plains.
By Morganawyn Faern Shaffer.

Providence it seemed had been slapping him across the face with a chunk of two by four.

"You know about this sort of thing?" he had enquired, mesmerised by the ethereal cover. A young man, sleeping, and his dreams a playground for his slumbering mind.

"Twelve dollars and ninety five cents," she had insisted with an outstretched palm. Her unexplained resentment meant there had been no easy ride to the truth. Reluctantly he had handed over the crumpled twenty dollar bill. *Homework*, he had assured himself. If he was going to work in a *Hippy* shop there would be a whole lot of it, consoling his niggling conscious that the superfluous acquisition was justified for broadening his skills in the world of new age retail.

Josh's stomach growled again as the exit for Edendale forced the lumbering bus to slow down. He realised the light-headed feeling he was experiencing was partially due to the lack of sustenance. *Be here for 8:45.* He would need a good night's sleep he told himself, if he was to make the early start with a fresh head and make the job vacancy his own, even if only until something better came around. He spotted the 7-Eleven store that heralded his stop was approaching. The woman's crabbiness was still a mystery, but as he slid the book back onto his lap he began to appreciate that fate was inexorable.

Back home Josh was thankful for the uneventful bus ride and slapped a half empty bag of frozen peas against his aching head. The closet stash of reenergizing white powder also popped into his mind, but he suppressed the desire to finish off the remainder of the class A stimulant by raiding his sideboard to appease his culinary appetite instead. All that was left was tinned and frozen, making him think twice about the limited funds he'd wasted on the book that he now tossed onto the breakfast bar.

While Samson circled his legs to the familiar hum of the working microwave, a quick re-evaluation of the day's events firmly planted it in the region of one of the worst on record. Josh leaned onto the bar and studied the book's cover one more time while he waited for the chicken soup to cook. A boyish man with a perfect beard and ponytail lay in a tranquil state of slumber at the bottom of the page, looking more dead than asleep, while around him ethereal pentagrams appeared as wisps among a dreamlike landscape. His dreaming spirit body ascended towards an astral ladder that met the book's title that was written in a Celtic font. *Hippy crap.*

In the mundane normality of his unkempt kitchen Josh wondered why on earth he had wanted to bring it home. Sarah had enjoyed a dabbling interest in the new age movement, though Josh had taken it as nothing more than a feminine interest in all things flowery and ornate. The store had simply dragged up buried emotions. Enraptured by the sweet, exotics aromas and ethereal imagery that had littered its interior, perhaps on a subliminal level he'd been reaching for a part of Sarah long forgotten. Samson leapt off the bar and followed his master's sudden departure into the bedroom.

Josh walked over to the bedside table and snatched up the prescription container. Every night for almost three weeks he had been taking the little blue pills, bracing himself to face what used to be an insomniac's inability to achieve just one good night's sleep. Sufferers of depression were supposed to sleep more, but not Josh. He couldn't even do that properly. He knew the reenergizing effects of Cocaine were not helping his condition, but it was only a part time vice he told himself, and the little blue pills had done their job, but perhaps too well. From the very first night he had fallen into a deep healthy sleep that had finally released him from the two year prison sentence of eternal consciousness. But the escape it seemed now came with a price.

He had been counselled the trial prescription could induce unforeseen side effects. However the warning had come with an assurance they would only continue until his body became accustomed to the newly developed complex of synthetic hormones responsible for stimulating the bodies natural sleep cycle. Josh didn't like the words *hormones* or *side effects* and the idea of another week of vivid symptoms appearing in his dreams no longer seemed an acceptable compromise. He tossed the container into the bedside draw and slammed it shut. *A few nights without won't hurt.*

The doppelganger that had appeared on the nocturnal bus of his dreams had seemed all too real. He wondered if that was how he appeared to the people on the bus; an edgy man at odds with the world. It was no wonder the man in black had stared so curiously at him, enjoying some private joke at Josh's expense. The distant beep of the microwave returned his sense of pride. For the moment at least, fate seemed to be smiling on Josh Brenin and the lacklustre soup would taste all the better for it.

*****

The special op training had educated the soldier about the hallucinogenic symptoms of prolonged sleep deprivation, but as Ben sat in the ornate chair spotlighted in the vast dark room, he knew he was facing a reality more bizarre than any delirium his mind could concoct. The phantoms from the past had found their way back into his nightmares, only to be replaced by new ones that had spilled into reality. As he sat in the vacant warehouse of oddities surrounded by the small militia, he knew that his dreams, and even his mind, were no longer his own. He was a captive in both mind and body. No longer able to run he had simply sat and listened.

The questions had flowed seamlessly from the mouth of the ghoul calling himself Monk and Ben had found himself answering them with a candidness that left him feeling violated, though liberating in a manner a murderer might feel when recounting past crimes. But he was no criminal. His keen sense of reason had told him the shape-shifting magician was the deluded one, lost in the void of his own fantasy. But that was the real misconception, for what he had seen with his own two bloodshot eyes had exposed this reasoning to be a vain substitute for the truth.

"*I told you I don't know who* Them *are!*" He had shouted the truth with the conviction of a sentenced innocent and eventually they had listened. Without any further elaboration he had guessed that whoever *Them* were they were adversaries to his captor's agenda. From the persistent questioning on the matter he had guessed it was no trivial matter to have *walked amongst Them*, but he hadn't.

Rumours of mercenary groups in the pocket of any one of America's enemies targeting military personnel on home ground now thrived in his imagination. The identities of elite personnel leaked into unfriendly hands through the sordid trade-fare of espionage and underground terrorism, had seen a score of ex military servicemen missing and presumed dead. But until that day he had thought that was all they were, rumours. Whoever his captors were, he now thought, they belonged to an organisation that existed at the highest echelons of the black book underworld. It was the only thing that made sense and he was sure it was one rumour he wouldn't live to spread himself.

"What are you waiting for?" he now goaded his silent captors as they studied his eyes for traces of subterfuge. "If you want to kill me then do it now." He had been coerced into answering their trivial questions through Monk's intimidating powers, filling a well with his life's blood as he recounted his career from his early days in the infantry until his commission in the Delta Forces unit. But the weeks of running from his own dreams, which these people had infiltrated and somehow commandeered, now left him taunting the hand of death to end the nightmare that was his life. "You'll get no more answers from me. Do it! Like I give a rat's ass anymore, I've got nothing left to give you." This time the affront was followed by silence. Monk then looked to the woman called Angelica.

"He's speaking the truth," Monk stated. Ben sensed the line of questioning had reached its crescendo. "A Nothos?" he then suggested to his blonde conspirator. The question had been asked with a tone of astonishment, though Angelica didn't look convinced by its enigmatic suggestion.

"A Nothos? What the hell is that?" Ben demanded to know. The woman then squatted down in front of him to look up into his tormented features, her eyes continuing to amaze him with their luminous spirit, holding his own in amazement.

"It means natural. He's suggesting you might be a natural," Angelica explained curtly, "which makes you one of us." She stared intently at him. "Does that mean anything to you Alpha?" The question eluded his sense of reason further. His assumption of their black ops background started to disintegrate. *These people are mad.*

"A natural at what? What the hell makes me like you?"

"Some people are born with the gift; some people develop it over time. But you, I'm not so sure of." She stood up, her fingertips trailing across his broad shoulders as she walked around him like a lioness circling its prey. "A man of your background, a military man, very much rooted in the cold hearted visceral world of *legitimate* murder, doesn't strike me as the life path a Nothos would choose." Ben listened with open ears, but the words may just as well have been in Greek for all they meant to him. "How long have you been able to live in your dreams Alpha?"

"My name is Ben," he declared. The derisive way they used his unit tag, and the silence the proclamation produced, conveyed they saw him as the Elite killing machine and not as the civilian Ben Wheeler. "Live in my dreams!" he then blurted. "Do you think that I'm some kind of nutjob? The only dreams I've had in the past eight months have been of the boy that wasted his own life for sake of taking mine. Every night I have the same dream of walking into the same desert hut and seeing the same Arab kid blow himself to bits, the same brain washed little kid responsible for making me so pretty! Now does that sound like living to you?"

He looked despairingly at Angelica. She loomed over him, her shadowed features revealing the enigma he represented them. They all shared the same blank expression now, one that suggested he was quickly becoming more disposable.

"I don't sleep, I suffer," he continued, hoping to invest some hard reality into the outlandish predicament. "Ever since I was discharged I haven't had a single night where I wasn't the same cannon fodder in my dreams. Even the Shrinks with their psycho bull couldn't save me from reliving that hell." His throat was dry, He paused to swallow, but there was little spit. "The only thing that blocked it out were the little blue pills washed down with a glass of Jim Bean. Guinea pig or not they did the job." He suddenly wished for a tall glass of his favourite spirit, but the change in Angelica's expression made him forget the indulgence.

"Tell me about these pills, what were they?" she asked intently. His captor's moods changed from indifferent deliberation to a renewed sense of direction. The renewed interest sparked Ben's own curiosity, allowing him to meticulously explain the psychological profiling, the reluctant referral to the specialist and his consent to take part in the pharmaceutical trial.

"What is the specialist's name?" Angelica asked enthusiastically. She was taking no precautions to conceal her interest. Black Ops interrogation specialists were trained to grill without emotion or humanity, but the delicate face and the crystal blue eyes no longer radiated a menacing aura. *Who are you?*

"If I tell you will you let me go?" Ben's question was impulsive and he resented its weak enthusiasm. The friendly consultant, who had listened to his nightmares, consoling him with the potency of the new drug he had to offer, was the catalyst it seemed that had brought him into the company of these crazed militants. *What if his name is my only ticket out of here?* Escape he knew was out of the question, compliance however may end it, one way or another. The name was unusual and therefore memorable. "Halberstram, Doctor Halberstram."

Angelica's reaction to the name was unexpected. She turned to gesture an acknowledgement to Monk then disappeared into the dark silhouettes surrounding them. Momentarily Ben wished he had retained the information and forced a bargain, but now it was too late. Monk stood, his body bathing Ben in shadow as the captive tensed for some final blow.

"Get up, you're coming with me," Monk then stated ominously. *This is it*, Ben thought. But against his better judgement he was sure his premature expiry date had been postponed, for if he was a *natural, a Nothos*, then surely his worth had suddenly doubled.

Chapter 4

The loud bang woke Josh with a start. The skin of his face clung to the varnished wood as he jerked his head up and realised he had been sleeping face down on the breakfast bar. He glanced through blurry eyes at the stainless steel kitchen clock bought by his Mom as a moving in present and saw it was ten minutes to eight. Matty was always ten minutes early. Rubbing the bewilderment from his vision he pushed himself from the bar and shuffled through the lounge and to the source of the commotion. Why Matty refused to use the doorbell was a mystery, and then he remembered it didn't work, it hadn't worked in months. Josh undid the latch as a matter or urgency and swung open the front door to find a six pack of export beer dangling in his face. Dismissing the sense of déjà vous, he sleepily took the contribution from his friend and carried it into the lounge.

"My God you're not going like that are you?" Matty said with a tone of disgust as he walked in and shut the door. Josh froze and looked at the old T-shirt and jeans he still wore and compared it to Matty's choice of attire. His usual executive chic had been ditched for a short sleeved black shirt embossed with a red Chinese dragon down the one side.

"No!" Josh replied protectively. "I was just…never mind." The skin of his cheek itched from where it had bonded with the tabletop and he cuffed the sensation away. "Take a seat I was just having some dinner." He pushed some old magazines off the couch to make room for Matty and the six-pack, then tugged a can free.

"Are you high? You look like shit Josh," Matty remarked tactlessly. In his half conscious state Josh hadn't realised just how lowly he looked to his image conscious friend. The half baked manner, the old clothes and the swollen face no doubt painted a picture of a broken man fallen into drug abuse. He forced a smile and tossed the can to Matty then took one for himself.

"A man's allowed to pig out now again. Don't tell me you don't walk around your place in your underwear picking you nose and scratching your balls." The quip was not appreciated.

"No I don't." His direct tone meant he wasn't joking. Matty was too suave for that. As he opened the can and started to guzzle the contents Josh awkwardly followed suite.

"Get mister perfect over here," Josh retorted. "Sit your ass down and relax." He put the half drunk can of expensive imported beer down onto the coffee table then walked off to the bedroom to change. "You hungry?" he called back.

"I've eaten" Matty lied. He slouched onto the couch beside the remaining cans, knowing Josh's hospitality would lack anything near adequate. "So you gonna tell Uncle Matt about this new job of yours or what mystery boy?" he hollered back. "For all I know you're moonlighting as a lap dancer in a titty bar."

"What!" Josh yelled back through the house, his ears muffled by the black long sleeve top he was pulling over his head.

"This week!" he turned and increased the volume. "The new job dickweed, what is it?" That time Josh heard.

"Yeah it's great, real great. Having the time of my life," Josh replied cunningly, wanting to avoid the inevitable. He didn't want to talk about work that night. That night was for forgetting who he was, pretending he was happy and drinking copious amounts of alcohol.

"What are you doing? Where is it dumb ass? Am I playing twenty questions here or what?"

"Just consultant work for a surveyors out on the Langley estate. The usual ball and chain thing. It's money." He dug out his best pair of jeans and hopped about the room as he tugged them on.

"Great, glad to hear things are working out." Matty drained the can. "It's about time." The last few words he muttered to himself. He looked around the dingy lounge and recalled how tidy and fresh it had been when Sarah had been alive. As Josh walked back into the room in some semblance of his former self, he respectfully took his feet off the glass top coffee table, only to inadvertently knock over a precarious stack of bills.

"Are we seeing that girl tonight?" Josh asked, looking up from rooting through his wallet. *Twenty three bucks.*

"We're gonna see loads tonight, what girl?"

"You know," Josh insinuated as he ushered his friend up from the couch and the evidence of his impoverishment at their feet, "the one you get the gear from." Josh did his best to drain the rest of his own can, but the fizzy beer made him retch. He generally distanced himself from the femme fatales that Matty consorted with, believing them to be soulless degenerates with no appreciation of the word morality. But that was the reason why his friend liked them. He was the clean-cut professional who lived a double life on the wild side of sensible, an eternal teenager in Josh's eyes. That was what made him fun to be around.

"Are we talking about Frazzle here?" Matty asked with a frown.

"The one with the…" Josh cupped his hands in front of his chest to mimic Frazzle's large endowments and they shared a boyish appreciation. At last the thaw had come.

The chauvinist reminiscence was interrupted by the distant sound of a car pulling up outside. Curious, Josh went to the front door and squinted through the small panel of frosted glass where he was able to make out a fuzzy figure climbing out of a cab.

"Get the beer we're leaving now!" Josh watched the long legged figure lean in through the passenger window and pay its fare. The new arrival was blurred and the voice mumbled, but he recognised the shadowy apparition as she straightened up and staggered across the overgrown garden. The taxi screeched off, short of its tip and Josh announced the intruder in an abhorrent tone. "Sharon's here."

Matty cursed. As Josh opened the door to find Sharon posed crookedly on the doorstep he assured himself she was the last thing his friend needed on the road to recovery.

"Forget it Sharon. Go home!" Josh greeted her curtly.

"Josh, Honey!" she replied, her senses numbed by the bottle of wine she had consumed. "Just in the neighbourhood, thought I'd drop by and see how you are doing." Josh looked past his lumbering girlfriend to see Matty's black Lexus was not parked in the street.

"Where's your car?"

"If you hadn't noticed this isn't granny's homemade lemonade I'm drinking here," his friend replied. "A piece of ass from work dropped me off. I got us a cab. It'll be here in…"

"Who's that? Who you got in there?" Sharon shoved the door open. As Matty was exposed he executed a perfect smile.

"You're looking lovely tonight Sharon, going somewhere nice?" The wide grin branded on the face of her social rival snatched Sharon out of her delusion.

"You!" she barked with a pointed finger, its long wicked nail threatening to gouge at his pampered face as she struggled to coordinate her anger. With Josh's help he cunning avoided loosing an eyeball as he slipped out onto the porch.

"Sharon!" Josh interceded as his friend escaped into the long grass out front, "For Christ's sake you can't pull this crap on me." Stepping out he slammed his door shut and locked up. His unwelcome guest then locked her arms around his neck, her enticing scent wafting into his face.

"Sharon you're drunk. Go home. Please!"

"But I want to be with you, I'm horny," she confessed slyly.

"And you reek of Booz, what kind of gentleman would I be if I took advantage of you in this state?"

"The kind who gets to screw me all night!"

"Look, how about you go home, have an early night and you come round tomorrow instead. How about it?" The cab arrived, pulling up to the curb in good time.

"Ready when you are buddy!" Matty called over as he crawled into its back seat. In the few seconds it took to wade through the grass towards freedom Josh believed the silence meant he had broken through to Sharon's sense of reason.

"Look at me!" He spun around to see Sharon had peeled off her jacket. "Don't you want to stay here with me?" Now hanging off her shoulders it exposed the strapless corset it had concealed. "I bought this for you!" she screeched. Her fair skin shone through the delicate fabric, revealing a vision of the perfect female form that intoxicated the two men and startled driver.

"I'm impressed," Matty commented slyly, but Josh ignored the bribe and shoved him back into the cab. As he slumped onto the slippery black PVC seat and tugged the car door shut, his ignorance only further incensed his inebriated girlfriend.

"You can't go without me!" Sharon's high-heeled shoes buckled beneath her as she lurched into the uneven, neglected lawn, causing her to fall embarrassingly to her knees in a drunken sprawl. Matty yelled at the driver to put his foot down as Josh stared out at the head and shoulders poking up from the sea of grass. Sharon looked on wretchedly as he was spurred away, still managing a feeble wave before collapsing out of sight amongst the grass. A pang of shame meant he suddenly felt like a bastard.

"Jeez Josh what are you still doing with that crazy bitch?" Matty blurted, dumping the remaining cans of beers onto the seat between them. "Nice mammaries I know but she's not playing with a full deck." Josh gazed out at the houses in his street as they zipped past, his conscience eating away at him.

"Give her a break," he said, turning to tug another can free. "She comes from a broken home," he lied, hoping to diffuse his friend's indifference to what he had just witnessed. The *shlook* of the opening can courted the driver's unwanted attention in the rear view mirror.

"How about she gives you a break? Look about this dinner I want to set up for this week; I want Serina to know I'm making an effort with her okay?" Josh had forgotten the answer phone message. The last thing on his mind was helping Matty get laid. "So you gotta bring someone nice, tell me you know other women."

"Well it's like you said," he stated calmly, his conscience quelled by the taste of the strong premium beer, "There's going to be loads of girls at this place tonight. The world is my oyster."

The driver, quietly irritated by his passenger's consumption of beverages, put his foot down and headed towards the hazy glow of the sunlit smog over downtown. A future with Sharon was beginning to look like a nightmare and Josh decided he already had enough of those. With the dilemma in mind he decided he would enjoy the night while it lasted. Tonight he would leave his nightmares behind, in search of his old self amongst the city's nightlife.

*****

The hospital lobby was over run with gunshot victims. Emergency staff summoned by a multitude of pagers and intercoms had been welcomed by a bloody scene of bandana-clad street soldiers who'd been the not-so-innocent victims of a drive-by shooting. A turf war over the rights to narcotic distribution in a back street battleground had resulted in the four half dead, blood drenched youngsters being carried in by their comrades, clinging to wasted lives against a frantic chorus of foul-mouthed pleas for help. As ICU and security staff were likewise rallied to deal with the explosive situation, an attractive blonde woman bypassed the unfolding chaos and carried on past reception into the clinical hallways. The unwelcome invasion of hysterical teenagers entering ER had been a welcome distraction. For what it was worth the daytime mission seemed less like the bad choice it had originally appeared.

Angelica paced freely into the wards, her white clothing easily distinguishing her as a member of the medical staff to the casual preoccupied viewer. Walking on without the usual interest such sights incited, she seemingly glided over the vinyl floor with an air of purpose as she hurried to her goal. Time was not on her side. In a war that was being won minutes at a time the loss of a single day could easily tip the delicate balance out of favour. Even on the other side of reality, amongst that ethereal world where time and space were irrelevant, ground was quickly becoming lost to the black agents. She and her comrades would need every head-start afforded them if they were to stop *the great work of ages* dead in its tracks.

An elderly man lay expectantly on a wheeled bed, hands clasped over a bloated stomach as if to help quell the pain in his abdomen. The sight of Angelica walking by, a picture of white, caught his attention. Mistaking her for a resident MD on her rounds he stretched out a hand gesturing for her to stop.

"Doc, I don't suppose you've got the time?" he asked attentively. "The big Samoan fella just left me lying here like a schmuck. I'm supposed to be in there like twenty minutes ago." He pointed a withered finger to a door marked *Radiology*. Angelica stopped and turned to look at the drawn, shrivelled face that gazed up from the pristine pillow case that exaggerated the deathly pallor of his skin. She said nothing, she simply smiled. The man then sensed something unreal about the vision in white. The blue eyes sparkled back at him with an otherworldly energy that was electrifying, an energy that then flowed from her palm as she clasped his outstretched hand. Intense warmth then surged into him, energising his entire arm.

For a few seconds the man was mesmerised by the Seraphim at his side. Before words could utter any emotion the large porter returned from the commotion in the lobby to find his previous charge now appeared strangely animated. Replacing the withered arm that grasped at thin air back onto his bloated chest, he wheeled the babbling patient into Radiology. The religious ones were always nutty.

"No sir I didn't, guess the angel must have flown back to heaven."

Angelica continued the journey, her pace quickening as she left the public areas behind and entered the back offices restricted from public view. The halls were quiet. They were new to her but instinctively she knew where to go. Her footsteps made no sound as she passed office after office, sensing the people inside were glued to their screens, administering the ongoing concerns of the hospital. Gazing up to the protruding lens of the closed circuit camera perched above her head she knew it would make no record of her visit and marched on. The door she sought was at the far end of the last corridor she entered. Two administrative staff came out of a nearby office, but too consumed in petty conversation took no notice of the white apparition walking amongst them as they left for a coffee break.

The flashing red LED above the card key slot relayed the door was locked. She had never seen the entrance before, but had known instinctively which one it would be and how to find it. Placing both her palms up against its cool surface she then closed her eyes. She didn't like to have them open when making an *Ephemeral Morphic Transition,* as Monk liked to call it. They instinctively preferred to be shut as her hands led the way, followed by her arms and torso as she then let herself pass through the barrier of metal and glass as though it were merely an illusion.

On its other side she found a much darker room, partially lit by low-wattage strip lighting that glowed from the edges of the ceiling. Angelica walked passed the humming cabinets containing the servers and network panels that fed the hospital's I.T. demands to sit down in front of a solitary workstation. She pushed the keyboard aside and placed her hands either side of the TFT screen, focused her psyche and began to access the database with the power of thought. Physic interfacing with electronic equipment was easy enough once you had mastered the moderately harder task of astral projection across hundreds of miles.

The digital information flowed across the screen at a speed no normal human could possibly comprehend. The entire network was at her fingertips, allowing her to navigate through the labyrinth of records that reflected in the mirrors of her eyes, bypassing *Read Only* protected files and minor security protocols within seconds. She could not necessarily read every single word or line that flashed on screen; that was impossible, even for her. Instead Angelica let herself join with the terminal as if it were an extension of her own unconscious mind, the server's electronic pathways an expansion of the neurons and synapses of her own brain. All she had to do was imagine the data she needed from the adopted brain and instinct would guide her through the directories, files and sub files until she found what she needed.

The doctor's name was Halberstram. It was the name Alpha had supplied, and now she had found it in the database. *Got you.* Aside from the record of his three month term at the Parasomnia clinic administered by the hospital, there was no photo or personal details relating to the agency stooge. Angelica wasn't surprised. Even the previous residency history she did retrieve was no doubt fabricated; the enemy was good at covering its tracks.

Ben (Alpha) Wheeler had been a patient of this puppet doctor, a name on a small list of referrals that were now on the screen in front of her. But it was the rest of the names that Angelica had come for. Effectively it was a directory of so called Low Grades scheduled to be tainted by the black light. A desperate optimism had her hoping the same names could be hijacked from the enemy to offer a much needed influx of turncoats, out manoeuvring the enemy before it tightened its grasp around their unwitting souls. For the battle was a race, and the winner would be the one who reaped the most powerful pieces on the chessboard of dreams.

*****

The queue outside the Helter Skelter was bigger than Josh had expected. The boisterous mob of waiting fans converging on the entrance to the converted cinema on Sunset Strip was in a formation more relative to a rabble than an orderly line. An ensuing bout of nerves made his legs jittery as he stepped out of the cab. Eager patrons keen to get inside the former purveyor of thirty five millimetre gems of pornographic smut were flocking to the lobby as though they feared the night's entertainment would be pulled out from under them by the Christian right that threatened to boycott the band across the U.S. But Bible-belt America and Los Angeles were several states apart. Above Josh's head the large red letters attached on the white billboards declared that the establishment was proud to present the night's act live for *one night only*.

The taxi sped off, leaving Matty and Josh on the pavement looking for a break in the rowdy crowd. The surly driver had tried to abandon his two fares several streets away from the notorious destination; the cause a spilt can of beer. Matty had intervened by flashing an extra twenty dollar bill as an incentive, but on arrival had refused to hand it over. Matty freed the two tickets from his back pocket and offered the crumpled one to Josh.

"Here you go buddy, your ticket to paradise." Josh took the small red voucher, looked disappointed at the cheaply produced piece of card and wondered whether it was going to be worth the fifteen dollars that paid for it. *Admit one adult. Devilwhore.* A sudden scuffle of frustrated fans caused the crowd to bulge out onto the pavement, but was quickly convened by the over enthusiastic door staff who recklessly grabbed the offenders from the crowd and threw them onto the asphalt. Josh hated the Helter Skelter Club.

"Matty you take me to all the best joints."

"Yeah you owe me for this one!" his excited friend replied. The sarcasm went unheard. Josh hadn't been to a rock concert in over a year and the youthful vigour that had once motivated him to attend previous gigs now seemed quite lacking as they joined the queue.

Amongst the teenage Goths and long haired head-bangers jockeying for position, he felt old before his time, out of place amongst a tightly packed crowd of misfits and miscreant music lovers. In the hustle of the mob he suddenly came face to face with an overweight woman with black number one dyed hair and matching lipstick. He smiled as she caught him looking up from the large breasts squeezed into the tight black bodice pressed against his chest, but she replied with a scowl and turned away to whisper in the ear of her girlfriend. Matty saw the discourse of gestures and laughed.

"What did you expect, they're everywhere!" his eager friend stated unashamedly. Funnelled into the lobby along with the migrating mob, they narrowly avoided a pat down search by the two eager goons that passed as venue security. Inside the doorway they then filed into a single line to hand over their tickets to the haggard weasel in the booth, his gaunt eyes glued to the robotic task in hand as his body odour escaped through the hand slot below its grimy glass. A finger prodded Josh in the back urging him forward. Matty was eager to enter the dark doorway in front, from which the familiar sonic distortions of heavy rock blared out of the veritable mouth to hell. Its humid air was laced with smoke and alcohol. Taking a deep breath as it bellowed out like the noxious breath of the Leviathan, Josh followed the voluptuous curves of the gothic lesbians into the darkness.

It didn't take long for the humid environment to turn the cheap beer in Josh's hand into something resembling urine. As he leaned against the back wall soaked in his own perspiration, he wondered how he ever used to enjoy the pogo head banging style of dancing commonly known as Moshing. Like the music it was manic, dangerous and invigorating, but leaning against the venue's back wall warm beer in hand, he realised just how past it he was.

Upon entering the dark under belly of the dreaded club the youthful vigour inspired by the power of hard rock mayhem had quickly returned. After following Matty through its dark, smoky interior to the front of the rebellious crowd Josh had found himself a slave to the instinct to join the gyrating mob of adopted peers. The support acts down tuned alternative rock had sounded okay, but after nearly losing his front teeth as they collided with a skinhead's shoulder, a fear of lost incisors had made Josh turn tail. Finding his way back through the dodgem of sweaty, pogoing bodies had been a fight against the tide, but he had made it to the bar intact and left Matty lost in the treacherous sea of flesh to revel in the moment.

He took another sip of the warm beer and tried not to think of the unsavoury likeness wafting from the squalid men's room door nearby. From the relative safety of the back wall he took stock of the manic surroundings, watching the rest of the show through the eyes of stability after deciding it was the best way to enjoy the night if he valued his anatomy. Matty had been right about the girls. Bored with looking at the four guys on stage Josh began to notice the bare skin exposed by the scant clothing of the young women returning from the neon lit bar. Against their dark clothes the ample show of skin seemed luminous in the dark sanctuary, though he doubted the licentious girls attracting his gaze were what Matty had in mind for the double date with his latest conquest.

Sharon's pitiable attempt to reclaim him from Matty sprang to mind. A part of him now wished he had stayed at home to take advantage of her intoxicated offer, though reminded himself he would see her soon enough before the rest of the shitty day came flooding back. Touching the crash sight that was his sore cheek he was relieved to find the swelling produced by Leo's punch had significantly reduced, after all Matty hadn't appeared to notice. Thanking his lucky stars for not being a bleeder, he recalled the humiliation of getting up from the diner table, then the army of strange faces who had witnessed his entire degradation.

It hadn't bothered him at the time, but reliving the painful memory made him wonder why fate continued to torment him. He abhorred himself, wasn't that enough? He had never envied his college friend's privileged background before, and Matty had shunned talking about the millions of dollars at his father's disposal. But standing in the dark venue alone with his festering frustrations, Josh was sure life had dealt him a particularly bum hand. That was why Matty was such a livewire. Privilege allowed him to be a libertine. Matty's outward contentment and success seemed to flow from a cornucopia of good luck that surrounded and protected him from misery. Career, Cocaine, fast cars, fast women, no strings, he had it all Josh though. He let the empty plastic cup plummet from his hand to the sticky floor. Even if he shared his friend's luck, he would deny it all for one more day with Sarah. Next thought.

The bookstore. The Mile at least still offered a chance for employment, the job was not what he had it mind but was as good as his. As he admired a raven haired girl resembling the less than friendly counterpart from the mystical store, Josh felt sure he could tip the scales of luck if he focused on shaping his future instead of dreading what it would offer as a substitute for a real life. Recognising the familiar bloating in his bladder, he then followed the smell of urine to the men's room.

As he pushed the swinging door forward a man blocked his way, his face buried in a woman's breasts. Before sliding past the amorous couple the man sensed Josh's presence and looked up as he pinched the white residue from his nose.

"So good of you to join us," Matty said playfully. Josh walked past to the urinal and unzipped, wishing he didn't have the audience while he peed.

"Couldn't put off draining the lizard any longer," he replied casually and stared down to watch his stream liberate the cigarette stubs towards the drain.

"Mr Josh, long time no see," the peroxide-blonde in Matty's embrace acknowledged. He looked up into the mirrored tiles in front of his face and saw in the reflection the familiar freckled skin and red leather jacket that signified Matty had found his dealer.

"Frazzle," he acknowledged, before Matty continued to nuzzle his face in her ample breasts to lap at the remaining cocaine in the luscious crevice. Confirming his conclusions about the imbalance of luck and fate he finished up and ignored the giggles of pleasure from the vixen as his friend's tongue teased her chest.

"What's the matter Honey?" Frazzle asked as Josh tried to edge his way out. Frazzle was no oil painting, but the writhing pang of envy was rearing its ugly head and he simply wanted to get out and wait out of sight and out of mind. "Somebody feeling left out? Here…" Josh paused by the door and looked at Frazzle as she produced a small glass vial and sprinkled the fine white powder over the exposed skin of her freckled chest. "…have a go Sugar, it's all good."

She arched her back to offer the narcotic on the platter of flesh. Matty watched on with an expectant grin, saying nothing, expecting everything. Josh had only met this particular lady of the night a couple of times before. Both had been brief while accompanying his friend to score coke. Her fair skin made her stand out amongst the usual Californian female archetype though without diminishing her allure. Her freckles reminded Josh of a Leopard and he sussed her personality was equally feline, a child of LA's back streets, a world away from the lives of the two college buddies to whom she offered the fleshy fix. Life was bizarre.

"Maybe some other time, I'm cutting down." Grudgingly he tore his eyes from her chest and avoided Matty's look of disappointment. Sometimes the righteous path was the best to take he told himself and exited into the dark humid environment of the club floor. The decision had been a fine line between sharing the fruits of his friend's good fortune and accepting he wasn't the kind of guy who licked his coke dealer's breasts. That was Matthew Nugent, he was Josh Brenin, big league and bush league, and as he leaned against the blacked out wall and watched the support act, at least he couldn't deny he had been true to himself.

The last song was met with a roar from the crowd just as Frazzle emerged from the men's room to pinch Josh's bum. The cheeky gesture stole his attention from the blonde in the crowd, on whose fair hair the stage lights flashed like a beacon amongst the blackened mob. He managed a civil smile as Frazzle walked off into the dark rabble, though darted his gaze back to the blonde vision to find he had lost her amongst it. Matty emerged with a beaming look of satisfaction.

"Here," Matty hissed into his ear. "Take care of this," Matty landed a bulky transparent gripper bag of white powder into Josh's palm and guided it behind his back. "You won't believe the deal I got on that." Fearing the considerable amount of class A drug would attract attention, Josh quickly fumbled the package into his jeans, struggling to slide it into his pocket without risk of bursting.

"How much?" Josh exclaimed as he deliberated the over enthusiastic weight. "You've got enough here to keep the entire Bolivian army marching for a year." He suddenly became aware he was secreting a small fortune of contraband on his person. Luckily the jeans were new and baggier than his regular ones, but the fact didn't make the burden any easier to handle. Security was lax inside the seedy club though their proven presence on the front door made him wonder why he was the one taking the risk.

"You can never get enough of a good thing my friend," Matty said loudly into his ear over the music. "Don't let anybody tell you any different." He pinched his nose again before giving Josh a suggestive wink. "You only get one life, don't waste it on missed opportunities. And that my friend," Matty patted the bulge in Josh's jeans. "Was a great opportunity." A long-haired youth caught sight of the gesture on his way to the men's and scowled a disapproval. "Problem dickweed?" Matty straightened to his full height, which was a good foot taller than Josh. Fearing his friend was riding a narcotic fuelled wave of elation that would get them both in deep trouble he grasped his elbow.

"Cool it tough guy," Josh urged calmly as the youth passed on Matty's offer and shoved the men's door open, "The last thing we need is you going all Scarface on me, let's get a drink and celebrate those great opportunities." Matty laid a heavy pat on Josh's back then followed his apprehensive friend towards the neon lit oasis of cheap beer. Adjusting the package into a less obvious position, Josh suddenly liked the idea of another bomb threat bringing the gig to a premature end.

*****

Devilwhore put on a hell of a show. In the darkness that had enveloped them like a mortuary shroud the sold out crowd had waited impatiently for the headliners to emerge onto the rock altar that was the stage. The dimming of lights to a near dark in the packed club had been suffocating and empowered the hellish red light that rose from behind the drum set to illuminate a large Satanic symbol of Baphomet; a goat's head inlaid into an inverted pentagram. As the intoxicated pilgrims sensed their Goddesses were about to make their ascension, Josh and Matty followed the surge of hot bodies towards the front of the main floor. The first entertainers on stage were two topless women who were greeted by the crowd's barbaric roar of appreciation as they slithered to centre stage sporting prosthetic devil horns and tails. As Josh watched them caress and lick each other's naked extremities he wondered what kind of show the fifteen dollars had really bought him. Then the music started.

The all girl band appeared on stage, instruments to hand after a second blackout had camouflaged their arrival. As the sonic glory of their music pounded the enthused audience at their feet the topless *devil whores* remained on stage, teasing the audience as they gyrated sleazily in their high-heeled latex boots. Matty looked more excited than Josh had ever seen him, and even though he enjoyed the perfect flesh on display Josh found the force of crowded bodies dodging around him too big a sacrifice and now fought his way out again to find his own space and more lukewarm refreshment.

Back against the safe seclusion of the rear wall the vibrations from the high volume music made it tremble against his shoulder. He quenched his thirst with deep draughts of the fresh gassy beverage he'd purchased at an inflated price. Josh decided the sound in his ears was no longer discernable as music; it had merely degenerated into a sonic fuzz of increased volume broken only by the high shrieks of the scantily clad vocalist. The band's controversial onstage appeal however more than made up for the shortfall. The mock dancing devils were effective in their tantalizing and he found himself hypnotised by the stirring of lust they notoriously created. *It's no wonder the bible bashers are pissed.* If he was honest with himself they weren't the most beautiful women he'd ever seen, but the licentious toys of flesh were just too enticing for any man righteous or not to take notice.

Searching the sea of bobbing heads below the hedonistic entertainment for Matty was futile. Knowing his friend's wandering attentions there was just as much chance he was scoring with one of the many pretty girls in a dark corner of the club. He glanced to his recalibrated Rolex for a time check. *One hour to go.* Looking up, one such pretty face caught Josh's attention.

The blonde haired women stood out amongst the crowd of dark bodies like a priest in a brothel. Apart from her choice of white rather than the dark, rock uniforms of those around her, she was also staring directly at him. There was no time for a double take. Her gaze had locked onto his, trapping his attentions with a will that seemed to enslave his own. His heart skipped a beat. Members of the head banging ranks passed between them on their way to mosh or frequent the bar, though the women's gaze remained unbroken. But neither did he want to break the connection. To Josh she looked like a gift from Venus, a gift that began to walk towards him. As she closed the gap between them it was as though she passed unseen by those around. None turned to look at or avoid the white figure that walked up to within a couple of feet of the awestruck loner. So overcome by the striking woman's presence Josh forgot his usual reserve and straightened to pursue her interest in him.

"Hi you come here often?" he hollered over Devilwhore's racket with a beaming grin. The old chat-up line was meant to sound satirical, but failed.

"I'm only here because you are here," she replied enigmatically, her words carrying across the sonic excess of distorted guitars without having to strain her voice as Josh had to.

"Is that so?" he mused curiously. *Matty, eat your heart out.* "Have we met before? I'm sure I'd remember someone as hot as you."

"You need to come with me now," the woman demanded abruptly but calmly. Josh studied her placid features. She looked serious. Josh thought the Gods had finally hurled a few lucky stars his way.

"I guess it must be my birthday! Did Matty put you up to this?" The look on her face remained grave as he remained oblivious to her intent.

"Look over my left shoulder."

"I'd rather look elsewhere," he joked, then straightened once more.

"Look," she persisted, "you'll see a man with short dark hair and sunglasses, wearing a black jacket." The mysterious request drew Josh to more sensible bearing on the encounter.

"Listen this isn't what I usually..."

"Look! Do you see him?" She had raised her voice and he realised her gaze was now far from alluring. The bizarre demand now sobering his take on the situation, he diverted his gaze to where she directed. Again he found his eyes locked onto another. Amongst the other dark bodies moving in the near darkness he saw the man's pale face, watching them from behind his shades.

"Yeah I see him so what?" he offered apprehensively.

"Do you recognise him?"

"No," Josh lied. "Should I?" He didn't like where the conversation was going, the lucky stars now turning into black holes.

"He's following you."

"Really?" *Just my luck; another nut job.* The man did look familiar, but Josh was ready to wrap up whatever it was that was going on. Fearing he might find himself on the wrong end of a blade for a second time, he humoured the attractive loony. "Somehow I don't think he's my type."

"Joshua you are in great danger and you must come with me now! Him and his kind are everywhere. They know you."

"Who does? How do you know my name?"

"We all know your name. You have no idea what you've become involved in. Leave this place" She was no longer asking, the beauty in white was demanding.

"I'm not going anywhere lady," he said defiantly. "Though if you're trying to screw with my head you're doing a great job," frustrated with the women's attempt at coercion, Josh slumped back against the wall. "So why don't you do us both a favour and go tell Matty or Frazzle or whoever the hell sent you that they're wasting their time, and yours." He turned away and took a long drink from the now less than cool beer. The oddball in the shades seemed to be biding his time. *Has he seen us?*

"Joshua!" His name echoed inside his head above the din of the club. "Come with me now or face the consequences." He looked into the blue eyes again, suddenly aware of an ethereal power that made the hairs on the back of his neck rise to attention. "On the other side there is no in-between or middle ground, only light and dark," she continued. "If you value your soul you must make a choice, or perish." As though she had tapped into some internal amplifier her rude petition resonated in his head. *Trick of the mind.* The surreal situation was now emanating an unworldly vibe, but his rational mind dashed the sensations as delusion. Someone was yanking his chain and his patience was wearing thin.

"Maybe you should save it for your friend in the shades; he's coming over to say hi." Over her shoulder the man in black was now closing in through the excited crowd and Josh expected the two nut cases to collide magnificently. Angelica caught sight of the approaching adversary, grimaced and swung back to her prey.

An invisible force suddenly gripped Josh's insides in a vice of cold steel. He was frozen, unable to breath. Her eyes were stealing his very life force; eyes he could now see reflected his terrified features in their mirrored surface.

"It's too late for you Joshua," her booming voice echoed inside his head. As suddenly as it had taken hold of him the icy paralysis suddenly relented its grip, releasing every muscle and causing him to slump back against the shuddering back wall. His first instinct was to draw a deep breath. Refilling his constricted lungs with warm smoky air the chest pain inflicted by the invisible grasp was instantly alleviated.

He looked up, expecting to see the macabre and inhuman silver eyes peering back at him from amongst the long blonde strands of hair, but they were long gone. He searched around for the loony's white clothes disappearing into the crowd, but saw only the electric beams of light falling onto the countless head bangers gathered in front. She had vanished, along with the oddball who had spooked her. As his chest pain dispersed into a dull ache it left him winded. He managed a brave face as a couple of young rock girls cruised by. *What the hell just happened?* His empty cup lay in a shining pool at his feet. Sluggishly he swiped the spilt beer from his jeans. The sizeable bag of cocaine still protruded against his leg like an enormous tumour and Josh decided there would be no more drugs that night, or ever. *I'm losing my mind.*

On top of the flashing lights that now seemed purposely trained to blaze into his eyes from the rig above the stage, he genuinely feared he had just experienced a psychotic episode, a narcotic induced short-circuiting of vital neurons in his brain. His chest continued to ache and he feared it the result of some form of cardiac trauma. *You gave up Coke for a reason.* But no, he recalled the blonde woman's face, she had been real enough. If anyone was an advert for saying no to drugs it had been her. A sudden punch to his arm made him flinch defensively. Turning to his assailant he was glad to see Matty's face beaming back at him from the shadows.

"Goddamn is there some talent here tonight or what?" Matty yelled into his ear with the enthusiasm of a child in a candy store. "I can't remember the last time I had my butt stroked so much, they can't keep their hands off me!" His smile dropped into concern as he studied his friend. "What's wrong?" From the dark strands of sodden hair plastered to his sweat drenched forehead, Josh guessed his friend had spent the most of his time amongst the sea of lurching bodies.

"Did you see that girl?"

"Girl? Girl? Gee, let me think…" he teased Josh with a mock gesture of wonderment, his voice sounding hoarse as he shouted above the music. "Are you kidding, there's pussy everywhere!"

"No, there was a blonde, in white just here a second ago, you saw her right?" He needed reassurance.

"What blonde? You were talking to someone?" Matty leaned against the back wall to watch the remainder of the lurid stage show. "When did you get so sociable?" He hadn't seen her. Josh suddenly felt nauseous. He checked the time again by raising the face of his watch to catch a beam of light and saw it was a little after eleven thirty. *Four minutes.* It felt like a lifetime had pasted since last he'd checked.

"So you didn't see her?"

"What are you talking about? Look around!" Matty finished the dregs of his beer and threw the plastic cup into the crowd. "We're wasting precious time back here, we're not going to score sitting on our asses." As Josh watched his friend run a hand threw his sodden hair in an effort to make himself more presentable to a petite brunette with a pierced lip, he knew they would remain to the end. "She'll do nicely, don't move!"

Following his quarry into the shadows he left Josh feeling exposed as a numb sense of fatigue descended upon him like a lead weight. Matty was still riding a wave of excitement, but Josh was looking for the nearest exit. *Who the hell was she?* Resigned to his fate he nervously shifted the bag in his pocket, kept his eyes peeled and hoped the night's sordid *opportunities* had all but run out.

Outside the club the summer atmosphere was warm but not stifling like the smoky den they'd eventually exited. The night was over and the horde of Goths, head bangers and miscreants were being ushered onto the Strip in a post rock exodus. Amongst then Josh wished he wasn't standing in a public sidewalk with several hundred dollars worth of cocaine in his pocket. Unable to shift the feeling of being watched he had remained dutifully against the ceaseless vibrating wall, paranoid and vigilant, until Devilwhore had finished their anticipated set with an encore of three degenerate songs. At its completion Matty had remerged in the brightly lit lobby, minus the night's trophy of flesh.

In the hectic migration of youthful fervour that now edged them off the sidewalk, a lingering chest ache reminded Josh of the grappling sensation he'd suffered by causes malicious or medical. Out in the fresh air he realised his ears were ringing, but this didn't detract his concern as he looked nervously around for cops and loonies alike. Around him the clamour of intoxicated chattering was muffled and alien in his sober state, while behind Matty played his last hand at chatting up two underage girls with a conceit created by a mix of pre-eminence and alcohol. Devoid of his usual charm and graces he failed miserably as a result.

"Rug Munchers," he spat derisively, stumbling down the high curb onto the street. "My ears hurt. Let's get a cab." He stepped a few paces onto the pavement and began hailing passing cabs with all the dignity afforded an inebriated individual who'd spent his Saturday night casting off self-restraint. Josh was happy to let his friend's bravado find them a ride home and took the opportunity to check his cell against the likelihood of missed calls from Sharon. There were none.

Unexpectedly Josh felt like his brain was being squashed. The disabling sensation caused panic. Impulsively he looked around for the blonde assailant, but near or far he failed to spot her. *What's is this?* The bizarre sensation worsened, intensifying until it seemed his grey matter would burst out of the top of his skull. He tried to call out to his friend, but as his mouth refused to cooperative, fears of a delayed concussion now quickly escalating into a grim reality. Josh could only watch as his staggering companion hailed down a cab then leaned in to blurt out the destination to its hesitant driver. The feeling in Josh's head then surged from the top to the side. As though drawn at the behest of some magnetic force the bizarre change in tack urged him to turn his head. *No not now.*

Not fifteen feet away Matty fended off three long haired youths, slumped into the back of the cab and called Josh to hurry. Josh began to walk forward, his head cocked at the unnatural pose, but his feet felt cumbersome. He was struggling against a disorientating sensation that thwarted his ability to make the short distance. Finally grasping the cab's roof with both hands he steadied himself, before succumbing to the cerebral tug of war that lessened as he looked across the noisy night-time street.

This time Josh didn't mistake the dark figure standing across from him. The pale face contrasted ghoulishly with the slicked back mane of black hair, black jacket and pants, while again the eyes remained hidden behind the same compulsory eyewear. *How did you do that?* It was the oddball who had frightened away his blonde assailant, the same he had spotted at the Mile, on the bus to Glendale and in his vivid dream. As Matty's calls to hurry went unheard, Josh suddenly realised there was something wrong with the picture. The stranger's face looked broader, the chin more prominent and the eyebrows seemed to arch unusually high above the shades. The world around Josh faded as the realisation hit home that coincidence was not to blame. It was not the same man he'd seen loitering in the Mile. The face that smiled wolfishly back at him was too dissimilar. *Two of them?* Disturbingly the stranger nodded a gesture of recognition. *Who are you?* As though able to read his thoughts the scathing smile grew across the pallid features, sealing the daunting effect of the insight on Josh's weary senses.

"Hey buddy, are you getting in or not?" The driver enforced the question by leaning out to look up at the tentative fare. "I ain't got all night." As magnetism converted to repulsion Josh slumped into the backseat and slammed the cab door shut. "Hey easy with the door!" the driver grumbled. He glared at his fares in the rear view mirror and scratched his flabby stomach.

"Just drive!" Josh demanded tactlessly.

"Whatever you say your highness." Shaking his head with disapproval, the portly driver pulled out into the street. The jolt of the moving car brought Matty out of his temporary drunken lull and he gave his friend a quizzical look. As they left the Helter Skelter behind Josh raised his head to glimpse out of the rear window, but the distant patch of sidewalk where the oddball had stood was now vacant.

"What's wrong? You spotted your dealer friend?"

"Nothing, forget it," Josh said, dismissing his actions as trivial before turning back to gaze out at the blurring sidewalk. "I'm seeing things." For all he knew he was.

"Whatever. Gimme the goods." Josh looked into Matty's alcohol deadened eyes and hoped the drone of the revving engine had muffled the words from the driver's curious ears. Reluctantly he freed the bag of white powder from his jeans and covertly handed it over watching the rear view mirror. "You've been acting skwirly all night what's up with you?" Matty snatched the bag from his hand.

"It told you, it's nothing." As he corrected his position on the slippery vinyl seat the taxi weaved dangerously through the traffic into the fastest lanes, causing him to slump into the door. His friend however was oblivious.

"And you look like crap!" Matty continued, trying to fumble the package into his own jeans. "I'll tell you straight Josh, you're gonna have to get your shit together soon because, I might not always be there to pick you up. You hear me?"

Ignoring the slurred rant as misplaced concern Josh gazed back out to the passing street, glad to be free of the sizeable bag of illegal temptation that Matty finally forced into a pocket. *What the hell is happening to me?* Josh mulled over the sights and sensations that had bombarded his psyche over the past couple of hours. He felt nauseous once more. His heart still pounded on relentlessly, but leaving the heart of the city behind he thanked whatever God was listening that the night was finally over.

Chapter 5

The taxi came to a brisk halt outside the neglected house. The jolt roused Matty from his drunken slumber. As he cuffed the drool from the side of his mouth Josh leaned forward and paid for the fare, giving an extra fifteen dollars and thirty eight cents to cover the extra distance to get his friend home. It was all he had. Ignoring the loose change the driver snatched the crumpled dollar bills and eyeballed his weary fare. Josh got the hint and gave Matty a nudge.

"You gonna be alright?"

"Yeah why shouldn't I be?" Matty blurted out, eyelids half closed over bleary eyes. "I'm not drunk. Where are we?"

"My place. I'll see you around."

"You're damn right you will, we gotta do this again soon." He grabbed Josh's forearm, "You're still coming to that dinner right?" The slurred question was delivered with an unfocused gaze past Josh's head. "You gotta meet Sabrina."

"You mean Serina," Josh corrected, pulling his arm free as he reached for the door handle.

"Yeah her," he agreed, chemically detached from his memory.

"I'll call you," Josh promised as he then slid out of the taxi.

"You do that. And don't go crazy with that gear," he tapped the bag of coke in his pocket. "Knowing Frazzle it's no icing sugar." Josh forced a smile. There was no point explaining he had kept none back for himself and shut the door in his friend's face. He was welcome to the lot.

The taxi sped off down the street and Josh realised he had forgotten to relay the second address to the surly driver. After watching the cab's tail lights make the right turn at the end of the street, he welcomed the silence that descended like a cool blanket on the quiet Edendale suburb. For a moment he half imagined to find Sharon still sprawled out on his lawn. Traipsing through the flattened patch of grass where she had fallen to his front door he was happy to discover she had long gone. Amongst the other insane things the night had provided, his friends had made the best anti drugs advert he'd seen in a long time.

Inside the smell of tinned Bolognese still permeated through the house. He purposely avoided its origins in the kitchen knowing a mess of unwashed pans and plates awaited his attention. He headed for the bedroom, waking Samson from a nap as he flicked on the main light. The friendly feline gave Josh a much needed sense of welcome home and purred loudly as his master gave him a long, cathartic stroke down the length of his arched back.

Before fulfilling the desire to fall onto the bed Josh went over to the closet and rooted out the shoebox. On the way home all he had thought about was the white slavery. Was it to blame for his unpleasant episode in the club? He emptied the nick knacks that served to put off the casual observer onto the bed and picked out the small clear bag of class A secreted beneath. As he held up the remaining amount of angel dust to the light he wasn't so sure of his conviction. *Just stress?* Coke had never affected him like that before. His conscience urged him it had to go, though Josh struggled to abate the fact he would be flushing money down the toilet. Samson mewed as if relaying an opinion of caution. Unable to bring himself to dispense of the expensive vice, Josh dumped it back in the Nike box and buried it at the back of the closet under a pile of heavy Architecture quarterlies he'd planned to reread, but likely never would. Something or someone else was to blame.

Deciding all he needed was a good night's sleep, Josh removed his top, draped it over the back of the regency style chair Sarah's grandmother had bought her for her twenty first birthday and collapsed onto the bed making Samson stand to attention. The heavenly sensation of calm flowed through every muscle as they relaxed against the soft mattress. He closed his eyes to enjoy the momentary bliss the first few seconds awarded him. *Yes, something else to blame.* The weight of Samson's front paws on his chest made him open his eyes. The curious cat was sniffing his face with the interest of a close relative.

"Hey buddy." The oversized cat stretched out his paws then lay across his master's chest. The deep purrs vibrated pleasantly through Josh's torso and he wondered if the dedicated friend ever missed his mistress. Animals may be dumb he thought, but if dumb meant not paying bills or having trouble sleeping he would happily devolve in his next life, that was if anything truly existed after death. With his luck he would come back as a stray. But at least then the only strange men and women with reason to chase him around would be from the pound. Perhaps he was a stray, Josh thought, a social stray who had lost his way. But the freaks who had recently intruded into his life were unlikely agents for keeping the peace.

As he closed his eyes again he saw the face of the man in black. He didn't want to think about him, or the femme fatale from the club, or any of the crap that had happened that day. Los Angeles it seemed was host to hundreds if not thousands of miscreants and disassociatives and, unfortunately for Josh, some of the city's finest had found him worthy of special attention. He rolled over onto his side to assist what should be a natural biological process, but knew he was in for an uphill struggle.

Something on the bed caught the tip of his finger. He raised his head to see it was the recently purchased book and picked it up to study its cover once more. Gazing at the boy-man snoozing against the ethereal backdrop he felt a pang of jealousy. Perhaps naively he had hoped the book's contents could offer some new age cure-all to his insomnia, after all Sarah had believed in all that *hippy crap* and she had been one of the most sincere and intelligent people he had ever met.

He flicked through the fresh white pages of the softback and ended at its contents. At first glance the chapter headlines looked pseudo academic. He wondered why on earth he was even attempting to decipher the new age jargon, but if it was as boring as it looked, at the very least it could only help.

Josh skipped the first ten pages in favour of getting straight to the nitty gritty. He passed on the first chapter's offer of *Your Journey Starts Here* and went directly to the first illustration he found. It was a crudely drawn pyramid schematic split into multi coloured horizontal steps that represented the different levels of spiritual existence. There were nine in total, the lowest level, number one, being the most material at the base of the pyramid and the highest level of existence number nine was at its apex. Humanity's current level was stated as number three. *So much for humanity.* Each level was illustrated with its coordinating colour, the subtext beneath it further explaining that each level, or plain, existed at a different *Vibrational frequency.* Again the higher the level the higher the frequency.

Josh squinted his tired eyes as he attempted to fathom the logistics. He considered himself an academic at heart, but the author was offering no scientific basis that could be justified in the parameters of any reality he could understand. Suspending his disbelief for a while longer, he turned to the accompanying main text and read on. His attention was briefly distracted by the distant clang of cutlery falling onto kitchen floor tiles. Samson had left to enjoy the remnants of the Bolognese on the breakfast bar. He smirked at the cat's greedy tenacity and continued his *homework*.

He wanted to find the link between the boundary stretching ideas portrayed in the schematic and the sleeping man he so envied. The flowery text described the higher levels above humanity as being the plains on which the astral travelling took place, a place that allegedly could easily be entered after first mastering basic meditative techniques. *Always a catch.* He flicked on further into the book too see just how *basic* the techniques were, but was faced with more of the pseudo academic jargon that alienated him from the core of its content. As he tried to let go of his preconditioned ideas and imagine the new world view the book was asking him to believe, something else extraordinary happened; his eyelids sealed him in a deep, natural slumber.

Josh woke, blinking his vision back into focus. *I fell asleep?* Something cool and hard was resting on his chin. He looked down and realised it was the top of the open spine of the book. He closed it and tossed it sloppily onto the bed beside him. *Why did I wake up?* He suddenly felt annoyed. Cheated prematurely of his well deserved reprieve he knew all to well it would not be easy to return to the dark blissful state. Then he heard the scream. It came from outside, a high pitch female call for aid that sounded close by. Josh sat up and focused his startled senses.

He heard it again, this time much louder. Distinctively genuine and sounding as though it had come from his backyard. His noble instinct aroused, he jumped off the bed to quickly make his way through the dark house, intuitively dodging his furnishings with the agility of a trained ninja and entered the kitchen. *This better be good.* As his feet touched the cool tiles he slowed his pace and listened out for another repetition, though sneaking across to the window to peer out through the blinds into his backyard he heard nothing.

Josh lurched over the pile of dirty crockery to extend his view into the neglected open plan garden. The bordering fences were relatively short and afforded him the chance to scour across a wide area of backyard suburbia. But through the cross hatch trellising mounting their tops he couldn't see or hear any evidence of a woman in distress. In the cool, deathly quiet darkness of his kitchen, he was now hit with a blatant realisation. *Did I dream it?*

The blades snapped back together as he retrieved his hand. Trying to shake the cobwebs from his mind he took in the shadows and silhouettes formed by the fine rays of light that penetrated the blinds into his kitchen. Everything seemed real enough. The smell of the Bolognese was reassuringly tasty and the cold steel of the basin rang true through his fingertips as he leaned against the solid wooden sides of the cupboards. If not for previous vivid dreams, he would have dismissed the thought as lunacy, but it was due to the very real nature of those dreams that now made him equally unsure. *Am I still dreaming?*

A shiny metallic knife reflected the faint light from the floor tiles by his feet, knocked from the table by Samson's eagerness for leftovers. But no sooner did he indulge his conviction of dementia; it was squashed by another definite cry for help. Someone was in trouble.

Josh fumbled the spare key into the back door, yanked it open and ran out into the night. He was sure the scream had come from behind the back fence that ran adjacent to the unlit alley and supplied access to the next street. Again the woman's shriek pierced the night. No longer calling for help, the victim was fumbling with an attacker.

Without thought for his own safety he vaulted over the back fence onto the asphalt on the other side. His feet landed flat with the hard ground, sending spears of pain across the soles of both feet, but there was no time for pain. To his right the alley stretched off into the darkness that led to some garages, but the sound of a foot dragged against worn asphalt made him turn to his left.

An overflow of electric light illuminated the silhouette of two people wrestling at the alley's entrance, the long shadow they cast dancing along the ground all the way up to Josh's feet. The streetlight blinked through the jerky movements of the four-legged apparition into his eyes, but he could easily make out the attacker as the taller of the two. The smaller figure of the woman was thrust hard against the wavering fence, the man's hand grasping her mouth as she tried desperately to prevent him yanking the small bag free from her grasp.

Her muffled scream made Josh's pulse race. The adrenaline and masculine bravado so lacking in his life now flowed through his entire body. Spotting a protruding piece of fence trim amongst the weeds by his feet, he picked up the makeshift club and manoeuvred behind the unsuspecting attacker, feeling an immortality built on necessity and rage.

"Shut up! You wanna die?" the attacker growled at the trapped victim pinned against the wavering fence. In the seconds it took to get behind the man Josh was now in a position to see he was similar height and build to himself. "Gimme the goddamn bag lady!" the attacker ordered franticly, oblivious to the lurking vigilante.

With the guilty pleasure that could come from such a violent act, Josh raised the makeshift weapon high and aimed for the top of the attacker's head. With a brutish swing he brought it crashing down onto his unwitting target. But to Josh's dismay the man turned and the piece of wood trim shattered in two across his shoulder. *Shit!* The wood was as rotten as his luck. He'd hoped the club would disable the attacker long enough for the cops to arrive. Instead the man howled in agony and turned to face him.

Josh clenched his fist around the remaining shard and sent a second crushing strike to the side of the man's head. The woollen beanie hat he wore padded the blow, but the force was enough to make the man yelp and stumble forward onto one knee, allowing the women to stagger free, out of breath and dumb with shock.

"You alright?" Josh asked, electrified by the experience. The woman simply stared at her doubled over attacker. "Did he hurt you?" he queried again. Again no reply. He turned to look at the wide-eyed woman still clasping her prized handbag. "Are you okay?" Josh repeated loudly, blood pumping wondrously through his veins. She nodded frantically, before her wild eyes betrayed a renewed sense of dread. Josh heard an ominous clink of metal locking against metal.

"Your dead man, you hear me? Dead!" the mugger grunted from his lowly position. Fuelled by an insane fury, he straightened to his full height and glared with a mania possessed by those prone to violence. "I'm gonna mess you up so bad your mama won't know you!" His dark features looked twisted in the harsh light that half hid his face in shadow. But it was the long, thin metallic object in his hand that now caught Josh's attention. Plucked from a hide hole in his jacket the enraged attacker now brandished a telescopic baton.

The woman screamed. Her ear-shattering shriek was a cataclysmic broadcast of Josh's own perishing sense of immortality and was quickly followed by her fleeing footsteps into the night. *Thanks Lady*! His adversary tightened his grip. The piece of fence trim Josh still held in his own moist palm now looked pathetic in comparison to the professional weapon. The attacker winced as he raised his wounded arm, and then sized up his brave opponent with a sense of caution. The slim built *Cracker* in the Berkley t-shirt posturing in front of him was a world away from the Latino hoods and clique's he had grown up around. Josh's decision to remain at the sight of his daunting weapon made him think twice. *Loco?*

The Latino lunged the agile baton at Josh, the swashbuckling whoosh sound it made ample warning for its intended victim to duck the steel pole in time. As it soared past his head, Josh retaliated with a lightening blow to the back of his off balanced mugger. The counter attack caused the man to crumple into a waistline tackle, the baton falling from his grasp to create a metallic clank that echoed into the quiet night.

The force of the unexpected grapple sent Josh stumbling back into the opposite fence that creaked under the pressure of the combined body weight. His head met the hard wood with a white flash of pain as the nauseating crush of his abdomen forced him to flay his arms around the heavy, awkward bulk that bulldozed his mid section before delivering a debilitating hook to the ribs. Winded, mouth gaping, Josh slunk to the floor in a heap of defeated limbs.

The individual pieces of grit in the asphalt created a dark, barren landscape as Josh examined it close up, his cheek pressed hard into the cool, jagged surface as he now lay demobilised, breathless and dazed. Again the hollow pounding exploded into his torso, this time nearer a kidney as he suffered the more unyielding impact of foot bearing into his exposed body. He was sure he heard a distant voice booming over him, but it seemed miles away as he lay mesmerised by the stark electric light that flooded down the alley to where he had fallen.

Josh felt his waist wrenched back, obliging the rest of his body to follow suit as he was rolled onto his back. Experienced hands patted Josh down, pillaged his pockets and rooted through socks in search of hidden caches while the wretched, winded agony left him in a distracted daze. The fake Rolex slipped off his wrist into the hoodlum's possession. Josh looked up, injuries no longer depriving him of focus as he wished he could rip off the street hardened face with his bare hands as it admired the watch in the streetlight. He realised then the attacker was in no rush to escape. He was arrogant enough to believe himself untouchable, a street warrior with the right to take what he wanted when he wanted.

"Piece of shit." The words barely escaped Josh's mouth, but they caught the man's attention as he hid the fake Rolex under his own sleeve.

"What d'you say?" the man snarled down at him, the familiar smell of weed sweet on his breath. An inferno of rage inside Josh had meant the curse to resound menacingly, but in the rash delivery he had forgotten his compromised position. Reminded of his victim's previous resolve, the mugger's face twisted vengefully into a mask of shadow and flesh. Without conscience he grabbed Josh's t-shirt and raised him from the asphalt. Josh knew what was coming next. In his apathetic daze he was content with his simple act of defiance, but grimaced as the Latino clenched his free hand into a fist and delivered a violent blow into his face. After a second flash of light its harsh electric counterpart was swallowed by oblivion.

*****

Heat. The ground against Josh's face felt warm. In the semi conscious state he was reminded of childhood tranquillity in the arms of a beloved parent. Then he became aware the increasing warmth was radiating onto the exposed skin of his face. He took in his first breath; the air was warm and dry. *Where the hell am I?* Realising his eyes were still closed he opened them to find they were blinded with sunlight, forcing him to squint until his startled vision adjusted to the unexpected intrusion into his consciousness. *I'm outside?* The revelation triggered an instant memory of the fight with the mugger. Shielding the sun from his vision with a raised hand he wrenched himself over, propped himself up and looked around expecting to find himself the centre of curiosity for the neighbourhood kids.

The local pre-teens used the alley behind his house as a racetrack, but that morning they had not come across the unconscious wreck of Josh blocking their speedway. Instead of the rasping noise they used to imitate their favourite motorbikes there was only a deafening silence. Squinting into the sun-baked surroundings he could see he was very much alone. His fingers dug into the soft ground. *Soft asphalt?* Propped on one hand he brought the other to his face to inspect the sandy grain that trickled out of his fingers in a fine rain. Josh's heart cramped in a throe of panic. The alley and familiar rickety fences of suburbia were gone. Instead of the Edendale 'burbs, he had woken into an isolated arid wasteland that was as barren as it was unknown.

He scrambled to his feet in a vain attempt to break the illusion. *Where the hell am I?* The desert plain on which he stood was truly lifeless. His scrutiny of the shimmering landscape produced no signs of plants or animals. He was struck with the sudden fear that he had died and gone to hell. *This can't be!* Josh told himself he was dreaming and clenched his eyes shut, shaking his head and the images from his mind, but as he stood in the hot sun, alone in the dark sanctuary behind his eyelids, he could sense that he was very much awake and in hold of his faculties.

An eagle shrieked way above his head. He looked up to search for the bird of prey in the bright blue sky and spotted it gliding away behind him. *Something is alive here besides me.* Following the path of the majestic bird towards the distant, dark peaks that lay on the horizon, he saw something more unbelievable at the base of the mountainous boundary. Shimmering in the distance not a hundred feet away from where he stood there was a building, a veritable oasis in the desert land. *It can't be, not out here?*

Isolated on the barren plain was a hazy mirage of a diner, the gaudy white on maroon motif of a large mouth baring down into a fat burger instantly recognisable as the motif for the Eat-A-Lot franchise. At first he was unsure if the vision was just that, a trick of the mind brought on by the exposure to the sun's rays, but after accepting he was no longer hallucinating, he was inclined to believe the dreaded diner was also just as real as the desert landscape it resided on. There were no discernable roads, no people, though he had to except it was real. The only other explanation was insanity, but unready to accept that dilemma, he took his first few steps towards confronting his confusion.

Josh quickened his pace as the sun rained down mercilessly on his unprotected skin. *Why dump me out here?* The wasteland looked strangely familiar. The Discovery Channel had widened his knowledge of the world in the past two years and he was sure he recognised the arid topography as that of the Californian desert lands. *Where else could it be?*

Cursed with pink skin tones rather than the more acceptable west coast tan, Josh knew he should be sweltering under the barrage of UV radiation, though as he approached the diner's gaudy frontage he felt surprisingly good, in fact felt better than good. Outside the miraculous structure he paused and stared, thoughts of harmful UV and kidnap were dispelled by the very real Eat-A-Lot franchise that now offered an ironic sense of relief.

A layer of dirt caked the maroon and white façade. Countless desert winds had obviously battered the building for some time; leaving the thick crust as proof the diner had been resident in the strange place for some time. Reaching out to touch the glass of the entrance, his fingertips were soiled in the fine dirt and confirmed the place was certainly no mirage. If not for the crooked *Open* sign just visible behind the dirty glass Josh would have forsaken the place as abandoned. In that place of death it was the only sign of life. As he looked around again at the barren sun-baked landscape he wondered why the hell he had been brought there. But such thoughts were irrelevant now, finding a way back home was all that mattered.

The Eat-A-Lot's door's beckoned him into the cool, sheltered interior, where instead of the deserted hideaway he assumed he would find; the bolt-down tables were taken up with a generous spread of people. In front a small family with two children enjoyed a Big Eat family meal. Without gazing up to meet the newcomer, the family unit continued their meal in pleasant seclusion as the row of booths to Josh's left and right housed a well behaved community of young courting couples and baseball cap wearing truck drivers. Of no apparent interest to any of the content diners, he weaved through the tables until he reached the long counter that stretched the length of the airy building.

The counter was one of the longest Josh had seen, but didn't have a single greasy faced teenager behind it to take his order. It then dawned on him he didn't know what he was going to say or do; after all he hadn't popped in for a bite to eat. He had woken up in the back of beyond with no recollection of how he had got there and with no; he checked his pocket, yes with no money for a drink or the phone. His thigh pressed up against the maroon vinyl of a padded bar stool. He decided to take the offer of a seat, the synthetic material making an embarrassing sticky rumble as it took the weight off his feet.

Slumping his elbows onto the counter he took a furtive survey of the uninterested faces quietly enjoying their food, taking reassurance from the lack of rowdy factory workers amongst them. He considered how crazy the whole damn thing was. Pressing a finger into the toothpick protruding from a glass vial in front of him he tested the bizarre reality. The pain it produced was real enough.

Movement then caught his eye. An employee was finally making an appearance, though as the tall sleek figure came closer he saw it was no ordinary adolescent burger flipper. As the young woman's long legs made light work of the distance between them, Josh found the maroon and white nylon Eat-A-Lot uniform in no way diminished her sensual allure.

"Hi welcome to Eat A lot, where good food and good service go hand in hand," she welcomed him, supplementing the scripted greeting with a broad smile that reminded him of a high school crush. "May I take your order?" The question flew over Josh's head. Her long fair hair fell down to her shoulders, framing big blue eyes that flashed with the spark of health and youth. Unable to prevent himself he darted a glance to the perked breasts he noticed were unrestrained by a bra. *Snap out of it.*

"Sure, gimme a cola," he replied. He didn't like cola. He was enthralled by the magnetic charm all beautiful women held over men.

"Original, cherry, lime, diet, caffeine free or banana?" she asked whilst maintaining the near perfect radiance. *Banana?* He liked Bananas. Out of a dishevelled curiosity he blurted out a request for the unusual choice.

"Okay would that be regular, large, extra large or Big Eat?"

"Better make it a Big Eat, I'm parched."

"Can I take an order for anything else sir?" The smile seemed permanently embossed upon her flawless face, which as far as he could see was not embellished by layers of cosmetic fakery. He felt the devil that was Lust stirring inside him, but he squashed the innuendo that was on the tip of his tongue.

"That's all for now, thanks."

"Anything you wish." With the cordial reply she turned tail to reveal her perked buttocks as she bent to retrieve an empty. Just as he had gotten enough of the wavering vision she rose with a huge garish plastic cup that was not much smaller than a bucket. *Holy crap.* As he watched her fill it with the humming stream of carbonated fluid Josh remembered his situation.

"Um, Miss," he interrupted, "on second thoughts, maybe I'll just have a water, tap will be fine." Expecting an unappreciative scowl he was surprised to find the baby doll eyes retained their sparkle.

"Anything you wish, handsome. Perhaps you'd prefer a beer?"

"You have beer?" he blurted.

"Sure. Draught, bottle...What would you like?" His conscience told him he shouldn't succumb again, but the offer of a cool beer made his saliva ducts melt.

"Bottle's good."

"Sure, anything you wish." She reached under the counter once more, creating an opportunity for an ample glance down the unbuttoned top of her nylon uniform. *Get a grip.* Her beauty was distracting, but not so much that he wasn't amazed by the feat of ingenuity. Before his eyes she clamped the bottle cap between her perfect teeth, twisted it free and slide the frosty beer towards him. "Enjoy, it's on the house."

"You're sure?" He didn't wait for the answer, but during the first few wonderful chilled gulps he took from the bottle he was sure he heard her acknowledge him. The cold refreshing liquid drained down his gullet until its chilly presence filled his stomach.

"I needed that," he uttered as he put the empty down and looked enthusiastically to the attentive beauty and her beaming smile. "Any chance the house's charity could extend to one more?"

"Anything you wish." In one swift moment the empty was removed and replaced with a fresh one, opened by the same oral vice as the first. Without a word of thanks he put the new bottle to his lips and drained it thirstily.

"Jesus, that's gotta be the greatest beer I've ever tasted," he exclaimed. The proclamation was no appreciative attempt at flattery. The two bottles of beer he had just guzzled in record time had truly been the most satisfying liquid that had ever passed his lips.

"We aim to please sir."

"Well you're doing a fine job, Miss." There was an awkward pause as he studied her face in the aftermath of the refreshment. It was in those fleeting seconds it dawned on him the attentive employee looked strangely familiar. "Don't I know you from somewhere?" he asked suggestively. The attentive blonde simply shook her head and grinned inanely. The more he studied her perfect features the more the niggling notion he'd seen her some place before took hold.

"You look familiar that's all."

"Anything you wish."

"Excuse me?"

"Anything you wish." The repeated enigma left him stumped. He looked at her beaming features and wondered if she was as dim-witted as she was beautiful. Then it hit him.

In his second year at Berkeley, a high school friend had visited with much needed supplies of alcohol and Grass. After the ensuing week-long binge he had returned home, leaving behind a collection of well palmed editions of Playboy magazine.

The blonde employee's unnaturally perfect skin had given it away, the unnatural perfection that could only be achieved by the ingenious use of air-brushing. Josh realised the employee's sensual perfection was the same that had drawn his attention to the blonde vision in the *Playmates of the Eighties* centrefold left on his dorm floor. Though not normally attracted to the WASP cheerleader types that set the Californian archetype for womanhood, the reprinted naked poise of Miss June nineteen eighty four had captured his male hunger in a shot. As he recalled the dorm wall favourite, he now realised he was looking at the same vision in the flesh.

Before blurting the revelation the logistics cut his enthusiasm short. *Miss June nineteen eighty-four!* The photo shoot had been over twenty years old, and yet she stood behind the counter in the prime of her youth, untainted by time. The penny dropped with a deafening clang.

"You're not real, none of this is real!" He remembered the distinct curve of the lips. The shape of the petite nose. The individual hairs of her head. He had studied that old shoot over and over trying to fathom what had made her so damned attractive. They were one and the same, he was sure of it.

"Anything you wish," she repeated herself. The employee could have been a doppelganger for all he knew, but deep down he knew he was looking at some physical projection from the recess of his memories. He wanted to touch her, to test the subtle warmth of her flesh, but the vivid authenticity of the world in which he now existed made the idea seem inappropriate.

"Un-frigging believable. I knew you were too good to be true!" he jibed at the Playmate. His electrified senses identified the virtual dream world as real. Defying all belief, the uncanny mirror image of its material counterpart was flawless and absolute. The counter was solid; the beer was cold and his excitement instantaneous. His bewilderment now converted to awe of the uncharted playground that was this inner world.

"How about some pie to go along with my beer Miss June? Apple! With fresh cream." She repeated her triple word catchphrase and produced a large slice of apple pie from under the magical counter, complete with generous squirts of whipped cream. Unable to prevent a grin, he picked up

Black Light

the fork she supplied, cut the nose off the pie and ate it. The sweet tangy apple sauce melted in his mouth. He swallowed it quickly and sliced off another ample forkful.

"Anything else I can get you sir?" she asked politely.

"Yeah a few more beers," he swallowed the second mouthful, almost choking. "And some ice-cream, if you got it. Chocolate!." Josh hadn't had the premium brand of ice cream in years. It was a luxurious and expensive treat, but his dreams were set to provide where reality could not. "This tastes so good!" he exclaimed. Like the beer, the apple pie was the best he had ever eaten. In the sensory overload of culinary revelry he quite forgot none of it was real, but as Miss June produced a king size tub of ice-cream he no longer cared. Josh pushed the half eaten pie aside. To his gleeful amazement his beaming servant bit into the side of the lid and prized it open with her teeth. The tub made a reassuring thud as she then placed it before him.

"Anything you wish." He rammed the spoon hard into the frozen delicacy, but like all tubs of the prestigious dessert it was famously too hard to eat straight from the fridge. Impatiently he eyed Miss June again.

"You say that a lot don't you?" he postulated, re-scrutinizing her beauty. "What if I wished for you to unbutton your top? What would you say to that?" The question had been an earnest one, but he hadn't prepared for its consequences. Without a hint of female prudence, she grasped either side of the uniform's plunging neckline and ripped the synthetic fabric apart as though it were made of tissue paper. Josh was left staring at the perfect pair of ample breasts he'd previously only appreciated in pictorial form.

"Now that's what I call service," he muttered as one hunger was taken over by another. "Play with them." With the same happy-to-please gaze she complied with his order, allowing Josh to carry on his experiment with the eagerness of a hormonal teenager. Forgetting his gluttony, past fantasies were playing out in the virtual world as lucky stars rallied to him like moths to flame. He checked behind for moral do-gooders. The happy diners around him remained uninterested in anything else apart from their food and continued eating in total ignorance of the erotic display. *Dumb bastards*. He gazed back at the perked breasts. Miss June continued to palm them, tweaking the nipples then licking her lips in a lustful anticipation of his next order. He couldn't resist.

"Take off the rest of your clothes," he ordered. Obediently the Playmate complied again, ripping away the drab uniform in its entirety until she stood completely naked. The blonde beauty leaned back against the maroon and white tiles of the back wall so that he could get the full picture as she writhed in a pornographic solicitation against the ceramic chessboard. But as she lowered one hand to tease her genitals, Josh was suddenly aware of another less interesting presence beside him.

*****

The empty glass fell out of Sharon's hand and landed safely onto the beige carpet. Its delicate thud was sufficient enough to wake her from her siesta. She snatched up her head from the couch arm, instantly rewarded by a shard of neck pain. The jolt to the system was enough to kick start her dreary senses in time to react to the dribble of black current juice escaping from the tipped glass. She reached down and placed the glass safely onto an old copy of Cosmopolitan and realised the sleep at done her some good. Blurry but not out, she felt her equilibrium stabilise from the effects of the bottle of red wine she had consumed before jumping in a cab to Josh's, only to be humiliated on his doorstep.

The smell of crushed grass still clung to her clothes. Her humiliation had been completed with Josh absconding in the taxi, leaving her the victim of her own self abuse as she lay in the neglected lawn like some homeless derelict. But damn it, the deadbeat had no right to treat her like a whore. Straightening on the couch to rub the dried crust of a tear from her cheek, she was reminded of her Mom's counsel that men used love to get sex and women vice versa.

After watching her man flee from her advances she had staggered part of the long walk back home. In her inebriated state her red stilettos had made the walk precarious and she had resigned to calling another cab to complete the return journey home. Sharon had ignored the driver's attempts at conversation. Instead she had been lost in her fear she was losing Josh. But had she ever had him? she thought. The memories of the pretty, dead wife still haunted her man's eyes like a black cloud. Even on the first night they'd met she had sensed the loss that possessed his heart.

The bagel's wrapper crackled under a cushion as she righted herself. The out of date treat had helped soak up the bottle of red wine along with several glasses of her favourite juice, but she hadn't planned on falling asleep. She also couldn't recall if she'd decided to live with only half of Josh's heart. Sadly even with half a heart he was still the best man that had come her way in a long time, job or no job she recognised the enigmatic winner residing inside. All that was needed was a little tender coaxing to bring it back to the fore. That had been her personal charge.

She checked her watch and saw it was late. Anger dispelled by the power nap, she reached over the back of the couch to lift the answer machine into view, hoping to see the little red light that signalled a recorded apology was waiting to be heard. There was none. *Bastard.* She grabbed her keys and went out to the car. She would be damned before she would let the black cloud befuddle their relationship. But as she climbed inside her Mom's little city car she couldn't shake the feeling Josh was happier to be distracted by the past than face reality. It was the past that drew Josh to her suave nemesis Mathew Nugent, a past she planned to deprive of power by being her man's highway to the future.

*****

Josh ignored the intruder's question. As Miss June writhed behind the counter in all her naked glory he could sense the patron sitting on the next stool, lingering like the burdensome personification of moral conscience, but the erotic display was far too much fun to let go. Josh felt as though he had waited his whole life to witness this event. He wished the annoying incursion away.

"You know you'll go blind if you keep this up Joshua," the man persisted. The mention of his name in that place suddenly made him feel uneasy. "And what use is a blind man to anyone? Least of all himself." Hoping the vision would not be lost, Josh reluctantly tore his attention from the Playmate to find the intruder at his side was wearing the same dark sunglasses and black attire he'd worn last time they met. The dreamer froze instantly as he scrutinised the ghoulish stalker from the Helter Skelter at close range.

"Do you know me?" Josh asked suspiciously. He admired the thick raven black hair that was brushed back from the stalker's high forehead into a crowning glory. His pale complexion was flawless, but revealed a mature man in his late forties with a well defined bone structure, offset by unusually thin, androgynous eyebrows that arched high above the reticent eyewear.

"You could say that Mr Brenin," the stalker grinned. The man in black stared at Josh with unseen eyes, his presence making Josh feel cold in the previously comfortable warmth of the make believe diner he'd been enjoying. Real or not he didn't like this man. One thing for sure, this was his dream, consequently affirming the stalker presence was as make believe as the rest of surroundings. "If you could spare a moment miss," the intruder then acknowledged the still writhing beauty. "I'd like a Cappuccino, De-Café." He looked back to Josh. "Don't want to be kept up all night do we?" he suggested, indifferent to the naked splendour that to Josh's displeasure walked away to fetch the order.

"Why don't you do us both a favour and get the hell out of here Mister?" Josh replied irritably.

"I'm afraid you can't tell me what do to Mr Brenin, that's not how this works." A feeling of dread suddenly smothered his previous excitement.

"How what works?" Miss June returned in record time with the Cappuccino and placed it in front of the dream world stalker. The outburst had little affect on the intruder's demeanour. Josh watched on as he casually stirred the hot drink. As Miss June returned to her previous writhing the man placed the plastic spoon into his mouth.

"Mmm, the Cappuccinos are pretty damn good here don't you agree?"

"I dunno I haven't tried them yet, do I know you?"

"Well unlike everyone else here I'm not merely a figment of your imagination. In here, as well as the outside world, I'm as real as you. You can sense that can't you Josh?" He asked the question with an air of mockery rather than interest.

"How do you know my name?"

"That's irrelevant. The real question to ask would be how I got in here." Josh felt his dream world spine turn into dream world ice. "After all this is your dream not mine." He raised the cup to his lips and drained the hot drink as though it were spring water. "That's very refreshing thank you," he said to Miss June. Confused and annoyed by the explanation, Josh felt the urge to crush the empty cup into the ghoulish face.

"If you're real then this can't be a dream!" Josh barked.

"Oh this is a dream alright," the stalker confirmed. "Where else but in your unconscious mind could a loser like you convince a centrefold to take off her clothes at the drop of a hat?" Josh ignored the slur.

"But I know this is my dream, I want to know what the hell you're doing in it!"

"Exactly! What *am* I doing in it Josh? Believe me I could think of much more appetising surroundings to place myself into. I'm not simply here for the wild roller-coaster ride through the unconscious cesspit Josh Brenin calls fantasy." He turned round to Josh, flicking the length of his black coat off his leg to reveal the collarless black satin shirt he wore underneath. "Why I'm here is much more important, to both you and me. Would you like another drink? Another beer perhaps? They're very good."

"I'll do without, thanks," Josh replied sharply. He swivelled round on his stool to face his enigmatic stalker. So far the black clad man had done nothing but entertain himself at Josh's expense. Sensing a menacing power emanating from the man's creepy aura he kept his disapproval in check. Josh wanted to see his eyes, to know what lay behind the shaded glass. For the moment he decided to resist the urge to remove them by force.

"Take a look around, do you see their faces?" The stalker gestured to the drones eating their fast food meals. "Pitiful aren't they?" Josh diverted his gaze from the man to look around the diner. No one else looked familiar, but all shared a blank apathy for what was around them. "The real world is full of such pathetic excuses for living beings," the man stated brusquely. "It's a wonder the world is still functioning at all."

For a moment Josh felt a stab of envy as he gazed at the young family contently finishing their bumper meal, wondering if he would ever enrol in the family ideal himself. The man's foreboding presence focused on Josh's bemused face once more.

"Tell me, don't you wonder if there's anything more to life than working nine to five, week in week out, accumulating electronic digits on an ATM screen that are reduced by the economic drain of merely trying to exist in the first place?" He didn't wait for Josh's answer, "We are a race of slaves, working to exist in a prison world, a world that eats away at the very thing that makes us extraordinary; our true selves. The outside world is a piece of shit Mr Brenin. The only sanctuary for true reality is inside." Josh pondered the spiel for a moment.

"None of these people of are real, except you?"

"Correct, but they are part the blueprint of your world as it has been stamped onto your psyche. At birth we come into this world unspoilt, clean. It is the world that soils us and makes us into what we become."

"And what is that?" Josh asked, aghast at the stalker's obvious contempt for his fellow man.

"Nothing, Mr Brenin." A cool silence followed as the two men swapped gazes. Josh was unconvinced by the condemning analysis.

"I'm sorry but I didn't catch you name," Josh said curtly. "I mean here you are running around my unconscious without the decency of an introduction." The comment made the man smile warmly for the first time. As he offered his hand in friendship the menacing aura around him momentarily evaporated.

"Of course, how rude of me. Galda Vey."

"Galda, Vey," Josh confirmed sceptically, perplexed by the exotic mantle. "That's your name?" He looked at the outstretched hand, its flawless skin ghoulish like a shop mannequin's. Josh declined to shake it. There was a brief look of offence from the man calling himself Galda, but the wily smile returned.

"At your service."

"And does this *service* involve stalking? Last time I checked it was a misdemeanour." Josh's belligerent tone instigated the return of Galda's intimidating aura. "I've seen you watching me, you and your buddy following me around like two psychos with a crush."

"It was necessary to help you understand the truth."

"The truth!" Josh blurted. "What truth? That you're both freaks? Well I've got a newsflash for you, Mr Vey, if that is your real name. I'm not interested in what ever the hell kind of bullshit you think it is you're selling here." He felt a surge of pent up anger flood out from somewhere and explode from his mouth, and it felt good. "But you're right, this *is* my mind and right now I'm busy enjoying it. So why don't you take a hike and find another *loser* who gives a crap!" Josh spun away from the intruder. Slumping his elbows back onto the counter he returned to enjoying the still writhing Miss June until Galda snapped his fingers.

The Playmate stopped her sensual gyrating. Josh turned to look at the raised hand responsible and then to Galda's shaded eyes from which he sensed a reciprocated vehemence. The stalker then gestured for him to look back. As he did he discovered Miss June's perfect vision of lust had degenerated into horror. More than halting the erotic display, the gestured order had transformed the blonde beauty into a decrepit specimen of elderly flesh. Smooth, sun kissed skin now hung loose from protruding bones, while grey, withered hair framed the baby blue eyes that had yellowed and sunken into a countenance of an old wrinkled hag.

Without warning the haggard female creature leant forward and clasped Josh's head between her wrinkled hands, forcing a hard slobbering kiss onto his lips. He tried to escape the awful grapple, but the women's hands were like a vice about his head and he was forced to submit to the sordid experience. After seconds of slobbering misery her mouth finished sucking at his. Releasing her grip Josh fell from the slippery vinyl covered stool onto the hard tiled floor, creating a roar of laughter from the onlookers. Looking up with revulsion he saw the old hag jeering at him, her huge sagging breasts spilling onto the counter as she exposed her slobbering, toothless mouth with a heckling cackle.

"Still enjoying yourself Joshua?" Galda asked derisively as Josh got on his feet to a chorus of laughter. The once quiet diners had forgotten their food and exploded into hysterics. "Surely the experience of age is better than youth?" Galda then sneered. As the faces around Josh creased with hilarity, their reproving fingers pointed his way, civility now distorting into a malicious unnatural amusement at his predicament. He felt his heart pound heavily in his chest, the blood in his head echoing the pulse as it forced the thundering affect into every limb.

"What are you laughing at?" Josh yelled at his hysterical audience. Still they continued unchecked by his rage.

"They're laughing at you Josh," Galda confirmed. He slid from his stool to walk into the centre of the eatery. "Ridicule; the plague of self esteem," he asserted in a venomous sneer, his expression stern and grim. "I can make it stop. But you must listen to what I say."

The distorted faces continued to heckle Josh with insane hysteria, distracting him from Galda's words. The once placid faces were now twisted into cruel masks of inhumanity, their laughter ruthlessly flaying his sanity from his soul. *This isn't real.* The crowd of jeering customers slowly fused together as they enclosed their victim like a pack of Hyenas. Searching their faces for a way out Josh suddenly recognised one. Like his adopted peers Matty's pampered features were stretched into a manic delight at Josh's discomfort, but deep down he knew the derisive features were not his college friend. He diverted his hatred from the caricature people back to the orchestrator of the malign engagement.

"Don't you get it? I'm not listening to you!" he yelled at Galda's callous face. "You, demonic bastard!" The black clad intruder remained rooted to the spot as the mob of laughing zombies began to close in around them. "You want my soul is that it? Well you can't have it!" Sunday School memories came flooding to his defence. "In the name of Father, the son and the holy spirit I command you to be gone!" To Josh's dismay the holy petition didn't succeed. Galda's features became sterner.

"Did you know the true meaning of the word daemon is wise one?" Galda's words carried over the encroaching rabble to stupefy Josh. "In that regard maybe I *am* a demon, for there is much wisdom that I can teach you. But first there is much for you to unlearn, before you can truly waken your dormant self!"

"What are you talking about you freak?"

"The service I offer is to show you how to exist. All this, is merely a cage that you call your mind. Let me give you the key to the lock Joshua."

"This isn't a cage this is a dream, it's all just a dream!" The mob's laughter increased at the feverish denial. They were all about him now, their vindictive fingers poking his body while their gaping mouths delivered their horrid wall of heckles. "You're not real, it's all not real!" In a vain attempt to block the deafening mockery out Josh clenched his head between his forearms, muffling his ears he hoped to thwart the incredulous onslaught that threatened to swallow him. Still the laughter pierced his desperation to resonate unhindered inside his head. Even as he closed his eyes Galda's face projected into his mind, the ghoulish countenance emanating from a montage of twisted, laughing faces. "You are not real!" he screamed again defiantly. Then the laughter stopped.

Josh opened his eyes and stared at Galda. They were now both alone in the diner. The mob of jeering people had vanished into thin air, taking the haggard Miss June with them into oblivion.

"If religion is your choice of weapon then so be it," Galda stated. "For in this domain I control everything you see." He clicked his fingers once more. The room around them suddenly caught fire. As the inferno sprang to life it consumed the counter, tables and chairs in a circling fireball, smothering everything in sight with the fires of Hell. "Everything you hear." His tormentor clicked his fingers again. The screams of thousands of tortured souls suddenly howled from the flames, chilling his blood. "And everything you feel!" Josh reeled in agony as he was stabbed with hot shards of pain. The flames were now licking at his exposed skin, causing him to scream in tune with the tortured chorus.

"You're not real!" Josh screamed again, his body searing in the flames that threatened to consume him in eternal damnation. Through the torment Galda's voice persisted.

"It's your mind, but I have the power to manipulate it," Galda's words pierced the pain. "But with the key I am offering you, you too can master it as I have."

Josh contorted in a desperate attempt to escape the burning torture, but with every movement the pain remained unyielding, all consuming. The incredible agony was more than he could endure. He screamed for mercy, but the inferno continued to bath him in the white-hot flames that fractured his mind.

"I am very real Josh Brenin," he heard Galda's voice declare above his screams. "And so is my offer. Accept it, and I promise to show you a realm beyond your wildest fantasy." Josh opened his tortured eyes to see the flames dancing around him. Amongst them Galda stood before him unscathed. Stretching out his arms into a mock crucifixion his tormentor then released a devilish laughter of his own.

"It's just a dream Joshua. Wake up!"

*****

Josh thrashed his limbs in an attempt to smother the flames. He opened his eyes searching for the hellish fire eating at his flesh, only to discover he was now free of the inferno. Raising his arms into the neon light glowing from above his head, he frantically searched his forearms for cauterised flesh. To his relief they had escaped unscathed. *It was a dream, I dreamt it.* The pungent chemical odour of clinical bleach suddenly made him take stock of his surroundings. Distracted from his terror, the abhorrent smell served to tell him he was no longer lying on his own bed. A door creaked open in a darkened corner. He turned his head to see a familiar young woman enter the sterile environment holding a cup of freshly vended coffee. *Not my room.*

"Hey you're awake," Sharon said thankfully, still wearing the same jacket that hid the sexy lingerie beneath. She placed the coffee down on the bedside cabinet and perched on the edge of the strange bed he lay in, a picture of calm and sobriety.

"What happened to me? Where am I?"

"What does it look like dummy? You're in hospital; you've been out cold for hours." The explanation further shocked his system. *Hospital!* Josh tried to raise his head in protest, until a spasm of pain filled his frontal lobe and forced him to relent. Sharon comforted him with a soft hand to his face, her warm scent, tainted with traces of wine and crushed grass, replaced the stench of bleach and helped him relax.

"My head," Josh complained. He raised his own hand to feel a numb swelling on his head and realised it was a medical dressing.

"Shhh don't touch it, let me get someone." Sharon urged his hand away and stood to leave. Realising something terrible must have happened Josh tried to recall it, but the only vision that leapt into his mind's eye was of the white hot flames licking his flesh.

"Was there a fire?" he asked.

"You don't remember?" Josh panicked, recognising his girlfriend's concern. *There was no fire. That was a dream.*

"Not really."

"Some crackhead tried to snatch your neighbour's handbag, that is until Josh Van Damme intervened."

"I did?"

"My brave little soldier," Sharon cooed. "The woman flagged down a passing squad car. They found you out cold in the alley. You had me a worried Josh." She leaned in close and gave him a lingering peck on the forehead. "Thought I'd end up dating a vegetable for the rest of my life." The warm sensation conflicted with a flashback of being struck by the hoodlum mugger.

"That happened?" he asked confused. Memories and dreams were swirling in a hazy mess of hallucination and reality. Suddenly there were no definable borders.

"Wait there I'll get the Doc." Sharon exited in a hurry through the creaking door, leaving the scent of coffee to permeate the otherwise clinical odour of the dim lit room. He was glad of the delicious alternative. As far as he was concerned the smell of hospital sanitation was a precursor to misery and death, and did little to calm his nerves. *A goddamn dream.*

The doctor who returned in her place was senior in appearance and not like the young, dashing medical heroes he'd seen on TV. Josh judged he was probably close to retirement. He was accompanied by a short oriental nurse, who after raising a smile went over to check the bleeping apparatus that had been monitoring Josh's vitals.

"Mr Brenin, I'm Doctor Stevens," the doctor said in a jovial English accent. He removed the small chrome cased torch from the top pocket of his immaculate white jacket. "And *you* are a very lucky young man." His smart, chiselled features looked satisfied with Josh's improved condition.

"Forgive me but I don't see how having my head cracked open can be seen as a lucky," Josh replied dryly as the bright light shone into his right eyeball. It remained there for a few seconds then went across to blind his left. Releasing a reassuring sigh the doctor returned the torch to the breast pocket.

"Lucky because this could so easily have been fatal Mr Brenin." He studied the wounds on Josh's head, touching them curiously with a concerned look as Josh winced. "Yes very lucky, how do you feel?"

"Like I've just been mugged."

"Nothing wrong with your sense of humour I see. Do you think you can you stand for me?" The doctor stood back as the nurse pulled back the bed covers and offered her arm to Josh for support. He didn't take up the offer. He preferred instead to slowly edge off the bed until he stood on his own merit. Apart from a headache and stiff legs he felt fine. *I'm not staying here.*

"Did they catch the guy?" Josh asked expectantly.

"I wouldn't know that's not my vocation. Close your eyes and put your arms out please." Josh did what was asked, making sure he performed the task as lucidly as possible. "Now take a few steps towards me," the doctor instructed. Josh felt an idiot as he walked blind in the hospital gown with arms outstretched, though the feel of the cold floor against his bare feet distracted his embarrassment. "Okay that's fine. Sit down." The nurse had remained close during his short walk and now guided him back to the bed.

"So what's the prognosis...am I going to be okay?" Josh asked. The doctor picked up the metal clipboard from the end of the bed and jotted down his unvoiced medical thoughts.

"You'll be glad to hear you won't need stitches, and you don't appear to be suffering any symptoms of concussion. So on that front you are quite okay. However I think we should get a CT scan done soon as possible, just to be safe." Josh didn't like the sound of the precautionary measure, but appreciated its necessity. "After all we don't want you toppling over in a week's time with an aneurysm do we?" Doctor Stevens looked up at the dutiful nurse. "Nurse could you give us a moment please." She smiled in acknowledgement and left doctor alone with patient. Josh sensed the requirement preceded something more negative.

"You've taken a few knocks to the body, but nothing looks broken. For the next dew days you'll be sore and bruised but it's merely superficial. As long as you go home, rest and avoid anymore heroics, we should be looking at no long term complications." The blow to the head Leo had inflicted earlier had been mistaken as a result of the second fray.

"That's fine with me."

"Though of course should you experience any head pain, nausea, blurred vision etcetera then you must seek medical attention at once."

"I understand." The imperial tone of the Englishman's voice had at first been comforting, but now the serious manner in which he described his condition made it sound intimidating. "What about hallucinations?" Josh asked. The doctor looked up from the clipboard with a quizzical look.

"Hallucinations?" He returned the clipboard to its perch on the end of the bed, "Tell me what do remember from before the attack?"

"I remember the club, lots of people and coming home," Josh replied. He tried to recall the attack in a chronological order of events, but all he could see was Galda's grinning features bathed in the fire. "There was the alley behind my house, I heard screams and found some guy attacking my neighbour." The ghoul's face continued to intrude on his recollection. He looked down at his clenched hand. "I think I remember being struck, but I don't really remember the fight. The rest as they say is a blur."

"And were drugs readily available at this club?" Josh looked up, his heart skipping a beat.

"Why do you ask?"

"Your tox screen shows traces of cocaine." He removed his glasses and studied Josh's reaction with his stern grey eyes. "Are you a regular user of controlled substances Joshua?" Josh reacted impulsively.

"No."

"I'm not here to judge or perform a citizen's arrest," he insisted as he replaced his glasses, satisfied his conclusion was sound. "Though I will advise that mixing leisure drugs isn't the brightest of ideas someone can have."

"What are you talking about?"

"Alcohol aside, we found traces of…" he picked up the clipboard again and continued, "…a substance similar to LSD."

"LSD! There must be some mistake. I don't do drugs. I mean I might take a bit of coke when I need a pick me up, but that's it." The doctor looked back at Josh and frowned. He was a man who stuck rigidly to the facts, and the fact he had already caught out his patient's first white lie made the second reaction all the less credible.

"What about other forms of medication?" the doctor then asked, deciding to humour his jittery patient who appeared genuinely bemused.

"Just some prescription sleeping pills but that's it, no Hippy drugs." It was the doctor's chance to look bemused. He re-consulted the clipboard.

"Really? I don't see any note of that on your medical records. Who's your doctor?"

"Some specialist, a Doctor Halberstram. I was referred to him through the Parasomnia clinic." Josh felt weak at the admission, feeling a bigger fool in front of the austere gentlemen. "I've been having trouble sleeping." The doctor abandoned the clipboard and came closer. He removed his glasses again in an attempt to assume a more personal interest.

"I'm not familiar with him, what was the prescription?"

"Some *Sleepeze* crap, pardon my French. It's some wonder drug he's trialling in the US. Basically, I'm a guinea pig for some multi-national pharmaceutical company, but hey it's free." Josh's flippant attitude didn't impress the doctor. Without concrete knowledge of the treatment he refused to offer any further interpretation. The high bleep of the doctor's pager then interrupted the awkward consultation. He studied its small LCD screen then resumed the formalities.

"Okay I'm going to prescribe some light pain relief, but it's only to be taken as needed you understand? And I want you to cease the use of *all* illegal narcotics, whatever they maybe, right away." His grey eyes looked grave. "If you think this will be a problem then there are some programmes here at the hospital which can help." The last thing he needed, Josh thought, was more drugs and psycho-babble.

"Thanks but I think I can take it from here." The back-handed comment received a look of disapproval, but all that mattered to Josh was he was going to be okay.

Sharon had been lurking close to the door throughout the consultation and swooped in eagerly as the doctor exited to answer the page.

"I thought he'd never finish, you gonna be okay?" She walked around the bed to face Josh.

"Yeah I'm fine. Just gotta get some rest." He noticed the freshly vended cup of coffee in her grasp then took it from her.

"I thought you'd given up coffee." The cup was hot, instantly reminding him of the seemingly real flames that had licked his flesh in the dream world inferno.

"Today's a good day to break old habits," he replied, raising it to his lips. "Besides, I'm parched." Sharon endearingly ran her hand through Josh's thick dark hair, and then watched her boyfriend's battered features screw up in disgust at the taste weak instant beverage.

"Take me home," he growled. Though he had woken into a world of pain it favoured immensely from the world of torment he had escaped in his dreams. Unsure if his sanity remained intact, he urged Sharon to find his pants for him.

*****

Unlike the previous morning's ride the zebra skin seat covers no longer worried Josh. He didn't care he was being taxied back to the quiet Edendale suburb in the garish little car, just as long as it got him home. Since signing out of hospital a cramping pain had crept its way slowly towards his frontal lobes, accompanied by the dread of facing the cold reality of his life. Along with the realisation the prescription painkillers were wearing off, the car's gentle movement empowered his misery with a lightheaded nausea.

According to his girlfriend's report he had been out cold for eight hours. The attack had happened around two in the morning and he had regained consciousness around ten. *Eight hours.* The afternoon sun on his face was soothing, but still he was unnerved by the thought of losing eight hours of his life, though grateful he hadn't been left bleeding in the streets for the local kids to find. *What the hell was that woman doing walking around at two in the morning?*

Sharon had returned to Josh's house that night in the hope of finding him in a more receptive mood. Instead her arrival in the quiet street had been welcomed by the flashing lights of the emergency services wheeling Josh into the back of an ambulance parked out front. As they stopped for a red light he turned to appreciate her good manner towards him. Sharon caught the glance as she studied the rear view mirror, gave a half smile then drove on as the lights turned green.

"You know the cops are going to want a statement from you," she explained, breaking the silence. "The woman he attacked was too hysterical to make an ID." The vice that was squashing Josh's brain worsened, forcing him to take a therapeutic breath and close his eyes. "You got any recollection of what the guy looked like?" They entered Josh's street and the familiar sight of home lightened his discomfort.

"He was just some unloved, crack smoking gang banger after rich pickings in the burbs. Good luck to them finding that guy." The jilt caused as the car mounted the sidewalk made him grimace. "Besides he got what he deserved."

"Oh yeah and what was that?" she asked, intrigued by his response as she braked in his driveway.

"A fractured shoulder and a fake Rolex." Sharon's abrupt appliance of the brakes made him wince against a numbing ache. He tensed against the door.

"Hey, you in much pain?" She touched his leg reassuringly. The question was answered with her green looking boyfriend yanking the door open to wretch miserably onto the asphalt of his drive.

He fended off Sharon's attempts to aid him as they walked into the house, male pride favouring his sense of dignity and independence as Samson greeted them eagerly by weaving around his master's legs with a feline elation that could mean only one thing.

"I think someone's hungry," Josh suggested. "Could you dish out whatever I've got left and bring me a glass of water?" He paced rigidly to the couch and lowered himself into the soft cushions, thankful for making the short trek without purging his stomach contents for a second time. *I'm not concussed, just need rest.* Pursuing the role of nursemaid, Sharon returned from the unkempt kitchen with a glass of water and bowl of tinned tuna. Josh was disappointed to find the pain relief he'd been issued was only prescription Aspirin. He popped the container lid and negligently chucked several of the small tablets into his mouth. The hospital's discovery of LSD in his system popped into his thoughts. *Bull.*

"Poor baby's ravenous, here," Sharon commented as she passed the glass and sat to watch Samson devour the chunks of tuna. "Anyone would think he hadn't eaten for week." Josh washed the tablets down with a liberal drink of the water, and then watched Samson empty the bowl's contents in several greedy gulps.

"To him a night without food *is* a week. You don't have to do this you know."

"Do what?" she asked surprised.

"This. Look after me like I'm the perfect boyfriend, especially after the way I left you out front." He couldn't avoid his conscience, even if she had acted like a drunken bunny-boiler. At the worst of times Sharon could be childish and neurotic, but at the best she was the sensitive caring person she was being at that moment, the person he had forgotten resided behind the big mascara laden eyes.

"I know," she smiled in the knowledge of her own misdemeanours. "But I want to. I don't know why, but I find myself with these annoying feeling of concern for you, or something equally stupid."

"Like what?" he asked, then immediately realised she was telling him she loved him. *Not right now.*

"Be warned the Doc said I should milk this for what its worth."

"He did, did he?" she asked half seriously. "And what else did he say? Did you damage any of the three brain cells you've got in there? I take it's not good you're throwing up everywhere."

"I'll live."

"Shame. For a minute there I thought all this would be mine."

"Well I promised I'd see you today didn't I? Josh joked. "So I postponed my untimely death, just for you." Sharon put her arm around Josh's neck, making sure not to touch his sore head. As she brought her face close to his they both ignored Samson's pines for another course. After a soft lingering kiss she slid down to lay her head against his chest.

"Let's forget about last night, it's over and done with. This is our time now. How's the head?"

"Better," he lied. He needed something stronger. "Though as we're on the subject of pain do you fancy accompanying me for a double date this week? My shout." He felt her hand tense slightly against his chest.

"Who's the double?"

"My *friend* wants to show off his latest piece of eye candy, someone with a sense of morality from what I can tell. How about it?" Sharon's nails dug into his chest. She raised herself to look coldly into his eyes.

"By *friend* you mean Matty right?" Josh felt the warm yearnings frost over.

"Well how many sexual predators do you think I know?" he joked. Sharon pushed herself away to condemn him from the opposite arm of the couch.

"Do you remember what happened last night? Do you?" she reprimanded him, the warm caring person disappearing again. "You got your head caved in after a night on the town with that Jerk. You aren't going *anywhere* this week buddy boy. You're staying right here and resting like the doc said, especially if it's just another excuse to go out on another coke and skirt binge with Matty!" The sermon of contempt flowed from her mouth with the venom of a spitting cobra, leaving him similarly paralysed. *I don't need this.*

"Hey I'm trying to make amends here," he defended himself. "Why can't you at least give this a chance? And just accept I have a life outside of us. The meal offer and last night are totally different, and you'll be there!"

"What to keep some silicon bimbo company while you and Matty score your latest bag from the Maitre De? No thank you!" She jumped up from the couch to continue the verbal attack from higher ground. *How does she know about the coke?*

"What the hell is this? Who have you been talking to?" he demanded to know.

"I have my sources don't you worry," she said slyly, leaning down to reinforce the message. "The fact your shoe box supply suddenly increases in size after a night out with that prick kind of gives it away." *You've been going through my stuff.* She was right of course, which meant he was caught red-handed without a credible denial. "Coked up last night were we?"

"You go a problem with the company I keep? Fine! You know where the door is; get the hell out of my face!" It was Sharon's turn to look stumped. His bruised male pride had ignited the embers of shame into a fire of defensive anger.

"What?"

"You deaf as well as stupid? Get your stupid little bag and leave." He picked up her furry handbag and threw it down at her feet. "The doc said a week of rest is required. As far as I'm concerned that means rest away from you. Get out!" Samson sprinted out of the room.

"Do you know what, Josh Brenin?" Sharon managed to say as she maintained her dumb-founded dignity. "You're the biggest asshole I've ever had the misfortune to sleep with!" Snatching her bag from the floor his distraught girlfriend stormed out. The mountain of magazines and unpaid bills toppled over as her leg knocked the coffee table. "Screw you deadbeat!" Sharon yelled over her shoulder from the hallway, "Have a great life!" The last words faltered as she tried to suppress her emotion.

"Shaz!" Josh called after her, his anger retracting from the sight of tears. The sound of the front door slamming loudly against its frame however signified the window of appeasement had shut along with it.

Josh stared at the mess on his floor. All he saw in the jumble of architecture journals and unwanted mail was a fitting metaphor for his entire life. At that moment the only thing left to do was to climb into bed, forget about the future that had stormed out of the house and reclaim the recommended rest that was rightfully his. If only it was that simple.

Chapter 6

In the smouldering blaze of a dying sun the empty street looked quite serene. But this time Angelica was prepared. The artificial canyon of imposing skyscrapers that ran either side into the distant horizon created an imposing landscape, both impressive as it was unreal. Though as she stood alone in the middle of its perfect pavement, dwarfed by the ravine of concrete, steel and glass that touched the synthetic heavens, she appreciated it was merely an astral backdrop for the latest encounter with the black light.

Behind her the sun's molten rays warmed the exposed skin of her neck and cast the elongated humanoid print of her shadow onto the asphalt far into the distance, back to where she had last convened with Them via the faceless electronic billboards. At first Angelica had fought the urge to return to the abandoned counterfeit Wall Street. She had recognised the distant call from the shadows of the higher dreamscape, taunting, daring her to attend and re-expose herself to danger. Though as she stood there again, dressed simply in the ethereal white robe that emphasised her precarious position in the virtual no-man's-land, Angelica now focused her conscious mind to adapt to the alien landscape and reminded herself she was a powerful servant of the light. Turning to face the large failing sun as it set behind the opposite horizon, she welcomed the approaching confrontation with the heart of a Zealot.

She fought her better judgement with notions of the sacred duty. Such open incitement of the enemy single-handedly went against basic rules of engagement. Essentially such lone gunman tactics were viewed as suicide. But their previous trap had been foiled when she had proved just how powerful a Nothos she was, smiting the grasping spectres of would-be assassins as though they had afforded no more of a threat than a mosquito. Though as their returning projections now polluted the orange light, she couldn't help but feel an impending sense of doom.

At first the enemy appeared as a distant swarm of black locusts on the horizon, heralding the arrival of darkness to the synthetic cityscape like an oil spill at sea. As they surged collectively towards her like some giant venous serpent the sun's warm radiance was in turn blocked out as they blanketed the sky above her. Angelica knew the black astral forms swirling above her like so many vultures circling carrion were projections of so called Low Grades manipulated into betraying their higher selves by the black agency. As she watched the swarm descend to ground in a macabre vortex to encircle her, she knew she and the few like her faced insurmountable odds.

Angelica braced her divine power for a merciless onslaught. Though one against many, she was ready to prove once again the superiority of the light. From amongst the hellish swirling army of black attired men and women whose metallic eyes were protected by the dark eyewear, a face surged forward to grimace at the loner with the vehemence of a snarling demon. The broad skull and high forehead of the devil man suspended before her indicated this was the black general Monk referred to as the Dark Architect.

"Who are you?" Angelica demanded to know above the babble of sneering curses and demonic shrieks. She focused her energy into a shield of light, cocooning herself in a protective barrier that kept the tornado of astral hyenas at bay. As pale hands clawed at the luminous shield, they were instantly retracted by an agonising contact.

For a moment Angelica thought the black general was about to answer. Instead he released a malicious grin that chilled her own projecting form. This black agent was no low-grade minion sent to impede or frustrate her. Angelica sensed the projection was that of a fellow Nothos, albeit of opposite polarity. He was a powerful conscious projection, but a servant of darkness that equalled, or God forbid, was superior to her own. Suddenly her breach of engagement protocol seemed like a real bad idea.

"You are nothing!" she hollered once more, aware she no doubt addressed the coordinator of their previous faceless encounter. Still the ghoul general remained silent. "What are you waiting for traitor? You cannot destroy the light!" The malicious grin returned to a grimace. Thin eyebrows arched freakishly high as he then raised his arms in a gesture that caused the swarm to slow around her and form a static barricade of zombified spectres. But the faces had changed. No longer a spectrum of tainted humanity, the black agents had all assumed the same recognisable features.

"Stay away!" the black general then warned, the demand distorted by the vehemence in which it was spoken. "Stay away from that which is not yours!" Angelica gazed apprehensively at the wall of identical faces. In a choreographed removal of sunglasses to reveal their golden eyes, they openly revealed the cloned features of the Low Grade she had tracked to the seedy real world club on the Strip. The warning was grave, the duplicated features meant to intimidate, but instead they only intrigued.

"This one is ours!" the black general then sneered. Unexpectedly his poised hands were consumed by a destructive ball of flame, but as he hurled it towards her she had seen enough.

In an instant she returned to ground in a strategic retreat across time and space. As she stared once more with mortal eyes at the mirrored walls of her real world sanctuary, she knew the threat had been left far behind in the dreamscape. The enemy's message was unmistakeable. But stay away from the Brenin Low Grade? No, she would follow her instinct. Like all Low Grades, this one had to be turned, or destroyed.

*****

Josh couldn't see any more faces in the ceiling. He had been staring at the same mottled surface for hours, looking for the faces his mind formed from its rough texture like a psychic artist. But as sleep eluded him for the umpteenth time, the hope he could somehow wear down his body's resistance to it soon faded. Rolling onto his side he closed his eyes and mulled over the misadventures of the past twenty-four hours. Like an internal cinematic showcase, his sleep deprived mind conjured flashbacks in a vivid show-reel on cue. Whether real or fashioned from a psychological desire to dream, he relived the faces, places and attacks over and over. The retrospective viewing quickly became nauseating to both body and soul. He then tried to blank the visions with other images, memories of happy times, but still his mind continued to race along and deceive his body into maintaining its alertness. *Goddamn it!*

He looked over to where the prescription container stood enticingly under the bedside lamp. He had resisted the urge to pop its lid and take one of the little blue pills. After the battering both mind and body had suffered, he'd assured himself how easy it would be to fall into the warm embrace of sleep without their aid. Begrudging the dilemma they presented, he stared at the container. The diner in his dream, the man, the fire, that hadn't been just any dream. Tales of hellish hallucinations and insanity induced by synthetic leisure drugs then sprung to mind.

But then it was still daytime outside. The closed bedroom blinds were glowing against the strength of the afternoon sun they kept at bay. Josh wondered if he should accept reality; sleep was something that happened to normal people. If the past twenty fours hours confirmed anything, it was that his life was far from normal. Josh plucked the container from the bedside table and studied the label.

Sleepeze 30mg Tablets
Take ONE tablet with water before sleep.
Causes drowsiness. Do not drive or operate machinery.
Avoid alcohol.
Provisional Batch 33 Ketron Industries.

He smirked at the obvious nature of the warnings, and then winced at the one to avoid licker. The white container still housed most of its original prescription. He pondered consuming the intimidating amount of trial chemicals, and whether it would cause permanent night terrors. Exposure to fire wielding demons in his dreams for the sake of a few hours of precious biological rest was swiftly starting to sound more curse than a cure, and one he was quickly re-evaluating.

The consultant, a friendly but persistent professional, had suggested Josh ceased with the trial if he experienced any disappointment. He hated to sound like a quitter but something was wrong. He would avoid mentioning the alcohol, and the cocaine, his conscience unable to indulge the probability the cocktail of drugs was responsible. *You gave up that shit for a reason.*

While Samson busied himself licking parts of his anatomy Josh would rather forget, he shuffled into the lounge to pick up the phone. The clinic's number was made up of a combination of three primary numbers and thus easy to remember. He punched it into the headset and ignored the flashing red LED signifying a message awaited his attention. Guessing it was Sharon, he focused on the call as a familiar voice answered.

"Yeah hi I'd like to speak Doctor Halberstram, its Josh Brenin." The receptionist's southern drawl was irritating. She patched him through to another extension that went unanswered. A change in ring tone then announced he was being diverted. To Josh's relief it was answered by a man. "Doctor Halberstram?" The camp voice that answered lacked any semblance to the thick set features of the man he'd met. The mistake was confirmed when he was diverted to another extension.

"Sleep ease my ass!" Josh muttered. The ring tone changed once more and the southern lady's voice returned to answer. "It's Mr Brenin again, you put me through but I got diverted back...he's not available? When will he be available? Well I've phoned before regarding my prescription. I just want to ask him if...yes I heard you the first time Miss, but its important that I speak to him...Can I at least leave a message?...listen could you tell him that I called and that I'd appreciate a call back when he's available...It's Josh Brenin...Thank you!"

He hung up and tossed the wireless headset onto the couch. Josh was sceptical as to whether the good doctor was truly indisposed or not. The only thing he was sure of was that his headache had returned. *Bastard's probably on commission.* He walked swiftly back to the bedroom, reached for the aspirin and threw two more pills into his mouth. The remains of the stale water tasted worse as he swallowed them. Back on his bed he took a deep frustrated breath and pondered what heinous crimes he had committed in his past life to warrant the events of recent days. He didn't believe in an afterlife, reincarnation or the existence of God, but in times of anguish and misery, the unwritten laws of karma and a retributive existence were the only things that made sense.

He gazed back over at the bedside drawer. *I'm not a quitter.* Josh didn't relish returning to the clinic, but without a professional diagnosis he didn't know if the *nightmares* were a projection of his own weakness or a by-product of the concoction of drugs. Josh imagined confronting the doctor in his pristine office, the impending look of disappoint, the smile that would hide the contempt. No, he would not face that yet. He wanted to know he was still of use to society, even if only as a lab rat.

Josh popped the container's lid and spilled the little blue pills onto his palm. He let one fall onto the table and slid the rest back inside. Opening the bedside draw he spotted the small Swiss army replica knife tool that had fallen out of a Christmas cracker at a festive corporate dinner Matty had sneaked him into. It was the virgin blade's first time out in the open and he used it to slice the single blue pill in half. *If one is too much then a half is enough.* One half shot away onto the floor, the second he prised from under the lamp base. After studying its dark insides he tossed it into the back of his mouth and forced himself to finish the dregs of the tepid liquid from the cloudy glass.

Josh didn't expect the wonder drug to knock him out instantly, though hoped the doctor's promise that over time it would permanently readdress the delicate imbalance in his body's natural sleeping process would become a reality. Whatever intermediate terrors he was to experience during the trail would only be a temporary tribulation he assured himself. Josh took comfort from the notion as he plumped the pillow into a suitable headrest. The whole thing was ridiculous, he was ridiculous, but when it was over he would be one step closer to normality.

Forsaking the random creation of faces in his ceiling he reached for the new age book, chose a page at random and began to read. The transition was smooth and stealthy. Before the chapter was finished his wrist went limp, the book slumped onto his chest and drooping eyes sealed his passage into an unconscious bliss.

Josh had no idea why, but he woke. The room was shrouded in the late evening light. He guessed he had been asleep for several hours, but was immediately disappointed it hadn't been longer. He felt unusually alert and wondered if another cry for help lay behind his heart rate's sudden escalation. Remaining still he listened for a repeat of last night. Happily there was none, except a niggling feeling of unease continued to crawl across his conscious. He looked around the bedroom. It was defiantly his room. Thankfully he hadn't awoken in another hospital bed or worse, but oddly he felt the cool sensation of being a stranger in a strange place. The feeling was unjustified; his bedroom was just as he had left it. Even the book was at his side where it had slid from his chest. Then he saw a validation for the unease.

The framed night shot of the LA cityscape had only been up on the wall a short period of time, a freebie from Matty, making the new addition against the wall's cream emulsion less obvious than it should have been. He looked up in wonder, blinked and stared, wondering how he had not noticed the foreign object mounted between the picture and the closet door. The words were unmistakable. *THIS WAY.* Gaze fixed at the alien object, he slid off the bed and walked up to examine it. The white letters embossed on the familiar green background were real enough, while the chevron arrow to the left pointed portentously towards his closet.

At first he imagined it an example of Matty's sometime bizarre sense of humour. Somehow his friend had sneaked in and placed the stolen street sign on his wall, but the only apparent explanation also seemed quickly redundant. It lacked the extravagance that went hand in hand with any of his college friend's pranks. As a result he found himself opening his closet door to peek inside.

Beyond the closely packed rail of hanging suits, shirts and an acute selection of Sarah's old clothes there was only darkness. It was to be expected, but Josh also sensed the darkness hid some new as of yet unexplainable opportunity. *But there's nothing here.* He speared a gap in the wall of clothes, only to be disappointed that nothing out of the ordinary lay behind them to reward his curiosity. Still the darkness continued to resonate an electrifying sense of the unusual that made the hairs rise on the back of his neck.

Impressions of childhood curiosity suddenly had their homecoming, of hours spent alone exploring the unknown hide holes in the undergrowth of the wooded area that had surrounded his childhood home. The same rush that had excited him on into those unknown thickets and overgrown ditches now edged him onto this new venture. Though he fully expected to crack his head on the back wall, reason and logic were dispersed by the draw of the unknown. He looked back over his shoulder at the unmade bed. The light was dying fast to shroud the room in night. Though it was home it felt like the essence of a bad memory. Enthused by the regression into his lost youth, he made the decision to bow under the chrome hang rail and crawl into the dark void.

Like all good dreams he expected this one to end at the most exciting part. A quick role call of his senses told him it was no dream, right then he felt more awake than he had in a long time. *I can't be dreaming, this is too real.* As he extended his hand out to feel blindly for the back panel of the deep closet, part of him hoped it would not be there. But when his fingertips met the cool, smooth surface he knew the fantasy was over. *Well that was fun.*

He felt like an idiot. He was crawling around in the back of a closet in total darkness, humouring dementia. He shuddered at his foolishness. *What the hell did you expect?* Josh turned warily to duck back under the rail. As his hand slipped down, a fingernail caught the edge of something metallic and he stopped dead. Josh swung his hand blindly in the dark to find it again, nothing. Ducking back in he tried once more, using both hands to caress the surface like a new lover until he found it once more. Yes, defiantly something.

There was nothing to see in the pitch dark, but in his mind's eye he imagined what the cold, square patch of metal inlaid into the wood looked like. As he caressed it with the proficiency of a blind man, he knew it was not essential to the wooden structure, too featureless to provide a joint for shelving or fitting. Instinctively he pushed it. To his surprise it gave way under the gentle force with a click. *A button?*

A dull halo of light then appeared around the edges of the back panel, seemingly released by the mechanism he had found. His heart clamped to a stop. His breathing froze and for a second he stood in total stasis. More of the light burst into the dark closet from around the panel. Josh was hit with the profound realisation of what he had discovered. *It's a goddamn doorway!* The light quickly forced Josh to squint, though he continued to push the back panel forward, ever open until the harsh light saturated the closet with its brilliance to blind and bewilder him. *What the hell is this?*

As the gravity of the situation took hold, his heart kick started, racing out of control as fight or flee instincts were replaced by the femme fatale that was curiosity. Unable to stop himself, he gave a final shove and the clandestine door swung wide open, forcing him to protect his sensitive eyes with a raised hand from the torrent of illumination it released. But as they slowly grew accustomed to the clinical light, he was to be further amazed by what he saw through the gaps of his fingers.

*****

The most extreme fantasy could never compete with what he saw. At first there was only the movement amongst the light, but as his eyes accommodated to its intrusive radiance he began to make out the figures that were walking within it. *This can't be*. The strange parade was making its way slowly past the doorway he'd stumbled across, the blank faces catatonic and oblivious to the dumbfounded spectator peering out at them from the dark alcove of the closet. Josh stood for a moment longer, blinking in the bright light. Comprised of adults of both sexes, the slow march was walking in a formal unison from right to left. *Where are they going?* An urge to call out to these passers-by was quickly dampened by a sense of anxiety that accompanied the eerie parade like some malign hanger-on. Cautiously he made the decision to step amongst them.

Entering the bright light he found himself standing in a long corridor of doors, constructed from a burnished metal that reflected the movement of the quiet procession but without a true mirror image. Again he was struck with the need to ground himself; to reaffirm the spectacle was firmly rooted in reality. Josh opened his mouth to ask a question to any of the nomadic community that would listen, but their rigid adherence to some unknown code of conduct made him think twice. At the far end of the shimmering passageway he could see the ensemble was congregating to form a single file queue. Though Josh wanted to believe his eyes, he didn't know if he could.

Suddenly everything felt very wrong. Curiosity was abruptly replaced by the urge to flee. *This isn't right, this can't be real*. But as Josh retraced his steps he found fate had made the decision redundant by covertly sealing shut his entrance. Stranded beyond the realm of reason, he panicked and tried to force the closet panel with his shoulder, only to find it had shut hard and fast. Josh stared at the black number seventy four embossed on its surface. No longer a closet panel, it was now one of the many matching doors along the unearthly corridor. Its austere branding empowered the fact his opportunity to escape had been stolen from him. With an impending sense of trepidation wearing anticipation down, Josh relented to the daunting walk down the seamless corridor to join the growing queue.

Along its length he passed identical sealed doorways, each marked with their own unique two digit number that suggested he was in some kind of a secure prison unit or equally institutionalised facility. As he joined the orderly line behind a middle-aged man dressed in a worn Raiders T-shirt and matching shorts, he began to question his sanity. *Is this real? Is this the real world? Am I insane?* For a moment he stood there with the crazed ideas running in and out of his brain. *This can't be!* Josh wanted to reach out and touch the black polyester of the Raiders shirt, to find if the black satin fabric would feel as it should. Unsure he was ready to accept whatever conclusions would be made from the act, he withdrew his hand. *What if it's real? What if I'm really here?* Recalling the past dreams however, instructed him it was another episode of vibrant delusion.

"This isn't real," he said out aloud. "I'm dreaming; it's a goddamn dream!" With a renewed confidence he poked his finger hard into the shoulder in front. The man's flesh was warm and subtle. As expected the rude gesture drew no reaction from its catatonic owner. "Insanity one, Josh zero." The queue's sudden movement forward distracted him from the world crushing revelation.

The door at the corridor's end had finally opened, allowing the obedient line of catatonics to filter slowly through into a dark neon blue light beyond. Impatiently Josh waited his turn. As the Raiders fan and his colleagues lumbered tediously onwards, a mixture of fear and intrigue gripped him as the blue light now enveloped his entry into insanity and the mysterious room.

It was nothing of the sort. In a way that was incomprehensible to Josh's architectural understanding, his discerning gaze discovered no discernable walls or corners, no superstructure or foundations. The dark luminous light appeared to compromise its entirety. It had no obvious source and was seemingly the very fabric of the illusion of infinite enclosed space. Simply put, the light *was* the room. To his amazement the only objects in the interior was a semi circular row of reclining seats, the highly polished metal chairs reminding him of the giant Lazy Boy chairs he'd seen on The Shopping Channel. The silent queue of people then began to sit down in these vacant seats, not an utterance of a single word as they slid into the ergonomic moulding of the space-age recliners. Following some untold protocol, Josh followed suit and slid into a remaining vacancy next to the Raiders fan. Doing so he turned to look blankly at Josh.

"I'm dreaming," he stated quietly. "Are you?" He slurred the question, his unshaved and weary features reminding Josh of the city's many homeless.

"Of course I am," Josh replied acerbically, amused by this first sign of interaction. "What else would I be doing?" The man's face showed no reaction to the belligerence and turned away to face forward. Josh's conceit was uncalled for, but as he sat in that otherworldly place somewhere between fantasy and delusion, he found himself enjoying the experience with the eagerness of a child.

He looked on with great interest at the spectacle that then appeared before them. A cinematic vision had taken form from the neon blue nothing. At first there had been a faltering in the interior's cohesive luminosity, one that had then morphed into a disembodied realisation of imagery in the shape of a giant screen, a voyeuristic portal back into the real world. The impressive diversity of images then manifested from nothing and began to play out for the submissive audience. *What is this?* Josh relaxed in his shiny seat and watched on as the world's cities, monuments and different races appeared to celebrate the nobility of humanity, its world, and its achievements. The performance was a veritable platform for humanity's own glorification. He studied the images intently, admiring the vivid spectacle that was an awe inspiring visual statement of the real world. *"And this is a dream!"* he mused to himself. But then Josh noticed their eyes.

At first he had thought nothing of the flickering in the corner of his own. Turning to investigate he was shocked to find its cause was the reflection of the imagery in the mirrored eyes of his fellow sleepwalkers. Josh flinched at the macabre sight. The reclined row of people had lost what humanity had projected from their glazed eyes and now stared on obediently as their minds seemingly sucked in the cinematic vision via chrome eyeballs. The eerie realisation was followed by a dramatic change in the cinematic display.

Josh could only describe what followed as visions of the apocalypse. Wondrous cities were now shown laid to waste, the happy, prosperous people now starving and dying, their corpses littering the scorched land and cities as the forces of nature conspired to destroy the world of man in a torrent of chaos and destruction. Noble coastal skyscrapers were lost to colossal tsunamis. The earth rumbled like a hungry beast and opened up to swallow the land and all upon it. Hell had come to earth. It was only as he turned away from the horrific spectacle he spotted they're hosts had joined them.

He watched the spectres stealthily approach their enamoured guests en masse from the dark blue periphery behind. Dressed in their black suits, shirts and pants the macabre welcome party now surrounded the arc of unsuspecting voyeurs in equal numbers. As each loomed over an unwary charge, the twelve dark figures placed white hands either side of the headrests supporting each mirror-eyed resident's cranium, their pale, blank faces reflecting no emotion or signs of their intent behind their sunglasses. The disembodied screen was now exposing its catatonic voyeurs to more gratuitous mutilations. Human butchered human in God-forsaken frenzy, civilised mankind reverting to an unrestricted bestiality in the face of calamity. As this imagery spiralled into bloody thirsty terror Josh knew their ghoulish presence was helping to focus some process of manipulation.

He tried to turn away from the obscenities, but found his body had surrendered its ability to cooperate with his mind. As he convulsed in vain again he felt the hands grasp him firmly by the shoulders. He it seemed had not been left unattended. Twisting his head around to look up above the shiny headrest that had covertly grown about his head like a glove he saw the demonic face of his custodian bearing down upon him.

It was the first time he'd seen Galda Vey without protective shades. The grisly sight turned his blood to ice as the dream spiralled into nightmare. In the shiny golden orbs that were Galda's eyes he saw the reflection of his own terrified features. The fiend was glaring down at him with a fiery stare; the blackened host struggling to contain his charge's fleeting interest. Josh let out a scream of panic, but the vice of Galda's grasp about his shoulders kept him locked into the ergonomic seat. Pathetically he tried to wriggle free, but under the ghoulish glare Josh found his will draining away and his body succumbing to a forced slumber. An inferno of rage built up inside him. It surged from the pit of his stomach and spread like a river of molten lava, flowing through his entire body to feed his stolen limbs. He looked back up at Galda's feverish face and screamed out defiantly once more.

Suddenly he was free of the chair. As he spun around he saw the chair had disappeared and Galda recoiling as if the recipient of some powerful blow. It was then Josh saw the mirrored eyes of the other sleepwalkers return to their previous human state. Their black attired custodians now also reeled away from the chairs as though an electric shock had daisy chained along the cabal of manipulation. Josh saw his chance and dashed out of the blue room.

Back in the corridor he became disorientated by the fact he was escaping to nowhere. Behind him he heard Galda's hellish roar as a brilliant explosion of light had replaced the dark blue aura escaping through his exit. The ghoul, the stalker Galda Vey, appeared in the doorway, arms stretched out against its frame as he braced his body upright against the force of light expelling him from his dream world layer.

"Joshua!" Galda roared down the corridor, his golden eyes creased in a furious agony as he struggled to fend off the potent torrent of light bursting from behind him. Josh's blood chilled once more. Realising a very real danger, he turned and ran for his life, but the corridor was quickly consumed in the intense white light, causing it to seemingly disintegrate underfoot. He continued to run. In the radiant, formless void he didn't know if his feet touched solid ground or not. Still he dared not stop.

"Joshua!" Galda's voice roared again from behind, demanding he faced the menacing presence trailing him like a ravenous wolf. Now completely encased by the light Josh was no longer running but leaping bounds across an unimaginable distance into an unknown sanctuary. He wished he was back home in the city, in the daylight and amongst people, and then realised that was where he was.

The peak of the US Bank tower in Los Angeles was the tallest building in the western United States. Recognising the real world again, Josh found he was standing on its tarred roof one thousand and seventeen feet high above the street below. He had always wanted to know what the view was like from the Californian tower of Babel. Now he knew. The midday sun beamed down on his face, the loose grit of the rooftop crackled underfoot and he gazed with amazement at the smog smothered cityscape wondering how the hell he had made the ascent.

"You shouldn't have run from me," Galda's brooding voice boomed abruptly from behind. Josh turned to face the black fiend. Instantly he was reminded of his last confrontation with this devil or whatever he was. The menace in his tone continued to cool Josh's blood.

"Just tell me who you are!" he demanded to know. "What do you want with me?" Josh shivered in the hot sun. Galda's anger was emanating from his very body like a noxious odour. His metallic eyes were hidden once more behind the sunglasses, but the ghoul's fury was not.

"We do not want for that which we already have!" he replied violently. Before Josh could unravel the enigma Galda thrust his hand forward to project an invisible projectile. As it struck Josh's chest like a canon ball the blow sent him soaring over the edge of the skyscraper. Falling backwards, dead weight and limbs flailing uselessly, he watched the rooftop rise above him as he plummeted to the ground and certain death.

"There is nowhere to hide Joshua," Galda's voice boomed around him in a sonic barrage. "We are your future!" No sooner had the words echoed in Josh's head, resonating throughout his entire helpless body, he struck ground zero.

Josh tripped over the shoebox as he leapt out of his closet. The contents scattered across his floor as he floundered then sprawled onto his bed like a startled bat from its cave to find himself wide eyed, wide awake and gasping for life's breath. *I'm alive? I'm alive!* Instead of the bone crunching solidity of the pavement he had found the soft cushion of his duvet. Panicking he looked for the street he had seen rushing to meet him as he fell, but it wasn't there. Instead he was greeted with the familiar silhouettes of his bedroom furniture in the negligible light.

Impulsively he gaped at his limbs, expecting to see them shattered and mangled by the horrendous fall, though was relieved to find them, and the rest of his precious body, very much intact. *A frigging dream, that's all it was.* The unexpected ring of the phone startled him. Josh scrambled across the bed and fumbled with the small bedside light. The small button at his fingertips resisted his eager touch, causing him to send the light tumbling to the floor. In the distance he heard the answer machine take the call in the lounge.

"Josh it's me," Matty's voice resonated from the loudspeaker. "I know you're there so pick up the phone!" Josh remained in the dark aftermath of the traumatic dream and listened. "You can't tell me last nights little shindig wore you out."

Flashbacks of the blue room and the hellish things Josh had seen came flooding back.

"Are you going to pick up or not?" Matty sneered before relenting. "Look, when you've decided to switch out of asshole mode, I need you to meet me at Sebastian's tonight around eight. You've got, an hour to pull your shit together and make an impression."

Josh remembered Galda's searing gold-eyed grimace looming over him and shivered. *Too real.*

"Serina wants to meet my friends. She thinks I'm too ashamed of her or something, you know what these women are like! I know I said it was going to be later in the week, but this girl is breaking my balls. So I really need you to make an appearance buddy, okay?" Sensations of running, fleeing something terrible, and then falling into thin air; the dream played back over in Josh's head like a demented horror film.

"If you're a true friend you'll want me to get lucky, just be there!" Matty commanded then hung up.

The long electronic beep followed the distant click of the concluded call, snapping Josh from his trauma. He massaged his stricken face then felt the dull ache returning to his head. The beating he'd received at the hand of the mugger now seemed like a distant memory in comparison to the vivid nightmare floating in his mind. *I can't go out I'm ill.*

He sat on the edge of the bed and centred his thoughts. *Keep it together Hotshot.* The doctor's allusion to the strange toxin in his blood meant little to him at the time, but now it all seemed to make sense. Josh stared at the prescription container on the bedside cabinet, proudly relaying its fraudulent mantle of Sleepeze. A swipe of his hand sent it flying across the bedroom to startle Samson as he entered expecting his next feed. His feline companion watched the rattling projectile until it came to a halt by Sarah's chair.

"What the hell is happening to me Sammy?" The cat then leapt over the upturned shoebox and ignored the small bag of cocaine to rub his face wantonly in his master's leg. Josh was happy to see some things remained unaffected by chaos and disaster. Getting up to cleanse away the nightmares with a cold shower, he decided some human company was what he needed after all.

*****

The taxi ride downtown to the exclusive restaurant cost Josh more than he could afford. Swallowing the negligent expense as deductible from his friend's charity, he tugged the vertical solid brass handle of its heavy glass entrance aside and entered. The gentle sounds of a Vivaldi concerto greeted his arrival in the marble finished lobby of Sebastian's. As he spotted the Maitre De's badly disguised look of aghast he secretly wished he'd spent the money on a bottle of hard licker. But it was too late for Dutch courage, he was there, it was real. He would have to deal with it.

Josh guessed the old suit and tie he'd thrown on didn't meet the usual house standard. He had swapped the hospital dressing on his head for a bandage of his own design, though he knew he still looked like crap. But he didn't care. His snooty greeter eyed him up and down, looked surprised he was part of the Nugent party, then reluctantly called for a waiter to escort Josh to the Nugent table, his conferred title of *gentleman* sounding more like vagabond. It was going to be a long night.

Josh had no taste for such high class eating. Preferring atmosphere over prestige, an authentic Italian pizzeria was more to his liking. He hid his thoughts behind his confident stride as he followed the young busboy into the lavish dining area, where the cream of the city's lawyers and accountants wooed their jewel encrusted ladies and business partners alike in the low, sophisticated light. Studying their prestigious seclusion Josh realised he was out of his depth. These were Matty's peers not his. Josh suddenly wondered why he had ever aspired to join their ranks. Money, he remembered, that was why, and hoped his credit card hadn't already maxed out.

"Josh! How good of you to make it," Matty greeted him sardonically.

"Sorry I'm late I fell asleep," he replied abruptly, sitting in a vacant chair opposite. Though previously busy whispering sweet nothings into the ear of the handsome woman at his side, Matty now looked at Josh with a curious amazement.

"No problem, we've only eaten the house out of breadsticks while we waited." The sarcasm caused a friendly smile from the woman as she nudged Matty playfully. "My God man what happened to your head?"

"A little reward for an act of chivalry I preformed last night, it's nothing," Josh replied dismissively.

"Nothing? I've seen better looking things pulled out of the grill of my Lexus."

"If you must know," Josh relented, "I got my head cracked open by some gangbanger trying to steal my neighbour's handbag. Can I get a drink?" Josh turned and called to the nearest waiter. "Waiter!" Matty stiffened in his seat. "What are you having?" Josh then asked.

"We're fine," Matty said dryly. While his friend's dishevelled appearance embarrassed him, he found his unorthodox behaviour unsettling. The waiter looked over dumbfounded.

"Yes you! Can I get a bottle of the house red over here?"

"Not sure about you though," Matty mumbled. The waiter finished serving his table and called back respectively.

"I'll tell your waiter sir," Josh settled back into the hard canvass padding of the sturdy high backed chair. The napkin on the starter plate in front of him looked like it had been folded with the skill of an origami master. As the present company stared on, he unravelled the coarse linen and placed it anxiously on his lap.

"Josh when you're quite ready there's someone I'd like to introduce you to, Josh this is Serina, my lady." Josh looked up, taking proper note of his friend's latest concubine for the first time. "Serina this is my good, though rather dishevelled, friend and colleague Joshua." Josh cringed. Except for his mother on formal occasions, no one used his full name. Awkwardly he reached over the shiny tableware to gently shake Serina's slender hand.

"Where are my manners? Nice to meet you, Serina," he said suavely. He had to admit, his friend did have exquisite taste in women. Far from the vampish, pierced vixens he had chased in the Helter Skelter, Matty had chosen for his present consort an elegant woman in her late twenties who's mane of dark brown hair, buttermilk skin and tasteful finery exuded class and finesse.

"Likewise, I've heard a lot about you," Serina replied courteously, her hazel eyes reminding him of Sarah's. Any other time he would have wanted her himself. "Is everything okay?"

"Yes fine, why shouldn't it be?" he responded cagily. Matty's covert glare rebuked the hasty question. Josh tried again. "Forgive me, I've been busy lately. It's been one of those weeks. Left me a little more *tense* than usual." Out of sight he wiped the perspiration off his palms onto the napkin.

"You know what they say, all work and no play," she replied with a broad confident smile.

"Quite," Josh agreed amiably and ignored Matty's gaze.

"So what is it you do?" Josh cringed again.

"I er, well when I say busy I mean I've had..." Matty jumped to his rescue.

"What he means to say is he's just started a new consultancy position in Glendale and been busy brown nosing the new boss and sowing a few wild oats with the female staff, isn't that right Josh?" The quip sounded like a decree and was impounded by a wilful stare. Serina laughed and gave Matty another playful nudge.

"Mathew you are incorrigible, down boy!" So is this true you bad boy?

"Um something like that", Josh responded with a fake smile of amusement. "I forget just how well he knows me, it's uncanny!"

"Yes he's quite a catch I'll say that."

"It's what you'll catch in return that you should worry about." The underhand retort at Matty's expense was not received well. Seeing how fond the latest catch was of his friend, Josh decided to bat for the home side. "But no seriously Mathew is a real, great guy, as you know," he offered lamely. *Smile, make her believe it.* "I'm just a bad boy in comparison to this pillar of the community, not worthy of kissing his, behind." *Great cover up, loser.* His words trailed off as he sneaked a sip from the glass of table water. *I'm too beat for this.*

"So Josh, how about you?" Josh put the glass down and looked puzzled. "You and this Sharon I've heard so much about, I can't wait to meet her. Matthew tells me you and she might have cause for window shopping for rings in the not too distant future?"

"Mathew did, did he?" Josh asked eyebrows raised, finding it hard to suppress his irritation. "Well Mathew's quite a joker sometimes, aren't you?" It was Josh's turn to glare at Matty.

"Ooh you little tease," Serina reprimanded Matty. "Just for that little lie I'm going to leave you." She plucked her handbag from between their chairs and stood, Matty panicked.

"Wait, Serina he's just..."

"For the ladies," she explained delicately. "You boys behave, I'll be right back." She trailed her hand across his shoulder as she passed, leaving Matty to appreciate her feline figure in the tight red dress as she walked down the aisle of tables.

"Shopping for rings!" Josh blurted out of earshot. "What the hell have you been telling that woman?"

"Exactly what she needs to hear. I told you, she's not like any of the other nymphets I invite into my parlour, she's..."

"Got morals!" Josh exclaimed. He was quickly deciding the best thing to do was leave the young lovers to their own fate, which he guessed would not last much longer than the morning after.

"No, I mean yes she's got standards; she's got class." Matty leaned forward onto the table, his features looking less self-assured than usual. "She's the kind of girl you take home to Mom and Dad." Josh looked blankly at his college friend, unsure if he had understood him correctly.

"I *must* be dreaming!" Briefly Josh looked around at the low-lit surroundings. Its tables of contented diners reminded him of the Eat-A-Lot in the desert. Ironically the prestigious restaurant seemed less vivid. *Maybe I haven't woken up?*

"Hey I may not like to admit it but I'm not the spring chicken I used to be." Matty's vague reference to the premature greying of his hair, convincingly died to its natural brown, brought Josh back into the revelation. "And when you, mature, certain things are expected of you."

"Mature? You! What are you talking about? You're only twenty-nine. You want to get married? To her?" Josh couldn't believe his ears. Matty leaned back into the chair and smoothed his tie against his chest in preparation for the impact of the next words.

"I love her," he admitted calmly. Josh had never expected to hear those three words from friend's mouth.

"You mean you'd love to bed her," Josh corrected rudely, the tactless statement ejecting from his mouth as their waiter appeared reverently at their table.

"Your bottle of the house red sir," the waiter offered respectively, feigning ignorance. "A nineteen ninety-eight Shiraz…"

"Could you give us a minute here," Matty interrupted the formality. The waiter looked shaken by the dismissal, but smiled courteously before exiting.

"Correct me if I'm wrong smart ass but didn't someone not too far from this table tie the knot when they were twenty?" Without risking offending his friend by accusing him of deceiving his way into Serina's bed, he decided to quit the debate.

"Whatever."

"We've all got to do it one day, might as well be before things start to sag. Look I don't exactly have a great track record when it comes commitment or celibacy do I buddy?" Josh began to feel the bleeding heart routine was leading up to something. "And that's the sort of thing that isn't going to impress a lady of Serina's calibre. Which is why I took the liberty of mentioning that you and Shaz were snugger than a bug in a rug, and," he paused apprehensively, "inviting her here to join us." Josh froze as Matty hid behind his raised glass of water.

"Tell me you didn't!"

"What do you want me to say? I'm desperate." It was the final straw. Josh removed the napkin and threw it on the table. Before making good his escape the familiar voice called from behind.

"Joshua darling." The woman's voice cooed across the restaurant floor. The waiter was showing Sharon to their table, the heavy stride and jangle of cheap jewellery enough to announce her arrival.

"I don't believe this," Josh said miserably as he stood and faced her. The waiter pulled the chair out beside him.

"I'm sorry I'm late darling, the traffic was hell," Sharon said in a flamboyant voice that caught the attention of the surrounding tables. "You're looking well," she added. Dressed in a black woollen off-the-shoulder jumper, black mini skirt and stockings, Josh no longer felt the sore thumb.

"Just sit down and behave." After half a bottle of wine Josh knew she could be unpredictable. The smell was on her breath and the exaggerated mood unmistakable.

"So charming to see you too lover." She kissed his cheek then took her seat. "So is everyone happy? What are we drinking?"

"May I open your bottle sir?" the waiter asked gingerly.

"Forget it," Josh snapped. He manoeuvred past to walk off and find the rest room, leaving Sharon to simply glare at the bottle of house red.

"Wine? We're supposed to be celebrating," she exclaimed loudly. No longer comfortable with his underhand tactic, Matty looked embarrassed. "Champagne," she ordered to the waiter. "The best my good man; we're celebrating."

"Yes, Miss." The waiter looked to Matty for authorisation. Reluctantly he gave a silent nod. Sharon grinned at her nemesis.

"So where's the poor girl you want to screw?" Matty resisted the urge to kick her under the table and smiled apologetically at the well-dressed couple to his right.

Meanwhile Josh entered the men's room. Instantly he was reminded of Tony Montana's opulent bathroom suite in the Brian De Palma film Scarface. The floor and the walls were fashioned from solid marble and the water fittings burnished in a garish gold plate, feeding the notion he had entered a sterile hedonistic suite fit enough for any king or city exec. A silver haired gentleman greeted him politely on his way out, but Josh's mood prevented him from responding alike. He had come into the imperial rest room to hide while he soothed his temper. If it proved impossible he planned to use the time out to prepare an exit strategy.

The restroom was now empty. Muttering his contempt for fate, he slumped over one of the magenta toned marble basins. Its golden tap spun smoothly in his hand and he took pleasure from the feel of the cold water that gushed against his skin. There was always something very cleansing, both physically and mentally, about washing hands in pure cold water he thought. He cupped a hand of the revitalising liquid to rinse his mouth and splashed the remainder over his face. Hands propped either side of the exquisite basin he then studied his tired features in the huge mirror. *Why me?* Suddenly he felt cold.

The sudden shiver made him think someone had entered, but the door hadn't budged. Guessing the air con had probably kicked in he thought nothing more of it. That was the problem with marbled bathrooms, he thought, the cool polished stone never attracted the warmth. Perpetuating its own cold austere essence, it was an inhospitable choice of furnishing that made Josh feel he was in a mausoleum. *Money never bought sense.* As he gave himself one more self study in the enormous mirror he sensed there was someone else in the room lurking out of sight.

He had been bowed over the basin long enough; the gush of the running water could have concealed their footsteps. Fully expecting to find another of the finely dressed executives standing over a marble urinal, he gave the last touch to his hair and turned to face a blonde haired woman.

"You!" Josh exclaimed in disbelief. "What the hell is this?"

"Again I am only here because of you," the white attired freak from the Helter Skelter stated calmly.

"What are you talking about this is the men's room! You can't follow me in here. I think you'd better leave." For a second she said nothing, her crystal blue eyes looking persistently into his. The white garment was more like a gown; plain, long sleeved and tailored straight to the floor to cover her feet. "Anyone would think you were stalking me," he added derisively. *She's an escaped loony.* As he made a move to walk around her she spoke again in the composed but impertinent tone.

"Did they get to you Joshua?"

"Who?" he asked, totally perplexed by the encounter. She didn't look dangerous he thought, but he sensed a brooding energy that seemed to electrify the very air around them.

"You know of those I speak."

"Miss, I don't know what you are talking about and you really need to get out of here before that pompous Maitre De finds you." Josh had made it to the door, his hand held onto the wide, gold plated handle ready to make his escape.

"The dark ones," she said enigmatically. Her back to Josh she stood her ground. "Have you walked amongst them?" He had been ready to pull open the heavy door and leave the pretty but strange creature where she had found him, but her last words troubled him. Curiosity rooted him to the spot. *She can't mean Him.*

"Who are you?" She turned her head to look him in the eye. Josh had never seen such crystal blue eyes in his life.

"A friend."

"A friend!" he echoed sceptically. He relinquished his escape plan to walk back over, the crystal blue eyes never leaving his as he did. "Like a friend you seem pretty familiar with my name and my routine, but I have no goddamn idea who the hell *you* are!"

"My name is Angelica, I am a servant of the light and you must listen to what I have to say. There is little time." Josh stared at her attractive but obviously deluded features. *She's a basket case.* He convinced himself she was the product of one of the post hippy cults still floating around in the Californian hills. *A joke's a joke...*

"My friends are waiting for me and I'd like to get back to them, so if you don't mind."

"The doctor entrusted to help you with your insomnia has involved you in something unimaginably dangerous."

"Excuse me?" His hand was now safely back on the door handle, but again her words served to prevent his exit. "How do know..." he trailed off. "Are you a nurse?" Angelica walked towards him.

"There is no time for questions. Come now before it is too late. If the dark ones take you first you will be lost to us. You must find me in this world; there are those who can protect you." Josh's hand tightened around the gold plated handle.

"Protect me?" he blurted. "This gets better! Miss, I think it's you that needs to find something, and that's reality and grasp it with both hands. Because right now you've got a serious nuthouse escapee thing going on here and it's really starting to bug me."

"You must resist them if they come to you!" she continued unabashed. "They watch you in this world and no doubt they have initiated their search for you on the other side. Do not listen to them; they are not what they seem." Her intensity began to scare him. Instinctively his arm drew the door open. "You must come to us Joshua, or face the consequences."

"Angie you're a loon. Stay the hell away from me!" He yanked the door open and exited quickly. No sooner had he taken several steps he stopped and looked back as the door slowly swung closed. His heart was racing again, making the head wound ache once more with a thumping pulse. *First the club now here?* Reason had told him the young fervent woman was the product of some self-perpetuating personality crisis, but her words had struck their intended target.

Galda, the Dark Ones? Turning tail he shoved the heavy door back open and re-entered. Planning to confront her, instead he found she was gone. *What the...*Josh bent and searched for Angelica's feet under the cubicle doors. In vain he shoved each of their doors open in a frenzy of frustration before scouring the marble walls for a non-existent window. After a fruitless search he had to except the cold fact Angelica had apparently vanished into thin air. The door creaked open. As his gaze veered to meet the suited high flyer that entered he found himself eyeballed suspiciously.

"You lost something buddy?" the man asked warily. Josh shook his head then quickly exited. *She was there I saw her!* The brisk walk back to his table across the main floor took half the time. With a hand covering the wound on his head he attempted to curb its thumping agony. *She was real!* Sharon spotted Josh's return and raised her head to greet him with a huge smile that publicized her content.

"Lost your Weiner?" she asked crudely. To her dismay he strode straight past the table.

"Josh?" Matty called behind him. "Where are you going?"

"Home, to sleep!" He projected the words without turning round and headed straight for the heavy glass doors of the opulent lobby. Serina's warm features dropped into concern.

"Is everything okay between you two?"

"I guess it's his time of month," Sharon replied. She shook off her boyfriend's ill manners and poured a fresh glass of the exclusive Champagne. "Bottoms up!"

*****

Ben had followed his captor without disputing the order to obey. He was perched on the edge of a low bed covered with a white duvet, time's progress seemingly faltering to a standstill as he sat in the brightly lit room and waited for the questioning to recommence. But the man calling himself Monk simply sat opposite in a wicker weave chair and studied the stocky ex soldier with an unwavering stare. They had abandoned the dark expanse of unusual furnishings and walked along a lengthy adjoining corridor to the light soaked room at its end where they now resided. At first its dazzling illumination had hurt his eyes, but they had quickly adjusted to the minimal surroundings.

"So you gonna tell what's with all these mirrors?" Ben asked, breaking their epic silence. They had sat without exchanging words for what felt like hours, merely lingering in silent convalescence until his thoughts had become his own one more. Now feeling as though he had woken from some psychic trance induced by his mysterious guardian, Ben was ready for answers. "What is this place?" he petitioned his silent custodian again. After a short deliberation Monk replied simply.

"Somewhere safe." Crossed legged and chin resting on peaked fingertips, Monk's hands were pressed together as he remained in silent but intimidating observation. To avoid the uncomfortable glare Ben looked around the minimalist interior and to the bare floorboards. Looking up he studied his haggard reflection in the mirrored surface of the room's only door. It had been days since he'd last seen it. *Look at you now tough guy*. He didn't like sitting in the compromised position, it meant the few extra milliseconds it would take to stand would create an ample window of warning for his competent guardian. Debating whether the option was viable, Ben thought he saw Monk grin. *Reading my thoughts?* His guardian was wearing a simple khaki shirt and jeans, his own reflection accompanying Ben's in the gigantic mirrors that adorned all four walls to create an unlimited reflective prism of doubles around them that echoed into infinity.

"Safe from what?" he persisted. Monk looked on and gave no reply. "Can you at least me tell that? And what's with the balls?" Ben referred to the four white burnished porcelain spheres placed in each corner of the mysterious room. At first he'd presumed them to be examples of the non-descript decor that cluttered the houses of people who had nothing else better to display, though something now told him they served some further purpose.

"They are what make it safe. Think of them as batteries." Ben was confused but intrigued. He wanted to get up and touch one of their shiny smooth surfaces, but under Monk's watchful gaze decided to remain seated.

"Batteries?" Monk looked momentarily bored with the line of questioning.

"They are made from a rare semi precious stone that conducts and stores natural Chi energy." The obvious question had to be asked.

"And what the hell is Chi?"

"Energy, pure creative energy, the same electro magnetic energy that binds this world together, flows through the veins of the earth, and also your own body."

"Like the Force?" Ben quipped, referring to Star Wars mythology.

"Quite," Monk confirmed remotely. He lowered his hands and interlinked them on top of his crossed thigh, making him appear the great intellectual. "The spheres store the Chi and act, for want of a better word, as sentinels. Collectively they act like an electro magnetic barrier that surrounds and shields us, do you understand?" Ben was unsure of the logistics, but understood the concept.

"Sure. Chi right? Chi is good, where would we be without it!"

"It will all make sense in time," Monk said reassuringly. "When your mind is reborn your world will follow." The enigmatic reassurance didn't quell the storm of questions. Though Ben no longer felt his life was in immediate danger, the talk of electric grids and Chi seemed totally inapt. He was a hostage of a small cell of eccentric militants with unknown allegiances, who had access to highly restricted intelligence and who also appeared to have unusual but deadly talents at their disposal. He felt far from safe, though humoured the idiosyncrasy.

"So they are protecting us from what? The Boogie man?" Ben asked suspiciously. For all he knew the only thing he had reason to fear was already sitting in the room with him.

"The black light." The solemn declaration from Monk's lips made the hair the on the back of Ben's neck stand to attention. His captor's face then stretched into a malicious smile as he recognised the dread he'd intentionally instilled.

The unexpected metallic clank of the door's opening mechanism made Ben flinch. As Monk's red headed cohort swung the mirrored door into the room she removed her hand from its palm print security interface, entered and pushed it shut behind. Monk uncrossed his legs and looked up at her undecipherable features.

"How did she do Calisto?" he asked, hands now clenching the wicker chair's arm rests. The red-haired Calisto acknowledged the query with a shake of the head. For the first time Monk wolfish features revealed a weakness, his look of disappointment contrasting with a previous bravado. Something had not gone well, presumably for their absent blonde haired cohort. Monk got up and stood next to Calisto. Both of them now looked down at Ben with a new sense of intrigue that unnerved the soldier further.

"Looks like it's just you Alpha. We best get started."

Chapter 7

The remainder of the Bolognese hadn't tasted so great. Josh had forced himself to eat the reheated leftovers, washing it down with a warm can of the beer Sharon had left behind while Samson looked up with eager eyes and a restless tail. Hoping to share in the makeshift meal, the cat mewed pitifully until his master acknowledged him by placing the cool plate on the floor.

Upon returning from Sebastian's, Josh hadn't been that hungry, but he hated to see food, good or bad, go to waste. Like a person who comfort ate due to boredom or grief, Josh had found picking at the processed sauce with his fork a welcome distraction from his thoughts. Now the meal was consumed the unwelcome thoughts returned. He tried palming away the manic tension from his weary forehead, hoping to incite some depth of clarity into the unworldly sights he'd witnessed. But the auto massage had little affect. The headache no longer bothered him due to the effectiveness of painkillers. In its place he felt a hollow recess carved out of his sanity. Samson pawed his leg in a desperate appeal for seconds. As Josh carefully prised the cat's claws from his jeans the phone rang, but unable to remove Samson's clinging attempts at persuasion in time the answer machine took the call.

"Josh?" A stranger's voice resonated from the next room. "…I dunno if I've got the right Josh Brenin, but how many of you guys can there be? Bro it's me, *Reinhold*." The prompt made Dink's voice instantly recognisable. "I uh thought I would look you up and see if you wanted to go out for that drink one time, grab that beer you know?" Josh was forced to lift the heavy cat and placed his bulk onto the breakfast bar so he could hear the curious message over the feline's wails. "That's unless someone doesn't wanna be seen hanging with an ex burger flipper like me? After all, I'm only the guy who saved your white collar ass from a good whipping!" Samson rubbed his face into Josh's cheek. "Anyway if you wanna hook up and get that brew sometime give me a call on 212-523-5469. Ciao hombre."

Josh was taken back by the call. He hadn't expected the brief work place friendship to spawn any future engagements. Flattered by the interest he was however not in a sociable mood. The cat's long whiskers then tickled his nose, causing a snigger that quickly fizzled out. He picked up the heavy cat and carried him through to the lounge. Dumping him on the couch he slouched down next to him and flicked on the TV. The best way to unplug from a mind full of tension was to switch on his second best companion. By scrolling through its many channels he would try and find something to catch his fleeting interest in the real life that still existed outside the four walls of his home. He was too tired to think anymore. All he wanted to do was switch off his mind and let the set guide him away from woe.

But the comedies weren't funny, the documentaries were un-engaging and the news seemed like the same old tragedies regurgitated into different lives and locations. An article in Men's Health had stated watching TV produced the same frequency of brainwaves as dreaming and, deciding the last thing he wanted to do was anymore dreaming, Josh switched off the set and turned his attention to the watch shaped patch of white skin on his wrist. *Frigging crackhead.* The digital clock on the answer machine declared it was ten thirty two. It was still early for a night owl like Josh, but the only thing that appealed to his weary body right then was reclining into his soft bed. *No dreams just sleep.*

Samson trotted after Josh as he walked into the bedroom. As usual the closet door was ajar. He went over, pushed it shut and irritably dumped a tan leather shoe at its base to prevent its gradual opening. Touching its smooth exterior he was instantly reminded of his adventure in the dark cramp space behind not a few hours previous. Josh had done his best to push the *incident* to the back of his mind, but the curious experience became fresh once again.

Kicking away the shoe, the closet door slowly creaked open, allowing the bedroom light to partially illuminate its interior. The bulb for the strip light inside had long blown and never been replaced, so parting the hanging clothes he wondered how he'd managed to walk so deeply into the cramped space. But then all that was a dream, right?

The breach it made revealed the back of the closet. Bending forward he bashed his clench fist against it to make a reassuringly solid dull thud. A strip of reflected light then caught his eye. Intrigued he bowed in further to closer inspect the square piece of steel and read the words imprinted on it. *Light Head Furnishings. Buffalo NY.* Josh realised the manufacturer's plaque had no doubt been the *lock* to the door in his bizarre dream. *So I'm sleeping walking now?* Unsure about his mind interpreting his surroundings into the delusion, he replaced the shoe at the base of the closed door. It was defiantly time to rest and forget.

Samson had found himself a comfy spot on the unmade duvet. Not wanting to disturb his furry companion, Josh lay down next to him and closed his weary eyes. *Relax...relax.* His eyelids jittered in frustrating spasms as his racing mind conspired to thwart his attempts at rest with flashbacks of his attractive stalker. *Was she real? She had to be real.* As crazy as the striking blonde woman had appeared in her white escaped loony robes, her tenacious sincerity prevented him from dismissing her totally. But if there was one thing that living in the city had taught him, it was he couldn't trust strangers.

Her questions bounced around his head. *The dark ones?* It was all too much for Josh to comprehend, but he had to admit whoever she had been, or was, she was privy to restricted information. Taking into consideration she was not the product of some oncoming dementia he shook his head. *No she was real.* Her disappearance stumped him. *There had to be another window, or something.* Samson's deep purrs echoed into the mattress. He turned to switch off the light then curled up against the drowsy feline. Before Josh knew it he had closed his eyes and drifted into sweet oblivion.

His body ached for the dark nothingness of deep sleep, but only minutes seemed to pass before his eyes were open again. *Awake. No must sleep.* A sudden pang of déjà vu urged him wide awake.

Samson was mewing loudly from the bottom of the bed. *Not now.* Expecting to find his cat pacing the floor to prise another feeding from him, Josh sat up and saw the large cat was sitting by the closet door, his bright eyes large and engaging in the low light. Before querying the unusual behaviour, the sign on the wall above Samson caught Josh's attention like a smack to the face.

He read the white on green words again. *This Way.* And realised he was back inside his mind. Sliding to the edge of the mattress, his senses energised by adrenaline, Josh studied the room around him just to be sure. It was his all right, right down to the tan leather shoe holding the closet door shut. But for some inexplicable reason it appeared more vivid than usual, as though his senses had been upgraded from analogue to digital. Samson released another poignant meow and Josh knew what was expected.

Inside the dark space of his closet he found himself up against the solid wood of the back panel and instinctively felt around for the metal clasp to his right. This time he knew what to expect. As the mechanism gave way under a slight touch it unlocked the secret doorway to another world. Again the light poured in through the opening seams and Josh prepared himself for the deluge of light that threatened to blind him once more. The brilliant glare filtered through the gaps in his fingers as he stood watching and waiting, a gush of warm air drafting in to surround him with its welcome embrace. As he slowly lowered his protective hand Josh didn't recall the cool surroundings of the austere corridor generating such pleasant sensations. When he opened his eyes fully he saw the reason why.

The diner was empty. Josh blinked at the familiar surroundings and froze. Instead of the clinical passageway of doors the portal had led him straight back to the sun baked desert diner. His sense of déjà vu was hijacked by apprehension. The diner held a more horrifying potential that quickly stunted his curiosity. Gazing around the beckoning fast food joint he saw no leering mob or hellish flames to seer his flesh. *Just me.* Safe in the belief he was alone Josh walked in as its one and only patron.

Reaching the counter he sat down on the stool, the flatulent rumble of the maroon vinyl padding going somewhere to breaking the icy trepidation. *Un-frigging believable.* He rapped his knuckles hard against the bar. The acid test hurt his knuckles and echoed throughout the large empty diner.

"Anything you wish." Josh backed off his seat as Miss June jumped up from behind the bar, topless and cordial. "Welcome to Eat-A-Lot Diners, where good food and good service go hand in hand." He was not alone after all. He stepped back to stare at the buxom beauty that had sneaked under his physic radar. "Can I take your order Josh?" she asked helpfully, smiling with the blank, soulless expression of a doll. If she was here, Josh thought, then maybe that meant He was too. Expecting the black eyed ghoul to come up from behind he spun around defensively. Pirouetting three hundred sixty degrees however he saw the diner remained free of demons and flames alike.

"Looking for someone?" The question made Josh's blood run cold. He could never mistake the lascivious tone. Turning back he saw his nocturnal nemesis had taken the Playmate's place behind the counter.

"This can't be happening again, this is a dream!"

"I'm afraid it *is* happening again Joshua," Galda confirmed sternly. He stepped towards Josh, his black form passing through the solid counter as though it were merely an illusion. "And this time you won't be jogging out of here in a hurry." Galda clicked his fingers.

A deafening thunder dragged Josh's attention to the windows. To his horror he saw sheet steel barricades slamming down over each. Like falling dominos they blocked off one after another in a thunderous succession, boxing Josh's ears as they sealed out the sunlight and his freedom. In panic he lurched back to the glass entrance, but faltered to a halt as he saw a brick wall now blocked his sole remaining escape route to the closet. *Trapped!* In disbelief he watched on as the tables and booths then disintegrated into the floor around him. The bar rotted and crumbled before his eyes into the void it exposed. The dream world was deteriorating into a black nothing. Just as he thought the encroaching darkness would consume him he was spotlighted by a single light that shone vindictively from above. Josh stood rigid, paralysed with fear.

"Abracadabra!" Galda stated theatrically. He emerged from the darkness to reveal his black attired form, a malicious grin stretching his pallid features and golden eyes hidden once more behind black lenses. "A cell within a cell." The cruel announcement made Josh want to flee the light and disappear into the black nothing that surrounded him. Whatever lay beyond in the dark unknown may have been certain oblivion, but right then it was preferential to being in close proximity to this demon. As though able to read his intentions, Galda moved to within a few feet of where Josh shuddered like a trapped animal.

"Don't waste your time with petty ideas of evasion; I assure you I have complete control." His ghoulish skin appeared made of pure white marble, unblemished, unnatural, emphasising the blackness of his high eyebrows and perfectly groomed black hair.

"What do you want from me?" Josh asked, trembling.

"Control of your mind, control of your life," the demon replied simply. Face to face once more with the unrelenting creature that had hounded him to the edges of sanity, Josh shivered. "Allow me," Galda waved his hand, gesturing for Josh to take the simple seat that had materialised out of thin air behind him. "Please, I'd rather not make you." Josh sat down in the miraculous wooden chair. Though he resented the unwanted hospitality, he didn't want to incur the infernal rage that simmered under the simple offer. Galda resumed.

"You want to know what it is I want with you. First let me tell you what this is about." Another chair appeared behind him. He sat with a casual, ominous manner, suggesting the encounter would be critical to Josh's survival.

"These charades you have witnessed are only a means to an end Joshua, part of a process of waking you from the slumbering experience that is your life. The methods are crude, but necessary to show you how you can control your *life* through controlling your *mind*. And though this *dream* exists in your mind, I possess a key that gives me control of it, and hence your life." The befuddling statement sent Josh's mind reeling as he listened with the ears of child on his first day of school. "Would you like the key?"

"That depends on what it will cost me," Josh replied pessimistically. He doubted the macabre individual was making the offer out of the goodness of his own heart.

"Nothing you wouldn't give gladly," he replied assertively. "Like the restraints that keep you imprisoned in a meaningless existence. Tell me, how would you like your freedom Joshua?"

"What are you talking about? Freedom from what? From you?" Josh said sarcastically. "Yes I'd like that!" The civility of this latest encounter was returning some of Josh's self esteem, even if it was only to argue back with a figment of his imagination.

"This is no joking matter," Galda chided him. "What I offer is something very real, just as this is all very real," his captor reaffirmed solemnly. "You are a prisoner in your own body Joshua and I am going to give you the key to the prison door."

"I didn't ask for this. All of this, it's bullshit."

"Is pain *bullshit* Joshua?" He got the threat, it needed no elaboration. The fires of Hell were best appreciated by their absence. He had Josh's full attention. "For symbolic purposes I could show you this," Galda persisted. He reached inside his jacket to pull out a huge golden door key that he then tossed over to Josh. The heavy object thumped awkwardly into his lap and he caught it before it fell to the side. "The key I offer you is not something material, you can't hold it in your hand like that one, but the true key is what makes that one real." Josh studied the weighty medieval key and tried to comprehend his captor's message. *Same as Sarah's.* His distorted face reflected in its smooth cold surface as he studied it, imitating his derailed perceptions of reality.

"How the hell can a dream be real? You, this key and the whole of this, *place,* is just some twisted nightmare cooked up by a brain pickled by drugs and deprived of sleep for too long" Josh looked around into the abyss that threatened to swallow him at any second and prayed the psychotic episode would end quickly. "All of this due to some key?" Josh asked sceptically. "This world, wherever the hell this is, is not reality! It just can't be!"

Galda raised his hand. By some invisible grasp he wrenched the golden novelty from Josh's hand back towards him, only for it to freeze in mid air between them.

"No this is certainly not reality. It is merely the first gateway on the long journey towards true perception, a veritable portal between two worlds" Josh stared at the magical display. *This can't be happening.* "The key gives you the ability to pass through. Acceptance of the key is what makes this real, and frees Joshua Brenin from oblivion." With a twist of his pale hand the suspended golden object then transformed before his eyes into a large colourful butterfly. From inanimate to animate it unfurled and flapped its wings, before fluttering away into the outer darkness. "So I ask: do you believe that it is not simply a dream, or delusion?"

"How do I know you're not just a personification of my own embittered twisted soul? Oh my God this is insane. Why am I even talking to you? You're not even real." The only reality Josh could comprehend was that he was the prisoner of a schizophrenic shadow of his own unconscious. *Get a grip Josh, focus.* He had never understood how the city's homeless crazies could hold entire conversations with imaginary companions, but now, unlike Galda's spiel of mumbo jumbo, it made perfect sense. *I'm going mad!*

"If that were the truth then what purpose would I serve?" Galda got up to join Josh. Before he could reel from the uncomfortable proximity of his tormentor sitting next to him, Josh became mesmerised by the interior of a city bus that morphed out from the darkness. Shielding them from the emerging sunlight, it wrapped its steel shell about them in a recognizable cocoon as they now seemingly travelled up the Golden State freeway to North Glendale. "Look familiar?" Galda asked with a suggestive raised eyebrow. Josh gazed around and recognised the diverse characters on the virtual bus from his ride to work.

"So it was you? You were sat in this very seat when that crazy woman pulled a knife on me," Galda smirked.

"To begin with you were the charge of one of my colleagues; it was He that you saw. But, seeing your potential Joshua, I decided to take a personal vested interest in your induction." Josh could see the effect of the revelation on his apprehensive face reflected in Galda's black lenses.

"Is that supposed to flatter me?" he asked dryly. Galda relaxed his smirk and gazed forward.

"Though what you saw appeared a thing of flesh and blood it was in fact a shadow of his material form. You are acquainted with the new age term Astral Projection?" Josh looked away from the sight of his favourite Taco Bell as it zipped past and studied Galda's unmoving profile.

"How do you…"

"It's your mind remember. If I wish I can access every synapses, memory and cell of your untapped brain." Josh looked appalled at the admission of his captor's ability to hack into his brain, his thoughts, and his soul. Galda turned to grin at his edgy captive. "Don't look so worried. There's nothing in there that could surprise me. Not after the things that I've seen, and maybe one day, you will see them to and appreciate just how futile *real* life has become." Josh ignored the gloomy comment and tried to distinguish the blurry mess of memory, reality and dream.

"So what, I was dreaming when I went to work?"

"No you were very much awake. The difference being just as my colleague and I can astral travel in your *dreams*, we also have the ability to project our astral bodies into the physical world. Dreams and reality are governed by a singular source…" he tapped his temple suggestively, "…the mind. So you see Joshua no matter where or how far you run, there is no escape." Josh didn't like the veiled threat, but his gut feeling told him it was the truth. As he turned away to the well dressed crazy woman muttering her one way discourse, Josh envied her psychosis. At least ignorance could be bliss.

"Surely that's impossible," he stated hopefully. Galda looked back and grinned slyly.

"Not with the key."

"So show me this key," Josh demanded fervently. "Enough of the crap already. Humouring the fact you might just be real, what is this key you keep talking about? I need to understand."

"So now you are ready to accept?"

"Yes I accept this is more than just a dream, just tell what's going on here."

"Good," Galda said, looking genuinely satisfied. "But such a milestone shouldn't be accepted so frivolously. Why not share this moment with a more, familiar face?" The ghoulish custodian raised his head with an air of complacency. "She's been waiting to see you Joshua."

Perplexed by the latest riddle, Josh followed Galda's gaze down the bus and immediately caught sight of the mystery passenger. Locking gazes with the young slim she woman rose from her seat and walked up the aisle to take the vacant seat in front of them. She drew close and his pulsed race excitedly as he marvelled at the Godsend. The cordial scent of Lavender wafted from her long straight brown hair as warm hazel eyes gazed affectionately into his.

"Sarah?" The mirage that sat before him living and breathing reached to touch his face then leaned forward to kiss him softly on the lips. "Sarah is it really you?"

"I am as real as I ever was Josh," she replied, her voice soft and kind, just as he remembered it. She then took his hand and held it to her warm beating chest. "Can you feel it?"

"Yes! But I don't believe it. You're dead; you died!"

"That is what you must overcome. Your disbelief is what holds you back from finding what you're looking for." He stared into the eyes of the young bride he'd lost and felt the misery and hardship of the past two years evaporate from his heart.

"I've already found what I am looking for, I've found you! You're really here?"

"When did you get so soppy?" she joked. "Haven't you been listening to what he's been telling you?" He sensed Galda had remained to enjoy the reunion, but for Josh he was no longer important. "This isn't the real world as you know it. This is only a gateway to the truth, and once you truly accept that truth then…"

"Then what?"

"Then you can have your hearts desire." As far as Josh was concerned he had all he desired sitting there in front of him.

"Who needs the truth when I can see you, touch you and even taste you" He reached over and placed his arms around her to hold her tight. "Sarah you're alive; you're really alive." Sarah pulled gently away.

"Look at me Josh. Look into my eyes. What do you see?" Josh blinked away the discharging emotions and saw his reflection in the gleaming hazel eyes.

"I see me."

"That is my point. This, all this, is locked away inside your mind. The only reason you can touch and taste me is because you are finally waking into this new world, Josh. Embrace this world and let him help you to break your caged psyche free." The intensity of her plea on Galda's behalf raised a sudden reservation.

"How can there be anything else to this?" He darted their silent, ghoulish observer a scowl. "Sarah what is the key?"

"The key is the truth, and the truth is that this is reality, the true plain of existence." He returned to Sarah, her eyes sincere, imploring, *but real?* "Your life, the life we used to live, is merely a reflection of this one. Once you truly accept this key and open the door of perception, then the path to immortality will be yours." He listened to the words coming out of her sweet mouth, but knew they were not her own; it was Galda's message, and his dead wife the medium of delivery.

"You're not Sarah!" Josh pushed the doppelganger away and sat back into the bus seat. "It's just a trick. End it!" he demanded of Galda. "End it now! How can this be reality it's just a frigging dream!" Josh watched in disgust as Sarah eerily morphed into Galda's own macabre form.

"Kissy kissy," Galda mocked him.

"I want out, let me out!"

"Out of where *Josh?* Out of your own head? I grow tired of playing these games with you; I want to know do you believe?" Josh glared back and wished he could beat the black clad devil into a pulp. "Answer me!"

Galda demanded brusquely. He raised his hand. Josh flinched at the sight of the ball of fire manifesting in the centre of the devil's palm. "Or maybe the flames of Hell might help to convince you?"

As much as Josh wanted the nightmare to be just that, he was sure even the deepest recesses of his mind could not be responsible for something so depraved and malign as this nocturnal nemesis. The offers of milk and honey were a temptation, but he had not seen or sensed any good from this creature that called himself Galda Vey. Reluctantly Josh was obliged to answer.

"I believe," he mumbled miserably. It was also the truth. After a momentary analysis of Josh's face Galda Vey grinned.

"Admirable," he replied. He concluded the tribulation with a click of his fingers that caused the counterfeit bus to melt away into the darkness and allow the familiar corridor of sealed doors to magically replace it. Standing once more in the middle of the sombre hallway, Josh looked quickly down the length of each end and saw they were alone within its shimmering walls.

"Go back to your room, return to your bed," Galda instructed. "Find your way *home* and ground yourself." Dazed but somewhat relieved, Josh turned around and opened the closed metal door that was numbered *74*. As he obeyed Galda's words resonated inside his head. "Upon returning to the physical world it will feel altered, strange," they continued, "Much like a faded photograph of ones past. But do not be alarmed." Finding his conscious state was declining into something that resembled sleep, Josh traversed the short passage until he was out of the closet door and back in his bedroom. "After you rise, leave your house and go out front. There you will wait, and with our help discard the chains that bond you, forever."

Walking back to the unmade bed he obediently reclined onto the crumpled duvet and closed his eyes. *Peace.*

As he opened his sore eyes the warm rays of a Californian dawn pierced the window blinds and relayed it was morning. He rubbed the sticky blur away and lurched up to gaze around the room he knew was his own. *I'm back.* The LED digits of the bedside clock said *6:24 AM*. A niggling paranoia toyed cruelly with his reasoning, but the absence of the *This Way* sign from his bedroom wall quickly dispelled his fear. With the visceral realisation confirmed, he wanted to write off the vivid nightmare as just another psychotic episode. Though this time he knew the impulsive speculation was folly. Whether he truly existed in a physical sense or not, Galda Vey was still a reality of sorts. He decided to put his sanity to the test.

The instructions were clear; leave the house and go out front. He had to do it, there was no better way to prove he wasn't deluded than obey and let fate prove once and for all the boundaries of his jumbled sense of reality. The sun rose quickly in California. Already its rays were moderate as they came through the small panes of glass at the top of the front door to warm the skin of Josh's face as he peered out. Unlocking the Yale bolt he opened the flaky wooden door, stepped out onto the porch and waded into the long grass of his lawn.

As expected the street was peaceful, just as it always was at dawn, miles away from the city's heart. Though unexpectedly something was different. Something was missing. He focused and tried again, looking for the source of his unease. Galda's warning then came through thick and fast. That morning the tranquil suburb felt as soulless and two dimensional as a photocopy. *He was right.* He took a deep breath. The air seemed a fettered void, drained of its usual regenerative power. At his feet the grass's usual vivid greenery seemed somewhat lacking, as though the contrast of his vision had been toned down. As he stepped towards the sidewalk the sound of his wading strides sounded muffled. *What's wrong with me?* Josh blinked, but the sights and sounds remained unrefined, indistinct. *A faded photograph.* He wondered if he was simply suffering the effects of a general malaise. *I know I'm awake.* Before he could decipher the sensation he saw the car approach.

Like a panther stalking its prey the black Mercedes made its slow advance up the lifeless street until it reached the neglected house. Not quite a limousine, but never the less designed for executive travel. The engine continued to hum quietly under the onyx hood as it came to a halt in front of Josh, an obvious invite to walk up and get inside the waiting chariot. Tinted windows were always a wary sight for Josh. This time was no different. The branches of the tall Maple trees overhead reflected in the blacked out glass and warped and twisted as he approached and found the back door unlocked. He cautiously opened the door, peered inside. Empty. Looking back at his house he formed a mental snapshot of his neglected home, inadvertently fearing it may be the last time he would lay eyes on it or the rest of Edendale. Swallowing a growing fear that gripped his racing heart, he stepped in and sat down on its luxurious black leather seat. Immediately his reeling senses told to him get out. *It's all real!* The presence of the car confirmed he was not delusional. Why would it be there unless He had sent it; a ghoul from his dreams! With the foreboding knowledge he still pulled the door shut. *What the hell are you doing Josh?*

The engine was then put into gear and the car drove off. A tinted protective screen divided the front and back of the car, meaning Josh was unable to see his chauffeur. He guessed the tinted obstruction was more for the protection of the driver than for his own privacy. The car picked up speed and Josh remembered to breath. Underneath him the seat's leather groaned as he adjusted to its ergonomic moulding. *I have to do this, I have to know.* After a quick look around the ample but confined space, Josh saw it was the only comfort on offer.

A sudden movement against his arm caused Josh to raise it defensively. The armrest had lowered by its own accord. A leather panel on its surface then flicked up to reveal a highly polished interior that housed a small wireless handset, on which a flashing LED indicated a call was holding. Alone in the gilded cage, Josh took the invitation and put the device to his ear.

"Good morning Mr Brenin," the lascivious voice greeted his ear. "I hope your transport is satisfactory." *It's him; he's real.* "I apologise for not meeting you in person but I am currently grounding myself after our little meeting just."

His host sounded fatigued, as though returning from a morning jog. The clarity of the voice slam-dunked Josh into the acute reality of his predicament, both mentally and physically, a notion reinforced as the tinted glass windows suddenly darkened completely until they blacked out the outside world. "Don't be alarmed," Galda assured him, sensing his apprehension. "It is merely a precautionary measure. I'm sure you can appreciate our reasons for wanting to maintain a certain level of confidentiality, for the moment at least." Josh found no reassurance in the words.

"Where are you taking me?"

"All will be revealed in good time. Patience is a virtue," his host added flippantly. Josh searched for a flaw in the mobile prison.

"I'm all out," he replied.

"Patience or virtue? After a hurried inspection Josh saw there was no inside door handle and realised his transport was built for the task in hand. "Either way, it's not necessarily a bad thing."

"Why me?" he asked. A few seconds of silence followed.

"It's going to be a long journey."

Galda hung up the line. Josh was left in a heightened sense of anxiety. *What the hell?* Imprisoned and unable to see the free world outside through which he was being effectively smuggled, he knew he was alone and faced an unknown future. A claustrophobic panic took hold. *What the hell were you thinking?* He had willingly accepted the ride, but trapped inside the dark restricted space, illuminated by the small interior light, he now wished he had stayed in bed.

Another motion from the armrest drew his gaze. A glass of clear liquid had been revealed in a second cavity. He knew what it was for. The unknown concoction was an offer of escapism. Though opposed to another voluntary imparting of good sense, he picked it out of its polished home and took a sip. The liquid was cold and sweet, refreshing. Within less than a minute he was unconscious and free.

As Josh was transported east out of the city a black clad intruder found her way into his unoccupied home. The front door had been easily traversed, her projected form passing through it like a ghost into the inert residence it guarded. In the Low Grade's hallway the blonde Nothos caught sight of the black form in the wall mirror and froze. *Not one of Them. Just a reflection. Keep moving.*

She had come to tie up the loose end Joshua Brenin posed; convert or destroy. Time had run out for the complacency of past engagements. She needed an answer and decisively she made straight to where her objective would be found fast asleep. Something had lulled her from enforcing her prerogative last time they'd met. Protocol had demanded she had prised her answer then, the Low Grade's stubbornness should have made it simple. But a niggling uncertainty had negated her duty. *Why would the Dark Architect risk exposure to protect this one?*

The sight of the empty bed however relayed one thing; They had been beaten her to the prize. Like a bad lingering odour Angelica could sense the cold negative vibrations of the enemy resonating from the walls of the vacant bedroom. *They were here.* For a moment she mourned the loss of another soul. But though this unwitting accomplice was a sacrificial pawn, a means to an unholy end, his loss now meant he was ostensibly her enemy. On the other side there no middle ground, no purgatory, only light and dark.

A large cat strolled up to meet the dark intruder and hissed an angry warning. Taking the hint she closed her silver eyes in preparation to ground her astral body. As she dispersed her projected form from the material world, it was in the knowledge it was all too little too late.

*****

Josh hadn't woken up in the back of a car since he was seventeen. That night he had driven out of town with his high school friends to get wasted on a crate of cheap beer lifted from the loading bay of the local 7-Eleven store. The hills had bled in the molten sunset that night and by nightfall they had been totally inebriated. This time however there was no dehydrated cerebral agony caused by a hangover, only the dread that accompanied waking from a deep sleep in a dark, strange place.

The black Mercedes had stopped under cover. Through the limited light Josh squinted and gazed out of its open back door. Someone had been there while he slept on the backseat. *No dreams.* Recalling the drugged beverage he was surprised to find his head surprisingly clear as he righted his body, the adrenaline flooding his startled brain no doubt contributing to the unexpected clarity of mind. Shuffling forward along the black leather he placed his feet onto the concrete floor. At any moment he expected to be greeted by the faceless chauffeur, but as he stood to take a look around he found the welcome party was nowhere in sight.

"Hello?" His voiced echoed into the dark void before him. The air was cool and dank; the depleting reverberation of his voice into the dark unknown verifying the underground space was of significant proportions. From behind the dwindling rays of dusk peeked in through gaps in the large battered doors that shut the parked car away from the outside world, giving the Josh impression he was perched on the edge of a concealed abyss that stretched out before him. *I've been out of it all day?* "Hello!" he called again. The anxious call bounced away into the nocturnal void for a second time. An ominous feeling of abandonment made him shiver. *They left me here?* Suddenly he was answered.

A floodlight erupted above his head, momentarily blinding him. Lowering his defensive hand, a second then followed it ten metres further away into the abyss. A third followed it, then a fourth, and another and another, dispersing the dark ten metres at a time. In a matter of seconds the lengthening corridor of light had extended outward to part the abyss in two. Frozen to the spot Josh watched the last overhanging spotlight come to life at the far end of what appeared to be a huge underground hangar the length of a football field.

The request was simple. Josh swallowed his anxiety and began the long walk forward along the illuminated path. The sound of his footsteps against the smooth concrete echoed and distorted as he made the cautious stroll to what appeared to be a dead end, he shivered again. Night time was crawling over what place lay above. In that underground place the accompanying coolness was reinforced by fear as he paced further into the featureless man made cavern. Along its distant shadow veiled edges he could make out the protruding steel girders that braced the walls against the living rock from which it had been cut. The vast, empty storage area appeared not have been used for years.

Josh stopped at its far wall and stared at the ancient metal door inlaid into it. From an initial inspection it seemed as corroded and idle as the rest of the remote place, a thick, brown crusted chain and padlock sealing it for posterity. A rust eaten sign bolted onto its blistered surface declared *No Unauthorised Personnel,* and after a careful dusting of the cobwebs from the flaky door bolt and latch, it didn't take a genius to see it hadn't been touched in decades. *What the hell is this place?* The wisps of dust and iron oxide suddenly increased as the door vibrated.

He stepped back and watched in awe as the corroded frontage then began to sink into the floor. *What's happening?* Out of sight a motorised mechanism was powering the foreboding sight with a deep reverberation that made the floor shake underfoot. Dumbstruck he watched on as the corroded facade disappeared completely into the ground to reveal the newly constructed, highly polished barrier that it protected. *A blast door?* The cavern's appearance of decrepitude and neglect was a front. Edging another step backwards, Josh watched as the modern security barrier then slid open effortlessly to reveal a large chamber furnished with the same highly polished metal. He'd found the secret face of Galda Vey's world, a clandestine world that existed under the slumbering noses of an unsuspecting mankind.

There was no going back now. Cautiously he stepped into the shiny interior he believed to be some form of elevator. The metal door slid shut, encasing him in the secret space and Josh held his breath. After what seemed like only a few seconds of slight gut wrenching movement he sensed it come to a stop with a slight judder. The notion was confirmed when the entrance slid open to reveal a long corridor jutting out before him.

The passageway's disorientating familiarity shot him back into the world of his nightmares. Though he had never been to this surreptitious layer in the middle of god knows where before, what lay in front of him was as recognizable as any memory of his suburban home. Josh took the first nervous steps into the clinical surroundings of the corridor of doors, its austere and institutional appearance as vivid as it had been in his dreams.

The elevator entrance slid shut, deserting him to the sense of déjà vu. *Keep walking.* He knew where he had to go. There was no other more obvious choice than to walk the length of the corridor to the closed door facing him at its end. The fact neither of the doors he passed were numbered didn't distract from an awareness of his twisted reflection following him on the surface of the corridor's shimmering walls, or that his feet made no sound when coming into contact with its floor. But none of that mattered as he came face to face with the door designated by the letter *K* embossed upon its cool surface. Feeling as though he were standing on the edge of some imaginary precipice, he placed his fingertips on its security interface. The lock mechanism disengaged with a click. Shoving the door aside it swung open to disclose an empty room. Déjà vu went out the window. *Not blue. Not the same.*

A table sat at the centre of the dark room, spotlighted from above. Cautiously he entered, unable to see the surrounding walls due to insufficient lighting. It was then he sensed he was not alone in the curious set up, but was prevented from bolting as the door automatically sealed him inside. He was Daniel in the lion's den, minus the faith in God.

"Welcome Joshua, please sit down." The voice projected from the surrounding darkness.

"Show yourself!" Josh demanded.

"Sit, down!" the voice returned fire. The harsh sentiment made him draw the chrome framed chair from under the table and obediently sit. The orator of the booming voice then stepped from amongst the shadows, revealing himself to his uneasy guest. "Comfortable?" Galda asked. He dragged out a second chair and sat down opposite. From behind the familiar sunglasses across the table Josh sensed sarcasm betrayed his host's macabre delight. Now he had Josh in the flesh.

"Not really," Josh relied coyly. "Where am I?"

"About to take the second step into reality. Would you care for some refreshment?" A glass of clear liquid was conveniently elevated from a hidden cavity in the burnished surface of the table. "You've had a long journey." Josh looked suspiciously at the miraculous beverage. "Go ahead, it has no added ingredients." Galda's black eyebrows arched deviously above his shades. Against the pale white skin of his high forehead his thick black hair remained as perfectly groomed back from his face as it had been in the dreams. With his offer declined, Galda reached over and picked up the glass. "I have to admit this astral travelling is thirsty work, don't you agree?" He raised the glass in a mock gesture of salutation before draining it. "You have to be careful to remember the needs of your mortal body," he said, replacing the glass on the tabletop. "It is so easy to forget those you leave behind. Though I find the more I am away from this mortal shell, the more of a chore it becomes to sustain it, as though its usefulness becomes redundant."

Josh became increasingly aware the shadows around them hid at least two more mortal spectres, who watched the parley in silent vigil.

"Once you taste the light you come to realise your body is merely a part of the darkness that exists around it," his demonic host continued enigmatically. "A shell that serves only to contain us while we exist on this earth." As Josh's eyes slowly adjusted to the surrounding gloom he made out the other black clad sentinels standing either side of them. "Unfortunately if your body is left too long in the darkness while you vacate into *other* places, it becomes photosensitive. Hence the necessity for protective measures." Galda tapped the sunglasses with a long, white finger.

"Well that sound's great Mr Vey," Josh interceded. "But what the hell has that got to do with me?" Unexpectedly a swipe of Galda's hand sent the empty glass soaring from the table, sending it to smash in the shadows with a heart wrenching clatter.

"It has everything to do with you!" he bellowed. "If you switched off your ego for one moment and opened your eyes you would be able to see that for yourself." Angrily Galda rose from the table and walked around to Josh. The captive stiffened in the chair. "We are offering you the key to a doorway you could never find on your own, the key to reality itself. Though still you refuse to accept the obvious. And yet you are here…of your own free will!"

Josh almost derided the latter comment with a heckling laugh of his own. His host manoeuvred behind and gripped his shoulders paternally.

"We are also asking you for your assistance," he admitted more amiably, tightening his grip.

"*My* assistance?" Josh queried the unbelievable. "What is this? Good cop bad cop? Just tell me who you people are, I have a right to know." The firm grip around his shoulders slackened and withdrew. "You're CIA am I right? You're too freaky to be FBI." Galda stared down blankly through the harsh light at his belligerent guest. "Is *this* even legal?" Galda turned his back on Josh and walked into the shadows. "NSA? You're NSA right?" Josh demanded to know, but was met with silence. "Right?" Josh then sensed the two silent cohorts edging closer to the table.

Though it was dark there was no mistaking what Josh saw next. His eyes tracked Galda as he walked to the unlit wall. With amazement they also watched as he disappeared through it like a ghost. Josh was wrenched up from his chair before he comprehend the marvel, the austere faces of the two henchmen appearing in the coarse light next to him, pale skin, shades, black suits, inhuman. One tagged something to Josh's top.

"What is that? What are you doing?" Without answering they grabbed his arms, ushered him from the table and then threw Josh at the same wall. Intuitively he braced himself for the inevitable impact of his face against the hard surface, but instead found himself flying though it and beyond. On the other side he corrected his balance with a disbelieving stagger. Just as Galda before him, he had unwittingly mimicked the supernatural feat and now looked up to find he was immersed again in the neon blue light of his dreams.

"What you just passed through is an alternating molecular portal," Galda explained, pre-empting his reservation for the miraculous passage. His ghoulish complexion was accentuated by the room's neon radiance. Josh looked from it to the so-called portal. All that was visible was a wall as solid as any other he had seen, blue but real. "Without the key card on your shirt you would have broken your face on the other side, just as you would any normal wall. Instead it regulated the wall's molecules to accommodate your passage through it. Just like magic eh, Joshua?" Readdressing his sense of dignity, Josh took the chance to study the new surroundings, which again were not that unfamiliar. The blue light emanated from a non-specific source to bathe the immeasurable interior; seemingly paralleled with the one he and his slumbering peers had been lured to in an assumed dream world.

"There's no such thing as magic. Only illusion and sleight of hand," he replied accusingly. Behind his black clad host the familiar chrome finished recliners were positioned in a semi circle arrangement. "This place is real?" he asked, looking for the cinematic display. But up front there was only the neon blue that created the luminous shell around the clandestine space.

"No illusion; fact!" Galda insisted. "Without the key card on your shirt you would not have made it through, just as without the key of knowledge, you cannot enter into the Leviscape." Josh looked down at the hurriedly placed badge stuck to his top. It was a small, squared tag and plain except for a dark square in one corner, reminding him of the personal radioactivity detectors worn by nuclear cleanup teams.

"The Leviscape? So what the hell is that?"

"In a nutshell, the Leviscape is an inter-dimensional plain of existence, on par with what is more commonly referred to as Dreamscape. Though unlike Dreamscape it is in fact the true plain of existence in this little thing we call the universe, known and unknown." Galda paced slowly towards the arc of shiny chairs. *Just as they were in the dream.* "Or to put it another way it is a conscious state achieved out of what we mere humans associate with the unconscious, where we exist outside the bio-mechanical cell we call our bodies."

"Still insisting my dreams are real?" Josh mocked. "How can they be? That's all they are, *dreams*. The only thing that's been making them seem more real lately is you!" Galda paused and glowered at his disinclined student. "Brain washing and mind control I understand, but dreams real? I think not," Galda smirked then continued.

"Since the beginning of mankind's relatively brief excursion from the primordial swamp of its pre history, he has sought to explain and reach out to this higher level of existence. At the core of every human's self-obsession and ego, lives a desire to be free of the constraints of this world. It was from this primal instinct that the world religions found their base to preach against the very sins that help lock humanity into this depraved world of flesh."

Standing in the blue void, Josh struggled to match the relevance of Galda's words to the mental angst he'd suffered.

"What if I was to tell you the Leviscape and heaven were one and the same?" Josh's lack of faith was suddenly reinforced. Josh Brenin agreed religion was the *opiate of the masses*. For the weak minded it filled the void left behind by lack of purpose. Scepticism, he thought was more righteous than naivety.

"So now you're saying you can get me into heaven?" Josh walked over to the nearest chrome chair. He placed a hand on its chrome headrest and caught a glimpse of the assortment of visual displays and interfaces flashing behind it. He failed to see how the outlandish technology could possibly link the heavens to the earth.

"What if it was true?" Galda asked assuredly.

"You *are* mad," Josh blurted, relinquishing the constraints created by fear. "Are you now telling me all this, these machines are capable of opening the gateway to heaven? This is what you brought me here for?"

"What you must understand is that you're conscious mind is still playing by the rules governed by this world." Galda declared as he walked close enough for Josh to see his own reflection in the blacked out lenses. "What you call heaven is a religious archetype, created by an institution to manipulate the masses into living their lives in a manner they see fit. Show them the yellow brick road and they'll dance and sing all the way to Oz! Heaven exists my friend." Galda put his hand reassuringly onto Josh's shoulder. "But it's is not the cloudy utopia of Christian fantasy. It is a real place, defined by immaterial rules, and already you've tasted its revelation. Throw away your misconceptions, suppress your ego and let me show you what freedom really is." Josh stared at his wide eyed reflection in the dark lenses. He hated himself for allowing the words to be sown in his confused mind.

"If this really is true, why me? Why go to all this trouble?"

"Because you are what we are looking for," Galda replied. He retracted his arm and strode towards the blank wall overlooking the reclined seats. "We need you and others like you to help us in our task."

He stopped and turned. "Our national duty if you will. *This* is what this is all about."

"What kind of help could I possibly give you?" Josh exclaimed. This is just so insane!" Galda glided back towards him.

"The only way to understand is to step onto the yellow brick road," he replied inexplicably. He slid into one of the chrome finished recliners and waved a pale hand over the vacant one alongside. "Take a seat Joshua."

*****

The muscles of Ben's legs ached as he stood up from the low mattress to face his captors. In the brilliant light he was able to study the red haired woman's delicate features properly for the first time and found their fragile beauty induced a protective stirring. In the clinical ambience of the mirrored bedroom she returned the scrutiny with her crystal green blue eyes, reciprocating a warmth as she gauged his thoughts. But as Monk held out his hand to reveal the small blue pill, Ben realised it was no time for pleasantries.

"Take it," Monk instructed. Ben looked bemused by the sight of the trial drug.

"What's that for? I ain't planning on going to sleep."

"Can you neutralise your conscious perception and project into dreamscape at will?" Monk asked with a mocking tone, knowing full well Ben was not skilled in the art of auto projection. The big soldier tried to fathom the pros and cons of ingesting the unwanted prescription. His split second analysis came back mostly cons. He tried to steal Monks agenda from his unsympathetic eyes, but saw only harsh sentiments that hid a lingering animosity. Calisto's fair skinned hand then took hold of Ben's and placed the blue pill from Monk's palm into his.

"If you want to know what's going on here Ben then you need to start trusting us. Cause right now we are the only things standing in the way of the people that stole your life from and put you on this dark path. We are the good guys here. Without us there is only slavery and damnation waiting for you." She closed his fingers over the tablet and raised his hand for him. Without refuting the gesture Ben let the gentle woman guide him. "Let us help you to understand, and in return you can help us to fight back against Them." He was always a sucker for a smile and pretty girl. He looked down at the pill in his open hand. "Trust us Alpha."

"Them?" he asked, gazing one more time into Calisto's crystal eyes. Ben had always been a good judge of people. He was sure the virtuous aura of the red head was genuine; of Monk he wasn't so sure. As a licensed assassin Sergeant Ben Wheeler had killed enough bad people with his own bare hands to know evil held no quarter in the young woman, and so foregoing his reply about the mysterious Them he was yet to encounter, he tossed the pill into his mouth and hoped his instincts remained intact.

*****

Josh slid into the vacant reclining chair next to Galda. The ergonomic form of the chrome seats made them surprisingly comfortable and Galda looked quite at home as he gently eased himself into the slippery moulding. Inspired to ask about the unusual choice of materials for their construction, Josh's apprehension however left him momentary mute. He followed suit and squirmed his own body into the chrome frame until comfortable, swearing the chair was tailored to fit as Galda's cohorts entered the blue room via the portal entrance.

"Don't concern yourself with them, they will monitor us while we project," Galda assured him, "There is nothing to fear." Josh didn't like having the two other ghouls out of sight, but there was nothing he could do to rectify it. Recalling Galda's golden eyes glaring down as he had struggled to escape in the *dream* made Josh's current position a tense one. After a quick glance behind he realised no one was poised to pin him down and relaxed as best his fragile nerves would allow. From a compartment under Josh's left hand a small translucent cube was raised from the armrest into his palm. Galda's raised his for Josh's attention, placed it into his mouth and swallowed.

"The transparent gel will liquefy in your mouth and aid consuming the pill at its centre. Take it."

"What is it?" Josh was unsure he wanted to be drugged again quite so soon.

"It's no different to what you've been taking for the past few weeks, except with a stronger sedative enhanced with a psychotropic complex that helps the mind to, free itself," Galda explained. He offered Josh a supportive glance across the short gap between the chairs, his sunglasses remaining perched on the prominent bridge of his nose. On that occasion Josh was glad they continued to conceal the macabre sight he knew glared out from behind. "The key card on your shirt will also emit low frequency microwaves that will regulate your brain's natural sleeping pattern," he continued. "Allowing you to achieve the perfect unconscious state."

Josh raised his gel cube and noted the small pill housed at its centre. The luminous neon blue light made it impossible to discern its colour, which he guessed to be blue.

"The stage is set; time to get this show on the road Joshua." With a gesture of his white fingers Galda instructed Josh to swallow the cube, which he did along with his good sense. As explained the gel liquefied on contact with his saliva and the small pill slid down his throat. Following Galda's example Josh relaxed his neck muscles and tried not to allow the headrest's slow, creepy enclosure of his head to overwhelm him.

An involuntary wave of slackening muscles throughout his body then made Josh feel as though it had also turned to liquid. Instinctively his heavy eyes closed as the tension ebbed from the core of his soul like a burst damn. The sedative was much stronger, and the bodies of captor and captive now sank into a rapid, deep sleep that unchained their conscious minds. *Sleep, precious sleep.* But this was no time to relax.

The transmutation from one reality to the next was so quick at first Josh believed he was still awake in the physical sense of the word. There was no need to blink. His vision was clear, his senses animated and vivid. As he gazed at the bookshelves that now surrounded and dwarfed him, the rustic smell of their timber mixed with the thousands of new and pre-loved books stacked upon them empowered the new vision as something very real, and not as he had hoped, a simple trick of the mind. *What am I doing here?* Recognising the counter that served the familiar bookstore, Galda sprang up from behind it with a theatrical open hand gesture.

"Ready to start work?" Galda Vey asked fervently. The question was meant as a double-edged jibe. From all appearances they both now stood in the shrouded world of the Mind Matters bookstore on the Fast Mile. The esoteric ambience of that place swamped his senses and overwhelmed his dishevelled mind with its visceral perfection. Josh focused his senses to test for flaws in the dream world counterfeit which he knew could only be a hallucination, but found the brooding pseudo-library of the occult was just as authentic as the original. Standing with his black clad guide in that very real emporium of secret knowledge bathed in sweet incense, Josh realised just how fitting a platform it was.

"It's amazing isn't it?" Galda asked enthusiastically. "It's a dream, but it's as real as any life you've ever known. This is the pinnacle of Lucid dreaming Joshua. Back in the material prison of the *real* world your body rests in the deepest sleep, while here, your mind exists in a parallel world, free of material constraint and more truly conscious of its true self." He lowered his hands and took a deep satirical breath of the dream world air. "Ah the wonders of modern science."

"So whose mind is this?" Josh asked. "You said you could read my mind, like one of these books, but are you doing all of this?"

"As I explained the truth is the key to all this and the truth is that this virtual world is in fact *reality*. Once you've used this knowledge to unlock your mind, this world is merely clay in your hands, though yes in this instance it is my hands moulding the clay of your unconscious." Galda then walked through the counter as he had done at the diner. With the freedom of a ghost his form glided through the solid barrier and stopped in front of Josh, who looked on amazed by the unravelling mystery. "Everybody and anybody can achieve access to the lower dreamscape, for every living creature is connected to the same universal core in the multi plain universe. We are taught that our dreams are the product of our unconscious, subjective minds playing out the ups and downs of life, and this is true to an extent." Josh watched as Galda raised his arm and caught a book that had floated from a shelf somewhere behind him. "However, for those like you, and I, who can penetrate this wall of sleep and are able to access the higher level of dreamscape, we can access a state of consciousness on equal plain to the purest level of existence." Though overwhelmed by a sense of awe, Josh tried to remain focused on the lesson's direction.

"The Leviscape?"

"Yes. All life is created and exists on that plain," Galda stated dramatically as the book levitated up from his open palms. Its pages fluttered open as though an invisible hand flicked through them. "Whether they are conscious of it or not is another matter."

"So this is Dreamscape not the Leviscape?" Josh queried. He took a step forward to examine the miracle more closely. The book then slammed shut under his nose and zipped past his head back to its home on the packed shelf.

"This is simply a twin existence, a stepping stone needed to cross the river of Creation, and one on which you must be perfectly balanced before jumping to the next," Galda's expression was stern again, reminding Josh of the zealous TV preachers proclaiming their profound mystical decrees.

"So what makes me so special I should be worthy of such a gift? Josh asked. "The only thing I've been special at lately is being a loser." Galda took another deep, cathartic breath of the dream air and began to walk slowly around the shop floor, studying the rows upon rows of esoteric literature.

"Two years ago you lost your wife in a tragic car accident," he continued formally. "After which you subsequently became unable to carry the responsibilities of your prestigious career for one of the city's top Architect firms." Josh bit his tongue and listened on. "Along with this fall from grace you began to suffer from depression and more importantly developed insomnia." The last two years of his life had been ably squashed into a nutshell. Intrigued by its inclusion, Josh buried his rising resentment. "After seeking aid for the condition you were referred to a specialist who worked under the alias of Doctor Halberstram, otherwise an agent of our organisation."

"So Sleepeze *was* responsible for this!" Galda paused by a box of unsorted books at his feet. The revelation confirmed the Doctor's mysterious unavailability.

"Do you understand what the term Remote Viewing means?" Galda then asked. He held his hand out to catch a book that floated up from the box and into his grasp.

"Yeah it's psychic spying or something. It was supposedly pioneered during the cold war to gather intelligence on the Ruskies." Galda looked up, suitably impressed.

"Sleepeze, as you know it, contains a highly classified complex of synthetic opiates called Ketron 115. It was discovered by chance by the military scientists working on the remote viewing projects of the fifties and sixties. Primarily used to aid the quality of the patriot's remote espionage, its true potential however lay dormant until the early eighties, when it was realised the complex could expand the mind's ability to traverse into new and uncharted territory, *this* territory." Galda thumbed his way through the new book hovering inches above his open palm via invisible hands. Josh recognised the slumbering man at the base of the ethereal font of the book's cover. The bookstore was the library of his mind, and Galda was picking and choosing his way at random through the memories archived on its shelves.

"Our highly funded black book project was founded to chart these unknown regions," Galda continued, "And just like yours and mine ability to project onto this plain, so does our agency exist outside the orthodox platform of the intelligence and security communities. By comparison we make the CIA look like a kinder-garden reading group."

Josh understood the ramifications of the boast. Outside the normal platform meant outside of the law, meaning Galda and his black book cohorts were children in a candy store holding a lifetime of credit. Galda couldn't have made it plainer; Josh's life now belonged to this anonymous spook agency, and he its custodian.

"You've been doing this since the eighties? I guess that means you haven't charted everything yet," Josh quipped. "So why the cloak and dagger routine? I mean why go to all this trouble? Surely you could have gone into partnership with some research facility or something? What's the big deal about mapping out some fairy tale kingdom when the real threats to national security are in the here and now? The Middle East, global terrorism, who's gonna fly a Boeing 747 with a nuclear warhead out of dreamscape?" Galda snapped the book closed and dropped it back into the box at his feet.

"Because that is where we made First Contact!" he snapped. The blunt reply left Josh stumped, unsure if Galda really referred to something so incredible.

"First contact," Josh confirmed. "You mean extra terrestrials?"

"*Ultra* terrestrials!" was Galda's corrective response. The impact of its significance was enough to stun Josh for a second time. Its implications sent his thoughts reeling back into the realm of disbelief. Even in the unreal world of dreamscape, the new tangent of the unravelling nightmare was too much for Josh's sensibilities. A fresh waft of the exotic incense made the dream world revelation seem all the more otherworldly.

"Wait a second, this is bull," he countermanded, pride and rage returning with a renewed tide of scepticism. "I didn't ask for this. You used me, tried out your wonder drug on me like a goddamn lab rat. You've intruded into my life, my dreams, trampled my civil rights and for what? Because you think you can get into heaven by talking to frigging aliens?"

"You and others like you are not a dime a dozen!" Galda retorted as he marched back towards Josh. "There are no obvious signs or factors that reveal the qualities we seek. We cannot simply give the Ketron complex to any bum off the street, just as we can't even hand it out to the highest ranks of the FBI, CIA or NSA! Not everyone is blessed with the ability to tune into and access the higher dreamscape. Not everyone is what we call a Nothos; a natural. For reasons unknown to us the symptoms of insomnia and other parasomnia conditions act as a catalyst for the transformation of conscious." Galda was no longer preaching to the deaf, but pleading for an objective mind to assimilate his words. "Though none except you achieved the immediate control and elevated state so quickly."

"You can forget the flattery for a start," Josh retorted dryly. It was his turn to wander amongst the library that lived somewhere deep within his unconscious mind, another world seemingly eons away from his slumbering body lying in state in the neon blue layer.

"No your initiation was perfect, more perfect than any novice before." Josh sensed the stroking of his ego. He tried to remain detached from Galda's enthusiasm. "Arranging the limo ride into the heart of our operation was not standard M.O. Our covert operation relies upon remote and absolute anonymity, yet we took a great risk in bringing you here Joshua, an unprecedented risk warranted only by your exceptional natural capacity for this work." And one that could easily be erased Josh thought. "Rather than allow me to manipulate and control your Low Grade induction, you were able to influence the dreamscape to aid your escape. A one in a thousand chance you were able to not simply access it, but truly exist within it from day one."

Josh stared at the long wooden counter in front of him. The touch of its worn, smooth wood told him it was solid. As he dragged his hand across its surface his nails picked out the individual ridges of the wood grain like a needle on a record. *How did he get through it?*

"The room with the chairs and the other people watching that screen, that actually happened?" Josh enquired.

"A fresh batch of recruits, each assigned their personal tutor to guide and aid the progression of their gift. Because that's what it is Joshua, a gift."

"So what about them, where are they now? They were people like me." He shuddered at the memory of the sickening vision. "And what the hell happened to their eyes?"

"Psychosomatic," Galda explained elusively, "Those who make the grade become unsuspecting volunteers to our cause. As far as *they* are concerned, it's simply all a bad dream."

"And those who don't make the grade?" Josh asked uneasily.

"Those who don't we return to their previous existence of drudgery, unblemished." Galda sensed his student's distrust. "Think of me as your spirit guide, and the dreamscape the school of life. The question is: are you willing to learn?" Josh withdrew his attention from the impenetrable counter and looked for hints of gold behind Galda's shades. "Graduation has many benefits." With a wave of his hand his demonic tutor made a black mortar cap appear on Josh's head. Its frayed braid dangled comically in front of his face. "Like assisting national security, I take you love your country Joshua?" Disgruntled by the magical feat, Josh removed it and threw it to the wooden floor, producing a small puff of dust that erupted in the sunlight.

"I love whatever gives me comfort," he replied dryly, undecided if his pale-faced *tutor* was truly a patriot or a misguided psychotic. "You've obviously gone to a lot of trouble to pull me into your parlour Mr Spider, what is it that you're really offering me? What kind of *assistance* are we

talking about here? You've made the big sell, let's hear the closing pitch."
He thought he saw a brief twinkle of delight in Galda's flawless features.

"Tell me; were you a fan of Star Trek the Next Generation?" The
question knocked Josh off balance.

"I thought you could read my mind, why don't you tell me."

"In one episode the crew of the Enterprise were plagued by
unseen entities who purposely caused ailments amongst the crew for their
own scientific ends. By sheer accident the Enterprise crew stumbled across
the incursion of the alien race, who while existing at a different frequency,
were affecting and interacting with them." A flashback of the blind
engineer stumbling across the unexpected parasites popped into Josh's
head.

"I remember. Jordy developed some kind of device that made
them appear. So what?"

"What if I was to tell you an inter-dimensional race of beings is
plaguing humanity at this very moment? And has been since the genesis of
our race." The question was asked with the assertive tone of man
determined to convert. "Existing on a plain outside the common realm of
man's perception. Manipulating him, exploiting him and disrupting his
natural evolvement?" Josh deliberated the new revelation. Visions of Jordy
and Ryker's shocked faces at the point of discovery played out in his
mind's eye.

"This is your first contact?"

"Mankind is at the mercy of a race of entities whose sole purpose
is to keep us beneath them and from finding our true place in the universe.
They are the bane of humanity." Galda spat the last sentence with a scowl
of derision.

"Who are they?" Josh asked nervously. He was unsure he wanted
to know. The truth hadn't been something he'd expected from this black
clad demon, but in the grand scale of everything Josh had seen and
experienced so far, the notion was not so absurd to be rejected out right.

"They are known as the Vanir. We want you to help us fight
them." As Galda made the grim statement, Josh saw from the grimace
contorting his pale face he was deadly serious.

*****

The concealment of suicide pills in the oral cavity was a necessary
skill, the risk of capture and torture before death being a valuable incentive
for its perfection. In the Elite military world of the Special Forces such as
Delta Force, honour was the only virtue a soldier could uphold after

detainment, even if achieved only through the strategic secreting and consumption of Cyanide tablets at the appropriate time. For Ben this had proven a useful skill, though one he'd hoped never to make use of. The small blue pill was lodged in a secure crevice between his top right wisdom tooth and his cheek. After feigning to swallow it, he handed the glass of water back to Calisto.

"So what now, you want me to lie back and catch some Z's?" he asked his captors coyly. Monk took it from him with a shrewd look of anticipation, making him feel all the better for non-compliance.

"Take a seat," Monk instructed. With another light touch of her hand against his elbow, Calisto urged Ben to resume his seat on the low mattress, which he did.

"Since I'm being so cooperative over here how about you people giving me some answers" He stretched his long legs out across the bare floorboards. "Like whom you really are and what the hell is going on around here?" Monk leaned against a mirrored wall, his reversed reflection propping him up in the infinite prism of light.

"As a professional soldier there is no one better qualified understand the meaning of war. For that is *what's going on here,*" Monk explained gravely. "Two opposing forces face off on a battlefield, and to the victor the spoils." Ben felt patronised, but listened all the same. "We are alike in that respect you and us, because we are also soldiers. Fighting in an unholy war where the forces of light and darkness battle for the souls of mankind."

"Well that's just great Mr Monk, but where do I fit into all this? You hoping to hire my professional skills? If so I'll tell you right now you're pissing into the wind. I've killed all the men I plan to in this life. No doubt I'll answer for it in the next, but that isn't me anymore. I retired before man's insanity cost me the rest of my face. So there's no way in hell, or heaven, I'm gonna moonlight as a mercenary for some black ops spook with a ponytail and a pocket full of magic beans." He leaned back and propped himself on his outstretched arms. In the belief he held the upper hand for the first time in the game of wits; Ben hoped to make the most of his keeper's relaxed guard.

"What if the battlefield *was* the next life? And Heaven and Hell the legacy of the spoils. Would you give a damn then Alpha?" The intense glare of Monk's sparkling eyes reinforced the declaration. "What if you were already a soldier in the war? Press-ganged into military service without prior consent or knowledge of its protocols. Before we intervened you were already being marched toward it, the obliging Dr Halberstram being your Uncle Sam. Whether you like it or not Alpha, you've been re-commissioned!" Monk's words stunned Ben. He looked down at Calisto, who smiled up from her crossed leg sitting position on the bare floorboards to his left.

"And what's your story?" he asked a little more gently.

"I am a soldier of the light. I didn't choose it but that's what I am." Her reply was florid but sincere. "And you also have no choice, because that is what you are destined to become. The only way to understand the light is to embrace it, just as we have. On the other side we can show you this." He found her placid, fragile tone soothing. Her contrasting appeal was dissolving his resistance to the inevitable.

"On the other side of what?"

"Reality," she replied with the chaste smile of young girl. "But only if you swallow the pill Ben." He realised then that the smile was actually the conceited grin of a woman who had caught him out. He looked over and saw Monk was scowling coldly at him.

"No fooling you guys," he quipped despondently. The saliva around the pill had dried away, causing it to stick to the inside of his cheek. Using his tongue to prise it free he finally succumbed to the inescapable path of fate and swallowed it.

*****

Standing amongst the monolithic bookshelves that rose up to meet the ceiling of the dreamscape bookstore, Josh stood transfixed in a purgatory of doubt and acceptance. In the brief moment he was afforded as Galda turned away to recompose himself, Josh leant against the hard wood of the counter and let the steadfast barrier ground his thoughts, before breaking the silence with a bemused query.

"So what, you want me to help you expose them? Is that what this is about?" In the spear of light thrusting into the main shop floor through the skylight above their heads Galda paused and span around on his heels.

"Where they are there is no time, no change," he responded enigmatically. "They have no planet, nor even material form, but they exist. By current orthodox scientific understanding their world does not even exist in the literal sense of the word, yet they are but, are not!" He paused to gaze up into the sunlight so that it blazed across the lenses of his sunglasses. "This is the foe that we face. We need your help to fight them on their own ground, beat them at their own game, infiltrate and annihilate."

"How?" Josh asked. "If all this is true then surely you can infiltrate them yourself? You and your buddies back there." Galda's gaze remained upwards towards the solar rays until seemingly he could stand it no longer, as though reaching the limit of his resilience he lowered his head down from the skylight. "You are obviously so much better at playing this game, you don't need me!" To Josh's amazement Galda then soared up through the air into the shadowy void above him, the only sound made by the super human feat the flap of his jacket as he landed on the counter to look down at Josh with the formidable presence of an avenging angel.

"If only this was a game!" Galda stated as he crouched down to Josh's level. "But the Vanir have their own allies here on earth. These converts aid them to track and undermine us, calling themselves Latronis, so-called servants of the light!" Levitating from the counter he then descended eerily slow to stand at Josh's side. "We have done all we can, but now we are known to the Vanir we are unable to access their realm on the Leviscape."

"That's why you need the drones like me to do your dirty work right?"

"Yes," Galda relented. "It is the only way we can find a way in to stop them now. Like a modern day Spartacus you must help us lead the slaves to victory against the enslavers." For the first time Josh didn't just see his own reflection in the dark lenses. From behind them he could now sense a weakness emanating via the sincerity of the explanation, the frank plea crushing any remaining doubt.

"I think I need to sit down," Josh said. The monumental burden that Galda Vey was laying on his shoulders was beginning to make his head spin.

"Do you?" Galda then asked haughtily. "Your mind is strong and this is reflected in your astral body. You needn't feel pain or want for nothing in this place, unless you desire to," he added mysteriously and Josh sensed his tutor's exhilaration building again. "For that is the cherry on the icing Josh, here you can do and be anything!" Galda waved a hand to the shop floor. "Go ahead, try it."

He then realised how obvious the request really was. This was his mind, a reality created by the blueprint stored in his own psyche, and like any good blueprint there was always room for improvement. Focusing his attention to the lighted arena created by the shard of sunlight he imagined a chair, a simple chair, a polished chrome frame, black padding, low back and armless like the one he had perched on at his last interview. Nothing appeared. He sensed Galda's eyes were on him, willing him on. *Focus.* For some reason the memory of his interrogator's beady brown eyes and the feeling of insignificance they had instilled suddenly discarded Josh's disappointment, and then it was there. As the sunlight bounced off the shiny chrome frame that had been born out of nothing he realised he had blinked and it had been created. Josh's amazement was overwhelmed with a sense of pride.

"Good!" Galda congratulated him. "Now something else." Like a child who had just learned to ride his bicycle the urge to show off suddenly took hold. The next creation had to be something more pleasing than a mere inanimate object. He focused his attention again to the lighted arena, the new object of desire had to be something more satisfying for the male gaze, and she was. Past lusts fuelling his thoughts the college dorm wall photo of perfect buttermilk skin, ample breasts and divine curves materialised in the form of the centrefold's perfection. As Miss June was reborn in all her naked glory Josh could sense Galda's excitement.

"Dance," Josh commanded. Immediately his creation of flesh and blood obeyed with a sensual gyration that quickly distracted him from his own sense of accomplishment.

"You don't have to command with your voice," Galda explained. "Use your mind; it is the master in this place." Enamoured with his new creation Josh walked into the light and sat on the chrome framed chair to better enjoy the fruits of his labours.

"Now this is truly amazing!" Josh exclaimed. Looking up at the buxom model she turned to tease him with her naked body, his thoughts her commands. Willingly she stopped her shameless dance, kneeled and looked up imploringly with her big blue eyes as the outstretched fingers slid up his thighs towards his crotch. The wave of excitement momentarily made him forget his place.

"I think we've had enough of that." Galda snapped his fingers and the naked vision disintegrated before his eyes. Josh frowned at the black clad killjoy as he joined him in the solar spotlight. "Power corrupts even the pure of heart. Stay focused on the task in hand Joshua, and then afterwards you can enjoy whatever your heart desires." With a passing command Josh retaliated against the intrusion by transforming Galda's black clothes into an evening dress his grandmother had once worn, his stern features contrasting comically with the flower patterned gown he now sported for his student's amusement. His tutor admired the achievement though the amusement was short lived. Asserting his superior skill he transformed the long old-fashioned gown quickly back into his black uniform and delivered his coup-de-grace.

"Can't have the student upstaging the master can we?" Galda explained slyly as the cage of thick iron bars materialised around Josh in an instant. "But you did do very well." The compliment was followed up with a malicious grin. "For a beginner." Josh stood and grasped the bars of the makeshift prison. Testing the strength of the cold wrought iron with a fervent shake he found it didn't give way even slightly. A second more ardent attempt strained the muscles of his forearm. The prison was solid and impassable.

"Let me out of this!" he demanded.

"Temper, temper, Mr Brenin. This is merely a little reminder to respect ones betters." Recalling his newly realised powers a new escape plan took form, though after several futile attempts of imagining the bars to be made of Styrofoam he realised his powers were no match for Galda's.

"What's wrong? Uncomfortable with your sexuality?" Josh ridiculed his captor, but the verbal attack went uncontested. The black clad ghoul grinned.

"I think that will be all for today," Galda replied and grasped his iron creation to peer at the trapped dreamer inside. "Are you ready to return?"

"And I thought we were just getting started here." His tone held its sarcasm and defiantly he sat down on his own chrome framed creation. "Plus I'm starting to like it in here, it's cosy." His confidence had grown throughout the ordeal he now considered to be the best adventure of his life. He was the child again, glowering at having to leave the fantastical playground.

"Don't worry we are far from done here," Galda admitted gravely, "This isn't the end, merely the beginning. But now you've heard my closing pitch, will you help us?" In all the excitement of playing God he had forgotten the real reason that Galda had brought him to that place.

"You mean help you and your friends overthrow an evil *ultra* terrestrial race of beings from enslaving mankind? Sure what have I got to lose?" Unexpectedly Galda reached in through the bars.

"Your soul!" he roared; his face twisting grotesquely. Josh reeled back from the unexpected advance but in an instant Galda braced his open hand upon Josh's forehead. Clasping the imposing wrist with both hands Josh tried to prise it free from his skull but just like the cage the ghoul's grip was like cold steel. A dizzying sensation then flowed from Galda's palm, making Josh's brain vibrate intensely.

"Wait!" Josh found himself screaming an appeal. He sensed the dream world around him was dispersing, transforming uncontrollably into the nothingness below that rushed up to meet him as the wrought iron hand covered his eyes and continued to push him down into the depths of unconsciousness. Before he knew it, the new world was gone.

Opening his eyes he recognised the open closet through his blurry vision, the morning sun filling the familiar room in which it stood in a warm, welcoming glow. *I'm back*. Josh was back on his bed, he was home and aware that he was fully awake; at least he thought he was. *My head*. Galda's powerful hand was no longer squeezing his frontal lobes but a curious feeling that his brain was expanding out of the top of his skull remained. Half expecting his tormentor to be lurking close by Josh lurched upright in bed, only to find that thankfully he was alone in his room.

A heavy thump on the duvet then made him jump. Samson had bounded onto his favourite bedstead after returning from a night of his own misadventures, the product of which was the small dead bird that flopped from his mouth onto the bed covers, a tribute for the master of the house. Josh gazed in horror at the pathetic corpse while the big cat purred its loud trademark rattle with a look of pride. He was definitely back home. *Did I dream it all?* The definite morning haze of post slumber lethargy hung over his conscious state like a hangover but whether the claustrophobic ride in the black Mercedes, or the tour of Galda's underground layer had been a part of the same dream trip he couldn't be sure. Samson rubbed his face against Josh's arm, another gesture of sentiment that assured him he was home.

"You miss me big guy?" he asked the lovable feline, still squinting in amazement that he was back. The digital face of the bedside clock then caught his attention. It was nine twenty three and already he was thirty eight minutes late for the first day on the job.

Chapter 8

It was fourteen minutes past ten before Josh found himself back outside the bookstore. His new employers on The Mile had instructed him to meet them outside to open up, though being almost an hour and a half late it meant they had been inside for some time. Had the garage fixed his car as promised he could have reclaimed at least part of the lost time but their call to his cell that morning had only confirmed his worst fears. Josh didn't have three hundred and eighty dollars in disposable cash; as a result he'd lied about going over later that day to make payment and hopped back on the next bus to North Glendale.

Reaching for the door handle he noticed the small card advertising the vacancy still prominently taped to the inside of the glass, shrugging off the bad omen he however found it substantiated as the door refused to budge. *What the hell?* He tried again and found the first attempt had not merely been a result of feebleness but thwarted by a deadbolt. He checked his watch again. *It can't be shut.* Above his head the golden eye of Ra gazed down in its condescending glory, a foreboding feeling took hold. With no visible buzzer he wrapped his knuckles hard on the blacked out window.

"Hello?" He knocked again, harder. "Hello it's Josh Brenin, I'm here about the job." After a few moments of uneventful silence he realised the job avert was more than an omen. *Two jobs in as many days. Way to go deadbeat.* Stepping back onto the pavement he scoured the building for a window into the secret world of Mind Matters. Pride wouldn't allow him to take the rebuke lying down but as he concluded there was nothing to gain by forcing himself where he was unwanted he cursed his stupid luck again. Like Adam expelled from Eden he began to retrace his steps. Amidst the roaring traffic and dull concrete buildings an imposing feeling of exile was exaggerated by the vivid nocturnal adventures imprinted on his psyche. His world was falling apart, or worse as he was beginning to fear, perhaps even his mind.

Under the renewed wave of melancholy he walked in the direction of the only other place on the Mile that offered any chance of redemption. Above his head the bar sign *Mike's Place* reflected the sun's glare into his eyes. It was ten thirty in the morning; he had never been to a bar before three pm in his life, though as he walked the short distance to the alleyway entrance beneath it, anything else seemed better than returning home. Besides what better place to bury his sorrows and mull over his dementia he thought. Leaving the lost opportunity behind he walked down to the alley to find its entrance.

Entering the dark establishment he found his instincts about Mike's Place were right. The drinking hole was inhabited by a close-knit society of regulars, but as he strode up to the bar illuminated by garish neon signs advertising the many brands of poison he didn't care. Taking an empty stool at the end of the bar he sat furthest away from the company of the beer-hardened strangers. Behind it a walking advert for steroids purposely took his time to finish polishing the glass in his hand. The barman's heavily muscled arms bulged freakishly out of the Chopper t-shirt that Josh noted was several sizes too small and made his head look similarly minute. Only after finishing the joke with a regular did he walk over to serve the stranger.

"What can I get you?"

"Lite beer," Josh replied bluntly. Uninterested in the young stranger who had wandered into his bar the barman turned to get the drink with a lethargic motion just as Josh felt his cell vibrate in his pocket. As he pulled it out, much to the interest of the middle aged regular studying him through a cloud of cigarette smoke, he saw a text message awaited his attention. The bottle thumped onto the bar.

"Three Bucks," the barman demanded monotonously. Josh pulled out a screwed up ten dollar note from his back pocket and handed it over. The short handed message from Matty read *THANX 4 BAILIN ON ME U JERK. WER DA HELL R U?* He had totally forgotten the aborted dinner date and immediately realised how rude his exit had been. Deferring the inevitable apology he decided to up his order when the barman dropped his change onto the bar.

"Could I get a double JD chaser with that?" The muscle bound attendant gave an irritated look then fulfilled the order from one of the large half drained bottles behind him. Usually such surly behaviour annoyed Josh but he had other things on his mind. Acting impulsively on the back of the text he decided to call Sharon, it was the down times when he missed her most, though after listening to the pre-recorded answer message suggesting he inserted his cell into his backside he hung up.

The barman took the difference in the change from the coins on the bar and left Josh the bronze-coloured spirit in a shooter glass. Draining the small glass he followed it down with the fizzy beer, and forgetting how much an un-cooled bottle of beer reminded him of urine, used the raised head perspective to survey the unknown establishment. A small group of pierced misfits egged on a companion to down a jug of beer though Josh sensed they and the rest of Mike's patrons were far from interested in the stranger in their midst. The bar was a place where people could come to be left in peace, to enjoy a beer or drown their angst in it. Whoever Mike was he owed him his gratitude though as Josh palmed the warm bottle on the bar he couldn't see how any amount of alcohol could drown his own.

The wasted bus ride that morning back up to North Glendale had been an alienating affair. He had taken a seat near the back, not far from where he and Galda had conversed in the dreamscape equivalent. The vivid dream, if that was what it truly was, had been indistinguishable from its real world counterpart, and oddly he thought, perhaps even more lucid than the reality it replicated. Though he knew the one had been a projection constructed from his own memory, translated through his senses via some hyper conscious state, he found its perfection a chilling perception that perhaps the real world was not all it seemed. Galda's fantastical claims came flooding back, the unexpected request for aid and the outrageous mission he had put to him, all amalgamating into the single machination of a lunatic. In the dark, smoky reality of the back street bar in north L.A. it was truly a world away though from the twisted feeling in his gut he knew had not simply been a dream. Material or not, Galda was real, all of it was real. Josh drained the rest of the warm beer and slid the empty bottle away with his fingertips.

The cigarette smoke from the portly middle-aged regular's constant puffing suddenly awoke his own desire for tobacco, but unfortunately he hadn't enough change to treat himself to a pack so settled for a deep breath of the second hand mist. The day seemed so pointless. Even if he stayed in the bar all day, watching the minutes tick away on the *Millertime* branded clock behind the bar, it would still end too soon. Then it would be night time, which meant only one thing.

Nature called. Unlike the opulent amenities of Sebastian's restaurant the men's room in the bar was quite literally a crap hole. Josh ignored the congealed black pool of dried blood splattered on the grimy floor tiles and walked up to the cleanest looking part of the communal urinal. Ignoring the fact that the drain at his feet was damned up with a blood-stained hand towel and a used condom, he took a calming breath of the foul air and finished up a quickly. As he walked away to admire the homemade bandage on his forehead in the blotchy mirror above a basin a pierced misfit entered to relieve himself.

The outside of the bandage had been soiled with a pink tone; still he sided with his curiosity and risked its removal. To Josh's surprise the wound underneath was neither moist nor bloody. As the final sticky edge stretched his skin as it was torn free he was pleasantly surprised with what it revealed. From behind the misfit watched the delicate operation with interest while he peed. Spotting his turned head in the mirror Josh ignored the unwanted audience that grinned back at him. Though the tattooed oddity finished up after blowing him a mocking kiss in the mirror Josh remained on edge as the men's room door swung shut after him. *Freak.* Instead of casting the soiled Band-Aid dressing into the nearest urinal he looked around for the wastebasket, which he found was under the dented condom vendor. A sudden chill made him flinch. Unfortunately the distance to the open bin proved too far for Josh's pitch and the dressing fell short.

"They've found you," the woman's voice declared. Josh spun around forgetting the dressing.

"Looks like so have you!" he stated back. For a second time the blonde haired Angelica had stealthily made her way into his company and the keen attempt to corner him made him feel endangered. Without warning she strode up close, making Josh back up against the basin. Her crystal blue eyes studied his like a hungry predator.

"You have walked amongst them on the other side!"

"The other side of what?" he asked sarcastically. "Sanity?" Her fair skin creased around her incensed eyes as she scowled.

"This is no time to play coy," she instructed threateningly. "Have they promised you the world Joshua?" Normally he would have considered such close proximity to an attractive woman an exciting prospect but instead felt genuinely intimidated by her tenacity.

"Angelica right?" he asked calmly. "I think you need to back off here. This whole stalker thing is getting old, so I'm asking you nicely, leave me alone." He spoke the last words as coldly as his nerves could muster though he sensed they had little or no affect. Careful not to startle him, Angelica slowly extended her arm and held out the palm of her hand so that it hovered a few inches from his forehead. "What are you doing?" he asked nervously, his own arms jittering from the fight or flight response surging into them.

"Don't move," she ordered. Her eyes revealed her concentration as the hand radiated a warmth from the exposed palm. After a few seconds she retracted the hand, her ethereal eyes then studying the skin above his brow.

"What is it?" he asked. As her scrutinizing eyes suddenly expanded in horror his spine turned to ice. "What's wrong?" Angelica took a step back from Josh, her gaze fixed to his forehead. The repulsion apparent on the young woman's face seemingly prevented an answer as she continued to step away from whatever iniquity it was that she could see. "Answer me!" he demanded.

"You ARE one of Them," she announced, still staring at his forehead. "You're one of Them," she repeated. Distracted by her reflection in the dirty mirror he turned to stare at his own. For a few seconds it was there, but no sooner had he seen it then the mark disappeared.

"One of them!" Josh exclaimed with equal disgust, Angelica's judgement condemning him with an icy denunciation that made him feel soiled. He had defiantly seen it. The mark upon his forehead had been there. He went to touch the warm perspiring skin of his forehead but it was too late as the black mark had already disappeared. Josh looked back to Angelica to see she now stood with her back to him, the faceless, ghostly posture adding to the dementia of the scenario. "What was that mark? What does it mean?" he pleaded with his now taciturn companion. Vigorously he wiped the sweat from his forehead with the back of his hand, wiping away the dirt, wiping away whatever had contaminated his body and soul.

"You want to know what it is?" Angelica asked ominously. "It is your death warrant!" The last words exploded from her twisted mouth. Before Josh had time register them he saw Angelica's white gown transform into black before his eyes. As the temperature around him suddenly dropped she spun back around to reveal her eyes had mysteriously glazed over with a shiny silver cataract. Before the macabre vision could take root an intense bolt of pain then pummelled into his chest. The bullet-like force sent him flying backwards into the vendor machine. No sooner had the flash of white light created by the tremendous blow vanished from his vision he was then aware of being grappled and heaved him up from the floor where he fell.

There was another flash of pain as the back his head collided with the wall. Josh opened his eyes to discover he was now being pinned up against the damp wall tiles; his numb legs dangling loose a foot above the floor. He looked down to see the chest crushing force holding him up was Angelica's arm. At first he had thought the violent attack had come from some second unseen individual, but looking down into the contorted face he saw his terrified reflection in the mirrored eyes and knew he had made a terrible miscalculation.

A plea for mercy went unsaid as the super human force began to slowly crush the life from him, dazed and in agony his hands grappled pathetically against his attacker's. The next thing he was aware of was being momentarily airborne again. Not content with a brutal asphyxiation Angelica had sent him soaring across into the mirror. After a split second of freedom there was another flash of light as his head crashed into its mottled surface, followed by the agony of falling hard onto the greasy tiles of the men's room floor for a second time.

There was nothing he could he do to defend himself. Disorientated and battered he was at the mercy of the angel of death who preyed on him with an inhuman aggression. For an instant he thought he saw Sarah, her warm hazel eyes, laughing and joking as she always had been, though as his blonde haired assailant rolled him over onto his back he was rudely woken from the hallucination.

"The light will always prevail!" Angelica roared triumphantly and he looked up at her black form. Blood was running into his eye but he blinked sufficient enough to make out the long, metallic blade that her forearm had transformed into. Her knee then crushed his chest painfully, needlessly pinning him down as she raised the double-edged blade to deliver the final blow. *Sarah.*

"What the hell?" a man's excited voice echoed off the tiled walls. Someone else out of view had stumbled into the violent scene. Distracted from finishing her lethal task Josh looked on as Angelica turned angrily to face the intruder. With a dismissive wave of the blade he was aware of the man's sudden flight from the doorway and his subsequent crumpled landing in the urinal. The last thing Josh heard was the muffled cracking of vertebrae. The last thing he saw was the blonde haired assassin look down and grin, her fair hair hanging loose about her face, and then there was darkness.

*****

Josh was keenly aware of being conscious again but still the blackness remained. At first all he sensed were the voices, angry voices shouting down at his lifeless body. Opening his eyes the first thing he saw was the bloody tiles. *My blood.* The tiles were then whisked away as his body was hauled from the ground and his head pulled back by the crowd of strangers. Held up from the ground, defenceless as a new born baby, a man shouted abuse into his face but the words failed to pierce his disorientation. His head felt numb and the sound of the people mobbed around him was nothing more than a muffled roar of indecipherable yells. As the crowd jostled him back and forth like a favourite toy he suddenly remembered where he was. *What's happening to me?* Through blurry eyes Josh saw a man point his finger accusingly at him before desperately trying to gain access to the men's room. The harsh fluorescent light bounced off the many shiny piercings in his enraged face but the enraged misfit was kept at bay by the squad of heavy handed men who then tried to manoeuvre Josh past the angry mob and out of the door.

Suddenly he became aware of a familiar voice amongst the confused babble. It was that of a young man's and his confident, streetwise tones were confronting the goons man-handling Josh away from the scene. Josh turned a bleary head towards the voice speaking in his defence, catching a glance of the boyish face as he shouted his reassurances into Josh's ear. He tried to reply, speak out against the furore but all he could manage was a vegetated slur. As he looked over his shoulder to his liberator his eyes stung. Blinking his profusely he tried to clear the sticky substance blurring his vision though could only catch a glimpse of a small crowd near the urinal.

"What's going on?" he managed to slur. The crowd were also surrounding another immobilized person. As they rolled him over the unnatural angle of the man's head filled Josh with dread.

"Get him out of here!" another man then shouted near Josh's ear. There was sudden jolt as he was forcefully ushered through the crowd of onlookers, their gaping expressions passing him by as the muscle bound entourage wrestled him out of the men's room back into the bar. To his right he recognised the big escort as the surly barman, whose agitated features suggested he was taking the stranger away from the limelight and out of public scrutiny.

Josh fell to his knees, the pain enough to emphasise the dark smoky interior had been swapped for the bright sunlight of the alleyway. Invigorated by the clean air, his senses began to recalibrate and he became acutely aware the two men were standing over him, like two soldiers deciding how to interrogate a prisoner of war. Alone, hurt and bemused Josh couldn't bring himself to look up at them. The young man's voice intervened again. After a quick ruckus with the two men Josh felt a foot slam into his ribs before a more slender build clumsily heaved Josh onto his feet and ordered him to walk.

"Tell me what is going on?" Josh pleaded through the chest pain, his feet finally finding their ground.

"You were about to be turned over to the cops! That's what buddy." The familiar voice eluded identification, though in the ensuing escape from the claustrophobic entanglement its identity was the last thing on his mind. As Josh tripped on an uneven slab his amiable liberator kept him on his feet. From the whirring rush of vehicles around them he guessed he was back on The Mile.

"The cops! Why?" His vision was returning in one eye, the other remaining congealed.

"For killing that freak back there!" his new companion exclaimed. "Lucky for you I came in to drain the lizard when I did. They were ready to tear you apart" As he rubbed his sticky eye he remembered the pierced man on the floor. *Dead?*

"I didn't touch that guy. I was attacked," Josh explained.

"So I see. Believe me it ain't a pretty sight. You gonna make it Brannigan?" The penny dropped.

"Dink?" he asked surprised.

"Who else white collar boy?" his liberator confirmed, his voice strained from supporting Josh. "This is getting to be a habit; me saving your ass, that is." In the ongoing escape the feebleness in Josh's legs began to ebb away and he found he was able to make the fast walk without relying so much on his ex Eat-A-Lot colleague. Cocking his head he recognised Dink's grinning features through his good eye.

"What the hell are you doing here?"

"I'm your guardian angel baby, God sent me!" Josh ignored the stupid answer, before bumping into a street bin.

"I can't see."

"It's just a bit of blood; you'll be fine. We're here." Dink edged him towards the curb as he slid open a side door and urged Josh into the back of a van. "Watch your head!" The outside world was shut out as the door slammed shut at his side and Josh found a makeshift seat in the form of an upturned beer crate. A strong smell of diesel then filled Josh's nose, producing a bout of nausea, and in the search for more comfortable seating his arms and legs only knocked over various boxes and crates. *What am I in a dumpster?* The driver's door slammed shut as Dink jumped in. After rummaging in the glove box he leaned into the back to offer Josh a rag.

"Here, it ain't what you call super clean but it's all I got."

"What the hell happened to me back there Dink?" he demanded to know as he took the bandana.

"You tell me! Hold it out." Josh tried to find the source of the blood and found the gash on his head had reopened. "Hold it out!" Dink instructed a second time then held out a plastic bottle.

"What is it?" Josh asked as he felt the liquid from the tipped bottle wet his hand.

"Something to kill the bugs. God knows what's lurking in those piss pots! Try it." Josh dabbed the sodden cloth to the gash on his forehead. It reeked of an alcohol-based spirit and caused a stinging sensation on contact, making him wince. The reaction amused Dink as he decided to down some of the improvised anaesthetic.

"I gotta get home," Josh said, still unable to open his eye.

"You look like crap Joshua. I tell you what I'll take you to my place its closer. Get you cleaned up first." He suspected Dink didn't know for sure whose place was nearer; the cheery young man had made the offer merely as a common courtesy. Dink turned in his seat to start up the van, the rumbling diesel engine sounded haggard.

"I'm okay, really, just drop me off."

"Not on your life," Dink stated as he revved the old van into life. "Besides looks like someone is taking an interest in your handy work." The distant howl of police sirens began to echo up the street and Josh was suddenly glad to be concealed inside the back of the dank, inconspicuous vehicle. Back at the bar Josh knew he had not been responsible for whatever had befallen the tattooed misfit, it had been Her. Whatever he was in the middle of was now following a more drastic path and he knew no amount of pleading with the authorities to the point could help his defence.

"Time to rock and roll amigo." Dink waited for the flashing black and whites to race past before slowly taking off in the opposite direction. Josh steadied himself against a metal toolbox, daunted by the possibility that the only place where he could seek answers, and asylum from arrest, was under the wing of his nemesis. The black clad ghoul and his cronies were above the law. It was because of their association that Angelica had dried to impale his head. *Did he put the mark on me?* Josh remembered the long murderous blade Angelica had wielded. For what it was worth he was suddenly glad he knew Galda Vey.

*****

Ben tried to avoid swallowing for a second time but the oral manoeuvre was too awkward to pull off convincingly. He was finding it hard to resist Calisto's smiling eyes. His instinct told him that Monk was a cold fish, under his holier-than-thou persona he was nothing more than an unseasoned idealist. But as the red haired woman watched him swallow the little blue pill for real her crystal eyes resonated the deeper sincerity of someone who had experienced both the yin and yang of the mortal coil. Ben handed the empty glass back to Calisto and resumed his seat on the bed.

"So what now? You watch me fall asleep and shave off my eyebrows or what?" Ben joked and leant back onto the white duvet. He had spent enough time with his captors now to feel relaxed enough to reveal some of his self-assured character. After weeks of running away from his dreams he no longer felt as though there was anything to fear, only to learn.

"We wait," Monk replied as he sat back down in the wicker chair. "And we will see" He crossed his legs, adopting the pose of an academic readying himself for a class with a promising student.

"So what about you two? You don't need any wonder drugs is that it?" Though he felt more at ease Ben still wasn't comfortable with the idea of sitting in front of two strangers as they waited for him to pass out. Voluntary vulnerability was not something a hardened soldier could succumb to easily, and secretly he hoped to thwart the effects of the drug by maintaining an intense dialogue.

"Sleepeze is only a stepping stone," Calisto added. "Once your mind learns to bridge the gap between this plain and Dreamscape, its consumption is no longer necessary."

"Kind of like riding a bike?" Ben offered dryly.

"Precisely, you'll never forget." He wondered what period of time was required before the brains adaptive memory cells could recall the magical skill without the aid of chemicals, though not wanting to appear naïve he kept the thought to himself.

"It is different for everyone," Monk declared. Ben looked stumped. "You were wondering how long it took to learn the skill of auto projection." Ben said nothing and blanked his mind fearing the pony tailed Monk was reading his thoughts. "Some people take days, some weeks or even months, but for most the years of materialist toil create a spiritual prison so absolute that they are powerless to escape, leaving their brains totally incapable of adapting to the new, higher level of existence."

"And for a Nothos?" Ben asked, remembering the foreign terminology.

"For a Nothos it is as easy as falling off a log!" Ben's head slumped forward. Instinctively he heaved it up again fighting the oncoming affects of the drug though from the smile on Monk's face he guessed he wasn't far from going under. Calisto placed a slender hand against the soldier's face.

"Don't fight it, relax," she said edging him to lie back.

"So are you coming along for the ride?" Ben asked as his head fell onto the pillow, unable to prevent the mischievous smile that crept across his face.

"Not this time, Monk will show you the way home."

"Home?" he asked lethargically. Before answering a new presence made Calisto turn quickly away. From the corner of his bleary eye he watched Monk rise quickly from the wicker seat to greet the latecomer.

"Is it done?" Monk asked the new arrival solemnly. Ben was quickly falling into a deep sleep but tried to hold onto the last conscious vision, Calisto's body however obstructing him from seeing the newcomer's face as he laid semi comatose on the soft bed.

"I was unable to complete the elimination but I made sure the authorities would contain him indefinitely." The voice of the woman's reply was familiar. "Where is the other?" Calisto looked back at Ben who continued to fight the affects of the powerful sedative, then moved aside so that the female arrival could get a better look at the incapacitated ex soldier.

"We were just about to begin his conditioning," Calisto explained. Ben didn't like the last word of the explanation but it didn't matter as he realised why he hadn't heard the door opening. Angelica stood in the mirrored doorway. He thought at first her to be standing in front of it though as his lumbering brain deciphered the vision he saw that she was actually standing behind the mirror's glass. She locked eyes with him as her white dressed form then glided through the mirror's surface and entered the brightly lit room. The sudden burst of adrenaline the sight produced was enough to delay the sedation.

"The Brenin Low Grade wore the black mark," she stated, walking up to the bed to inspect Ben as if he might pose some secret threat. "He is lost to us; I had to prevent them from using him against us."

"If you are sure the mark has tainted his heart then you did the right thing", Monk said paternally, though sensing his blonde-haired comrade was hiding some reservation. Returned to her benign form Angelica's mind was no longer influenced by her aggressive duty.

"You did what was necessary. We still have Alpha," Calisto said offering her assurance as she looked down at Ben with a spark of pride. The conversation was becoming distant, Ben's eyes had sealed and only the echoes of the voices now registered in his head.

"But is it the mark that taints the heart?" Angelica suddenly asked. "What if the heart is too strong?" She had preformed her duty according to the code of light, the code of law that governed their sacred cause. If the Low Grade wore the black mark he was to be removed from play like a pawn in an inter-dimensional game of war. But as she stood in the presence of her peers she couldn't explain the uneasy feeling that picked at her soul. The code had not been broken but her dogmatic reliance on it had begun to unravel in the aftermath of her murderous task. *The code is the law.*

"Sister?" Calisto asked anxiously. "Something wrong?"

"Rouse him," she replied abruptly. "And meet me in the Solarian."

"As you wish." With the unyielding instruction Angelica's form then dispersed from the mirrored asylum, leaving Calisto and Monk to administer Ben with the rarely used stimulant.

*****

Josh looked up the dimly lit stairway and wondered if he had the energy left to ascend the steep steps. Dink had parked the battered van with a melodramatic caution then hurriedly bundled his charge into the doorway of his apartment building. Its musty hallway stank of stale urine, making Josh feel he had simply been transported from one grimy establishment to another, but by the time Dink led the way up the dark staircase Josh at least began to reclaim a sense of mental stability.

"My place is on the third floor, you gonna make it?" Dink asked, a little amused at the bloodied straggler following him onto the first landing. Josh ignored the concern.

"What's wrong with taking the elevator?"

"The Super was shot last week," he explained dismissively. "And I can't see anyone else coming to fix it in a hurry." Josh waved his guide on.

"I'm not an invalid just lead the way." He felt tired but not from the physical exertion the harsh steps demanded. The combination of sleep deprivation, grievous assault and mental trauma had all taken their toll on Josh's unlucky body and now it was begging for a chance to switch off and re-energise.

"You know you're one lucky son of a bitch, do you know that?" Dink asked as he continued the climb to the third floor. "There are some crazy bastards out there; I mean you could have been wiped out man."

"Funny you're the second person to tell me how lucky I am to be attacked. I can't say I share everybody's enthusiasm for grievous bodily harm."

"Mind the screw," Dink warned just as Josh's hand brushed the protruding shard of metal on the handrail. As he pulled his hand to safety the sickly smell of iron rose from his clothes. Splattered as he was in his own blood he realised he would undoubtedly look terrifying to anyone they were unfortunate to pass, but the unlit stairway remained thankfully empty. Making the third floor Dink swiftly inserted the key into the flaking door at the top of the stairs, cringed at its creaking joints and then urged his charge inside.

"Welcome to Dinksville!" he announced, shutting the noisy door behind them. Josh took the lead into his new companion's home while Dink put both set of latches and several chains into position to ensure their privacy. *Must be a great neighbourhood.* Josh shuffled his blood stained sneakers across the bare floorboards as he sulked around randomly placed boxes and crates to the centre of the barely furnished room, quickly surveying the squat Dink called home.

"It ain't much but it's mine," Dink said joining Josh in the open lounge that consisted of a tired looking couch and a small TV perched on a derelict washing machine. "Sorry about the mess it's the maid's day off," he kicked an empty beer can away, "It's not much to look at I know but it's cheap, keeps the rain off my head and even the cockroaches feel at home."

"Cosy," Josh said sardonically. He particularly admired the strips of sun-bleached wallpaper hanging from the tired walls but did his best not to show the lack of enthusiasm. "Where's the bathroom?"

"Through there buddy, I'll get us some drinks; you're thirsty right?" Dink disappeared through the hanging beads covering the doorway into the kitchen as Josh manoeuvred to the door in question. "Give it a shove!" Dink then shouted. The odd instruction became clear when he found the bathroom door offered resistance to his first attempt to open it, though the second more ardent attempt remedied the problem. He entered the cramped, tiled room and bolted the door. "And don't get blood all over my stuff!" Dink's muffled voice ordered from the kitchen.

Josh took one look at the dirty sink and wished he had followed his instinct to go home. The vinyl floor was also littered with soiled towels and clothes, leaving him little choice but to stand on the damp rags as he saw his bloodied reflection for the first time. As he looked at the grotesque mask that resembled Josh Brenin he felt his heart fall again like a bowling ball of a skyscraper. Smearing away the damp fog from the mirrored cabinet's surface he saw the streaks of scarlet tar that decorated his pale skin to make him look like the walking dead.

"Do you wanna a beer?" Dinks distant voice asked. "I've got beer, cold ones to." Josh studied the fresh wound on his forehead and wished for a nurse instead. He spotted a towel hanging from a dull metal loop to his left and wrenched it free to douse it in the water that gushed from a squeaky tap. Applying the sodden towel in nervous prods he hoped to remove the dried crust and reveal the unblemished skin underneath. It took several more anxious dunkings of the towel before the congealed goo began to relinquish that which it stubbornly hid, though eventually the reassuring unblemished white below the crimson gore appeared little by little. Back in the kitchen Dink shrugged off Josh's silence, popped the lid from a bottle of beer and greedily guzzled the icy liquid.

"You know the Super, God rest his fat ass, already had me down as a dealer or a hood or something. Had he seen you coming in here like that he would have freaked." He finished the bottle and reached for two more before closing the fridge. "How's it looking? You still in one piece?"

"Gimme a minute," Josh hollered back. He had begun the slow, wearisome task of freeing his sore eye from the coagulated glue. It was a tedious operation but the cold, damp towel felt good against his bloodshot eyeball and thankfully made light work of the hideous ordeal. Taking time out he stared into the hollow eyes looking back from the mirror. *What's happening to you Joshua Brenin?* Against a sudden onset of light-headedness he closed his eyes and focused on the past.

The rising sun was warming his elbow as it protruded from the passenger window. Brought into the moment by the pleasant recollection Josh looked out to the sun-drenched streets of downtown as they passed him by. *The morning of the crash.* Not the best choice he thought, but to his left Sarah drove, chatting in the buoyant manner she had always done.

"Remember Josh," her voice suddenly said, turning grave. "The light will always prevail." In his mind's eye Josh turned to query his wife's pronouncement though to his shock found Angelica's silver eyeballs glaring back at him. Before he could react she swung the long shiny blade to his throat.

"You still alive Whitey?" Dink's query roused Josh from the macabre daydream. "There's a lonely looking beer with your name written on it out here." Dink could hear the running water gushing into the basin and guessed the clean up detail must be monumental. He thought he heard Josh whimper. "Can I come in?" he asked. The tap was then turned off and the door given a brusque tug inwards.

"I'm almost done," Josh said as he gave his face the final cleansing with a double handed rub down of his face. Dink edged the door wide open to let the daylight fall onto Josh's battered features.

"Jeez, look at that. Anyone for Pepperoni?" he joked.

"Sorry about the mess, I'll pay for a new one."

"Screw the towel it's not even mine. What about the uh…" Dink pointed to the wound. Josh had managed to clean away the dried blood but the open gash on his forehead continued to ooze a pink syrup from its crater.

"It's going to need the stitches put back in but I'll live. I couldn't find any gauze"

"That's because there ain't none. Hold these." Dink gave him the two opened bottles then reached in to open the mirror door of the cabinet. "I've got some medical tape which I swiped from the Eat-A- Lot first aid kit, but can you believe it, no frigging Band-Aid."

The profane confession was answered by the sound of the two bottles smashing onto the floor. Dink turned around expecting to see his bewildered guest making a second apology. Instead he saw Josh lying unconscious on the floor in a growing puddle of beer.

*****

Calisto and Monk guided the stooped figure out of the mirrored sanctuary and back through the unlit corridor. Though sensing they had re-emerged back into the large clustered expanse that had acted as his interrogation room, the second pill's painful side effect however now prevented Ben from appreciating the collection of oddities and furnishings it contained.

"It will pass," Calisto's soft voice assured him through the apparent discomfort, though he doubted it would soon enough. The fiery sensation that incapacitated his eyes felt worse than any chemical attack he had endured as part of his Delta Force training. Like a newly made war widow the tears streamed down his cheeks, drenching his face but failing to cleanse his eyes of the offending agent that was internal rather than external in origin.

His leg brushed against an ornate chair with a high carved back of untreated wood. Ben made the brief recognition through the watery blur of his vision and guessed the vast room was a showcase for the extravagant furnishings, but there was no time to appreciate the mystery handiwork as he was quickly bundled down another passageway and onto a fire escape. The weight of his floundering body made the metal stairway rattle, a wave of fresh air alleviating his fiery symptoms enough for him to concentrate on speech.

"What have you done to me?" Ben asked, wiping his tear soaked face in his sleeve as Monk freed an arm. "If this is your idea of a *dream* you guys are in serious need of a shrink."

"We only use the stimulant when it is absolutely necessary," Calisto explained, grasping his elbow as she guided Ben down the stairway. "The cool air will ease it until it passes." He let himself be led by the petite woman, though sensing he was near to the ground he over compensated and stumbled on the last step.

"It isn't bad enough you people torture me in my dreams, you have to torment me while I'm awake!" he cursed. She was right, the cool air had dampened the debilitating burning and after squinting away the last of the tears he was able to catch a glimpse of remorse in the red-head's pale features as she checked his fall with a slender arm. "What the hell is the Solarian?" Ben then demanded to know. Calisto's compunction turned to surprise as she realised the partially sedated giant had registered the word through the hazy effects of the Ketron sedative. Pausing their progress, she remembered his mind was the astute and disciplined one of a professional soldier.

"Why don't you see for yourself," she offered mysteriously then gestured back up the adjoining alley. Up ahead Monk strode on, his lengthy ponytail wavering down his back as he paced gracefully in front of them. At first all Ben saw was a back street littered with refuse and dumpsters. Though his face was soaked in tears his vision had returned in their recession, still he saw nothing out of the ordinary. Sensing his short-sightedness Calisto looped an arm through his own and resumed her guidance. Before Ben could voice his confusion Monk strode up to a large silver RV parked at the far end of the alley.

"A van?" Ben exclaimed as they joined their escort by the huge people carrier. The obvious comment made Calisto smile. As she retracted her arm Monk, who was keeping guard with a stern upwards survey, looked back from the surrounding rooftops with a look of mock bemusement.

"What did you expect Alpha?" he queried sarcastically. "A spaceship?" Monk revealed his perfect set of teeth in a large grin and tugged back the RV's side door. "Hop on board, your chariot awaits." Though not used to mockery without reciprocating with physical retribution Ben swallowed his pride and stepped up into the vehicle's doorway and hauled himself in.

As Monk jumped in behind, Ben took a convenient seat above the wheel arch to his left. Sitting with his back against the side of the refurnished RV he was surprised by how much larger the interior appeared, but far from being an open storage vehicle or simple people carrier he could see from the range of electrical equipment imbedded into its structure that he was now in the obscure militia's mobile command centre. *Bingo*. During a variety of special ops tours in the Far-East Ben had seen plenty of advanced Intel and Com rigs, though nothing like the set-up that he was now privy to, the most ambiguous feature being the two space age reclining seats mounted in the centre of the windowless vehicle.

"Are you sure you won't come with us?" a woman's voice asked out of nowhere. Its source became apparent as the reclining seats swivelled around to reveal one was occupied by Angelica.

"You know me I'm a creature of habit," Calisto replied as she stood outside the waiting RV. "I prefer the home comforts." Angelica, though looking weary, smiled warmly at the reply.

"Send them our regards sister," Angelica replied enigmatically. Calisto smiled back at her blonde comrade, then caught Ben's lost look.

"You not coming along for the ride?" he asked again, this time with sincerity.

"There is something I must do first, look after yourself. All of you," Calisto added gravely before taking a step back. Standing on her own against the backdrop of the city alley she appeared all the more fragile to the ex soldier, much unlike her more austere colleagues. Calisto's seeming frailty and warm manner had sparked an unexpected connection in Ben's tormented heart and suddenly he felt it strained by their parting of ways.

"It's what we do," Monk stated matter-of-factly. "Merry meet merry part." Offering a respectful nod he slid the door shut, severing Ben's parting glance. As the RV's engine rumbled into life the soldier felt the cumbersome but agile vehicle take off to its unknown destination, and his questionable future.

*****

The late morning sun flooded into Josh's bedroom through the half opened blinds. Woken gently as it warmed his exposed legs he stretched his arms out across the ruffled duvet, forcing the sleep from weary muscles and rose slowly onto one elbow to survey the homely sight. The trousers he had discarded onto the floor before beginning the night's passionate adventure had now been placed tidily onto the bedroom chair. Recognising his lover's domestic compulsion produced a smile on his face. The sudden aroma of bacon and eggs then made his stomach growl abruptly as it drifted in from the hallway. Kicking the duvet away Josh scrambled to his feet and followed the delectable sizzling to his kitchen, where he found the pretty brunette standing over his stove.

For Josh there was nothing sexier than a naked woman concealing her mystique in one of his own shirts, especially as this particular sexy woman had vowed to be his until death did them part.

"So how would you like it this morning?" Sarah asked, sensing her half dressed husband was admiring her from the kitchen doorway. Josh had hoped to sneak in and surprise her, though happily settled for sliding his arm under the shirt and wrapping his arms around her slender abdomen.

"Is that a decent question to ask a half naked man at this time of the morning?" he joked, nuzzling his face into her loose hair. He never tired of his wife's scent and took in a deep intoxicating breath.

"Only half naked!" she joked back, feigning disinterest as she continued to slide the bacon in the hot oil with the chrome tongs. "What use is a man in clothes to a young woman?"

"Well I'm sure I could remedy that if you come back to bed." Sarah turned around in his arms, seductively pressed her body close and placed her arms around his neck.

"Don't you want your eggs my darling?"

"The only thing I want to put inside my mouth right now is you," he replied. Holding her tight he kissed her ardently on the mouth. "Sunny side up." The hunger in his stomach was quickly replaced by another and he reached around to turn off the stove.

Playfully Sarah broke away from the amorous embrace and ran back through the house to the bedroom. His pulse racing Josh followed suit and found his spirited mate poised on all fours on the exposed mattress. As he pounced to seize her however she unexpectedly counter moved by pulling the fallen duvet up over his head. Under the makeshift trap he heard her muffled giggle, followed by the sound of the closet door being tugged open. Tossing the heavy duvet away the swaying of recently disturbed shirts on the closet rail revealed her bolthole. *Hard to get, huh?* Unable to contain the heated expectation of laying his hands on Sarah's warm body Josh followed the trail, only to find the cold smooth surface of a corridor floor as he stumbled through to the other side.

In the lingering excitement he still expected to see his wife's spirited form running playfully away.

"Sarah!" he called, his voice echoing off the shimmering walls, though as he recognised the long deserted passageway of doors he suddenly realised she had never been there at all. He was back.

Behind him the door marked with the number seventy four was still ajar but he knew there was little point in ducking back inside the dreamscape closet. None of what he had seen, or now saw, was real. The sudden chill exuding from the austere surroundings reminded him of his nakedness; quickly he remembered what he had learnt by imagining himself fully clothed. The dream world complied with a satin shirt, corporate suit, pants and handmade leather shoes, his proficiency at mastering the formative skill also going some way to instil a new confidence that made the once lonely walk to the ominous door at the end of corridor all the less daunting.

As he approached it, his shoes creating a confident soundtrack of rhythmic echoes on the burnished walls, he noticed for the first time that unlike the others it was marked with a strange emblem rather than a number. He didn't need to wait till he closed the gap before recognising the unusual mark, for it was the same black character that had mysteriously appeared and disappeared on his own forehead. The neon blue light escaping through the opening door then pushed the realisation to the back of his mind. *Home sweet home.*

Except for the number of individuals who were busily employed and unperturbed by his entrance the blue room was just as he recalled. At the far side of the wall-less expanse, Galda Vey stood, overseeing his black clad subordinates as they performed their clandestine duties upon a full gathering of recruits sat in the semi circle of reclining chairs. With hands placed on unwitting shoulders his lurking *tutors* were simultaneously restraining and coordinating their slumbering charges from behind, whose mirrored eyes absorbed the apocalyptic images from the holographic display before them. Amongst the civilian test subjects were men and women of varying ages, though none looked older than middle age Josh could see no race, creed or body type was impervious to selection for the secret army that sat comatose and oblivious to their manipulation in the illusory training facilities.

As Galda had stated the body was just a shell. It was the soul of a person that determined a person's strength, and the alternate reality of dreams provided the perfect vetting ground. Seeing the covert operation through the sober eyes of a spectator now made it appear all the more inhuman, filling Josh with a new sense of iniquity and guilt. *I'm a part of this now.*

Galda turned to see the concerned look on the new arrival. As he made his way over to offer his paternal company Josh was the first to speak.

"What are you doing to them?" he asked without turning to his shades sporting tutor. He knew the mental hijacking did not exist in the real world as he understood it; still he needed a rational justification for the unholy venture.

"Such direct schooling was ultimately unnecessary for you," Galda explained subtlety as he gazed back proudly to his legion of dream manipulators. "They however," he then referred to the press ganged collection of dreamers, "Must learn to adapt to their new level of consciousness, or as we now know it, reality." Josh found it hard to accept that a dream could be reality but let him continue. "Reality is defined by consciousness Joshua. But even though these Low Grades are near ready to aid us, they will never be truly *awake* like you or I."

"So what does that make us?" Josh asked cagily, holding back his frustration. The luminous blue light reflected from the lenses of Galda's shades, making his implication harder to interpret.

"We are the Elite," he replied with a conceited grin. "Welcome aboard."

"I didn't take the pill, why am I here?" Josh asked, suddenly finding the situation overwhelming. As though the question's lack of insight irritated Galda he took several paces towards his occupied colleagues then turned to face Josh.

"The Ketron complex acts as a bridge. After a period of time the mind learns, as it does with all repetition, how to recreate the crossing without the need to re-ingest the complex. As we see you are a quick learner, a natural." The disembodied display continued over Galda's shoulder, making it harder to concentrate on his words. Josh tried to blank horrific images from his mind. "The question is Joshua, are you ready to take the next step?"

"How can anyone be ready for this?" Josh blurted as his doubts began to seep back into his soul. "How am I to know when I am really awake for Christ's sake? Two worlds, one mind. This feels so wrong."

"Disorientation is to be expected but I assure you this world is very real. Like the many radio broadcasts flying through LA's airspace, different plains existing at different frequencies can cohabit the same physical space. Think of this as the premiere station. Right here, right now, you are more *alive* than ever before."

"Wait…so there are more of these plains?" Josh asked cynically. "So why this one? Why here?" An image of panic stricken Asians being burnt to ash in a thermo nuclear blast temporarily distracted Josh.

"This dreamscape exists at a higher frequency than your nine to five, twenty-four seven world. Above it there are a further six higher plains, each on ascending frequencies, the fifth being the highest that can be infiltrated by those currently tied to a mortal body."

"The Leviscape," Josh stated as he focused his eyes away from the continuing carnage projecting from behind Galda.

"Correct, the land of light!" Galda proclaimed with a sardonic wave of the hand. "Do you like you're new watch?" The question stumped Josh. He followed Galda's gaze to his wrist and looked down to the counterfeit timepiece that had mysteriously returned to its owner. Josh raised his arm to inspect the gold look Rolex. Even in the unnatural blue haze he could make out the small chip on the glass where he had cuffed it against the handle of his front door.

"Nice try but mine was stolen."

"Yes an unfortunate night by any standards but here is where we make dreams come true," Galda announced, walking closer to Josh. "And I'm not talking about winning the lottery or a lifetime of blowjobs from

Miss June nineteen eighty-four, this is about returning humanity to its core by giving it what it needs."

"And what does humanity need?" he asked sceptically. "Maybe unlimited bank accounts and casual sex is all humanity dreams about." He raised his arm to flash the timepiece back at its creator. "Because that's all *this* is; a dream." With a quick focus of will he made the Rolex disintegrate from his wrist.

"The problem with humanity is that it has forgotten the dream," Galda stated solemnly. "Lust, greed, sloth, apathy, the seven deadly sins if you will, are the destroyers of the dream. The dream is what has been taken from us and our aim is to return it." Josh listened to the sermon and tried to understand how the ghoulish man, or whatever he might be for he remained unsure, was able to take the moral high ground regarding a clandestine operation that undermined the free will of its so called Low Grades.

"So you need my help, to restore this great dream we've all forgotten!" Though he hated to acknowledge it, a niggling curiosity was making Galda's message harder to renounce. But any validation for the subterfuge would have to be damn good. "So enough with the bull, why don't you just show me exactly it is you want from me." Galda walked up and placed his hands upon Josh's shoulders, the unexpected gesture feeling all too paternal for comfort. Josh was unconvinced that his new mentor was really smiling behind the dark sunglasses.

"Now we are ready to proceed," Galda said and turned back to his stooped cohorts who continued their guiding vigil. "Across the US alone thousands of people are unreservedly using Sleepeze in total ignorance of the freedom it offers. Insomniacs mostly, though in essence any form of neurosis or stress disorder is treatable with our wonder drug." Josh followed Galda as he paced behind the other agents, like a drill sergeant inspecting his parading troops. "For every single patient it guarantees the same pay out; the psychological equilibrium that can only come from regular periods of deep, healthy sleep. But for us this is where the wheat is separated from chaff. Under our influence the gifted ones are summoned to this place where they are shown these crude images of abominations, to appeal to their sense of humanity and their duty to prevent it, and thus into aiding us." Between each of the bowed tutors Josh could see the mesmerised faces of the Low Grades as their mirrored eyes absorbed the images and tried to void the thoughts of wrong doing for what could be the greater good. Aware of the conflicting emotions Galda continued the inspection undeterred.

"They *want* to help us Josh. We are not brain washing, we are not forcing them to act against personal moral codes. We are simply appealing to a lost sense of duty, enhancing a natural desire for prevention."

"But they are passive," Josh interrupted. "They are Low Grades because they are not truly awake! How can they really know what they are doing?" Galda came to a halt at the end of the row of metallic chairs and turned to confidently answer the accusation.

"To them it is still only a dream, and it is this which allows us to operate without detection. As I told you before we are known to the Vanir, leaving our kind and our task compromised the moment we project into the Leviscape. Hence the only way to undermine our astral foe is for us to operate undetected via these Low Grade Trojan horses." Galda paced into centre stage in front of the holographic display to continue his animated justification.

"We cannot simply converse with these people," Galda stated, gesturing towards the row of catatonic Low Grades in front of him. "The sensory overload would fracture their under exposed minds. So they must be programmed, over weeks, months, until their unconscious minds accept the unacceptable." Dutifully his black clad peers remained at their posts, stooped like malevolent familiars their eerily pale faces remained fixed on each of their charges, leaving Josh to cast judgement unhindered.

"It still sounds all too much like brain washing to me!" he said disdainfully.

"It is direction!" Galda retorted. "Their lives, our lives, *your* life, the fate of mankind is affected by what is taking place here. If only they had your gift! None of this would be necessary." Josh joined Galda centre stage in front of the holographic display. Images of a barren apocalyptic wasteland haunted it now; destruction absolute. He looked up into the morbid representations as the three dimension pictures floated about their faces.

"You still haven't told me why a loser like me is special enough to warrant this wonderful gift."

"Fate. Destiny. Luck. God's will. Take your pick," Galda replied unceremoniously. Josh picked up on the unexpected last suggestion.

"You believe in God?" he asked, expecting a miraculous answer to a subject he had long written off. "Where does God fit into all this?" Galda responded with a shrug.

"All I can tell you for sure is that you are our secret weapon in a war against the Vanir. You who have the astral presence of one of us, but are unknown to them. You can go where we cannot. This is your charge."

"My charge?" Josh exclaimed as the effects of the disembodied images of carnage and misery began to have a disorientating influence. "Whatever you say, dungeon master! Even if I could infiltrate the Vanir's extra terrestrial…"

"ULTRA terrestrial," Galda corrected him.

"Whatever, what's to stop them recognising me as one of you?"

"Before you project into the Leviscape we will lower your consciousness," Galda explained. "And when you reach the heart of their reality you will be able to raise it once more. You will go unknown to them I assure you." Angelica's aghast features then flashed into Josh's mind.

"And what about the mark?" he demanded of Galda, hoping to topple his confidence.

"You mean the Tsadeh?" Galda confirmed as he pointed to his own forehead. The same black symbol Josh had seen appear on his own now materialized upon his tutor's white brow. "We all wear this mark so that we may recognise each other. This is our badge of honour," he pronounced. "Wear it with pride, Joshua. We are the Elite and this is the symbol of our allegiance." The unusual emblem dispersed from Galda's forehead, leaving Josh unconvinced that the hand of fate, destiny or whatever it was that was guiding him along the dangerous path was something that he wanted to give his allegiance to.

"I don't know if I'm ready for this," Josh relented. "Whatever this is, to act as some kind of spook, floating around in the cosmos spying on an inter-galactic race of gremlins. I wish to God this was just some frigging nightmare, and you the result of eating too much dairy products before going to bed. I don't want any of this!"

"Look at the images Joshua, look at them!" Galda's voice returned to his earlier mania. "Do you think mankind wants any of this?" he snapped. Josh looked closely at the untold thousands of stricken faces surrounding him. Lifeless bodies, deathly white as his tutor's, dashed in the familiar dark crimson splatters were being paraded by bestial mobs of men and women revelling in degradation and butchery, the fall of man heralded by catastrophes both natural and unnatural.

"This is the future of mankind Joshua. This is what awaits us if we sit back and do nothing. The Vanir are its beginning and its end. War, pestilence, chaos and genocide, all are their gifts to us. But we have a chance to spurn them once and for all."

"It's just the way of the world." Josh protested. "Just because the world is screwed up doesn't mean that some malevolent force is at the centre of it. It just is!"

"Is it?" Galda asked, his black eyebrows arched high above his shades. "We've been down for so long we don't even realise we can stand up. How can you know what light is if you've lived your whole life in the dark?" The declaration was reasonable but Josh still doubted the intent behind it.

"All of it?" he asked staring once more at the morbid visions. He didn't want any of it to be true but his conscience craved assurance. "They can do all of this?"

"They have and they will continue to do so," Galda confirmed. "We have a choice. We can sit back and accept the *way of the world*, or, armed with the knowledge of truth, we can fight our way out of the darkness." The images disappeared. For the row of Low Grades the show was over and Josh watched their mirrored eyes return to their human but catatonic glaze.

As the other tutors straightened themselves and appeared to see Josh and their superior for the first time a white guiding hand was placed on his shoulder.

"Don't you feel like getting up off your knees and finding your true place in the universe?" his enthused tutor asked him dramatically. "Escape your chrysalis and be reborn as something worthy of claiming residence amongst the Gods. This is our time now Joshua." Galda's hand braced his shoulder more firmly and Josh looked at the eerie pageant of identical crusaders staring back from behind their sunglasses. "Help us to take back what has been denied us since the genesis of our race."

"Liberty and justice for all?" Josh asked ironically, before turning back. "And what about my other stalker? You're not the only ones wanting to be my bosom buddies right now." He had waited until the final pitch before revealing his knowledge of Angelica. Now was the time for answers.

"It was unfortunate that they found their way to you, but not unforeseeable," Galda replied as he let his hand slip away.

"She tried to kill me!" Josh retorted. Angelica's eyes had been silver, Galda and his black legion were gold, and both were equally disturbing and inhuman. "What's to stop them from finding me again?"

"That particular irritation my friend is currently being remedied, for good," Galda announced coldly. "They are renegades," he added, sensing Josh's curiosity. "Feeble-minded hosts to an unholy delusion. Allied to the Vanir they help them to undermine us, but their part in this is soon to come to an end." Josh gazed back to the black clad army of capable individuals supporting Galda in his secret war. "So what is it to be?"

Gradually his self-proclaimed tutor's confidence had instilled the desired empathy. Not only did he offer fellowship, but answers to the greater truths of existence. Josh knew he was dreaming but he had also accepted he felt more alive right then than he had his entire life, acknowledging that his traumatised mind was incapable of creating such a vigorous delusion. Perhaps the world of dreams was the last frontier and the Leviscape the holy grail of spiritual existence? Doubt had clawed at his conscience though it was now smothered by a desire to surrender to the inevitability of fate.

"I guess you'd better show me the way to the yellow brick road." For a second he thought Galda would show some sign of satisfaction. Instead as the catatonic Low Grades stood and filed out of the blue room in an obedient line he guided Josh towards his new ghoulish colleagues; the black clad elite. Now it was show time.

Chapter 9

Ben estimated they were travelling north. The only window that allowed him the necessary viewpoint of the sun's position was directly through the windscreen, but the view from his back wheel arch seat was a blinkered one due to the length of the populated RV. Under the watchful gaze of Angelica who sat facing him, he was only able to sneak the occasional tell tale glimpse when the cumbersome vehicle turned onto a new street. Forsaking the vacant recliner next to her, Monk currently sat crossed legged on the RV's floor. Though his head was turned away Ben speculated from his nemesis pose that he was residing in quiet contemplation, of what he could only guess.

"How are the eyes?" Angelica asked, removing her feet from the chairs stirrups. Ben could tell by the astute look in Angelica's crystal blue eyes that she was aware of his instinctive curiosity, though evidently found it inconsequential. "That caffeine bomb has a real bitch of a side affect." Stopping his sore eyes from darting back to the front of the RV as it turned onto a new street he looked up at the attractive blonde perched on the reclining seat at the RV's centre.

"Better," he replied cagily. "Though a glass of cold water would have done the trick." His eyes were still tender but he didn't like to show feebleness in front of the *weaker* sex as he saw it, and so swallowed his damaged pride.

"If that worked we would have." Relaxing back into the purpose built chair her cool eyes studied the ex soldier. "The wake up call is used in extreme circumstances and only on the strong and healthy. Both counts were in evidence." From the glitter of perspiration on her brow to the slight flush of her cheeks Angelica looked as though she had taken part in some rigorous exercise before their meeting. Ben guessed the art of auto projection was no stress-free adventure and was quietly amazed by the blonde woman's abilities, as well as her appearance.

"What you did back there," he said, referring to the mirrored bedroom. "That was something pretty amazing. How long have you…" He trailed off, a little uncomfortable with the personal question.

"Most of my life," Angelica replied openly. "For a Nothos, perfecting the gift is like learning to walk, except the urge to travel from A to B in the least distance and time is instinctively attained by stepping out of the physical parameters of this world." She raised a hand to her brow and smoothed away the small beads of perspiration with the back of her hand. "However, stressful excursions on the higher plains can also take their toll on the body." Ben felt the RV slow down as it came up to a busy intersection.

"That might be all fine and dandy but how does that make me a Nothos?" he asked sceptically. Angelica smiled.

"The gift, skill, power... whatever you want to call it, develops at a different rate for everyone, though fully manifests for reasons unknown by the age of thirty three." The RV's massive engine revved up again as the traffic began to edge forward. Ben looked back up towards the windshield, reminding himself he was only a year away from the landmark age. The driver's arm appeared from behind the huge high backed chair to shift the gear stick and he caught a glimpse of the arm of a second man in the passenger seat.

"So are they Nothos to?" he asked referring to the as of yet unknown members of the dreamscape militia.

"Hey Jonah!" she suddenly called over her shoulder. "He wants to know if you're a Nothos!" Ben saw the arm of the man in the passenger seat grip its arm rest.

"Hell yeah!" was the man's unexpected response from behind the chair. "Lean, mean and proud to dream!" The RV took off with an unpredicted burst of acceleration. Ben looked back into Angelica's grinning face and wondered what tangible qualifications the small squad really possessed.

"I'll take that as a yes," Ben said dryly. He was starting to see that the squad of spooks as maybe nothing more than a trumped up gang of self trained mercenaries and was bitten again by the bug of apprehension. "So are you going to brief me on the nature of these extreme circumstances that required me to have my eyes burnt out? Or is that classified?" he asked sarcastically. The RV now found a fast moving stretch of freeway Ben recognised would take them to the north of the city.

"To tie up a loose end." Monk spoke for the first time, his stern answer exposing an underlying tension though indicating a certainty that he passed onto Angelica with a dour glance. Saying nothing in reply she swivelled the chair around to face the front, Ben guessing so she could hide a growing apprehension rather than to watch where they were heading. Taking the hint the soldier stretched his long legs and wished he had never laid eyes on the damn blue pills.

*****

Josh followed the Low Grades as they were rallied into an adjoining room lit by an overhead white light that created an arena at its centre. To his left he felt Galda's lingering presence urging him to join the catatonic volunteers as they then formed an orderly line. Finding his own space in between an athletic man in his late teens and a rotund middle-aged Asian woman he became aware of a sense that his mind was drifting from its previous state of awareness. There had been no prep talk, no briefing and no strategic planning of how the inter-dimensional mission was to unfold, yet as he stood with the assorted line of entranced individuals in the light that cocooned them from the surrounding darkness, the tutors remained in the shadows, encircling the mesmerised parade in an archaic ceremonial formation.

Josh tried to focus his mind on what was happening around him, trying to analyse the logistics of the situation and what was to become of him, though as he stood submissively within the line the bright light that blazed from above seemed to drain him of this vigilance. The black clad ghouls around them disappeared from his conscious thoughts as he let himself be taken along with the wave of peaceful radiation from above. With eyes closed his weary mind welcomed the tranquil moment.

"It's time to stand up and be counted," Galda's voice resonated in his mind. He knew he wasn't hearing his mentor's words, for their minds were now bonded by a telepathic link that melded their conscious thoughts. "This is the path you have sought your entire life and now is the time to take your first steps along it," Galda's voice continued, its hypnotic tones instructive but not overbearing. "On this journey you will be like the others. Your mindful state will decrease to be like the others. You will travel in this state as you traverse the path of light onto the Leviscape, from where I will guide you to Hyperborea, the world of the Vanir." Josh took in the words finding them reassuring and alluring, even hearing the name of his destination filled him with an ecstatic elation that he was finding increasingly hard to suppress.

Josh opened his mind to the endless possibilities that were being offered him by his private guide. "Ascending time and space you will not literally travel to your destination, but their will be an intermediate period where your conscious projects and seeks Their world before merging with it. Only then will your conscious state be raised and you able to govern once more." Josh's own thoughts withered from the core of his mind as it emptied and let itself expand into a serene oblivion. "Are you ready for the future?"

"I am ready," Josh replied rashly. If Galda had told him he was about to walk over the edge of a thousand foot precipice it wouldn't have mattered. Josh had given himself over totally to the will of his tutor, he and the Low Grades were ready for anything. Unknown to the peaceful line of recruits their tutor's then raised their arms and focused their will to create a ball of pure light that encompassed the line completely like a giant egg. As they created the luminescent protective chamber, the ethereal power of their collective will channelled by their upraised palms, the dark space before it morphed into a celestial wormhole, penetrating space and time. The sphere of light slowly moved into it, carrying its catatonic passengers along into the spiralling vortex and another dimension.

For a brief moment Josh was aware of travelling at great speed into an unknown trajectory. He was unable to open is eyes but didn't care due to the serenity that encased him in an infallible sense of security.

Then it appeared. Not before his eyes but inside his mind. The image became clearer as he embraced the vision. The sphere of light, surrounding him and the others in a suspended line along its horizontal axis, was being propelled through a celestial tunnel. Focusing his control of this disembodied vision he forced it to escape the confines of the spherical chariot to see that the wormhole extended out between the fabric of the physical universe and towards a distant sun. But as the journey continued at an infinite speed he saw through his soaring foresight that the sun was actually a cluster of nebulas surrounding a vast astral metropolis. The sight was too vast to assimilate at once. Several other small moons appeared in orbit around the vast luminous world that was seemingly both gaseous and animated by a shroud of primal light.

Like a bullet down the barrel of a gun the sphere shot down the tunnel of light towards the centre of the new world. Josh saw that theirs was not the only tunnel but one of countless many that spiralled off like so many celestial highways into infinite black regions. Again spheres of light shot through these inter-dimensional corridors to and from the world of light as though it served as the nerve centre for the very cosmos itself. Fearing that he might become permanently separated from himself Josh drew his vision back down to the sphere, just as it entered the enormous hub of divine light that then enveloped them totally.

The next thing Josh became conscious of was being inside a vast portal that seemed made of the very light that emanated from its interior. The place was a hive of activity and as his conscious abilities began to draw him out of the waking dream he saw that he and his companions were not alone. Small orbs of varying coloured lights flew around them like so many firebugs, appearing and disappearing at random before he could study them properly. He couldn't explain why but he knew they were living, thinking beings that existed and propelled themselves under their own free will. Then he saw the tall ones.

Though humanoid in form they stood four to five feet above the height of an average man, their elongated necks supporting luminous heads aloft above the flux of travellers coming into their world. Like customs inspectors these slow methodical creatures were scrutinising the filing lines of people and beings of light as they passed, reaching out to touch them momentarily before allowing each to proceed in turn. A small ball of light flew manically around the head of one of the elevated gate keepers, though as it raised its elongated arm to touch it with a long, extended finger it paused, and then tamed was allowed to pass. A nervous sense of apprehension crawled up Josh's spine. The overwhelming scenario was waking his senses like an adrenaline bomb, and no more so as the elongated being then appeared at his side.

Before Josh realised it had reached out and touched his chest. He looked up in awe at the placid face that hung above his own. Its crystal eyes were of a violet colour and gazed curiously into his own as its finger seemed to penetrate his torso. Whether shock or the effect of the contact, Josh was momentary paralysed as he stood gazing up into the mesmerising eyes. The violet orbs set in an otherwise featureless face, for he saw no openings for a mouth or nose, revealed no emotion as the luminous creature studied him, exuding a serene integrity as it held him in a hypnotic trance.

It may have only been seconds but for Josh the experience lasted an eternity. *What does it see?* The next thing he realised he was standing in a vast hallway. *I'm in?* He had passed the gateway into Hyperborea and was now seemingly free to roam its unearthly spaces. He looked back expecting to see the lofty creature following him into his guarded domain but behind there was only the influx of newly admitted life forms. He recognised a few of their faces as his fellow travellers, overwhelmed by the fantastical stream of coloured lights that shot from behind and into the world of the Vanir. *This is first contact?* He had crossed the boundaries of time and space and arrived in a place affected by neither. Like some momentous rite of passage Josh felt reborn, akin to Dorothy he had followed the yellow brick road and now stood in the hallowed halls of Oz. The experience with the gate keeper had left a tingling at the centre of his soul though as he stood in that celestial place he understood why his ghoulish tutor and his colleagues would not be welcome. Hyperborea was a realm of light and no place for something at home in the shadows of dusk. Then he remembered he was one of them now and was amazed he had found his way through at all.

Josh looked up to the white expanse that rose above his head. The white light illuminating the interior made it almost impossible to see the vaulted ceiling. It was so high above his head it might as well have not existed, if truly it did at all. The immense hall swiftly reminded him of a celestial airport, an intermediate place where beings gathered before parting ways. Just existing in Hyperborea amongst the light seemed sufficient to those who had made the epic journey, even his Low Grade colleagues had walked on passively to join the many gatherings that appeared to be taking place in the blissful expanse.

He looked on as a slight built young woman whom he recognised as one of the Low Grades went up to a tall custodian. She appeared to welcome the contact with the gangly creature and openly placed her raised arm up towards the creature's mid section. Without query it raised its own slight arm to touch her and the two seemed to enjoy a joining of beings, the open bonding gesture benefiting each of them in some spiritual embrace that was both platonic and mystical. For a moment the two beings, human and Vanir, were locked in a mutual sharing of energies and then parted with a courtly nod of farewell. It was only when Josh looked more intently around that he saw the same divine embrace happening everywhere around him. Human and human, human and Vanir and also the flying orbs of coloured light seemed to share in the activity, leaving Josh with the notion that it all fitted into the grand scheme of oneness, a universal ideal that all living beings were linked to each other by unseen bonds and Hyperborea was the melting pot for this cosmic fellowship.

Not sure he was ready for such personal one to one contact he decided to walk further into the open space, towards the source of interest that drew the small gathering of beings together at different locations. The groups appeared unstable as each member manoeuvred closer to whatever lay at the centre of the crowd. As he approached the outer rim of one such group a faint glow of violet light seemed to radiate from its centre. Respectfully making his way through the placid attendants the flashes of violet light became more apparent. Other humans past him on their way out from the centre and allowed others to step forward and take their place. Josh tactically moved his way in further and was swathed in the growing intensity of a violet glow.

At the source of the interest he found a monolithic crystal that drew each of the attendants like moths to reach out and touch it. As they did so the violet haze would seep out via the extended hand and swallow the arm and body in a nourishing flood of energy. When a sufficient bathing of energy was taken the recipient would let go and turn to leave, radiating a sense of fulfilment. He didn't know why but he panicked. Movement from behind was urging him forward, forcing him to stand firm so as not be pushed too close to the strange crystal that drew its quarry in an eerie ritual, that to Josh resembled a cult-like adherence.

A hand on his lower back gently urged him on. He looked down and saw it was the fragile looking woman who had taken part in the bonding ritual. She looked back with an innocent look of encouragement, her fair skin and sincere expression made her appear virtuous in the haze of violet but he rebelled against the offer and made his way back out of the crowd, feeling elation at avoiding some unknown obligation. Josh checked around him and saw no other being had taken notice at the change of heart. The elongated Vanir stood out above the heads of the human masses but took no notice of the loner who stood bemused on the outskirt of the group. Though he sensed no malicious intent in any of what he had seen a natural apprehension prohibited him from taking part in such outlandish occupations. Then he felt a soft hand take his own.

"Do you remember me?" a woman's voice asked him gently. Josh's gaze followed up from the hand to the young woman's inquisitive face. She had followed him out of the crowd and now sought his attention in a clingy manner that immediately made him nervous. A thick, wavy head of red hair hung loose upon her small shoulders to frame her gentle face, making her look quite at place in the celestial surroundings.

"Yes you are one of us," he replied cagily. The question had been a subjective one but he had sought to shrug off the tender intrusion with an impartial response.

"And who are we?" she asked, cocky her head slightly as she edged to stand face to face with him. "Are you like us?" The woman's sparkling green eyes studied his own.

"We travelled here together," he replied, still choosing to remain impartial. He took another look around, hoping to avoid any third party attention, then back to her own fey-like features. The rest of the Low Grades had been drawn in an obedient fashion to wander the vast hall of light, join in the bonding sessions or seek the violet haze from one of the many crystal monoliths. "Are you awake?" he asked, the question making her cock her head slightly to the opposite side.

"Are you?" she asked suspiciously. It was the only explanation that made sense to Josh and her nonchalant reply merely confirmed that he was not the only elite dreamer amongst the recruits.

"This is a dream," he said, fearing his cover had been blown by his refusal to follow the protocols of visitors to Hyperborea.

"We both know it isn't." The reply was damning and sharp enough to cut through his charade. In hindsight her bonding gesture had appeared more personal and lasting than any other he had seen taking place and now he knew why. *Galda sent two of us.* "Trust me," she then said, raising her hand to touch his chest. Before debating resistance he was filled by a sensation of warmth that vibrated into the centre of his body. The sudden surge of euphoria produced by her actions brought with it an ecstatic rapture, similar to that which he had heard addicts describe their experiences on heroine. Though as she took back her hand the euphoria vanished.

"What did you do to me?" he asked, his body tingling from the rousing experience.

"Joshua I am Calisto," she announced with a new look of certainty, her knowledge of his name astonishing but not surprising. "You have a tumour in your soul," she continued ominously. "It is a ball and chain around your neck and it cages you from finding your higher self. You shouldn't be here." The warning unnerved him but the bemusement it created unsettled him further. After all they were batting for the same earthly side.

"I have as much reason to be here as you, Calisto." He had hoped to make the use of her name sound derogative but he found it impossible to degrade something so seemingly gentle and sincere.

"Don't be so sure of yourself. You wear your heart on your sleeve, which makes your true identity all the more easier to spot. This isn't you Joshua," she pleaded. "You seek the path of light but it has been hidden from you by Them, and now you must return." Josh looked at Calisto and was struck with the realisation that she was not one of Galda's secret dreamscape elite.

"Who are you?" he demanded but the force of the requirement was lessened when he saw that they had become the centre of attention for several of the Vanir, who standing out above the heads of the people they surveyed, now began to make their way towards them.

"There isn't time. Go back to their dreamscape layer but let them learn nothing of this place from you. Only through inefficiency can you discourage their interest." Her plea became more intense as she sensed the Vanir were forming rank around the two humans. "When you return to ground seek me out in the real world. We need you." Over her shoulder he saw the tall, slow moving creature stride up from behind to take a more stern interest, its presence now emanating a new menace that made Calisto's words seem all the more imperative.

"Where will I find you?" Josh asked but the request was interrupted by the sudden decomposition of their surroundings. As though an undeveloped film reel was being exposed their presence began to fade as an intensifying light swallowed their consciousness.

"We are being drawn back," Calisto declared as the hall and its occupants were blanketed in bittersweet nothing. The approaching member of the Vanir was rubbed out just as it reached them, its lofty expressionless face shrouded in the white mist as they were pulled away from the world of the Vanir. "I have a shop in the east side," Calisto's voice resonated in his mind, her form also fading in front of him, voice straining to relay the message in the unexpected withdrawal. "Remember me and tell them nothing!" In an instant Calisto was gone. As her voice trailed off into the brilliant haze that had enveloped them Josh felt it pilfer his grip on that world.

For a brief moment he was aware of being sheltered once again in the sphere of light as it hurtled from Hyperborea, through the Leviscape and back to its creators. As it made the urgent return leg through the fabric of reality Josh tried desperately to hold onto the picture of Calisto's fragile features. *She wasn't one of us, one of the others.* And her candid instruction; *shop in the east side*, but as the slumbering recruits were drawn like flies into the spider's parlour, the Elite's psychic influence eradicated her from his thoughts as their dark dreamscape layer took form once more around them.

The Low Grade scout party was back under direct control of their black clad tutors. Instantly the dreamscape welcome wagon deteriorated into a fast track debriefing of the catatonic travellers. The sphere of light dispersed as the dark recess was replaced by the eerie blue room. Low Grades were re-seated once more in the row of reclining chairs, tutors, eyes golden and menacing, quick to leech onto recruits to drain visions from their heads in a frenzy of psychic pillaging. Through an unshakable haze Josh watched on from his own chrome recliner until he felt the large pale hands brace his head. His turn. Galda's ghoulish face was grinning as it raided Josh's mind and soul, the visions he sucked free nurturing an insatiable need he was powerless to stall. *What is this? No, stop! I want out!* But no sooner had it begun, it was over.

*****

"Josh!" a voice yelled at his face. Waking him from the nightmare he quickly realised it was Dink's. Eyes wide open he stared up into the youngster's concerned features and realised he had just escaped another unpleasant bout in the arena of dreams. "Christ's sake buddy, can you hear me?"

"Yeah, yeah, I'm fine," Josh groaned, ushering Dink away with a limp swipe of the hand. "I just..." He raised his head to find that the soft base he was lying on was the tired looking couch. As his sore eyes adjusted to dank real world of Dink's apartment he realised the blue room was gone, million miles away across the labyrinth of his tortured psyche.

"You just passed out that's what. For a second there I thought you'd had an aneurysm. I was just about to roll you in a rug and leave you in a dumpster!" Dink joked.

"Thanks," Josh replied sardonically. "How long was I out?" His faculties were returning quickly, but so too were the vivid flashbacks of his unbelievable adventure. *It can't be true.*

"Long enough," Dink commented gravely. Brushing some ready meal packaging off the top of a nearby crate Dink took a temporary seat on what had previously served as his makeshift dining table. "I think it's time you saw that Doc," he then stated as the worn out cushions of the red couch made his guest feel as though he was being swallowed alive by a giant mouth.

"No doctors," Josh stated. "I'll be okay I just need some rest, that's all I ever need." His hand sank into the soft cushions as he tried again to haul himself into a sitting position but was forced to abandon the attempt as an unbearable cramping sensation in his head forced him into submission.

"No I'll tell you what Brannigan. You just sit the hell back and relax. Tonight you're staying in the Reinhold Motel, on the house." Over his host's shoulder Josh saw the dark pool of spilt liquid on the bare floorboards.

"No Dink, really I…"

"Here, I saved you one," Dink interrupted, holding out an open bottle. Josh stared at the cheap beer and concluded Dink had dragged him to the couch after he blacked out.

"Try swapping it for a glass of water and some painkillers."

"Funny," Dink replied sardonically and took a big swig from the unwanted bottle. In the reassuring light of a dying sun Josh's nightmares stuck to his conscious thoughts like tar to white satin. From the midst of the ethereal apparitions one thing had scored his mind. *It is the badge of our allegiance.* He touched the cool damp skin of his forehead. At first he thought it had been the letter *Y*, or from recalling Sarah's adherence to astrology during college, the symbol for Aries. But in the clarity of hindsight a niggling sensation made him feel he had seen something like the black mark before, a mystical symbol, a letter from some ancient dialect but he couldn't be sure.

"Time flies when you're having fun eh buddy?" was Dink's flippant response to the strange act. Josh realised apologies and small talk were to be expected but through the half daze of a kick started brain he was far from a participating mood. He slumped his weary head into his upturned palms. "You looked like you were having a good sleep over here." Flashbacks of his celestial journey were now discharging into Josh's minds eye like a torrent of hot lava, scorching his sanity, but he hid his reactions behind the protective wall of his wrists.

"Yeah you could say that," he replied mundanely, massaging his forehead and wishing he was back home.

"A hell of a trip I bet." A wave of second hand fumes blew over his upturned hands. The pungent smell of the rolling tobacco aroused an unexpected bout of nausea in Josh's gullet. He thought about Dink's odd observation for second then dismissed it as a quirk of the young man's streetwise nature.

"Yeah hell of trip," he repeated. There was a pause where Josh sensed a little excitement in his host's shuffling of feet.

"So what was it like?" Josh lifted his head to lock eyes with Dink.

"What was what like?"

"The trip!" Dink reiterated. Josh looked quizzically into his young friend's eager eyes and wondered if he was smoking something a little stronger than tobacco. "Come on Bro, you know what I mean," Dink insisted seriously before taking another big drag from the roll-up. Josh watched its end flare up as the influx of oxygen fed the smouldering light then sat back into the couch to quiz over the accusation.

"I'm not sure I follow."

"Oh come on don't play me like that. This is me you're talking to not one of those retarded grease monkeys from Eat-A-Lot." He blew out another plume of smoke that enveloped Josh's head. "Don't worry you're in safe company, you can talk to me." He lowered his tone, joviality converting to intimidation.

"Talk to you about what exactly?" Scrutinising Dink's sudden intensity Josh expected the crossed lines of conversation to unravel at any moment.

"The big trip, the cosmic parade," Dink replied elaborately. "The stairway to heaven baby!" To imitate the journey he swished his pointed hand through the cigarette fumes like a fish through water. "I want to know what it was like!" Josh stared dumbfounded at his exuberant host, then concluded years of drug abuse had taken their toll. "What? You didn't really think I just happened to be passing that dive just as you were busy killing faggots in the rest room did you?" Josh felt a chill of realisation creep up his spine and explode into his neck. "Don't look so worried, chill out," Dink instructed, trying to counsel his guest against the bombshell he had dropped into his lap. Seeing the pale look of astonishment on Josh's face he jumped excitedly over onto the soft cushions next to him. "Relax, we're bro's. We're on the same side you and me!"

Josh glared into the young face. It was exuding a stern collectiveness that came with solid conviction, and in this case, a conviction of something most profound. *He knows!* As Dink casually replaced the roll-up onto his lip Josh struggled to find words as the realisation made its full impact on his psyche. For a second he tried to convince himself that Dink couldn't possibly be referring to dreamscape or Hyperborea, but the odds were stacked coincidence. After all his experienced scepticism was becoming short in supply.

"I haven't the faintest goddamn idea what you're talking about, and if you don't mind I think it's time I got back to my own place." Swinging his arm in front to help lever himself forward he caught a glimpse of the gold bracelet around his wrist.

"Don't be so such a grouch. You've got nothing to worry about I'm your buddy, I'm here to look out for you." Dink's assurances went unheard as Josh pulled up his sleeve to reveal the gold face of the Rolex. "It's a present," Dink explained, watching avidly as Josh's manner changed tack.

"What is this?" Josh stood and raised his wrist to catch the last of the sunlight coming through the tall, unveiled window behind the couch.

"Gee I dunno," Dink replied morosely. "I think some people call them watches Josh."

"I can see that but what the hell is it doing here?!" His raised voice was not projecting his confusion at finding the shiny trinket on his person but rather that it was no ordinary watch. As the evening sun reflected on the protective glass it revealed the small chip where it had been scratched against a door handle. "This is my watch! Where did you get this?"

"They told me to give it you," he explained. "Next time you went under." The use of the word *They* was used all too casually. "Something about it helping you cross over. Though if you ask me the least they could have done was replace it with the real thing. I've got three just like it in the drawer."

Slipping the fake Rolex from his wrist he knew he was looking at the stolen watch bought him by his father. Such a personal everyday item was uniquely marked by constant wear, every fine imperfection in the gold plating familiar as he inspected it now in the failing light. With bitter irony the counterfeit was genuine.

"If you ever want the real thing," Dink continued from his subdued position on the couch, "I know a fence in the dock area, he can get hold of the real deal for a fraction of the price, plus he owes me. It would be a real gift," he leaned forward and stubbed the small remains of the roll-up out on the crate. "From a friend to a friend." Josh mused that Dink may have gotten the watch from the Latino. Perhaps he was a cohort and they had planned the whole thing as another dirty trick on down and out Josh Brenin. But that path didn't sit straight for Josh. "He said you'd be a little spooked."

"And who is He?" he asked snidely.

"You want me to spell it out for you?" Dink said as he jumped up from the couch's grasp. "The dude calls himself Mr Vey. Says he's a close friend of yours, so why don't we drop the whole amnesiac act, all right buddy!"

"Somehow the word friend seems a little inappropriate," he replied sullenly. Josh didn't know how but Galda had obtained his stolen watch and given it to his adolescent guardian to vouch for his affiliation to the Elite, no doubt as proof of his tutor's own omnipotence. He turned to pace across the floorboards, before turning back to face his new brother in arms silhouetted against the setting sun that flared up behind him. "So what's going on here Reinhold? You're a part of this? You're just a kid!"

"Careful you could hurt my feelings," Dink joked. "Let's just say appearances can be deceptive." Josh looked out over Dink's shoulder at the jagged backdrop of buildings enshrouded in a late evening smog. *I've got to get out of here.* "Would it make you feel better if I told you I was only eighteen months younger than you?" The revelation made him look back to the boyish features, now blacked out by the molten sun shining in Josh's face.

"Bullshit," he blurted. "You can't be a day over nineteen."

"What can I say; I'm blessed with good genes, so why don't you take a load off and take a seat so we can have a civilised talk about our mutual friend Mr Vey." The latter part of the reply was a perceptive comment to help stem Josh's instinct to leave; still he took a step back.

"No I think it's time I left." Josh looked around for the entrance to the run down apartment and saw it several feet away in the shadows of the hall behind him.

"Where you gonna go?" Dink stepped around the crate and slowly closed the distance between them. "I mean it's not as if you can hide is it? A word from the wise there IS nowhere to hide from Them." Dink's tone was unusually unyielding, his darkened features emphasising the grim insight as he paused a short distance in front of Josh. Josh assumed a posture of obstinacy and turned his back on his host as he made for the door. Dink pushed past him to raise an arm to the hallway wall as an improvised barrier, blocking his way.

"I'm sorry buddy I can't let you do that," Josh stared at the defiant expression in the low light. "Even if I did you can't really go anywhere can you?"

"Watch me," he replied sternly but found Dink's arm resisted the force of his chest as he pushed against it.

"Josh just listen to me," Dink continued more diplomatically. "I mean, if you're gonna be a part of this then you might as well have a buddy, someone on the level. Am I right?" For the moment Josh accepted the intimation of reason on offer.

"How did they get to you?"

"I've been riding this wave right from the start amigo. I'd been washing floors and flipping burgers in that shit-hole for months before you turned up. Then what do you know, some dude pops into my frigging dreams, offers me the keys to the cosmos and hey presto, offers me a slice of the pie if I keep an eye out for his little padowan here." Dink relaxed his arm slightly as Josh realised the extent of the conspiracy. "You, me, that Eat-A-Lot dump; it's all part of the grand plan. You see that's the thing here Josh, this is bigger than you and me. Frigging Hyperborea man!" Dink exclaimed the closing sentence with all the excitement of convict in sight of parole, though the enthusiasm was wasted on Josh.

"Get out of my way Dink," he instructed sternly. His patience had waned but so had Dink's.

"For a college boy you don't listen too well do you! I just can't let you walk out of here right now." There was a tense pause as Josh recognised an unpredictable menace in his host's features.

"Get out of my way," he repeated. The order sounded feeble to Josh. Dink, picking up the tell tale signs of weakness, savoured the obstructive power he wielded over the older and taller man. His instructions were clear; reveal the extent of the Elite's influence over Brenin's life, make sure he understood that they controlled everything in both worlds and detain him until accomplished. Making the next grade was all that mattered to Dink now. His life was a pathetic waste of oxygen. He had finished with the material world and was ready to move onto something greater than class A drugs or cheap thrills.

"If I let you walk out of here I'm putting my balls on the chopping block," Dink stated, defending his big chance at making the grade. "Now they said you might be little upset, but personally I'm feeling a little offended over here, buddy. I mean I offer you my hospitality and a friendly one to one and you throw it back in my face, after everything I've done for you! That just isn't very friendly is it Joshua?" Dink straightened and lowered his arm. "What can I say? You're forcing my hand here. So at Mr Vey's behest I'm gonna have to insist you park your ass down."

To Josh's dismay Dink lifted his shirt and pulled out a small black device from where it had been tucked into the inside of his jeans. It was a small foreign object that fitted snugly to the shape of his closed palm. As he raised it towards Josh the thin neon blue strip at its forefront glowed in the near dark of the hall. Taking a defensive step backwards Josh stared in horror at the tazor-like device.

"What's that for? You planning to zap me now!" Josh blurted. Dink edged forward, exploiting Josh's fear of the unknown device to force him back into the unfurnished apartment.

"This? This is a nasty little device that our friends in the agency gave me in case you tried to fly the coop. As I've explained I can't have my chicken flying the coop before the eggs have hatched, my balls are all too precious." Josh bumped into a crate as he edged nervously back across the floorboards. He had no idea what the nefarious little device was or what it could do but from the way Dink wielded it he sensed it was capable of inflicting terrible pain.

"So what are you going to do?" Josh asked as the back of his thighs pushed up against the arm of the couch. "Hold me hostage till the cavalry show up is that it?" Dink remained silent, unsure of his agenda though determined in his cause. "You're right; I can't hide from Them. They ARE everywhere, in this world, in my life, in my frigging head, so why keep me here? They can just as easily track me down in my own kitchen because that's where I plan to go, to sip an ice cold beer then cook some pasta and meatballs." From Dink's steadfast glare he could see his words were ricocheting off his captor's conscience. "Unless you want me to stay for more *personal* reasons why don't you lower that thing and let me go home and feed my cat." The setting sun had immersed itself behind the concrete tower horizon, its failing light struggling to fill the inhospitable room as the shadows seized hold to make the weapon's blue light glow more intensely.

"I'm not going to ask you again, buddy," Dink threatened as his thumb pushed down on the rear of the black device. The high pitched whistle of the charging device was enough to coerce Josh to obey. As he sat down on the couch's worn arm the loose fitting Rolex slipped down his wrist. "Now that's so much better isn't it?" Dink said as he retook his seat on the opposite crate. Josh was aware that his hand was juddering nervously as it rested on his thigh. Amongst the angst of violent possibilities that could arise from his actions in the next few minutes the exit strategy took hold.

"Always the good friend eh Dink?" Josh said as the shaky right hand picked at the clasp of the returned watch. "Always there to help out a friend whenever it was needed. You're right. With a friend like that I should be honoured, and the friendship appreciated." The unpicked clasp allowed the watch to slip over his left hand. He caught it by the bracelet strap and then offered it to Dink. "That's why I want you to have this."

Dink looked suspicious as it dangled from the outstretched hand. He envied Josh the gold faced Rolex. Even though it was counterfeit Josh was also Their golden boy, the watch was his crown and Dink wanted the prestige for himself.

"Take it," Josh insisted. As Dink reached out to snatch the prize he let it fall clumsily onto the wooden boards with a ruinous clunk. His host only diverted his gaze for a split second but it was all Josh needed.

Exploding from the couch like a sprinter from the blocks Josh lurched for the weapon with both hands. For a brief moment they wrestled for the weapon in a freakish dance but as Josh jumped up from the couch his momentum toppled Dink from the crate. The sound of his host's head hitting the hollow floor echoed around the room. Josh had managed to stun his opponent but needed to secure the device to win the bout. He struck his fist into the soft tissue of Dink's face, the impact splitting his work buddy's lip. As the blood gushed from the small wound Josh prised the small black weapon free of Dink's clasping fingers then stood victorious.

His breathing was heavy, his own blood rushing to his throbbing head. Momentarily the pounding gave way to a bout of giddiness as his exhausted body came down from the adrenaline surge, but it didn't matter. Master of his own destiny once more, he looked at the strange prize in his hand. The space age looking weapon had no determinable weight. Its shiny black exterior was ergonomically designed to sit comfortably in the palm while its simplicity reminded Josh of a child's toy. With no lettering or identifying markings to reveal its manufacturer the cold neon blue light still emanated menacingly from the slit he guessed was its muzzle.

"That's a hell of a punch you've got there white collar boy!" Dink moaned, before rolling over to spit out a string of bloodied saliva onto the floor. Sliding an arm out from underneath he then lifted his head and assessed his bloodied mouth with a cautious hand, then started to laugh. "And here I was thinking you were a Sissy!" Josh tightened his grip and levelled the strange weapon on Dink as he slowly stumbled back up to his feet. "Now the question is, are you ready to dance again buddy?"

Revealing his blood coated teeth in a malicious grin he upped the stakes by pulling out a flick knife from his back pocket. As its thin, sharp blade shot out from its handle Dink's eyes glistened with a new hatred.

"Do you really think you can just walk away from this?" Dink exclaimed, swapping the vicious blade to the other hand as he crept forward in a predatory stance. Nervously Josh edged back. "It's all in here!" his host explained manically, pointing the knife to his own head. "You can't walk away from your own mind. They're in here, we are them, they are us, it's all one big happy family all pulling together." Though remaining defiant Josh let himself be coerced towards the tall window. "There's no room for slackers who are aren't strong enough to grasp the future, and you Josh Brenin ain't grasping, which means you ain't got no future!" Staring into Dink's feral eyes Josh saw for the first time that none of what had transpired since his waking had been part of the *grand plan*. Galda had under estimated this particular Low Grade's ambition.

"Is killing me a part of the grand plan you little prick?" Josh yelled at Dink. "There's nothing to gain from this so back off!"

"Oh there's plenty to gain Josh. With you out of the picture maybe Mr Vey will lavish a bit more time on me! Freedom is what I get out of this, freedom from this stinking rotten world. This isn't reality," he continued as he tossed the blade back into the other hand. "This is a bad frigging dream, and unlike you I'm ready to break the chains and ride the cosmic parade all the way to the top." As Josh backed up against the window he shuffled to the side so that they both stood level in front of its rotting window frame. Time was running out before a decision had to be made. He sensed Dink's eagerness to lunge the shiny blade of steel into his ribs. Before long the time for words would end and the struggle for life and death would begin. *He's lost it!*

"Dink this is crazy!"

"Do you want to know what crazy is Josh?" He ignored the question and stood his ground preparing for the worst. "Crazy is someone who chooses to lose."

"You're a fool if you can't see that they are using you, using US, and God knows how many more to do their dirty work. All for some freak, black book government project that might not be anymore real than a wet dream!" Josh retorted, his arm steadying as he gripped the weapon tighter. "You are not in control of your life they are! *That's* crazy!"

"Would it surprise you Josh If I told I've always wanted to know what it would be like to puncture a man's heart with this knife." Dink's grim and sincere confession sent a final chill of dread up Josh's spine. With his finger tightening on the weapon's trigger he knew there was no time left to weigh up his own conscience against the necessity to defend himself. If he turned and fled into the dark room he knew the blade would almost certainly find its way into the vulnerable muscle and skin of his back. So reluctantly he accepted what had to be done. *Maybe it'll only stun him!* "So I guess it's ciao buddy." Dink sneered gleefully as he edged forward, forcing Josh into the darkness of the corner behind him. "It'll be quick," Dink asserted gravely. "For an extra ten bucks the guy who sold me this was good enough to instruct me in its most effective use." Josh's gaze drifted from his would-be killer's shadowy grimace to the wicked blade, unable to understand his continued resilience to the threat of being *zapped* by the mysterious weapon now in his possession. "Night night sweet prince!" Dink's knuckles turned white as he gripped the switchblade; necessity urged Josh to finally squeeze its trigger. But Dink's bravery was explained as his hand suddenly flared up with white hot pain. Yelping like a kicked dog, Josh dropped the malicious weapon onto the bare floorboards.

"Hand recognition amigo," Dink explained. "Bites don't it?" The electric shock had left his hand numb. Stunned by the trickery Josh grabbed the tortured hand, glaring at his assailant as he tried to squeeze the life back into it. The weapon had never been a threat to anyone except himself. Standing with his back against the mottled plaster, he realised his last line of defence had vanished along with the misconception. "If it's any consolation," Dink added slyly. "Mr Vey played the same trick on me. Except this time, someone's going to die."

What followed next happened in the blink of a disbelieving eye. With the uncoiled ferocity of a panther he saw Dink lunge at him. The shiny blade sought its target with lethal conviction, but the blow was not delivered. Paralysed with fear, Josh had expected to feel its cold sharp steel slash into his upraised arm, or plunge into his exposed chest. But instead he watched on as Dink was uprooted by from where he stood and thrown from the window across the room.

His short pathetic squeal was silenced by a grim heavy thud. Following his assailant's trajectory across the dark room Josh's unbelieving eyes were then spellbound by what they found. There in the low light of the dying sun Dink now hung helplessly like a wall painting against a dank wall. Half concussed from the potent blow to the back of the head, the invisible force continued to crush his chest as it restrained him several feet above the floor. With the window frame's shadow projected across his scrawny body, it looked to Josh like the crossbars of some supernatural prison were responsible for the intervention. But as Dink's wide eyes relayed, he too was struggling to comprehend the source of the unnatural power pinning his suspended body to the mottled plaster. For in the dark veil of dusk around them, nothing else was seen to move.

Dink groaned as the invisible press continued to crush the very life out of him. A ghoulish dull crack then signified a bone had been shattered. The same terrified eyes then bulged as the clunk of the switchblade falling from his hand resonated across the room. *They are here.* No sooner was Dink relieved of the blade then the same invisible force sent him flying forward, and crashing out through the rotten window. Josh recoiled from the effects of the collision, his heart skipping a frantic beat as Dink's brief wail was then cut short by the impact of the three storey fall. For several seconds the shards of broken glass echoed their shattering chorus as they followed the young man down into the adjoining alley, before being followed by a deathly silence. It was as Josh's stunned senses suddenly re-ignited, he knew the young killer had just been out manoeuvred by something much more deadly.

*****

It took a moment for Josh to assimilate what he'd witnessed. He'd seen the same demonstration of lethal supernatural power once before, though that time he had been its victim, not a spectator. As a tingling sensation of electrified skin on the back of his neck relayed there was something watching him from the darkness he didn't have long to wait before its source made itself known. The figure emerged from the shadows like some pallid spectre and walked into the dying light so that she was visible from head to toe. The blonde hair was pulled back tight away from her face and shimmered in the molten light as she stopped in plain view; her blue eyes boring into his soul as she offered her hand.

"Follow me." Her voice resonated in his mind, delivered by some psychic power that both overwhelmed and impressed its receiver. The last time he had heard that voice it had ordained his own demise, but now confusingly, it offered salvation. *Angelica.* No sooner had she appeared then she retreated back into the shadows, her outstretched hand the last to be swallowed by the dark as she enticed him forward with a beckoning finger. He wanted to ask why she had helped him but suddenly it didn't matter. The would-be killer had been foiled and he was alive. At that moment it was all the reassurance he needed. Stepping forward Josh's foot kicked a small object into view. The shiny black surface of the strange weapon beckoned him to pick it up. As he scooped it up and placed it into a pocket he gave thanks he had not been the human missile that had created the jagged void where the window had once been.

Walking towards the exit it took several seconds for his eyes to adjust to the denser shadows. As he palmed a nearby wall for guidance his leg bumped into a crate. In the heat of the bizarre and revealing exchange between Dink and himself time had passed quickly, night had replaced day, death replaced life, though pushing onwards his outstretched hands quickly found the back of the door. With eager hands he fumbled with the multitude of Yale locks, bolts and chains before finally freeing himself from the confines of the temporary prison. The faint glow of the corridor's low wattage light was a welcome sight. Cautiously Josh ducked his head out the doorway to check the musty landing for loitering tenants. *Empty, no one will see.* Surprised the ruckus of the brawl had not drawn unwanted attention; he pulled the door shut behind him, tugging it gently into the tight fitting frame until it squeezed back into place. Outside Dink's apartment his conscience made him pause.

Dink was dead. *I witnessed his murder.* Recalling his own brush with death Josh swallowed the festering guilt and stepped towards the unlit stairway that descended ominously before him. *He tried to kill me.* By any standards being linked to the death of two men in one day was quite an accomplishment and taking his first shaking step down he imagined himself advancing up the LAPD most wanted list. *No one knows me here.* He reassured himself with the idea that as a stranger in a strange place he could disappear into a void of obscurity. The tired building sported no closed circuit cameras; even the Mile was thankfully free of big brother's ever watchful eye. Apart from the tragic memories of a bunch of misfits and alcoholics that could link him to Mike's bar, all he had to do was inconspicuously exit Dink's apartment block and no one would be the wiser.

"Quickly," Angelica's voice suddenly commanded, urging him on. Before him the stairs descended into an unending darkness. Though he couldn't see his new guardian he realised she remained close by, watching, waiting for her disadvantaged adherent to continue. As a heated argument was liberated for a nearby apartment through an opening door, Josh pressed on with the descent. After several hasty but attentive steps his mind grew accustomed to the spacing. With the aid of the handrail he was able to climb down the subsequent dark stairwells with relative ease, the adrenaline fuelling his accelerated heart rate now improving his coordination. Each floor was seemingly deserted. Behind the unmarked doors muffled sounds of hip hop and traditional Latino music reminded the prowler he was on the wrong side of the tracks, an alien place inhabited by people he didn't really know existed or chose not to. The ruffled carpets underfoot, disturbed by intent or neglect, now also helped to muffle his footsteps as he reached the last flight of stairs and stared down to freedom. From the top of the stairway Josh thought he glimpsed Angelica in the main entrance. No sooner did he see her she was gone again, enticing him on, reminding him to remain cautious. As Josh cleared the final steps in eager bounds, he hastily grabbed the door handle and followed her outside to find the unfamiliar street bustling with life.

An intoxicated local was slouched against the apartment railings, surveying the passing night life with a glazed but disgruntled glare. With his back to the doorway he was unable see the look of panic on the pale stranger's face as he exited the building and sneaked away down the sidewalk. As Josh's jittery legs carried him along, not even the anxious walk they produced was enough to distract the loitering drunkard as he raised the contents of the brown paper bag back to his thirsty mouth. *Keep moving.* Josh egged himself on, making sure to avoid the brooding glares of two youths from under their hooded tops as he swerved to avoid their approach. When Dink had guided him to the building, dazed and half blinded with blood, the street had seemed quiet and mercifully threat free. But now the dark shroud of night had descended onto the neighbourhood, it had seemingly drawn out an army of nocturnal natives who could sense the outsider's apprehension a mile off. *Don't bother them and they won't bother you.*

Forcing an upward glance he saw the poorly lit street was filled with apartment block after apartment block as far as he dared to see. *Project housing?* Across the street two major fast food chains fought for supremacy, both acting as magnets for the small gangs of youths he noted were crowded outside their brightly lit exteriors. Underfoot the sidewalk was uneven, its neglected flagstones thwarting his every step to vacate the area as his feet scuffed every protruding corner or dip. Vacate to where exactly he wasn't even sure. He had no car, no idea of his location and doubted with certainty he would see any cabs touting for custom in the run down vicinity of wherever the hell he was. He quickened his pace. In the open air with its unfamiliar sights and sounds, fear had banished any thoughts of his elusive guardian. That was until he saw her striking figure propped up against the streetlight mast ahead.

Bathed in its orange aura her sleek black attired form appeared solid and real, her casual pose suggesting she had been waiting for some time. *Where did she come from?* Approaching the unexpected sight, the hint of a cruel smile upon her lips instinctively made him slow his pace once more. Cautiously he closed the space between them. A myriad of anxious thoughts were racing across his bemused mind. *Who are you?* But just as he reached speaking distance she was gone.

In disbelief he managed to track her blurry form as it raced carelessly into the busy road and over to the opposite curb, before again disappearing out of sight behind a large vehicle. *What the hell is this?* For a moment he stood dazed on the street corner. *Did she just do that?* The feat had been superhuman; a mere blink of an eye and the exploit could have been missed, but seen it he had. Instantly he reminded himself he had to be witnessing some form of projected image or spectre, one that had previously attempted to kill him. *This is so crazy!* Paranoia hijacked his reasoning. What if instead of leading him to freedom she was merely guiding him into some new diabolical trap?

A gunshot suddenly perforated the street air. He turned to see a gang of youths were quickly scattering away from the crowded drive-thru parking lot, spilling into the street like a flood of startled wilder beast. The victim of the discharged weapon lay dying on the spotlighted asphalt as his friends and peers also made good their escape. A second gunshot rang out as the shooter then walked over to the body and fired the fatal headshot in a casual execution. Josh ran across the street, making for the dim lit sidewalk where he had seen Angelica. The killing fields in that part of the concrete jungle had just claimed a second victim that night and he, like the retreating youths, wasn't planning on sticking around.

Gliding between the hood and trunk of two parked vehicles he reached the opposite kerb only to find his blonde guide was long since vanished. A rush of feet relayed he was about to be railroaded. Stepping back against a tall vehicle he was prevented from being bulldozed on the sidewalk as the mob of startled youths fled past and dispersed into the night. Leaning back forward from the tall chasse, he decided that night ranked as the most insane he had ever experienced, and now he just wanted it to end.

Behind him a heavy side door suddenly whooshed open. Josh turned in time to see the formidable stranger squatted in the dim interior, but not the strange device in his possession. As its energy bolt struck his mid drift all feeling and cohesion was stolen instantly from every muscle. Paralysed in a heartbeat, his body crumpled to the ground where he stood. He looked up from the cold concrete as this new assailant then lowered the weapon and stepped out of the vehicle to claim his victim. For a moment Josh was aware of powerful hands grasping his arms and shoulders, until oblivion claimed his stunned mind and stole the world from him. His numb mouth unable to voice any resistance, he welcomed its bitter-suite embrace and the dark nothing that followed.

Chapter 10

The viewer's protected eyes scoured the translucent display suspended in front of his face. As he scrolled through the latest project stats the holographic display was mirrored on the dark lenses of his sunglasses as he sat alone in near darkness. Even when viewing the disembodied interface, projected in front of his pallid features from the tabletop at his fingertips, the sunglasses remained a discouraging necessity. The years of required service in a dream world reality had taken their toll on his mortal shell. For Galda Vey, project principal and senior Nothos of the black light Elite, even the dullest of lights produced an inhuman aversion to that which had once been normal. The only time the senior agent ventured without protective eyewear was during the few hours he took to sleep, a dreamless sleep that passed quickly and afforded his body the necessary rest it still required.

At times he even pondered if he was slowly becoming like Them, the true elite, the secret legion that offered unimaginable power and technologies in return for Elite aid. Their time was coming, but for Galda it couldn't come soon enough. Already he was weary of his earthly role and ready to discard it for a place at Their side. Focusing his attention through the dark lenses at the unfolding events relayed before him, he curbed those thoughts for a moment and appreciated the omnipotent power he currently had at his disposal.

The holographic display technology produced a live 3D schematic of the field of play, the adopted sunglasses providing a convenient pointing device while the sensors under his hand enabled him to scroll and select at will. He had wanted to lead the delicate operation unfolding on screen for himself, but the mortal body he now re-inhabited had been too fatigued from his last Leviscape assignment, and so he had remained a distant observer as his dependable field agents executed their deadly mission.

High resolution military satellites had provided detailed voyeur capabilities of the battlefield. In conjunction with the space age bio-interface technology at his fingertips it was also possible to reproduce the east side of Los Angeles in a virtual holographic environment. At its greatest magnification the schematic could identify a rat dropping from several miles above the city. These impressive abilities however were currently closed in on one particular venue at the centre of the Elite's attentions and Galda watched on as his crack team of black clad agents surrounded the warehouse block and cut off the fire escape to the adjoining alley.

The squad of Elite field soldiers had travelled to their objective the old fashioned way, by car with chopper support, and were now waiting to make their final strike.

"Perimeter secure," the field commander stated impatiently over the comlink. Galda double checked the thermal sensor readout on screen. The target was alone and lying down in a large room to the rear of the premises. As the figure lay there in an apparent slumber it had no idea it was only minutes away from a quick, merciless death.

"Execute primary field objective." Galda felt his pulse escalate as he issued the order. In one coordinated swoop the agents now entered the building with lethal agility. A second disembodied panel then opened to Galda's left, its red holographic frame indicating it was a priority Stream. Reluctantly he turned his attention to it. The Stream ID denoted the flagged relay originated with the LAPD; an alleged one eighty seven had occurred at a project housing estate in the north of the city, a rundown neighbourhood of neglected buildings ruled by small time gangs who vied for supremacy of its streets. *What is this?* His impatient attentions switched back to the unfolding military strike. The lethal field agents had secured the main rooms and were positioned to take down the target, who he could see from its thermal signature, still slumbered in peaceful ignorance of its fate.

"What are you waiting for?" he demanded over com. The order was transmitted in a split second and the response equally swift. As two agents surged through the adjoining hallway and burst into the small room at its end, Galda increased the zoom for an improved view. The ruckus produced by the strike's forced entry however didn't create even the slightest of stirrings in the body that lay on the bed, its bright crimson form appearing otherwise lifeless as they closed around it, weapons posed for the kill.

These same weapons released no heat signatures as they now discharged at the defenceless target. Its body jerked repeatedly from the multiple impacts before returning to its previous stagnant pose as the agents ceased firing. The target was dead, mission accomplished. *At last.* Relieved at its ease Galda closed the holographic panel down and returned his attention to the remaining red frame. The name of the homicide victim was flashing across the disembodied screen, *Daryl Reinhold.* Recognising its significance his moment of gratification was immediately destroyed.

*****

The jolt of the braking RV drew Josh back from the welcome slumber. At first all he could sense was hard steel pressed against his face.

Then the voices echoed in his ear as he became aware his body was slowly joining his waking mind. *A dream?* Feverishly he wanted the restful existence to continue, but just as the life crept back into his doubled up limbs the familiar sound of the woman's voice urged him to concede to reality. Without moving to aid the recovery of feeling to his hands and feet, he slowly opened his eyes and surveyed the inside of the RV from its floor.

A thick set man was crouched by the side of a reclined swivel chair at its centre. The small LCD display he was studying on its side reflected in his frowning eyes as he checked his balance in the swaying environment, one hand grasping an armrest the other modifying the unseen instrument implanted in the occupied recliner. While Josh studied his face to determine friend or foe, two voices in the background debated the ups and downs of the previous night's Laker game. The sound of a shuffling foot then resonated through the floor into his ear; someone had leant over to check on their immobilised guest. The man's ponytail of dark, shiny hair hung over his shoulder as he gazed down and grinned at Josh. Josh reciprocated with wide upturned eyes and recognised the stern features as the last face he seen prior to the paralysis. *You shot me.*

"Rise and shine!" he goaded the captive. As he leant back out of view the strange comment caused his heavy set colleague studying the LCD to avert his gaze momentarily to the strange detainee.

"Your Flyboy's back on earth," the second captor added dryly, then returned to study the LCD as Josh tried to turn his head, only to find he was prevented by the awkward angle of his body. The LCD was whisked away from his face as the swivel chair then spun round to bring the occupant's legs into Josh's view. A slender hand touched Alpha's in thanks for his attentive presence.

"You know you really should be more careful when choosing your friends Joshua," the familiar voice stated. "True friends are a rare gift in this day and age, especially in that part of town." The sardonic tone was uncalled for, but could have expected worse from his former attacker. Josh stretched his legs, straightening his aching body so as to raise himself and see it really was the blonde haired stalker who sat in the reclining throne. As all eyes now fell upon Josh he chose to remain silent. "Friends who can look after you," she continued. "And who care what you do with your life." He detected the cruel irony in her words, though sensed it served some further purpose. Righting himself until he sat with his back against the rear doors of the RV, he was finally able to see the three captors properly for the first time. The heavy set man, whose broad suspicious features were unfriendly in nature, kicked over a silver crate, suggesting Josh used it to sit on. Making himself comfortable on the makeshift stool

Josh watched the stocky captor stand and lean against the recliner's headrest for support.

"Angelica, I presume?" Josh asked with equal disdain. Though his mind was unhampered by the after affects of the paralysis the slow responding muscles of his mouth made him slur his words slightly.

"In the flesh," she confirmed acutely. "And these are my friends Alpha." She raised a right hand to the foreboding giant propped against her chair. "And Monk," she then gestured to the wolfish captor sporting the ponytail on her left, who now pensively rested his chin on a spire created by two raised index fingers. "And the two characters you can hear up front are Jonah and Dex." Still unsure of what new cruelty the fragile but deadly woman had in store next, Josh was momentarily relieved to be off the streets and away from the crime scene she had perpetrated, in the flesh or not.

"And what about my *friend?*" he asked, avoiding Alpha's intense stare.

"You mean is he dead?" she asked correctively.

"Well going out on a limb I'd say the three storey fall did a little more than clear his head," he retorted. Though it sounded like compassion, Josh was using Dink's demise as an act of rebellion.

"The life of that unfortunate fool is no longer a concern of yours," Angelica chided him icily. "Your only concern now is for the future." He stared into Angelica's blue eyes and thought she looked weary, like Galda had been when they had met for the first time *in the flesh.* The art of projection had seemingly taken its toll on her also.

"Unfortunate?" he blurted. "You killed him!" He looked up at the scowling face of the big man she had introduced as Alpha, then briefly to Monk's intense features still contemplatively posed upon his finger spire. The subject of death remained close to the mark. "Besides last time we met you didn't exactly act like you wanted me to have a future, period. In fact if I recall properly you tried to decorate the men's room with my brains." The RV banked heavily to the right as it traversed a street corner at considerable speed. "Where are you taking me?"

"That's not important," Angelica stated bluntly. She leaned forward in the mysterious recliner, her unkempt golden hair loose about her face, reminding Josh of their violent last encounter on the tiled floor. "What you should be asking is *why* we are taking you."

"I'd like to think it wasn't for the purpose of killing me," Josh replied hesitantly. Alpha produced a black object from his pocket. The ergonomic hand grip of the small bulbous weapon was instantly recognisable as that of Galda Vey's present to Dink.

"He had this on him," Alpha stated. He handed it to over to Angelica who looked surprised by the sight of the foreign weapon. In her slender hand it appeared like a malignant growth, foul and wicked. For a moment Josh thought she would translate his possession of the device as a threat thwarted, but unimpressed she simply passed it back to Alpha and looked down at Josh with a look that betrayed concern.

"You look older in real life," she declared, blue eyes producing mixed feelings in their captive. "The world has taken its toll on you."

"Getting your face rearranged repeatedly has a way of doing that to you," he replied acerbically. "So why all this?" he then asked. "Who are you people? What the hell is all this about?" The RV banked to the left as it turned into another unknown street and Alpha scowled as he was forced to check his balance again. Angelica gazed up and insisted he relaxed. Reluctantly the big man sat down on a wheel arch, though continued to scrutiny their captive suspiciously.

"For weeks, perhaps months," Angelica explained as she sat back into the swivel recliner. "The black agency, as we call them, for no one knows who they really are, have, via astral projection and unsuspecting *Low Grades* like your friend Dink, been manipulating you and your life. Like a boa constrictor winding its cold hearted coils around you they have progressively tightened their hold on your mind, body and very soul, until your every move and thought was a product of their own collective consciousness." Angelica's words rung true. Still their profound revelation left him dumbfounded.

"For what purpose?" he managed to ask after first clearing his parched throat.

"For the sole purpose of assimilating you, or more accurately, your gifts, into their organisation. And too that end they have already succeeded." A few cold seconds of silence followed the condemnation.

"Wait a minute," Josh snapped. "Wait a goddamn minute. I didn't want any of this. You think I'm one of them?" Immediately Josh wondered if the black mark, the Tsadeh as Galda had called it, was blazing upon his forehead once again for all too see. Any affiliation with Galda and his agenda had been coerced. But then he recalled how after Angelica had seemingly killed the misfit in Mike's bar, his *tutor's* kinship had given him a sense of security. Perhaps he had succumbed? Suddenly he feared again for his life. "Stop the van!" he demanded. Another grave silence followed the order. "I had no choice!"

"The majority of their converts don't even know there is a choice Joshua," Angelica replied, breaking the deadlock. "That's the point. We are Latronis, servants of the light. We represent that other choice."

"Latrine," he echoed rudely. "Servants of the light, or whatever the hell you people call yourselves, how do I know you're not this *black agency* running another mind job on me?" Angelica scrutinised her captive's eyes.

"I think you already know Joshua," she replied intensely. "You're just too afraid to admit it to your self."

"What? All I know is that I'm no convert," he reasserted. "*You* murdered Dink after making an attempt on *my* life!" His confusion bred an irrational desire to persecute them, just as the vying factions had persecuted him. "You don't exactly strike me as the good guys here!"

"So would you prefer to be dead Mr Brenin?" Monk intervened bluntly. Josh's thoughts returned to the wicked blade of Dink's knife. For a moment he had seen the depth of death's black soul in the young man's eyes. Angelica had undoubtedly saved his life, but Galda had warned him of other's who would try to undermine his righteous war with the Vanir.

"Let's cut the crap," Alpha then blurted coarsely. "We need information." As the RV came to a slow halt approaching an unseen crossroads the reason for his detainment bemused him further.

"Information?" Josh sensed the low muffled hum of other vehicles either side of them, a distant radio blared out from a nearby car. As Angelica gestured to Alpha to back off, Josh's gaze darted to the opening latch of the slide door.

"Why are the Black agency so keen to make you one of them?" she demanded, rejoining the interrogation.

"I thought you were the one with all the answers here, why don't you tell me?"

"Potential recruits come and go," she continued unabated. "Thousands are covertly induced into their Sleepeze programme so that the one in five Low Grades amongst them can be assimilated into their unconscious army of drones to fight their war on the Leviscape. So what makes you so special that they are willing to risk exposure by contacting you in the physical world?" Josh thought about the disclosure for a moment. She was right. Galda's attention had extended beyond that bestowed on the other Low Grades. While they had been forced to endure their tutelage in a catatonic state, he had remained conscious, and that he realised was the reason for his special treatment. He was a natural; his gift both curse and blessing. As a burgeoning member of the black Elite his case warranted extra attention. Undeniably it also made him a greater threat to these so-called servants.

"Answer the lady's question," Monk then instructed menacingly. Josh gazed over to his austere features and shivered.

"I don't know what do want me to say?" he retorted. "I'm a victim here, right?" he petitioned Angelica. Josh hoped to impede the line of questioning with belligerence. He no longer cared who was good or bad, who was right or wrong, he just wanted out. That was until then he felt the steely grip suddenly crush his throat.

At first it felt like an ice cold hand had seized him from nowhere, but as none of the three kidnappers had moved a limb he quickly realised the malicious vice was more supernatural in nature. As his body convulsed to regain access to oxygen the vice-like claw remained solid about his larynx, its grip unyielding while his own hands pawed at nothing about his throat. His bulging eyes pleaded with Angelica's unsure gaze. From her chair she was watching the assault with a vacant detachment while her colleague maintained his invisible grasp. Josh's strained gaze then fell upon his tormentor. Monk returned the look with the cold and calculating air, focusing his incredible power over life and death like a cat toying with an insignificant bug. *He is not a projection, how can he do this?* Just as Josh thought his gullet was about to collapse, the invisible claw relinquished its victim and Josh sucked in the first wonderful draft of air he had breathed for over a minute. Slumping forward onto his hands he felt the blood pound back into his skull and pulse violently at his temples.

"Answer the lady's question," Monk's callous voice repeated the previous demand as though nothing untoward had occurred.

"Ask Calisto!" Josh sputtered between breaths, fighting the light headed sensation that crept across his reeling brain like a wildfire. "She's one of you, right? Ask her, she knows what this is about!" Josh remained on his hands and knees until he regained his composure. Head slumped forward he couldn't bring himself to confront his humiliation.

"Calisto?" Angelica blurted in return. Her voice sounded stunned.

"How do you know that name?" Monk asked, making this second demand sound more potent.

"I met her," he replied in a rasping voice as he sensed Alpha's approach. Clearing his aching throat he continued. "I met her when the black agents sent me into Hyperborea. She was there with us." He slumped back onto the crate and glared back at his heartless blonde interrogator. *Beauty and beast.*

"By *us* you mean the other Low Grades?" she asked eagerly.

"Yes. Before we were drawn back, to wherever the hell the agents had us. She told me to make contact, here in the real world." There was a pause while the unexpected information settled with his captors. Though Monk had withdrawn his invisible stranglehold, Josh could still feel its lingering impression about his throat.

"And have you?" Alpha finally asked. Josh darted a contemptuous glance to Monk before answering.

"I haven't had the chance! But she's one of you, right?" He was aware of some personal interest from Alpha, who he sensed was holding back an urge to beat further information out of him. Angelica avoided the question.

"Did *they* see you conversing with her?"

"How the hell do I know?" Josh chided her boorishly. "We were drawn back, all of us and they, stole our thoughts or something."

"Did the agents see you with her?" Alpha growled as he lurched closer, fighting the urge to crush Josh's throat in the flesh. Angelica raised a calming hand once again, though looked on intently for the answer.

"I don't know! She mentioned a shop, on the east side of town. That's it, that's all I remember." A flashback of Galda's devilish face drawing out the Hyperborean visions from Josh's mind via the two hands he'd clasped either side of his head exploded into his mind's eye.

"I...we were tested on or something, he was in my head," Josh struggled to explain himself. "They fed on my memories; the visions were like some great prize to them. We were mules, used to smuggle out sights and visions they could not see for themselves." The flashback left him with a hollow impression his very soul had been robbed of something magnificent, thus pillaged he found he could recall very little, if anything of the city of light. The draw of Josh's body against the back of the RV indicated Dex or Jonah was speeding the RV ever onwards. The lack of stops and turns suggested they had hit a freeway and were free of the labyrinth of streets interlinking the project housing estate they had left behind. Alpha looked intently at Angelica, who continued to look curious by the developments.

"She could be compromised," Alpha stated uneasily, his tone calmer and respectful as he addressed his petite colleague.

"We don't know that," Angelica replied, somewhat lacking in conviction. As Josh looked into her crystal blue eyes he saw insecurity for the first time. His unexpected revelation had taken the militia by surprise, as though the very keystone of their grand design was suddenly about to collapse around them.

"Calisto would not have risked exposing herself if she knew it would draw Their attention," Monk stated surely. "As you know she is more a part of that plain than any of us. She knows its limits, its dangers." Monk looked back at Josh with a curious gaze he could only decipher as distrust. "She would not have risked revealing herself during an infiltration of the Low Grades, not for him," he added cynically. "Unless..." His words trailed off as he studied Josh's face. Monk's stern eyes bored into his as some new trail of thought took hold.

"He's one of them!" Alpha suddenly blurted out, his eyes wild and fearsome. Josh stiffened at the outburst. "It's a trick, he never met Calisto, he's a mole. Monk's right, she would never risk herself for him!"

"Alpha!" Angelica reprimanded the outburst with a grimace of denial. "She would have made it through," she explained with a forced certainty. "She's strong." Talk of the mysterious Calisto had abruptly shifted the interrogation's momentum into new territory. Instead of relief, Josh felt a sense of dread in its place. His life still hung in the lurch.

"Is she in danger?" he asked lamely. His only response was the brutal glare of the imposing Alpha. It was as Angelica called for the driver to stop the RV Josh realised just how profound his disclosure had been. As their cumbersome vehicle came to a halt with a squeeze of the brakes its heavy chasse banked unexpectedly. Up front the passenger seat swivelled round until its occupant faced the spacious interior and his comrade's sullen faces. The man's broad cheeks gave the appearance his olive skin was stretched tightly over his youthful face, while his dark eyes shone with the vivacious youth of a child from under a crown of short dreadlocks.

"What now Boss?" he asked. To Angelica, who sat in an ominous silent deliberation of grim possibilities, the answer was obvious. Her anxious glance to their co pilot was ample response for him to signal the driver to take an unplanned detour to the east side of town. As the RV's powerful engine roared away from the kerb it was with the brooding certainty the war of opposites verged on an unpredicted escalation.

*****

In a bid to avoid the unwanted visitors, a spooked cat leapt from a dumpster and skittered into the shadows. From a murky refuge its slit corneas scowled back at the huge vehicle that had appeared at the alley's mouth. From inside Monk slid its heavy side door open, allowing Angelica to pounce out and see dusk had transformed the back-street into a haven of darkness. As Alpha grabbed their captive by the elbow and yanked him up from his seat, Monk followed her out onto the asphalt and joined in her reconnaissance for the unknown. Forced into the ranks of the apprehensive team, a sullen pride urged Josh to snatch his arm free, though sensing a continued animosity from his unyielding custodian; he decided subservience might just postpone an untimely demise.

"I don't like this," Monk stated, glaring into the shadows that waited for them. As though some primal instinct was guiding his instinct, he took a deep breath of the night air. From his subsequent scowl it appeared his initial evaluation had been sound.

"Wait here," Angelica instructed. "This doesn't need all of us." Monk looked surprised by the proposal, and then stepped back into the RV to continue his vigil into the back alley with an obedient reserve.

"And him?" he asked referring to Josh. "He's not one of us."

"He's coming along." Angelica reached back into the RV and retrieved a small hand held device that Josh decided was most likely a weapon.

"What happened to this choice you were telling me about?" he asked slyly. Staring into the partially lit alleyway before them, he wondered what gauntlet awaited them amongst the dumpsters and crates positioned along its shadowy length. As Alpha's steel grip tightened above his elbow, he realised there was no choice, only compliance. Monk then threw a second device to Alpha, who catching and toying with the small device in his palm, decided it was too tiny to be of any real use. To their captive it appeared this undersized, capricious squad of dreamscape warriors possessed their own strange technological arsenal. He wondered if the five man militia represented a mere slice of a much larger mercenary pie, but as Alpha shoved him forward as an indication to follow Angelica into the shadows, such thoughts became irrelevant.

The drive from the freeway had been a sombre affair. As the RV had journeyed at speed towards the east of the city, Angelica and Monk had swapped reassuring glances, except Josh now realised he had mistaken apprehension for confidence. Little had he known but his Hyperborean meeting with Calisto had tilted the malicious scales of fate and thus sealed his own, which now rested on his captors finding their colleague safe and sound.

Through the single security light that struggled to illuminate the dark alleyway Angelica strode confidently on ahead. Behind, the two men followed observantly, the mysterious handheld device in his custodian's possession ever ready as Josh was marshalled to the metallic skeleton of the fire escape that now spiralled above their heads into the night. A toppled bottle crashed onto the asphalt, causing Alpha to flinch before cursing the cat's shrieks of warning. By the time Angelica had cautiously began the climb up the exposed stairway Alpha had released his grip of Josh's arm. Deciding his military instincts were better suited to the task if unhindered by the unnecessary responsibility, he allowed his captive to begin the ascent behind their blonde leader, who reprimanded their first heavy steps on the reverberating fire escape with a reproving glance.

Reaching the first storey fire exit after a silent climb, Angelica took the opportunity to survey the alley from above. Certain no hidden enemies lurked in the chasm below them she returned her attention to their sealed entry point. Nudging Josh aside Alpha insisted on being on point, except Angelica was in no mood for chivalry. After tugging the fire door open she urged the ex soldier back into rear guard and disappeared into the unlit void it exposed. As Josh looked into the black oblivion on offer, a bout of fear threatened to glue his feet to the spot. A sharp jab of Alpha's palm sized weapon into his ribcage however quickly cleared the blockage.

Inside the dark corridor the captive was obliged to rely on his sense of touch as he shuffled into the unknown. At first the light scuffing of Angelica's feet striding confidently before them was assurance enough no dangers lurked in waiting, until unexpectedly the wall to his right ended. Wrapping his fingers over its corner he feared the security blanket would be taken away and he lost in the black void. From behind the incessant prodding ceased as Alpha sensed Angelica was out of their limited sensory range. An unearthly silence followed as the two men stopped and waited, listening for a signal. Suddenly it exploded in their faces. The brilliant light had come out of nowhere, blinding the two unsuspecting men who raised their hands in defence of their sensitive eyes. As the beam dropped safely to illuminate the floor at their feet a familiar voice hissed through their misery.

"All clear," Angelica declared. She swung the torch beam away and out into the large expanse around her. The last time Alpha had been in that place he had been the captive, but now due to the unexpected reversal of fate he commanded Latronis' latest hostage.

"Move it Flyboy," he ordered, urging Josh to close the distance between them and Angelica. Sweeping the brilliant beam across the warehouse of unusual furnishings, her blank features glowed in its harsh afterglow. As she scoured the warehouse for unseen hazards Josh was somewhat relieved by the device's mundane reality. His anxiety momentarily abating, he watched as the powerful beam emitted from her palm revealed a vast collection of ornate chairs, tables and furnishings that filled the entire floor.

"This doesn't feel right," Alpha stated gloomily. His highly trained senses were unsettled by the unearthly silence. "We should have brought back up."

"There's no time. Give me the thrower," she replied, hiding her own brooding sense of doom behind a wall of tenacity. In the radiating aura of the torchlight her out stretched hand looked like white marble as it waited impatiently for the device in his possession. From the word *thrower*

Josh guessed she wasn't asking for a second torch. Alpha stared at the woman half his size. He wasn't used to taking orders from pretty, pint sized women. As the only professional soldier amongst them he decided to utilize his intrinsic talents. But Angelica's impatience had no time for pride. "Give it to me Alpha," she demanded. Reluctantly he tossed her the weapon. "Wait here. Holler if you get spooked." With military zeal he nodded obedience and turned to adopt a rear guard defence. "And you," she said turning to Josh, "you come with me."

With the thrower in her other hand she strode off again, winding her way amongst the ornate tables and intricate light stands until she reached the doorway spotlighted in the torchlight at one end of the vast interior. Josh was unsure of his unwanted privilege. But should they be walking into a trap his custodian's instincts were no doubt urging her to keep him close, and if proved to be one of Them, the first to appreciate the thrower's destructive capacity.

Josh followed his blonde guide into the second blacked out corridor. Mimicking her stealthy pose he trailed her like a lost puppy until their final goal revealed itself at its end. Angelica cut the torchlight as it brushed the door. The light spilling through its tight frame gave sufficient illumination to warrant retiring the torch to a back pocket. Approaching the only seemingly occupied room in the building, Josh reciprocated Angelica's increased caution, her backwards glance warning him to stay within range. *What is this place?* Josh swallowed a parched throat. With the thrower expectantly poised to the side of her head, Angelica's focused features were hard to read in the leaking light. After one last glance behind assured her the reluctant captive offered no unexpected threat, she shoved her outstretched fingers forward.

The unlocked door swung open slowly and silently, causing a flood of light to scorch its way down the corridor as the two squinting prowlers invaded the sanctuary of brilliant light. Unwelcome thoughts of Sharon equally assaulted Josh's mind. Realising he was entering a secluded room with a beautiful woman he new she would be far from impressed, stepping inside, its apparent function immediately justified his misgivings. *Someone's bedroom?* Between Angelica's legs he saw the white linen tucked tidily around the low lying mattress at the room's centre, then as his irises contracted he noted the soles of the two dainty feet upon it that greeted their arrival.

The reason for the bedroom's radiant environment was explained as he recognised his own haggard features creeping towards him from the black doorway reflected behind the bedstead. Mesmerised momentarily by their intrusive reflections in the mirrored wall he was oblivious to the horrors that awaited him, and that which currently held Angelica in a grave, silent shock. As their synchronised doubles entered left and right in the opposite wall, Josh realised these single reflections were being mass produced in the surrounding mirrored walls that created a never ending and disorientating chasm of reflections reflecting reflections into infinity. At first he believed the crimson streaks were a continuation of the same avant-garde themes he had witnessed back in the showroom, much like the erratic works of modern artists that relied on colour and composition to create an aesthetic work without form. But as the unusual nature of the room dawned upon him he then saw the red streaks and splatters upon the mirrors for what they were.

Josh had seen enough blood and witnessed the gory affects of ruptured, split flesh several times in the past few days, but nothing prepared him for the nauseous mess of human remains that lay on the bed before them. The young woman's body looked like it had been butchered. Laid on her back, her thin, straight legs were positioned together while her arms were outstretched to create a mock martyrdom of the fragile body. At first the exposed skin of her legs against the bloodied white material made it look as though she lay partially covered in the bed sheets, but as the gruesome sight began to imprint itself upon Josh's weary mind he realised the victim wore a matching frock of pure white. Drenched in the blood that had spilled from the open wounds on her slim torso, the distinction between frock and sheet had blended into a macabre shroud of dried plasma that caked the entire scene and reflected into infinity via the mirrored walls.

Josh tore his eyes from the nightmare. In his captor's rigid face he looked for comprehension for the horrific scene. All he found was the same dumb struck horror imprinted on her rigid face, blue eyes unable to believe the extent of the bloody scene they had discovered. In her hand the thrower trembled uncontrollably; revealing the harrowing effect the sight was having on her traumatized gaze. As Josh followed it back to the porcelain features of the victim the profound nature of the discovery hit home.

"That's her," Josh whispered breaking the silent vigil. "Who…?" he asked, failing to control the jittery muscles of his mouth. "Who did this?" His words were impulsive, disorderly and no sooner had he asked the question the answer became obvious as Angelica turned to him with a tear soaked face. At first he had seen condemnation in the wide, watery eyes. But then as she returned her saddened gaze back towards her dead friend the true nature of their war was defined even for the blindest of captives.

The Elite had killed Calisto. In strict contrast to the fatal and gratuitous assault she had suffered, her eyelids remained closed, her fragile features relaxed and at peace. From her tranquil repose it was as though death had come with the gentle touch of a lover, not with the excessive brutality relayed by her wounds. But it was the locks of red hair about her face that stamped the cruelty into Josh's psyche, and rammed his shameful naivety home like a freight train into a brick wall. Calisto had told him to seek her out in the real world, and there she was, butchered, bloodied and dead. They were too late. From the dark congealed patches of the gruesome pools formed from the multiple gaping cauterised entry points over her body, it was obvious she had lain in state for several hours. The smell of iron diffused into the air and filled Josh's nostrils, making the urge to vomit all the more worse.

"Why?" he asked imploringly. Angelica remained silent as though distress blocked her hearing. His question had not been aimed at the reason for the butchery, the enmity he had witnessed in the past few days had been evidence of the gravity of the existing feud between the Elite and these servants of the light calling themselves Latronis, but rather why the young woman had been so grotesquely despatched and left to spoil in the uninhabited warehouse. *This can't be real.*

"She was a sister of the light," Angelica said in a weak voice hindered by emotion. The dramatic explanation was a title of endearment, though he sensed the two women had retained some universal bond created through intense experiences of comradeship. Stepping forward she stroked the dead woman's face. The touch of the cold lifeless skin jaded the warm gesture and she retracted her hand. The answer to *why* was apparent. The gory manner in which the defenceless woman had been executed had been designed to terrorise and intimidate whoever laid their eyes upon the atrocity. From the dejected way Angelica's spirit had broken, the task couldn't have been more successful.

Watching his blonde captor lean forward to gently kiss Calisto's forehead, he still couldn't believe that Galda would turn his hand to such extremes. But that was the crux of the matter, he didn't know Galda and he didn't know these people who now kept him in their self righteous custody. The war was not all that it seemed.

"We must leave here," Angelica announced abruptly. Josh looked up to see she had changed her attention to the smeared blood on the mirror behind the bed.

"But," he replied, unable to comprehend the inhuman reasoning, "What about Calisto? We can't just leave her here like this!"

"Rest assured," she continued, still gazing at the crimson splatter on the reflective canvass. "She is now in a much better place than this. We are all prepared for death's release." Josh looked dumbfounded at Angelica's profile, unable to understand what garbled logic was running through her mind.

"We!" he blurted, emphasising his own part in it all. "*We* can't just leave. We can't leave her like this, she…" Again the words failed him. He followed her gaze once more to the fouled mirror. "She tried to warn me. I'm the reason…" His words trailed off, but not for lack of conception, but because amongst the grotesque arterial spray he saw what had captured her attention. At first glance the mirror was a bloodied vestige of the woman's murder, though amongst the crimson streams he could see a finger had been used to smear a single word. *Iscariot.* The word meant nothing to Josh but to Angelica it offered a vindictive motivation for her friend's murder. Turning back she saw his sudden silence was caused by the unsettling graffiti and walked over to take him by the arm.

"This is not your fault," she asserted, "there is more to this than you can see. And we must leave here, now!" She squeezed his arm at the elbow. The renewed grip of the tender muscle tore him away from the macabre sight and he looked at her with a bemused revulsion.

"This woman was your friend!"

"She still is," she replied enigmatically. "But if we stick around any longer it'll be the others mourning *our* departure." She saw his conscience was burdened by a lack of perception. "Josh, this is a war of extremes, and one that can only be won if we are strong. We don't expect you understand what we are, what we know, or our faith here and now, but believe me when I say the strength it gives us is all we have left to save mankind!" Josh's manic thoughts were suddenly interrupted by the muffled sound of approaching footsteps.

Alpha's large form appeared in the dark door space. Angelica turned to meet him, surprised to see the soldier had disobeyed her instruction. Seeing the look of horror on the big man's face she pushed Josh roughly towards him.

"Alpha no," she pleaded, hoping an inherent dedication to duty would make him guide their captive back out, but the hope was in vain. She had sensed the soldier's attraction to Calisto's fragile beauty and she now watched on as the steel of martial stability cracked under the weight of human frailty. Eyes staring, tinted with hidden emotion, Alpha edged past them to stand over the bed he had not so long before sat himself, and gazed upon the type of bloody inhumanity he had hoped never to see again.

"No, not like this," he murmured, shaking his head in disbelief.

"Alpha she's gone!" Angelica pleaded. "This place is compromised. We must leave, now!" She watched as he raised a hand, an extended finger poised to touch the smooth white skin of Calisto's upturned palm. Before he could complete the one and only act of intimacy, she grasped a fallen bed sheet and hurled it over the corpse. "This where it ends," she said facing him across the bed. Josh looked on mesmerised at the soldier's meek transformation. "Listen to me!" she yelled. "She was ready for this. All this does is prove that we must never stop, not until our task is complete. If necessary we give our lives to do so, such is the path we follow." Her words bounced off Alpha's misery.

"We should have been here," he stated distantly, his desolation evolving to anger. "We could have protected her!" In a lightening strike the big soldier sent a huge fist hurtling into the bloodied mirror with a mighty crash.

*****

The collision startled Josh. Until that moment he'd been locked in a daze created by the onslaught of exhaustion, confusion and shock, but the impact of Alpha's fist with the mirror caused his heart to skip a beat. For a moment the soldier kept it against the cracked surface. The cathartic pleasure of breaking something with brute force had helped to dampen his anger. Head bowed, he then lowered his arm and gazed at Calisto's congealed blood that now mixed with his own as it oozed from the fresh cuts on his knuckles. The collision had created a spider web of jagged fractures spiralling outward from a central crushed core, leaving a permanent statement of fury upon the bloody canvas. As he turned to Angelica, his eagle eyes revealed a new steely determination that echoed a desire for retribution. If he was to leave that place of mirrors, then it was with the cold hearted agenda of a highly skilled killing machine seeking vengeance. Satisfied with Alpha's silent conviction, Angelica urged Josh to leave with a subtle prod. But as the new fissure heralded its development with a definite crack the Latronis strike team paused.

Before their eyes the new fissure continued its progression. From the original impact it began to splinter out horizontally in a sharp unsettling chorus of splintering glass across the mirror wall. Alpha stood back and watched in amazement as the unstoppable fracturing continued to the corner of the room and onto the adjoining wall. Josh joined their scrutiny of its jittery, stunted progression across the second wall until it travelled to the third, unimpeded by the ninety degree change in trajectory.

"I think it's time to leave," he announced ominously. The notion of remaining as a storm of shattered mirrors rained glass shards upon them didn't appeal to his delicate sense of preservation. But the advice went unheeded as his two captors were mesmerised by the shattering fracture that continued to encircle them like an escalating crack in weakened ice. At first it had been slow in its progress, but as it traversed and spread to the final wall its speed increased until it rejoined its source at the sight of impact. In the aftermath of silent amazement, Josh was the first to state the obvious. "Something is very wrong here people." Braced for the inevitable collapse, the soldier's calm focus distracted Josh as the mirrors refused to give way. Defensively Angelica reached over to the open door and pushed it shut. To her amazement the fissure had continued across the breadth of its mirrored surface, completing the three hundred and sixty degree circuit and confirming the event as freakish and unnatural. Josh shivered. The huge weakness created by the horizontal fault was enough to bring the large reflective surfaces crashing down around them. But it was as their continued stability revealed the source of the unholy presence that had descended upon them, that everything suddenly made horrific sense.

Josh was the first to see him. Recognising the fear in the captive's eyes gazing over his shoulder, Alpha turned to face the dark intruder that loomed into view from behind the bars of crimson streaks above Calisto's head.

"Ladies and gentleman," Galda announced melodramatically. His voice echoed across the room, the recognition of which sent a chill down Josh's spine. Angelica turned from the door to face their adversary. "Elvis has entered the building." Galda Vey had come to claim his cruel glory.

"You!" Angelica spat the condemnation with a surprised derision. Behind the mirror's glass, Galda's form appeared like a reflection. Even with no physical form to reflect, only his shadow body projected from his slumbering body, he was still just as real and present. Manoeuvring his head to peer at the them from between the streaks of caked blood, Galda reminded Josh of a roused cobra swaying to the inaudible music of his own self conceit.

"Angelica, face to face at last," he said smugly with a mocking courtesy. She straightened at the sound of her own name.

"At last," she concurred, "except I don't have the pleasure of your name." The comment appeared to amuse Galda as he glanced quickly to Josh.

"My name is everywhere," Galda continued, moving from behind the arterial spray to gain a better view. "And I am also nowhere." His form began to pace anti clockwise around them, like a lion circling its prey, seemingly unable to pass through the walls of the mirrored cage. "Ask your friend sleeping beauty here," he gestured to Calisto's body, forever mocking as he paused to admire his trapped quarry. It was then Josh noticed something was missing. As though the very molecular fabric of the mirrors had been changed by the fracture, the Latronis reflections were no longer present, only their adversary's projecting psyche trapped behind its surface. "She knew what it meant to know my name," Galda continued vindictively, "But alas it was not something she could endure." The wicked boast was enough to melt Alpha's cool. Without warning he released his wrath from the muzzle of his returned Glock revolver.

The three shots fired in rapid succession into Galda's form. At such close range the shots were highly accurate and their spread of two to the head and one to the heart would have expertly dispatched any mortal enemy. But as Galda stepped aside from the behind the three new minute spider webs to reveal he was totally unharmed, it was with a look of amusement on his ghoulish face.

"Such hostility!" he said as he clapped his hands. "Most admirable." The gesture provoked the soldier to raise the gun again, only to have Angelica's disapproving hand thwart the offensive.

"Wait! The mirrors are what are holding him back." She explained the phenomenon while glaring into Galda's protected eyes. "While they remain intact he or his kind cannot enter." Alpha lowered the weapon, feeling a fool for almost compromising their safety. Galda's callous laugh then filled the room.

"And there I was thinking you servants of the light were the embodiments of benevolence. But you are nothing!" Galda cursed them. With a tilt of the head he reached out to the invisible barrier between them. Against its durable surface his pale hand fanned out as he attempted to force it through, but snatched it back with a snarl of frustration when his analysis was unfavourable. This was not the cool, charismatic tutor who had approached Josh with offers of kinship amongst the black elite, but a crazed, rabid creature, whose bestial mannerism was slowly revealing itself in all its unholy glory.

"It is you that is nothing!" Angelica yelled back. She pushed past Alpha so that she stood face to face with her nemesis, inches from the protective barrier that held Galda at bay. "You have betrayed yourselves along with your race. You are blinded by your own distorted vision of the truth and all the evil and iniquity that it breeds. It is you who are the slaves, and hell is your home!" Like a striking cobra Galda lurched forward, both hands spreading up against the mirror as his adversary lay just outside of his infuriated grasp.

"It is better to rule in hell than serve in heaven you pretty little fool," he quoted with a proud obstinacy. "The latter being a place you and your colleagues are closer to right now than you realise." As he backed off the approaching swarm that joined him behind the reflective surface confirmed the ghoul's conviction. No longer a singular representative of the black light he personified, a legion of identical clad spectres now began to materialise around the trapped militia. As the white faced, black-attired reinforcements positioned themselves into a dark wall of hatred, Galda bowed his head in solemn appreciation of their superiority.

Within seconds the encroaching spectres completely surrounded the protective cell. As their poker faced principal leered inward at the outnumbered enemy, the widening grin of malicious intent across his pallid features then relayed he was readying himself for some new onslaught. Instinctively Alpha, Josh and Angelica backed away from the walls. Forming a back-to-back formation they stared on at wavering walls that darkened as the legion of Elite projections solidified their perimeter. The enemy's number appeared infinite, and for Josh he was struck with the realisation he was no longer the Elite's protégé. *He didn't even acknowledge me.* Galda's ignorance had written him off as a traitor. The judgement was unfair but Josh's shame was short lived as he acknowledged he held no devotion to the macabre army that now threatened to engulf them. However as the Elite general looked up, the notion of his malevolent power and fury being unleashed in combination filled Josh with an ice cold dread.

His features grim and focused, Galda began a second assault on the sanctuary's wall. Drawing power from the concentration of Elite presence that weakened its mystical barrier, he felt it waver under his escalating power. In horror Josh watched as Galda's hand speared its way into the fabric of the faltering mirror. As though glass had transformed to rubber, its surface stretched inwards up to a black elbow.

"This is a place of light!" Angelica roared at Galda as she watched his arm spear deeper into the room. Under the strain his face contorted into a furious grimace. "And you may never enter it!" Though the declaration seemed vain denial, Josh was amazed to find it more than a boast, she was right. Galda's features further distorted with rage as his entire macabre strength failed to breach the mirror's pliable skin. Still he persisted. Driven by a furious mania, rooted from a deep seated hatred of those standing in his path, he signalled to the black legion to join him.

Josh felt Angelica and Alpha's bodies push up against his own. As they stared at the army of limbs and hands now seeking to penetrate the wavering walls where their master had failed, only then did Josh sense true fear in his captors. At first they had merely been trapped, Angelica had known this, but now as she grasped the hands of the two men she too realised the cell of undying light may actually succumb.

"Whatever happens next, you follow me," she instructed as the swarming mass of grasping hands now found they could infiltrate deeper into the obstinate barrier. Overhead the lighting flickered ominously. To his right and left Alpha saw the protective white Chi balls were beginning to dull in colour. As he saw the appearance of black veins beginning to corrupt their perfect surfaces Angelica pulled her hand free and fumbled for the device in her pocket.

"What are you doing?" Josh asked. Though he'd seen Angelica's immense power at first hand he knew the insurmountable odds they faced would easily overwhelm even her, but not without a fight. He flinched back as an intrusive claw swiped at his chest, missing him by inches. "Whatever it is you're planning do it fast!" The leering faces of their invading assailants were shielded from the room's light by protective eyewear. Though they sought to enter and destroy what lay within the sanctuary of light, the Elite horde remained weary of its power, fear like ignorance paving their path to hatred.

"Get onto the bed!" Angelica's order echoed through the room. Breaking ranks she leapt onto the bed. The two men quickly followed suit until all three balanced on the low mattress, careful not to trample the sacrosanct form under its bloodied sheets. The legion of belligerent, grasping hands continued to swarm ever inward, encroaching to the shrinking room's centre where the trio now made their last stand. With the aggressors reach only several feet short of their goal, the mirrored barrier was now stretched to the brink of perforation. It was then Angelica pulled out the thrower and pointed the device at Galda's seething form. "May the light protect us," Angelica muttered the words and tightened her grasp on the weapon's trigger.

Before Alpha could reciprocate her own warning a white flame consumed her hand. Both generated and contained by the thrower's mechanism that sat flat in her palm, the ball of destructive light hovering in her hand was now at her disposal. With a reciprocating malevolence Angelica raised her arm back, goading Galda's stunned glance as he dared to believe she would be so imprudent. Poised to deliver the act of foolishness she held it aloft and watched the fireball's reflection dance in the enemy's black eyewear.

"Do it!" Alpha hollered. Swallowing her apprehension with desperation she then hurled the fiery projectile at its target. The trapped trio cowered as the collision imploded against the mirror, covering them in a hail of glass shards as demonic screams relayed the black projections had been caught in the blast. In an infectious chorus the snarls and shrieks unfolded around them as the Elite assault was corrupted by the break in their circle. Instead of attacking Galda, Angelica had turned at the last second to throw the lightening bolt at the mirrored entrance. In a brilliant flash the door had been obliterated instantaneously. Lowering their arms as the aftermath subsided in an ensuing chaos; the trapped servants of the light saw the creation of a fleeting window of escape.

"Move!" Angelica shouted. Leaping from the bed she disappeared into the gaping passageway. The sonic blast had left the attackers reeling. Intrusive hands had recoiled in agony, but the retreat was only temporary. With the barrier of light breached the Elite vultures were free to flood Calisto's room and bury it in darkness.

Disappearing into the blacked out passageway after Angelica, Josh trailed Alpha in a desperate tangle of leaps and bounds. Unaccustomed to the dark he tumbled against a wall, letting fear guide his legs back into the showroom and away from the nightmarish horde on their trail. Behind, a cacophony of fiendish howls heralded the sanctuary had been plundered. Like a torrent of black floodwater escaping a breached levee he sensed the surge of Elite ghouls filling the vacuum they left in their wake. Running for his life Josh bulldozed a path through the arranged furniture. Around him unseen obstacles were sent cashing into the shadows in a desperate attempt to flee those that pursued them. Within seconds of skirting tables and toppling chairs he was back into the first passage.

The glow from the outside security light acted a beacon as Angelica held the fire door open, guiding the two men to the iron stairway and their only chance at freedom. But instead of racing down its steps Alpha paused on its mesh platform to face the evil. Josh blundered into the soldier as a chilling roar reverberated from the showroom.

"Go Flyboy!" Grabbing Josh by the arm, he forced their captive down the iron steps and shoved the door shut. Removing a boot knife he jammed its thin blade into the door's bolt. Now impossible to be opened from the inside he raced down the steps, pushing Josh ever onwards. He doubted it would hold for long, but any advantage was greatly appreciated. Their heavy footsteps went uncontested now as they scurried down the metal stairway like rats from a doomed vessel. Jumping its last four steps to the alley floor a sprawl almost cost Josh his ankle. Stumbling to the cracked asphalt he looked up to see Angelica's blonde hair disappear into the night as she ran on ahead. A strong hand then grabbed his belt, hauling him onto his feet.

"Keep moving!" Alpha bellowed. "We're not out of this yet." A loud boom from above interrupted the surprise camaraderie. Both men jerked their head skywards to see the purged fire exit door had been blown off its hinges. A howl of demonic roars followed its tumultuous fall into the alley before it crashed onto a dumpster. "Holy mother of God," Alpha gasped as he saw the black forms gushing from the mouth of the now gaping fire exit. The dark bodies that clawed their way out in pursuit were humanoid but not human, their movement swift and serpentine. Behind the shades perched on the pale, snarling faces of the Elite spectres, shiny golden eyes were now searching for their loitering prey.

With terror piercing the heart of morbid mesmerism, the two men took flight and ran for their lives. At the alley's mouth the RV was still parked in the shadows, its side door open as Monk stood half out guarding their only means of escape. Behind them the thunderous noise of an army of feet threatened to shake the fire escape from the warehouse wall, the howls degrading into a chilling chatter of devilish glee as Alpha and Josh dived into the RV.

"Get the hell out of here!" Alpha yelled. From a backwards glance Josh saw the asphalt had come to life. The Elite army had emerged from the dark alley like a pack of wild demons; the only thing between him and them was the enigmatic Monk, who snarled back at the black forms that slithered out from the shadows. With a wave his arm up and down he traced the sacred symbol in the air.

"Veita okindra alla ilska!" Unknown to Josh the incantation had brought an invisible power to life. In the seconds before Monk finally tugged the heavy door shut, Josh saw the black horde reel upwards like a torrent of crude oil as they collided with some unseen barrier. Before he knew what was happening a heavy stamp on the gas peddle lurched the RV from the alley and sent it hurtling off into the night-veiled streets.

Josh tumbled around on the floor as it banked left and right like a boat in a storm. For a cumbersome vehicle their getaway vehicle felt as nimble and swift as any car a third its size. Finally backed into a corner he sat and prayed they were finally delivered from the enemy. They had done it; they had escaped by the seat of their pants, though for how long depended on how fast they could loose Galda and his legion of black agents. Angelica, panting from the exertion to freedom, was back in her reclined seat. At her side Alpha had joined her in its adjoining chair. The big soldier was staring ahead, a blank stare that hide a myriad of bottled emotion. Angelica took his hand in hers and gave a reassuring squeeze, but the gesture was little recompense for the void left behind by their joint loss.

"Calisto?" Monk suddenly asked, his exposed emotion curtailing his previous austere manner. He already knew the answer. They had returned without their sister, but pride demanded it was made official. Angelica, bereft of her usual vivacity, shook her head and looked away. They had lost her, and in doing so almost lost themselves in the trap her sacrifice had created.

*****

Only a block away Galda waited furiously inside the black, unmarked Government Issue van. The first to ground his projected shadow body back into its mortal shell of flesh and blood, he watched and waited as the pale skinned bodies around him were reanimated by their own returning astral projections. The foiled attack had merely inflamed the principal's desire for vengeance, being forced to return to their slumbering bodies prematurely had made a mockery of the calculated efficiency he so prided his success on. Drawn by their fallen comrade the Latronis militia had been trapped and outnumbered; still they had escaped.

The Elite had known of the red head's infiltration of the Low Grades for sometime, the strength of her Nothos spirit paradoxically leading to her exposure. Had the bond between tutor and the Brenin Nothos not been fashioned by some ascended compliance, he may never have been able to draw her image from Josh's mind, or the valuable instructions she imparted during their Hyperborean rendezvous from his unconscious. The servants of the light had over played their hand one too many times. Josh Brenin was no Low Grade, his star was yet to shine, a black star that would sit at the principal's right hand into eternity. Still, as his reanimated soldiers now turned to their master for instruction, the failed display of the black light's supremacy had inevitably helped to secure his unwitting protégé's allegiance with the enemy. Galda still had his ace in the hole.

The Elite driver's grim features slackened with fear as Galda yanked the Smith & Wesson revolver from its holster and reached over to ram its muzzle against the back of his cranium.

"Catch them or die!" Galda hissed as the Elite van in front pulled away to give chase to the fleeing RV. It took less than a split second for the order to register. The driver obediently joined the pursuit with a screeching of tyres. The Nothos traitors had to be eliminated, *They* would not grant the keys to immortality until it was done, and thus Galda remained poised for the coup de grace.

The powerful Nothos who had cast the stumbling block had been unknown to Galda, but the last second show of power had marked the long haired Latronis renegade for an exceptional death in Galda's eyes. The light wall had been impenetrable. With his black legion unqualified to breech its opposing energy at the quantum level, its power, though fleeting over time, had obliged the Elite attack into an unplanned detour. Forced to continue the assault on the mortal plain they had returned to their entranced bodies waiting in the two blacked out field ops transports.

In a re-enactment of the red head's termination, a subordinate agent had suggested they storm the building on foot, though Galda, preferring the covert security that astral projection afforded them, had preferred to unleash their unholy gifts on the outnumbered enemy. *Strength in unity*. But now as he sensed this subordinate agent return to his mortal body in the second unmarked van up front, he knew his ambitious underling would be quick to exploit the situation. The secret masters, the ultra dimensional coordinators of Project Olympia would only advance its principal agent to the highest accolade. Should failure dog his progression of their great work of ages, then Galda would find he had a battle for supremacy much closer to home for the greatest of prizes. Failure was not an option.

Chapter 11

Dex handled the Solarian's bulk with the master skills of a professional getaway driver. He knew every nut, bolt and inch of steel on the speedy RV, which in turn he had tuned, built and rebuilt with his own bare hands. As he weaved between the heavy traffic of late night downtown L.A., he knew exactly what she was capable of. The heavy vehicle was powered by a mammoth ten litre engine, customised with handmade components devotedly manufactured in his dead brother's workshop. Before the fatal crash on the Indianapolis speedway, the corporate sponsored workshop had maintained his older sibling's pride and joy, though in its burning wreck of steel and florescent body kits, that dream had died with his own flesh and blood. But now his brother's legacy served a new family, and one he was charged with transporting to safety.

The nocturnal streets were busy, making Dex's duty all the more harder to uphold. As he banked the RV into every free space as it appeared in the traffic lanes, he made the most of what freedom the road offered from what he had no doubt still pursued them. At his side Jonah relinquished his grip on the passenger seat armrest and looked back into the Solarian's interior.

"What happened back there?" he demanded to know, his question aimed at whoever would break the silence.

"Darkies!" Alpha growled. "Frigging Darkies, they were everywhere!" The answer was blunt; it was bitterness hiding true feelings. Fury was the cap that allowed him to bottle those feelings and avoid the obvious question.

"What about Calisto?" Jonah persisted. "Did she get out?" Alpha's silence answered a question no one was willing to answer. Their comrade had been murdered. "She's dead?" he asked.

"What do you think brainiac?" Alpha growled back. "She isn't here." Jonah looked mortified. "They killed her you dumb bastard!"

"Enough!" Angelica intervened before the simmering emotions boiled over into a distraction. "There's no time for this, everybody just empty your minds. After projecting amongst us for so long they can still trace our astral signatures. Until we with have a big enough physical gap between us and them, everybody centre your thoughts." Her instructions, spoken calmly and concise, diffused the sad truth threatening to crack the frail sense of security. Jonah turned back around in his seat and stared out of the windshield at the passing traffic. Outside there was an unsuspecting world caught in the no-man's land of a battlefield they didn't even know existed. Couples walked the streets, bars and fast-food joints purveyed their services to endless clientele, a bearded vagrant picked up a half eaten box of fries from a garbage can. It was the world that lived in a dream.

The loss of their sister was the first blow the small militia had suffered. Angelica knew the hollow space left behind by Calisto's death threatened the cohesive bond that, up until that point, had made them feel untouchable.

"There will be a time to reflect once we are out of the woods," she added then watched Monk and Alpha reverently lower their heads. The Latronis militia turned to silence again in an attempt to thwart their zealous enemy. Apart from Dex and Jonah who remained unexposed, the others used a technique perfected by necessity, closing their thoughts to retract their presence from the psychic web that conjoined all living creatures on the universal higher plains. But one amongst them remained curious.

"Where are we going?" Josh asked concerned. His heartbeat had finally calmed to a comfortable rate and now, as he perched once more on the crate in the back of the fleeing RV, he realised he wasn't going home. Alpha turned sharply to answer.

"What's it to you Flyboy?" he replied coldly. He was still carrying the discharged revolver his hand. His grip suddenly tightened around its handle as his steely gaze transfixed on Josh. "We should get rid of this one," he then suggested with flick of the gun.

"Alpha relax," Angelica ordered.

"Something's not right!" he retorted. "He's not one of us!" The captive felt his blood turn to ice as he sensed the frank vehemence resonating from the bloodshot predatory eyes. Josh found the twitching of Alpha's thumb against the revolver's hammer particularly disconcerting. Intrigued Monk turned to Josh, but said nothing in his defence. "Think about it, Calisto would still be here if it wasn't for him," Alpha declared coldly, "her blood's on his hands!"

Alpha abruptly raised the gun to Josh's forehead. Unable to retreat Josh banged the back of head against the rear door, the cold revolver's muzzle pinning it there. The jolt of the cocking hammer then reverberated into the captive's skull. Unable to vent his fury on the *Darkies* that had murdered Calisto, Alpha had turned to what he saw as the next best thing.

"Alpha put the gun down!" Angelica barked. The order went un-obeyed. Josh stared past the big fingers grasping the gun and into its owner's frenzied eyes.

"Wait!" he pleaded. As the ex soldier pushed the muzzle harder into the thin skin of Josh's forehead he saw Alpha's grey corneas contract his jet black pupils.

"You weren't one of us, remember?" Angelica reminded him. "He is not the enemy; the black agents are the evil responsible for Calisto's murder. Killing him will only help to diminish our small numbers further. We need him." The pressure of the muzzle relaxed slightly.

"They are the Elite," Josh blurted, hoping to verify Angelica's claim. "The black agents call themselves the Elite." Unexpectedly the muzzle was spitefully reapplied to his temple, hard enough to twist Josh's head to one side.

"It's his fault!" Alpha growled with a renewed fury. He placed an outfacing palm behind the cocked hammer to shield from the spray of blood and brains that would accompany the close range execution. The trained killer had been used to despatching Uncle Sam's enemies without a conscience; the fury of the alpha man was not to be deterred. That was until Monk intervened by raising a thrower to Alpha's own head. Again the muzzle's pressure relaxed.

"Calisto isn't dead Alpha!" Angelica continued. "Even the blackest of nights cannot smother the light of a single flame, you know this. All of us will all meet again" Though Alpha doubted Monk would discharge the powerful weapon inside the RV; he took note of the proposition behind it. Lowering the revolver with a look of defeat he sat back in the second recliner.

"I hope you know what you're doing," he snarled. Josh righted himself on the crate, his look of dread quickly followed by one of loathing as he rubbed life back into the bruised skin of his forehead. "For all our sakes." The ominous prediction was cause enough for Angelica to glance at Monk for reassurance as he lowered the thrower. Their captive had been compromised, Calisto's exposure the result of the psychic bond that chained tutor and Low Grade. In a court of logic, Alpha's judgment would have been sound, but something about Joshua Brenin refused to condone her similar condemnation. Inside the down and out's weary body she sensed a hidden power, a power she was sure Galda Vey and his black Elite would kill to reacquire. *But why?* Still overwhelmed by the confrontation, Josh decided that neither side, Latronis or Elite, offered much in the way of hospitality.

"So this *Elite* we face, what else do you know about them?" Angelica asked with stern curiosity.

"By their own admission they consider themselves the best at, whatever this is!" Josh replied a little coyly. "And my impression is that their arrogance is well founded." He didn't mean to sound condescending, but his opinion was the self styled Elite held all the aces, and from their last display, particularly in sheer numbers.

"Their arrogance is their weakness," Monk stated solemnly. "By exploiting it, we will be their undoing." This second prediction echoed with vengeance. Josh searched his features for mockery; though found they carried the same bemusing certainty.

"I'll take your word for it," Josh said dismissively. He caught Angelica's blue eyes scrutinising him again with a combination of scepticism and curiosity. As she unlocked eyes to stare into nothingness he realised he found her stubborn confidence admirable. The noble manner in which she carried herself amongst the male dominated militia radiated a rare charisma, one like no other women he had encountered before. His heart would forever belong to Sarah; though in the company of the blonde haired Angelica Josh saw a woman whose defined strength commanded a similar enigmatic respect, but a respect that could quickly degenerate into fear.

His mind still raced with unasked queries. *Calisto not dead?* From the RV's calmer manoeuvres he guessed their driver Dex had escaped the crowded streets and made it onto the freeway. But in the tranquillising hum of the bulky interior, Josh sensed it was merely the calm before the next storm.

*****

Galda re-holstered his weapon and released an impish grin. Glaring through his windshield into the night the escaping RV had been easy to spot, its lumbering chasse dwarfing the hatchbacks and people carriers that comprised the heavy stream of traffic up ahead. Thrusting the revolver into the driver's neck had not only disconcerted the accompanying agents, who's reanimated faces continued to stare respectively away, the incentive had also won them first place in the pursuit of the Latronis getaway vehicle. With the second blacked out Elite van now tailing his lead, Galda urged his driver to decrease their speed. From the RV's steady pace along the freeway he guessed their prey had been lulled into a false sense of security. But Galda could sense apprehension, apprehension meant fear and fear was a useful tool for aiding an enemy's destruction. Retracting his astral reconnaissance, he sensed it trailing from the fleeing transport like the necrotic odour of a rotting corpse.

"Ready yourselves," he instructed and strapped himself into his seat. It was time to finish what had been started, to clear the path for his glorious destiny. The twelve Elite agents bowed their heads as if in silent prayer, their black clad bodies strapped upright into their seats so their vacant shells would not be harmed if the van made some hasty manoeuvre.

"And not too close," he warned the driver, before assuming an identical meditative pose. Like all highly skilled tradesmen their skills were second nature, honed to perfection from years of training. As the agents closed their minds to the material world, their projected forms would be free to ascend time and space, enabling them to apply their fatal trade upon the servants of the light in a matter of seconds. "Remember," he prompted, "all are to be extinguished."

"And the Brenin Nothos, Sir?" an agent asked.

"If he dies, then it proves I was wrong." Death was ready to stalk the light for what was to be the last time.

Inside the Solarian, Angelica raised her head and stared blankly at the rear door. Since they had escaped the clutches of the Elite she had capped her higher conscious by imagining a mirrored shell cocooning her body, reflecting unwanted attention to the light that was her immortal essence. The technique had taken months to perfect, though Monk had learnt it within a matter of days. The pokerfaced Nothos had been traversing the astral plains since the age of seven, conversing with disembodied entities at the age of nine and playing mindless pranks by projecting his shadow body to relatives living hundreds of miles away from his San Diego home by the time he was in junior high. As an adult his highly receptive conscious could adapt to whatever level of existence he desired. As the second most powerful Nothos in the Latronis ranks, he could channel, amplify and propel pure Chi energy into a protective or destructive form while still grounded in his body, something the rest could only accomplish while projected in astral form. But today, Angelica had out done her mentor. Their recent contact with the dark essence of the Elite ghouls had left a trace contamination, inadvertently acting like a fleeting homing beacon, its originators could tune in and triangulate location across time and space at will. It was as Alpha followed Josh's concerned gaze to Angelica expanding eyes, he saw she had been the first to sense Their return. But the forewarning was too late.

The first Elite projection cleared the half mile distance between the two vehicles in milliseconds, its spectral form clasping onto the RV's silver exterior like a leech to warm flesh. Though unseen through the vehicle's metal hull, the black agent's presence was like a boiling hot coal landing in a tranquil lake, the astral tremor it created sufficient to wake Monk from his deep internal refuge. Two more grasping shadow bodies quickly followed the malignant hijacker. Then three and five more, their numbers swelling until a small army of black clad attackers had pounced and attached to the vehicle's exterior and now attempted to claw their way in. Though their prey sped on through the lanes of unsuspecting traffic, the

Elite forms clung to its surface unaffected by wind resistance or G-force, their immaterial forms existing outside the laws of the physical world, giving them the freedom to release their hate in a rabid frenzy seen only in nature's wildest predatory pack hunts.

"Light us up!" Angelica instructed to Monk. Immediately, he slumped back into a meditative trance and enforced the command by projecting an invisible shield of Chi energy about the vehicle, thus making it impossible for their assailants to enter. It worked. The Elite had hoped a surprise attack would make for any easy slaughter. But like Calisto's room, an unseen barrier that had impeded their every strike now protected the RV, its duration dependant on Monk's psychic stamina. The metal exterior above Alpha's head suddenly warped and stretched inwards as a twisted hand forced its way in from the outside. Unable to breech the Solarian's hull, the Elite's polarised power was simply weakening the very fabric of the steel, transforming metal into an eerie rubber that began to shrink around the occupants. As he jumped from his seat another hand grasped ghoulishly inwards. The sound of his fist punching this second swipe boomed throughout the RV as flesh and bone struck solid metal.

"What the hell is going on?" Alpha demanded, squeezing the pain from his bruised knuckle as the writhing hand retreated.

"What does it look like? It's them!" Josh yelled. Angelica strapped herself into the swivel mounted recliner and turned to the cabin.

"Dex! Keep us moving; don't stop for anything!" she ordered. Already surmising their salvation depended on maintaining high velocity, Dex floored the accelerator. "Jonah, outside!" Leaping from his passenger seat as the RV banked to avoid a four-by-four; their dread locked co-pilot jumped into the vacated recliner beside her and locked the heavy body straps over his broad chest.

"Up to our asses in it again," he joked as he relaxed into the chair. But Angelica didn't hear. Already her shadow body had left her mortal body to do battle. With little time to plan strategy or tactics, the parasites would have to be removed fighting fire with fire. As Alpha ducked another ghoulish arm he tugged his revolver free and pistol whipped the grasping limb into retreat. Unable to auto project he was a spare part, a tin soldier, and so he watched on as Jonah closed his eyes to join Angelica on the RV's exterior.

In a matter of seconds a legion of grasping arms turned the calm interior into a mobile hall of horrors. Its walls were now a writhing, clawing enemy that sought to harm the trapped Latronis. Not until Alpha suddenly released a visceral growl that quickly degenerated into a frustrated gargle did Josh realise one had succeeded. Looking up he saw the big man struggling to free himself from the grip of the successful metallic arm that had clamped like a vice around his neck. He jumped up and tried to pull the hand free, until a sudden swerve of the RV caused him to stumble to his knees.

"Hold on!" Josh shouted, righting himself as Dex straightened their trajectory. Again he tried to prise the solid hand from Alpha's neck, but found its hold retained its steely composition and was as formidable as a statue. The revolver fell with a thump to the RV's floor as its owner's face began to redden. Even their combined strength was no match for the murderous limb and Josh realised there was little he could do to prevent Alpha asphyxiating.

Outside of the speeding RV another battle raged. Angelica and Jonah were outnumbered five to one, but the Elite projections had been ill prepared for a counter offensive. Attired in the ethereal uniforms of servants of the light, they stood on the Solarian's roof like the avenging angels they were. Around them the stream of disbelieving traffic hurled past at over eighty miles an hour as their mirrored eyes targeted the astral parasites glaring back with vehement golden equivalents. Out in the open their fanatical Elite opponents began to encircle the two Latronis projections, their black forms jockeying for position as they eyed up their overdue victory. They sensed an easy kill, a chance to prove the supremacy of the black light and eradicate the one thing that stood between the Elite and immortality. But Angelica and Jonah were not there to defend this day. Necessity demanded they fought for their lives.

The first defeated agent reeled back as the invisible bolt struck its chest. Cast from the blonde woman's palm like a canon ball it body's cohesion destabilized before being plucked free of the steel hull as it was forced back to ground. Casting projectile after projectile Angelica quickly began to cleanse the vehicles exterior. With one hand she sent out a Chi bolt to strangle an Elite ghoul; watching it struggled like a hooked worm she blasted another into its torso. As its screams pierced the night like a crushed cat it shook it cohort's blackened faith. Thus began the cleansing. The furious fight between contrasting powers was quick and aggressive. Two Elite forms took on the mighty blonde Nothos at once, but with a raised arm she sent forth another psychic shockwave to crush a pale snarling face and blasted the other away before it reached her.

Angelica was a powerful Nothos, a servant of the light and on that day the powers of light were strong. Jonah too enjoyed a similar success. His shadow body attached to the RV's side like a fridge magnet, he had begun to wrench the black parasites away, enjoying their demonic yells of defeat as they disappeared into the night. He was not as strong his blonde partner. For him the invisible destructive force did not hold the same potency, so he relied on crushing necks with his astral hands, his vivacious will power reflecting in the strength of his shadow body and making him a formidable hand-to-hand opponent.

One by one the Elite projections were being scraped from the Solarian's bulk like barnacles from a ships hull. But the fight was to take its toll on Jonah. After dispatching so many of the demonic parasites, his astral body had been weakened by the very opposing powers it had overcome. As he sensed his focus slipping it was too late to issue a warning of his retreat. Her name faltered on his lips as he sunk through the reinforced steel underfoot. Forced to return to his slumbering body inside, he reluctantly left Angelica to dispel the final few on the RV's exterior. But seeing the Latronis numbers halved, the remaining ghouls saw their chance.

The four agent spectres regrouped to face off against the mighty Nothos, only by combining their strength could they hope to defeat her. Still, the distance they kept betrayed their apprehension. As the murderous pack closed in Angelica watched the streetlights dance on the lenses of their shades as they zipped by overhead. Behind the protective eyewear she sensed the golden eyes reflecting an insane fury. While the RV continued its dangerous weaving amongst the freeway's traffic the astral combatant's feet remained rooted to its metal chasse. Cars and trucks were being left in the RV's wave as Dex sought to maximise every inch of chance for evasion from the hell that pursued them. Out of sight however another Elite agent was unrelenting in its grip through the vehicle's malleable roof.

Alpha's lips began to blue as his brain was starved of precious oxygen, the soldier's eyes rolling up in their sockets as Josh's attempts to wake Monk from his induced trance continued to fail.

"I need help!" His plea went unheard. Attempts to remove the vice at the soldier's neck were quickly becoming in vain. Alpha's face now a dangerous shade of purple he knew the big man's time was quickly coming to an end. But as Dex swerved to avoid a motorcycle, fate intervened. Josh looked down to what had knocked into his foot. Expecting to see another grasping hand instead he saw Alpha's revolver. Picking it up by the muzzle he then hammered its handle down hard on the elbow of the clasping vice. In a vicious frustrated attack he pummelled the relentless arm, each strike creating a booming clunk of synthetic polymer striking living metal, until suddenly it released its victim. Half dead the soldier slumped into his arms, but as the RV banked again the soldier's bulk toppled Josh into the interior wall. With a violent bang to the head, the liberator was knocked out cold.

Outside the pained agent retrieved its arm from the RV's roof, aching from whatever had managed to strike it so hard. But as a colleague's snarling projection shot past and disappeared into the traffic, the agony quickly became the least of his worries. Before he had turned to face its evictor two other agents were wrenched from the RV's roof by unseen projectiles, their reeling shadow bodies joining the rest of the failures as they were sucked away into the night. Standing his ground, he was now the sole remaining Elite agent waiting to face the mighty blonde servant of the light. As mirrored eyes locked with his golden orbs, her grin dared him to advance.

"Angelica," he sneered her name. No sooner had he inched towards her the same invisible force that had dispatched his cohorts blasted into his chest. Ripping his magnetic foothold free, he was sent soaring backwards in their wake. But Angelica's elation was short lived. As her mirrored eyes looked up into the night she saw the pawns had been sacrificed to clear the path for the black knight.

*****

The Elite projection soaring downwards from the black heavens was no avenging angel. Galda Vey's projected form made a deafening clang as it landed on the RV's roof, stunning Dex and the others underneath who instinctively reeled in panic. With a sallow, devilish face he looked up from the permanent indent he'd made in the sheet metal to Angelica, and grinned with the guilty pleasure all predators enjoyed before devouring their prey. Facing off like astral gladiators on top of the speeding vehicle, Angelica knew there would be no sardonic wordplay. This time the furious black agent was ready to make his final offensive.

The first strike came like a bolt of lightening. Galda's arm moved so fast it was merely a blur as the ball of energy struck Angelica's midriff. The collision sent her ethereal projection soaring backwards. Brutal as it was, Angelica's contrasting power absorbed the blow like a sponge, negating its destructive energy as her projection surged back to its previous stance as though tied to the speeding arena by some elastic cord. Surprised but undeterred, Galda propelled the brutal force to wrap its invisible claws around her astral neck and squeezed. Again her mighty form writhed and shrugged it off like the arm of a discarded lover. Down but not out, she followed up by reciprocating in kind. The first bolt she cast Galda managed to sidestep with supernatural ease, but the second blast caught the Elite ghoul full in the chest. The collision made his black projection warp and twist freakishly before her mirrored eyes, but with an eerie immortal cohesion quickly returned to its original brooding state.

"Touché, my little angel," Galda hollered over roar of the slipstream. "I'm impressed." He made the admission with a raised eyebrow. "You know in some cultures that might be seen as foreplay." His initial fury spent, he returned to debasement while he searched for a weakness.

"You're nothing, can't you see?" Angelica retorted confidently. "You are as puny as your pathetic minions. Go back to your pit where you belong!" Though she felt hatred for the murderous creature that now confronted her on equal grounds; the killer of her friend, following the path of light meant forsaking such thoughts. Instead Angelica channelled the negative feelings with the euphoria of victory. But as she scrutinised the obvious might of the contrasting Nothos, she knew the battle would be far from easy.

"I'm just warming up my dear, and besides," he continued his leering taunt, "Daddy's got a whole new bag of tricks." With a wave of his hand he sent a new evil to take its toll on the defiant servant of the light. Suddenly her feet were gripped by an icy sensation. Looking down she saw to her horror that the RV's metal roof was morphing up into her own shadow body, her own feet becoming one with the shiny silver surface that had liquidated on command. The extreme cold continued up her shins as the metal continued to slither and blend in with her astral form. Angelica struggled to free her trapped feet, except her vast strength was no use against this new magic threatening to engulf her. The magician laughed malevolently as its grisly progress began to swallow her thighs.

"Ever wondered what it would be like to be the tin man in the wizard of oz?" he goaded his victim. Desperately she needed to countermand her absorption, yet she knew of no remedy for the unstoppable metamorphosis. "At least you'll have your heart," Galda leered as he stepped closer. "For what is a servant of the light if he or she has no heart?" Angelica tried to cast another bolt but the progression to her abdomen had served to drain her of all her vital strength. Under the manic gaze of the principal black agent she began to fear for her life. Her arms and mind were all she had left, but within seconds she would have neither. Frantically Angelica searched for a way to prevent her total absorption.

"It's been a long time coming," Galda continued, admiring his handiwork on the trapped Nothos. "But now at last we shall be rid of you. In a blink of an eye you will cease to exist, and with a second your wretched kindred will follow you into eternity." In an unheard of gesture, the Elite agent removed his sunglasses. In the artificial light of the passing streetlights his golden eyes glistened like two molten suns. Naked and inhuman they failed to lose their malignant resonance as they focused on his dying prey. "Yes, They will be pleased," he assured himself. The distant wail of police sirens momentarily distracted the principal, though amusement turned to bewilderment as his victim produced a conceit smirk of her own.

"I hate to be the bearer of bad news Galda," Angelica hissed as the freezing metal absorbed her chest, "but death loves the living." The timing was everything. With a final discharge of her depleting energy she sent forth an invisible hand to wrench the cable free. From the corner of a terrified eye she had eagerly watched as the power cable running along the stretch of freeway finally crossed directly over the RV. Within reach she drew it down through the night and coiled it around the agent's neck, around which it tightened like a giant black boa constrictor, spitting blasts of discharging electricity that flashed and popped from its dislodged end into the shocked shadow body.

Galda's let out a surprised howl as the cable delivered its twenty four thousand volt payload, but the counter attack was not enough to dispatch him. As his projection deformed and cauterised under the demobilising surge, pale face contorting in agony as his metallic eyes glared wide and soulless, it was the actions of another projection that finally evicted the parasite. The new shadow body rose through the RV's roof and swiped at Galda's feet, the underhand manoeuvre enough to dislodge the black agent's magnetic foothold and send his howling form reeling away into the night traffic. With its coordinator beaten, the creeping metal retreated back into the roof and the two Latronis projections returned to ground, exhausted.

Dex saw the light turn to red and put his foot down. The black and whites had been tailing the speeding RV and the Elite transports on their tail for the past two or three miles, over which their ranks had continued to swell. Choosing to abandon the freeway for a random turn off, Dex followed it round through an underpass to a crossroads. From behind sirens blared and lights flashed as the cross traffic ahead was released by a set of green lights. *Can't stop.* With the skilled split second assessment of an Indie car racer he banked and weaved the cumbersome RV through the leading cars. A sudden jolt to the tail end relayed its rear bumper had taken a direct hit. Darting a glance to a wing mirror he saw the unfortunate people carrier responsible spin to a halt at the intersection. Straightening up the RV with the knowledge he'd made it, he realised their escape had been secured by a stockade of halted, honking cars left in his wake.

The Elite vans had only been less than twenty feet behind. The first tried to follow the RV's precarious path, but was brought to a premature halt as it clipped the nose of a Corvette and was railroaded by a surprised Cadillac crashing into its flank. Upon seeing the carnage the second Elite van screeched to a stop. As the wailing squad cars blocked it in at the lights, several armed LAPD officers now rushed out on foot to greet the first immobilized van with handguns and orders to vacate the wreckage. Stepping out, Galda walked through the pile up and police threats to see the Solarian's silver bodywork disappear over the horizon into the night.

"Stay right where you are!" a cop ordered. "You take another step and I'll shoot you where you sta…" The cop's voice trailed off when Galda turned his ghoulish face to greet his with a crunch of dislocated neck cartilage.

"Good work, Sergeant," he replied coyly. "I hope you like Alaskan winters!"

Josh returned to his body with such a jolt it felt like someone had stamped on his chest. He had woken to find a pressing weight was smothering him, though instead of some vicious foot bearing down he found it was Alpha's unconscious bulk. As a helping hand then pulled the big soldier away Jonah's anxious perspiring face peered down.

"You still with us Flyboy?" he asked. Josh nodded and crawled up from the RV floor to find he was host to another glorious headache. As Jonah inspected the now groaning Alpha Josh saw the pale exhausted shell that was Angelica sitting motionless on the reclined chair. The last time he had seen someone look so white and sullen was the pathetic, though serene remains of their fallen sister.

"What about her?" he asked concerned. "She gonna be okay?" Alpha grunted at Jonah and pushed him away, leaving him free to turn and inspect his exhausted comrade.

"She's fine," he replied dismissively. "Ain't nothing this girl can't handle." The reply had been accompanied with an effervescent smirk that seemed inappropriate in the aftermath of what had transpired. Jonah gave Monk a reassuring slap on the knee. As he appeared to awake from some deep trance it was with the grim satisfaction he had protected them all from disaster. He reciprocated with a solemn nod and glanced quickly to Josh before getting up. The long-haired man's continued austerity surprised the captive. Seemingly unconcerned by the pleas for help Josh had yelled at his face he went to join Dex up front.

"He did all he could." Josh looked over to see Angelica's assurance was aimed at him. Mistaking her furrowed brow as a sign of ailment, Jonah gripped her shoulder warmly.

"We nailed those bastards right?" he asked. Kneeling beside her he wiped his own perspiring brow. Angelica replied with an up stretched thumb of approval and smiled, though it was Josh's eyes she had locked onto. "That's my girl," Jonah said, then stood as Alpha coughed and spluttered.

"Darkie bastards!" The soldier growled and coughed again, massaging his bruised neck. "They almost killed me!" As he got used to breathing freely once more his flushed complexion began to return to normal.

"Living is a luxury my friend," Jonah retorted with his jolly persona unblemished. Reaching out to assess the purple handprint left behind on Alpha's sore neck, the fatigued soldier pushed his hand away with another grunt.

"Let's just hope Calisto didn't sacrifice hers for nothing," Alpha replied sullenly. With his pride as bruised and battered as his neck, his bitterness was undiluted by Josh's aid. After darting a resentful glance at the stranger who may have saved his life, he quickly turned away to splutter once more. Angelica's crystal eyes however remained on Josh, her forehead shining with perspiration. The Low Grade had shown his true colours, a fact she approved with an appreciative wink. It was then Josh knew the swiping of Galda's feet had been no optimistic dream.

*****

The Montana apartment building was one of the most desirable locations for young, successful executives seeking residence near the city's financial district, but it had been Matthew Nugent who had paid the small fortune to secure unit 142 at its summit. The penthouse styled apartment boasted large airy rooms and a separate kitchen, its surfaces topped with the finest Italian marble that appealed to the assumed sophistication of society climbers who had little appreciation of its origins. But it had been the extended veranda with the excellent panoramic views over LA's downtown cityscape that had clinched the purchase for the young accountant's sense of pride. As the morning sun now gradually climbed the distant jagged horizon to silhouette the skyscrapers that funnelled the city's wealth, dawn's molten radiance was channelled through its towers of concrete, steel and glass to warm the black lace thong that hung from the arm of a hand-crafted recliner. The envy of colleagues, he religiously kept the prestigious residence for his own exclusive appreciation, and for whoever shared his bed.

The trail of discarded clothes ended by the open terrace window that led into the bachelor's bedroom. As the creeping shadows lengthened stealthily towards a discarded pair of Calvin Klein hipsters on its tiled floor, a wireless phone rang subtly from underneath them. A despondent groan from the king size bed suggested the caller's timing was greatly misjudged. Beneath its black satin sheets the two lovers chose to ignore the call, opting to allow the pre-recorded voice in the next room to answer in the homeowner's supercilious tone. As the machine delivered its brief greeting he rolled over and decided red wine was not his drink.

"Matt?" the caller queried from its speaker. "Matt I don't have much time, if your there I really need you to pick up." After a short pause he blurted a curse and relented to leaving a message. He knew the accountant would check the machine several times each day without fail; his words would not go unheard. But back in the bedroom the exhausted accountant was already revisiting his dreams. That morning the caller had no idea the message was going to go unheard for some time.

"I need you to look after the house. By that I mean feeding my cat," the caller elaborated, "I need to you feed Samson while I'm away." His voice was calm but purposely hushed, relaying the sense of trouble he hoped to avoid. "I know it's short notice but something's come up and I can't get hold of *her*!" his words trailed off as the hastily planned speech quickly faltered. The last thing he wanted his friend to think was cocaine abuse had fried his faculties. "I met someone, last night. One drink led to two then three!" he quipped, hoping to break the ice of concern that the message would so obviously create. "We're heading out of town for some R&R; I just need you to look after my place while I'm away. I…" He was a bad liar and his college friend would see straight through the pretence. A part of him wanted to tell the truth, but the truth was insane. "I'm not sure for how long." He paused while he thought how to tie up the ridiculous message. "I'm relying on you buddy. I…" The caller's message was cut short by the dial tone, seconds before the slender hand could press the Conference button.

"Who was it?" Matt's croaky voice called out from the bedroom to the naked woman hovering over the machine. The garish bracelets she had forgotten to remove after collapsing in a post coital bliss clunked gently together as her hand slipped curiously away.

"Our mutual *friend!*" she replied acerbically. Her bare feet pattered on the cool tiles as she walked back towards the large bedroom.

"Josh? What did he want?" The woman slid her naked, feline body back onto the bed and placed herself enticingly on top of her boyfriend's best friend.

"He wants to know why you're screwing the love of his life."

*****

The cell phone screen flashed *battery low*. As it went into hibernation Josh slipped it slyly back into his pocket, hoping no one had seen. The glare of the early morning sun had made the display hard to see, but as he squinted back to the barren horizon from which it had risen, he decided the inhospitable parched landscape it slowly resuscitated was preferable to the violent deaths they had evaded. Jonah stepped out of the RV to stretch his legs. Pulling out a fresh packet of cigarettes he stripped away the clear plastic wrapping and offered one to Josh. It was the first offer of sustenance he'd received from his custodians and he accepted it thankfully. A silver Zippo lighter then flashed before the captive's eyes purveying a naked flame, but Dex's rebuke came loud and clear as he thumped his hand on the side of the RV. With a rigid finger he pointed out of the driver window to the *No Smoking* sign above the gas pumps. Jonah laughed off his negligence and returned to the security of the Solarian as he spotted Angelica and Alpha leaving the gas station with two full grocery bags. The sight made Josh hope Matty wouldn't let Samson starve to death. Slipping the cigarette in his shirt pocket he followed him back inside.

After successfully evading capture at the hands of the Elite, Dex had kept the large RV, nicknamed the Solarian, floored until reaching the arid outskirts of the city. Driving through the night they had left the familiar surroundings of the concrete jungle behind and exchanged it for the desolate, sun-baked landscape of the Californian desert. Stopping at the remote gas station on the edges of dawn had only empowered the feeling of escape. After the long, silent drive in the RV's contained environment, stepping out onto the desiccated ground to see the stretch of traversed highway disappear into their past, it felt as though they had fled from the night itself, and all its hidden dangers past and present. As the athletic blonde and the big soldier stepped back into their waiting chariot, the whoosh of the shutting side door now reverberated with a sound of hope rather than dread. With a twist of the keys Dex reanimated the powerful ten litre engine and continued the drive onwards into the rising sun.

Returning to their seats Alpha was the first to hungrily pillage the large grocery bags. Even though he'd been trained to survive hard times by living off the land, which usually meant eating very little, he loved food and resented being deprived of it. His big hands plucked out various treats of pre-packaged foods and tossed them to his comrades. The station's refrigerator had been well stocked owing to its relative proximity to the city, its selection of fresh fruits and baguettes a welcome sight. Taking a double helping Jonah passed the extra supplies onto their dutiful driver.

Josh however began to feel left out. His stomach rumbled as he watched the food parcels passed amongst the others. After a cynical glare Alpha reluctantly tossed a shrink wrapped packet into Josh's lap, and then tucked into the tuna baguette he had bagged for himself.

"Corndog, my favourite," Josh thanked him sardonically. He ripped open the noisy plastic wrapping and took a bite from the not so healthy snack. Josh was hungry though perhaps not hungry enough to enjoy something he had hated since childhood. "Great way to start the day, you guys eat out often?" Monk darted him a disapproving look and slurped at his bottle of water. The mood had lightened after the grisly night of misadventure and Josh hoped to use the elevated feeling to initiate some much-needed Q&A. He needed to know what lay ahead. Too many questions remained answered, and now he was sure that killing him was low on their agenda, he hoped to get lucky. The corndog dehydrated his mouth. "Could I get some of that cola?" he asked, gesturing to the unopened can of soda at Alpha's feet. Alpha reached down, opened it and took several big gulps of the fizzy drink. "I guess not," Josh said as the crushed, empty can then landed in his lap.

"Here," Angelica offered the bottle she had been quietly drinking. "Try some water, it's better for you." He offered his thanks and took it from her. After several mouthfuls of the precious ice cold liquid he handed it back and noticed she had not helped herself to any food. "You on a diet?" he teased.

"Eat your corndog, it's a long journey," she answered mysteriously and placed the resealed bottle to her side.

"Journey to where? Where are you taking me exactly?"

"We're not *taking* you anywhere," Angelica replied with a frown that implied he was close to offending her. "You come of your own free will."

"Free will?" he blurted back. "What part of kidnap and hostage don't you understand?" The exclamation ended in silence. Monk continued to drink; Alpha looked amused while Angelica gazed at him with an air of pity.

"We're not kidnapping anyone Joshua."

"Then what the hell do you call this?" he demanded, gesturing to the RV that had been his mobile prison for the past eight to nine hours. "A road trip?"

"You are taking a journey," she continued with the same benevolent air, "a journey on the path to truth, and if you believe in it, destiny." For a moment he thought she was reciprocating his mockery, then sensed she was deadly serious. "A path you want to follow is it not?"

Monk now looked at Josh with a curiosity enticed by what must have been a momentous question. It had been taken for granted he was now a willing participant in their bizarre war games, but after sitting in the Solarian's confines, taxied to some unknown destination, he felt far from free to exercise his civil liberties.

"I wasn't aware I had a choice in the matter," he replied dryly. Angelica's cool blue eyes flashed with indignation.

"Dex, stop the van!" The unexpected order brought the RV to a halt at the side of the desert road. Reaching over Josh, Angelica shoved open the rear doors. The early morning sun blared down onto his back as they swung wide, blinding him as he stared behind at the long grey snake of asphalt that shimmered against the parched landscape. Suddenly his options had doubled.

"There's your choice Mr Brenin!" she stated formally, "You are not our prisoner and we are not your jailers. If you want to leave then go right ahead we won't stop you." Gazing at the barren road back home he was tempted to place a foot onto its weathered surface. *It's gonna be a hell of a walk.* Angelica's face hovered above his own; the sun embellishing her golden locks as they hung about her face. "Though ask yourself this question," she continued, sensing the temptation she was laying at his feet, "where do you want to be?"

"Right now? Back home in bed!"

"In your life!" she reprimanded. "Who is Joshua Brenin? Is he back *home*, squatting on his own in the dark? No money, no job, no hope. Or is he an example of the divine architect's master craftsmanship; a Nothos, standing with his fellow Nothoi in the light?" The melodramatic speech would have seemed madness had it not been delivered by Angelica, but in the short time he had known this mysterious woman, he had found her serene sincerity eradicated any notions of insanity.

"You're saying I'm free to leave? I can go?" he asked, expecting to see one of the throwers being freed from a pocket.

"You can get out; you can walk back down that road. But what is freedom Joshua? For most it is merely an apathetic vision of a world through limited perception, a mirage created by the media as it secretly advances the Elite's agenda right under their noses. But that hypothetical freedom comes with a price. Without the responsibility we owe our *true* selves, humanity is doomed to fail." He looked back to where the road vanished into the horizon. Watching as it danced in the heat waves rising from the asphalt Josh felt her rational strike a familiar heartstring. Suddenly the way back home looked just as warped and twisted. Perhaps the blonde woman knew him better than he realised after all? Perhaps the home he was leaving behind really was a misshapen dream of regret and depression? But who were these people to make that decision for him?

"What the hell do you people want from me?" he demanded. Josh knew he was on the threshold of something monumental, but he was being torn in two by the opposing sides of a past he knew and a future he didn't.

"All we want is what you want!" Angelica replied paradoxically. She retook her seat in the recliner. "If you look deep enough inside you will see this, we want to help you find what you're looking for."

"My *true* self!" he exclaimed sardonically. Josh was beginning to tire of feeling like a pathetic miscreant, a fool of his own design. "I didn't ask for any of this!"

"We didn't ask for this either Josh," she replied sternly.

"All I wanted was to be left alone!"

"Was it?" was Angelica's obstinate reply. The truth was nothing hurt more than being alone. The truth was he hated how he had to pretend that existing was possible without Sarah, and his blonde confessor could read it on his soul like an open book. "If there was a child who didn't know right from wrong, wouldn't you want to teach it?"

"Is that how you see me...as a child?" Alpha kicked the crushed cola can out of the RV where it bounced and twirled on the asphalt until it came to a stop at the centre of the road.

"If he wants to go, let him go!" he growled rudely. "Let him roast out on the road, we've no room for losers anyhow." The coarse remark made Josh want to ram the crushed can down the soldier's neck.

"A child is only a child because he doesn't have the accumulated wisdom that accompanies age," Angelica continued, ignoring her associate. "The world must teach him this wisdom by good or by evil. But time is something we have little of, and so we ask you to trust us." Josh looked back to the road, thought of home, the past, Sarah, then back at the faces of the people who called themselves servants of the light.

"The future beckons the brave," Jonah called out from the passenger seat. "Whet's it to be Flyboy? The clock's a ticking."

"After all you've seen; all you've experienced..." Monk stated unexpectedly, "...do you still want to be a slave?" Josh stared into his wolfish features and saw the hint of compassion for the first time. "The only way you'll ever taste real freedom is to come with us. The key to unlock the chains is at the end of your journey; let us help you to help yourself."

"Why?" Josh asked, looking back at Angelica.

"Because you are one of us." The reply was blunt and overwhelming. Back in the city that lay some hundreds of miles behind him, he had been alone and constricted by the walls of his past. But with these mysterious strangers he saw an opportunity to take fate by the hand, the future they held in the palm of their hands was an offer of redemption. Somewhere deep inside a voice screamed for him to relinquish doubt and embrace the unknown. LA had nothing left to offer Josh Brenin, fate had vindictively entangled his future with them, wherever they were heading. Deciding fate was a bitch; he reached round and pulled the doors shut.

"Prove it."

*****

Beneath the desert plains of the Sierra Nevada, Galda entered the dimly lit room and took his seat at the metal table at its centre. Spotlighted under the single low wattage light, he removed his shades and squinted around the room. He had no reason to remove the protective eyewear except to test the sensitivity of his eyes to the murky light and to try and remember what it was like to walk around unshielded from the daylight, something he had not done since being initiated into the higher echelons of the intelligence community and been consumed mind, body and soul into the Elite. Forcing himself to stare up into the light source it soon became too uncomfortable to endure. Even in the low luminosity his stubborn irises refused to adapt naturally, such were the rewards for his sacrifice. He then replaced the shades as he waited in silent contemplation for those that would answer his summons.

A glass of fresh water rose up from table. Raising it to his pale lips he drained it before two subordinate agents finally appeared in the doorway and took their seats after first offering a respectful nod. Another agent entered the dark room via the alternating molecular portal behind him. Striding over to occupy the spare place to Galda's left he took the opportunity to remove his own shades and blink his own weary black balled eyes. The two earlier arrivals gazed at their colleague in dismay. Such lack of respect was unheard of in the presence of the Principal and it was Galda's stern look of disapproval that persuaded the agent to replace them with a half-cocked smile. The belligerent agent relished the time when he would stand as the Elite's commanding officer, but until such moment as he surpassed Galda Vey's accomplishments, he would bide his time.

"Gentlemen we have a problem," Galda began the proceedings solemnly. "The enemy has assimilated another Nothos into their ranks. A man, who would have been of considerable use to us, and our great cause, has been lost to the other side." He waited for the motive behind the assembly to take hold before delivering its pre judgement. "He must now be eliminated."

"Principal, if I may," the belligerent agent known as Kladar declared, "if we had followed protocol to the letter then perhaps we would not have lost him so easily to the light." Galda picked up on the condemnation of fault and glowered at the obstinate subordinate. By *we* he had meant *you*. Kladar was the agent behind the suggestion to storm the butchered Nothos's building, rather than send their projections to dispatch the cornered Latronis militia. Galda had dismissed his idea as reckless, though the lower ranked agent was now enjoying the Principal's suggestion of damage control for his ill conceived choice.

"If *you* were half as powerful as he *could* be," Galda retorted, "then we would have no use for him in the first place. Latronis are now a potentially much stronger force and we must destroy them before they unlock the newcomer's potential and become too powerful."

"What makes you so sure of this Brenin Nothos?" another agent queried. "There is no certainty he will ascend."

"Even if he does we are still many to their few," Kladar interjected derisively. "I think you over estimate these servants. The only thing preventing our crushing of them so far has been luck. It hardly denotes that even with the Brenin Nothos they could defeat us, should we meet them again." The last line was meant to bait Galda's disgrace.

"His ascension is inevitable," Galda declared, maintaining his insight as superior. Kladar's strategy to undermine Galda's command in front of his peers was becoming an ongoing struggle, but he needed the abilities of shrewd witted agents such as Kladar if he was to finally defeat Latronis, fulfil his role in the eyes of the secret masters and thus receive the highest accolade. That was what mattered in the long term and so he postponed eliminating the pretender to the throne until such time, something in which he would take great pleasure. "Our brothers over seas assure me of the global network's integrity and nothing must prevent us from achieving the ultimate goal now that we are so close to completion," Galda continued, contemplating his own personal ambition. "A window of opportunity has been offered to us," he then revealed, "to deal with the renegades and offer their destruction as an additional tribute. Only when everything is in place can we step up and take our rightful place alongside Them."

"When the time comes will *we* mean us all?" Kladar antagonised his superior further. "I can't speak for my colleagues, but for such an exceptional risk, how can we be sure They will maintain their side of the covenant?"

"Has not what we have received so far been proof enough of their commitment?" Galda chided him. "For us, the possibilities are infinite." However Kladar was not so easily swayed by the Principal's confidence, preferring devils advocate he continued.

"After we hand over control how do we know we will not be left behind to share in the fate of the uninitiated?" Galda glared at the agent's pale face wishing he could rid himself of the line of questioning, but now the enquiry had been made it had to be answered.

"Faith," he replied acerbically.

"Faith?" Kladar asked in amused disbelief. He removed his sunglasses, his glare challenging his superior's sanity.

"Faith, like respect, should be shown at all times," Galda explained coldly. "Faith is what makes the world go round. Faith is what makes miracles possible." Galda raised his hand to issue his command over the laws of nature. By unseen hands the agent's shades suddenly sprung up from the table and landed abruptly back on their owners face. "Faith, in your superior's superiority!" Galda's glare then conducted the shade's frame to bend forcefully against Kladar's face until the lenses were close enough to crush his wide, panicking eyes. "Do I make myself clear?" Kladar's colleagues watched on with passive interest as the eyewear began to crush their colleague's temple.

"Absolutely," Kladar murmured, the word escaping through gritted teeth before the invisible vice relaxed its hold. Galda stood up from the table, followed regimentally by the two other agents, leaving Kladar to straighten the shades on his aching face.

"Find them!" Galda then ordered bluntly, before turning to exit through the portal. His second engagement was destined to be equally as trying, but the consequences were potentially much more grave.

Chapter 12

The Solarian continued its journey into unknown. Since leaving the gas station Dex had kept the RV moving at a steady pace across the increasingly barren landscape, only alleviating the accelerator as a freight train now made its own lumbering journey across their path. Josh saw the huge metallic boxcars pass before the windshield and studied them for clues as to where they may or may not be heading. But as it was unlikely they were either from, or going to, the same place as his new comrades, he simply diverted his imagination to what might lie inside the monstrous convey.

"How can he be one of us?" Alpha suddenly piped up. His opposing attitude to Josh had changed little since he had freed him from the murderous metal arm. Instead it appeared to have only instigated a new rivalry fuelled by his growing resentment.

"There was a time when you asked that about yourself," Angelica reminded him as she palmed her fair hair back against her scalp. "You didn't know it at the time either. You had to be shown the way, like the rest of us."

"Except my enlightenment didn't come at a price!" Alpha's renewed reminding of Calisto's demise fell on deaf ears and he was left to mull over his bitterness as the last boxcar passed by with a rhythmical roar. Dex put his foot down and set the RV cruising onwards again.

"Do you still have trouble sleeping?" Angelica asked Josh as she tied her long hair back from her face.

"Can't say I've had much chance for it lately," he commented ruefully. The question seemed silly, though as he looked into her upturned eyes he realised it was rooted in an obvious fact. If he hadn't sought treatment for his insomnia then he wouldn't have been ensnared by the Elite's subterfuge. "And when I do I'm usually being chased by some Bozo with a serious case of anaemia." Then he realised the importance of her question. "That's how you found me isn't it?"

"The man you know as Doctor Halberstram is an Elite stooge," she confided, confirming what Galda had already told him. "He uses many aliases right across the US, under which he is appointed prime placements within suitable recruitment clinics by the Elite. Along with the others like him, he never remains in the same state or identity for more than several weeks at a time, leaving him free to spread his black work anonymously across this country like a cancer."

"Son of bitch. Even national heroes aren't exempt."

"Quite," Angelica agreed, disregarding Alpha's attempt to detract the conversation from Josh. "As a specialist practitioner his roster of patients is primarily made up of people with parasomnia conditions. The active complex in Sleepeze called Ketron only has a catalytic affect on those suffering with sleep related disorders. Whether it correlates to an imbalance in the body's chemistry or not we just don't know, but it doesn't stop Sleepeze being handed out like candy to thousands of unsuspecting guinea pigs nationwide as they search for unwitting soldiers to fill their ranks."

"So, all those things that were chasing us back there, they were all people like me?" Josh asked, concerned by how close his own fate was entwined with such grisly apparitions.

"Predominately," she replied simply. "The longer they play host to the Elite's black influence the more consumed by it they become. The ones that attacked us were Ascended Ones, Low Grades that have risen through the ranks so to speak, but the final attacker had been a Nothos, a blackened parallel of ourselves."

"His name is Galda Vey. He was my tutor!" Josh admitted ashamedly, gladly unburdening the knowledge. Hearing the name of her archrival, Angelica nodded thoughtfully, but added nothing to the revelation. The dark architect's name was a curse she couldn't forget; not since Calisto's. "My guess is he was the one responsible for your friend's death." Alpha looked down broodingly at his feet.

"Not all who take Sleepeze are converted," she added, "Thanks to the detailed records of the complex's authorised distribution and application, we are given a chance to neutralise their work, though admittedly one step behind their lead."

"Records?" Suddenly Josh's pride felt desecrated.

"They make no effort to hide the wonder drug from the authorities. After all, the pharmaceutical companies are forever pushing out their latest concoctions onto those that maintain the eager market that supports them; supply and demand. But the Halberstram's of the world are never around long enough for the drug's results to be verified. As a medical trial its success or failure is relative only to expectation. Subsequently the in-volunteers are psyched out on the lower Dreamscape and manipulated through their dreams," Josh listened attentively. He had hoped that just as Galda had shown his true colours then perhaps the extent of his macabre influence had not been so extensive. But everything Angelica now explained in the seclusion of their mobile command centre only confirmed he was part of something that extended throughout the very back bone of the country. Just as the physical parameters of a physical reality meant nothing to the black projections, law, order and morality also meant just as little to the Elite.

"Those unlucky enough to have the highest states of consciousness are consequently press-ganged into undertaking missions into Hyperborea. Under the remote power of their tutor's psyche, these Low Grades become their unwitting puppets, performing the Elite's dirty work on the Leviscape."

"So how many of these puppets are there?" he asked pessimistically.

"The Elite has existed for decades, their ranks have continued to grow three fold each year and their kind exist across the globe. I'm no mathematician, but I'd say the number isn't small." Angelica picked up the bottle of water, unscrewed its top and took a sip. Josh imagined an endless legion of clawing black agents threatening to swallow them. Suddenly he felt insignificant. "Like all armies there is a hierarchy," she continued after replacing the bottle. "At the bottom the Low Grades provide the majority of their infantry, a battalion of pawns. Above them, more powerful but less in number, are the Ascended Ones that provide the cavalry. While at the top are the few, these are the Nothos, the black generals." *Trained by a general,* Josh mused; *I'm honoured.*

"I saw how they recruited people," he admitted. "A blue room full of zombies who didn't know reality from dream. But that's the problem; if everybody's dreaming how the hell are they supposed to know what's going on?" Josh's frustration exploded into a rant, "Or that they're being used as mindless slaves, to undermine some goddamn aliens!" He slumped his head into his hands and gripped his dark hair between his fingers. *I want my life back.* The realisation that his life was changed forever was a desolating thought.

"Has his head exploded yet?" Jonah suddenly interrupted as he joined them in the back of the RV.

"Not yet," Angelica confirmed playfully. Jonah ruffled Josh's hair boisterously. He looked up into the grinning olive features and found the look of amusement frustrating. Their co pilot was a similar age, though from the exotic looks and generous scattering of small scars across his face guessed they had lived very different lives.

"Believe me when I found out about that crazy inter-dimensional entities jazz, my brain was ready to pop to." Jonah squatted down to root through the groceries bag but found only empty packaging. "We never get enough food around here." He crushed the bag with a powerful punch and looked directly across to Josh. "Believe it or not it'll all make sense in the end. Us, humanity and the Vanir, we're all part of the same grand plan my man. You want some?" The question referred to the half empty packet of spearmint chewing gum he had pulled out of a back pocket.

"I'll take a double Vodka if you've got it," Josh joked as he took a silver stick from the crushed packet. Jonah smirked.

"What it boils down to is this," he said tapping his chest. "It's about what's in here, that's where the truth is. Don't listen to this," he then tapped his temple, "You'll go mad. You just gotta go with the flow." He stood and returned to the RV's cabin. "He doesn't look convinced!"

"He should be," Angelica stated. "Galda Vey isn't the type of miscreant to chase after a Low Grade on a whim." Josh guessed from her serious tone they had reached the objective of the interrupted Q&A. "You must have made quite an impression on him." Recalling the black architect's threats to stay away from Josh Brenin, there were some answers she had to have.

"My good looks and winning charm?" he said drearily, hoping to shrug off the interest. His projection during the fight with Galda had proved to be the letting out of the cat from the bag. Previously her interest had reflected her fear the crestfallen Low Grade held some undisclosed secret in the Elite's plans. But now she'd seen his potential, Angelica understood her curiosity was well founded. Unable to avoid the inevitable he started from the beginning.

"I hadn't been sleeping properly for some time," he began, "We've all been there, just lying there looking into space waiting for the sandman. As it turns out he was on vacation. My Dad used to say it was a sign of a guilty conscience, not being able to sleep. But that couldn't have been the case because he slept like a log every night." Josh purposely skirted around the roots of his insomnia, not wanting to sully his precious memories of Sarah with his current nightmare. He wasn't willing to share those parts of his soul with theses strangers.

"After a few months of waiting for the son of a bitch, the sandman I mean, I decided to get myself checked out, just in case I had brain cancer or something. After some preliminaries I was referred to your man Doctor Halberstram at Saint Johns."

He recalled the glass doors that had led into the clinic's lobby. The abhorrent smell of clinical bleach that swamped all medical institutes had greeted him as he entered, before slumping into a low armless chair with a well palmed copy of National Geographic. His morbid curiosity had been ensnared by an article detailing Japan's illegal whaling, though he had been prised away from its gruesome pictures by a pretty nurse telling him to go on through to room three. Halberstram had been a tall, middle-aged man who had greeted him with a strong handshake and the offer of a more comfortable seat. Above his top lip a lustrous moustache had sat like a huge black slug.

"He seemed a pretty genuine sort of guy, kinda reminded me of my uncle. Just one of those people you take an instant like to you know?" Angelica nodded formally wanting him to continue. "I explained my situation and he told me about this experimental wonder drug from Europe. He held the sole US license for its prescription and had achieved an eighty five percent success rate. I'm no pill popping quick fix junkie, but he spun a pretty convincing case."

"If you can't trust your doctor who can you trust?" Alpha supplemented the monologue bitterly.

"Right," Josh agreed, suddenly aware that Monk was also taking a keen interest after abandoning his meditative pose. "So I went home, gave it a shot for few days and it did its job, I slept. Except the wonder part of the drug was a goddamn lie."

"How so?" Monk asked, his chin resting on a spire of two up pointing fingers.

"Unlike the other sedative drugs on the market it was supposed to permanently rebalance my body's natural chemistry and induce a healthy sleep pattern without the need to re-ingest the blue pills after a month. The best part is he said to stop taking them if I experienced any ill affect!"

For an unknown reason Josh realised he couldn't remember any intricate detail of Halberstram's features. The silly facial hair aside, he remembered the doctor had been ordinary in appearance, though the more he forced the memory, the more the face disintegrated. "Except every time I tried to get in contact with this Doctor he was unavailable," he continued. "From what you told me, he was probably long gone, heading out to his new post to dupe some other poor bastard." The practitioner's smiling face continued to elude him, only a familiar warmth replaced the void in his memory. *I need some rest.* The RV slowed and banked to the right as Dex turned the big vehicle onto some new unknown road. Josh hoped there was not much further to go. His butt was getting numb from sitting on the hard crate and he yearned to stretch his legs.

"How long before the dreams started?" Angelica asked.

"Dreams? I've never had dreams like that before," Josh wondered if he would ever enjoy another perfect night's sleep. "A dream is when you wake up and realise that's all it was, a dream. But those, visions were too…" he racked his brain for a fitting word.

"Involving," Monk offered with an insightful glance.

"I thought it was just me, one too many knocks to the head," Josh joked, omitting his concerns of cocaine abuse. "It all seems so wrong now." Alpha was feigning disinterest as he carefully stripped his revolver down. He glared at the nicks in the gun's finish, created by the strikes against the liquid metal arm. Josh's story sounding all too familiar, he preferred to ignore his own wonderment by appearing to look useful.

"Wrong is one word," Angelica replied suggestively. "But don't beat yourself up; you were under their influence from the second you were referred to their Pied Piper." Her face suddenly revealed a dark thought. "Did they take a blood sample?"

"That's standard practice, right?"

"Show me your arm," Angelica instructed, a little too bluntly for comfort. Alpha's skilled hands paused in their well versed task.

"Why?" Josh asked, bemused.

"Roll up your sleeve and show me where the needle went in." The second request was brusquer. He detected an urgency in her tone that made him nervous.

"I don't see how…"

"Do it!" Reluctantly he undid the buttons of his sleeve. Monk's stern features returned to a distant glance as Alpha picked up something from behind Angelica's chair and handed it to her.

"We should have checked him out before deciding to bring him along," Monk reminded her. "Kristos is going to be pissed."

"Well Kristos isn't here," she retorted dismissively. She waited eagerly for Josh to reveal the hypodermic's entry point. "I can't think of everything." The mood inside the RV had iced over once more.

"Are you going to tell me what this is about?" Josh asked as he tugged the rolled fabric high above his bicep. He had endured the nurse's needle as a matter of necessity and was unenthusiastic about being violated again. Angelica revealed the new object and held it over the skin of his arm. Her hand partially hid it from view as she used the unknown device to study his arm. Its transparent centre resembled a magnifying glass, further intriguing him. "What is that?" he asked nervously.

"Hold his arm," Angelica instructed. Alpha reached over to perform the task with a keen grip. She was hovering the device over his skin while her thumb manipulated its control to enhance the instruments ability. Josh felt a cold sweat pass down his back.

"What are you looking for?" he demanded, his interpretation of Angelica's frowning features doing little to reassure him.

"Well?" Monk asked. The device emitted a small beep and its display illuminated in Angelica's blue resolute eyes.

"I can see it," she announced. Josh felt the cold turn to ice.

"See what?" A nightmare scenario of contamination by an exotic disease was flashing before his eyes. As a child he had associated syringes with drug use. Public health films had programmed his adolescent mind to equate needles with the passing on of diseases, and now the communal interest in whatever they had found relit those past phobias in a flash. "What are you looking at?"

"You're tagged," Alpha stated ominously. He gripped Josh's arm with both hands to prevent fright from retracting it. The melancholy silence that followed the announcement had sealed its certainty and Josh looked to Angelica for deliverance.

"Hold him I'm going to neutralize it," Angelica stated as she used her other hand to twist the device's lens until the red light it emitted reflected in her eyes.

"Wait!" Josh pleaded, "Can't you get it out?" The word 'neutralise' intimated pain, urging him to seek other options.

"Believe me," Angelica said gazing into the luminous display. "It's much less painful this way." Josh leaned over to see whatever the device was revealing, until Alpha's thick forearm locked itself around his neck.

"Wait!" he bawled again, but Angelica's thumb had already pinched down, sending the disabling signal into the foreign chip imbedded in his skin. As the soldier's grappling hold constricted the rupture of pain made Josh yelp like a kicked dog. The device's discharge was like a hot poker thrusting into his arm, its molten agony remaining for a couple of seconds before Angelica removed the device and covered the tortured area with her palm. "Let me go!" he demanded.

"Be still, we need to make sure." Angelica replaced the device over the skin. There was a pause as she studied his arm for traces of the foreign object, until finally she removed it relieved.

"It's dead," she stated and tossed away the offending device. Satisfied, Alpha released Josh and shoved him back onto the crate.

"So is my frigging arm!" Josh snapped, massaging away the remnants of the hot pain that still smouldered. A quick glance to his exposed arm revealed a small gathering of haemorrhaged cells.

"Don't be such a baby," Alpha growled and sat back to pick up the half stripped revolver from the RV's floor. Reassembling the gun in seconds its top slide clunked into place in front of his face. While Angelica opened a small medical kit he gave Josh a sly look of amusement.

"There, there," she teased, her frowning features now showing a childish glee as she spread some cooling balm tenderly onto the afflicted skin. The RV juddered as it hit rougher terrain. Josh wondered what other delights awaited him at their unknown rendezvous. "Sorry, I'm all out of lollipops." Angelica finished the act of mercy by applying a patch and smoothing it down with her thumbs.

"What did you just do?"

"We just debugged your sorry ass," Alpha answered for her as he finished buffing the revolver's surface and pocketed the gun in his jacket. "So quit moaning, we could have done it the old fashioned way," he rebuked.

"They implanted you with a chip," Angelica explained. She retook her seat and reached again for the bottle of water. Ignoring Alpha's animosity Josh stared at her with disbelief.

"What? through a frigging needle?" She offered him a reproving glance as she sipped from the bottle then lowered it.

"How else?"

"That's impossible," Josh stated. He looked at Monk who had returned to a post traumatic trance, then back at Angelica. "They can't make them that small."

"Who says they can't?" she replied, offering him the bottle. He took it from her and gulped down the rest of the lukewarm liquid. "Just because it's not broadcast on CNN doesn't mean it doesn't exist, quite the opposite. The society we live in is the plaything of the media, disinformation is its propaganda and it's the truth that suffers for it." Josh thought about her comment for a second before returning to the point.

"Okay let's just say for a second you know what the hell it is you're talking about! If that thing you just fried in my arm was a tracking device, that mean they know where we are."

"It wasn't a tracking device," Angelica replied, closing her eyes warily. "Via the astral plain they can find you anytime they want. The chip we just fried attracts microwave signals that regulate your brainwaves."

"For what possible purpose?"

"To manipulate emotion, to influence you. That sense of ease you felt at your meeting with Halberstram?" she asked, opening her eyes but remaining in the reflective pose. "For want of a better word you were being bombarded with happy vibes." Initially Josh concluded she was deluded, the explanation too outlandish, but again his baptism of fire suggested evidence for her claim. Yes he had felt an uncommon ease at his consultation. After it was over he had felt more relaxed than he had in weeks, but was his recalibrated perception of events fuelling delusion?

"By hijacking existing communication transmitters," she continued, "The Elite has the ability to discharge ultra low frequency waves onto specific targets, kind of like armed watchtower guards in an invisible prison. Finished?" Angelica asked for the bottle's return. He handed it back. There was little left but she drained the last few drops and finished her spiel. "Via the chip they can triangulate GPS position using localised cell phone networks and global satellites and emit the signal, positive or negative, directly to the host anywhere on the planet."

"The host being me," Josh confirmed, glad in the knowledge that he was no longer at the mercy of the malicious technology. "So if you know about these transmitters why don't you do us prisoners a favour and destroy them?"

"Big words for a little man," Alpha sneered.

"Because it's a roaming technology," Angelica affirmed. "No same network or pylon is used for more than a day at a time. Sometimes they use mobile transmitters. The latest we heard the Elite were localising miniatures by exploiting common household electrical devices such as TVs and cell phones." Josh remembered his counterfeit Rolex, and Dink's disclosure it held the very technology she spoke of. He thought about what his father would think if he knew the gift had ended up on the floor of a murder victim's crummy apartment, a victim who had tried to kill him for the same counterfeit gear and had been thrown out of a three storey window by a dreaming blonde. His arm began to itch under the patch. "It's going to swell up like a balloon," the same blonde warned him. *They're not taking* my *cell.*

"Great, another addition to my war wounds," he replied dolefully. Josh felt the RV begin to shudder as the deserted road underneath its wheels became increasingly uneven. Making the same realisation, Angelica turned to holler up to the cabin.

"Jonah?"

"Fifteen minutes," the co pilot confirmed back. Getting up to join Jonah and Dex she left Josh with the realisation their road trip was about to reach its end. *Fifteen minutes to where?* Seemingly unimpressed by the news, Alpha and Monk remained in quiet repose. From the big soldier's blank, staring expression Josh guessed his thoughts still dwelled on their absent comrade.

"So what was the old fashioned way?" Josh queried, referring to the cause of his aching arm. Averted from his thoughts, Alpha produced a flick knife. With a nudge of its release catch its long, deadly blade snapped into place in front of his face. He was right, Josh thought, the new way was better.

*****

The lone black clad agent was sat alone in the blue room. In the centre of its arched row of silver reclining projection chairs he remained in silent contemplation. Behind the sunglasses that protected his sensitive eyes the lids were shut as he mentally braced himself for his next confrontation. Galda was a powerful Nothos, an elite amongst the Elite, though as he prepared himself for the things he was about to see, he felt insignificant. For decades he had followed the dark path that had been his destiny, but still the memory of his first encounter with the secret masters had never diminished. So much had changed since that time, within and without both the project and its leader, but the anticipation of confronting such beings again was something to fear as well as relish.

As the Principal agent of the black book project it was his sole responsibility for conversing with its true superiors. He took a deep breath and plunged into the well versed techniques he had mastered as a young man, permitting his mind to separate from the bio-mechanical shell that was his body and thus free it from the chains of the material world. On the astral plains his higher conscious, his true self, could soar into the ascended plains of existence. Though as he made this particular journey, his body now slumbering as though in the deepest of sleeps, he was regulating his shadow form to join Them in the recesses where light met dark.

Like all government funded black book projects, the Elite did not officially exist. As an unofficial offshoot of the NSA it existed outside the boundaries of the intelligence and national security communities, a self perpetuating cell of exploratory modern warfare that was under the jurisdiction of the most powerful men in the world. But unlike their official peers, their allegiances to western security had deteriorated into less than compulsory. Funding had depreciated over the years, diverted to the many secret wars taking place across the world in the name of freedom. But in contrast the Elite's work had continued to progress from strength to strength, along with its allegiance.

For the eyes of their Washington superiors, project achievements were purposely stunted, its reports enticing but noncommittal due to its otherworldly and indefinable science. For a new covenant had been created, and with its inception, project resources had been assigned to more personal goals. No longer was the accumulation of ultra-dimensional technology its primary objective, for in the eyes of the dreamscape pioneers responsible for its discovery, it had become apparent such material gain was ultimately fruitless. Now it was the self promotion of its highest agents into ranks of the usurpers themselves that would be its greatest achievement. This was the prize that Galda Vey sought; a chance for immortality itself. But its realisation was dependant on results, and results were lacking at this time.

The physical world that housed the blue room several layers beneath the Sierra Nevada desert had now been absorbed and replaced by its dreamscape counterpart, a mirror image that existed on a higher vibrational frequency above humanity's material prison. Galda opened his eyes. Everything looked the same, the world around him looked unchanged, but he was no longer in the realm of men. In the alternate blue room his conscious mind had now tuned into an ascended level of existence. Getting up from the silver chair he readied to receive his prestigious guests in the astral chamber that would act as his greeting hall.

Their presence was always slow in materialising. He watched the blue aura before him warp and twist until finally it contorted into the celestial wormhole that would afford Them passage. The gaping portal stretched like a black hole into infinity, an unstable vortex across space and time that would link the world of man with the unknown. From its furthest recess he watched the six approach. The secret masters had never inhabited a physical body. As thus their writhing spectres would not manifest into any definable form. Since time immemorial they had existed as such, dark gaseous entities both desolate and dreadful to behold, personifications of limitless power to create or destroy. Galda stood tall as he welcomed these secret masters to the inter-dimensional rendezvous, and prayed he could quell their expectation.

*****

In the RV's stifling interior Angelica removed her top. As she discarded the unnecessary clothing Josh found it hard not to admire her athletic body. Seeing the prudent manner, in which he respectively turned his head away she smiled, both amused and flattered. His own reciprocating smile however was quickly dissolved at the sight of Alpha's protective stare.

For the last fifteen minutes the small militia had returned to silence, each member lost in their internal worlds where they buried emotion and anxiety. In that time Angelica had spoken briefly to Jonah, joining in his search of the arid surroundings for the first signs of home, though before Josh had plucked up the courage to ask Monk a question, she had returned to her seat and his query dissolved on his parched lips. He had wanted an explanation for Angelica's comment about Calisto not being dead. Not wishing to appear insensitive, he had hoped for Monk's enlightenment, a willing detour from the anxieties over what might lie ahead. But as he wrung his clammy palms together and gazed at the stern features crowned by the long black hair, he realised an enigmatic dismissal would have been his most likely answer.

The RV veered heavily to the right as Dex suddenly swerved off the desert road onto an even less subtle track. From the increasingly ruggedness of the terrain Josh wandered what kind of civilisation could possibly exist in the barren and inhospitable landscape they travelled deeper and deeper into, away from civilisation, away from reality itself. What he'd seen of the empty the sun baked topography through the distant windshield hadn't proved inspiring. In the molten light off the setting sun the dusty arid surroundings were as lifeless and lonely as his own tired soul, and perhaps a fitting end to his pointless existence. However these morbid ruminations were put to the test as Dex finally brought the Solarian to a halt.

Josh tensed as Monk yanked the sliding door's handle. Dragging its smooth gliding action aside into a gaping exit in the RV's flank, the heat from the scorched earth entered like a warm caress against Josh's face. Monk stepped out to embrace it, quickly followed by Alpha who was glad to stretch his long legs and gaze at the dying sun on the distant horizon. Angelica's hand touched Josh's elbow, suggesting he followed suit, his knees creaking and neglected leg muscles complaining as he stepped out of their getaway vehicle into the foreign landscape. Glad to be free of the claustrophobic environment, he took a deep draft of the clean desert air, only to have the distinct smell of gasoline fill his nostrils.

Monk tugged the door back into place before the RV took off without them, leaving Josh free to study the secluded desert plain they had driven almost a day to reach. The silver RV headed towards a distant dilapidated lockup constructed from a ramshackle of rusted iron sheets nailed against a wooden frame. With shake of Alpha's head Josh was urged onwards. He could see the isolated rendezvous was a cluster of similar degraded buildings that hadn't seen a fresh lick of paint in decades. The small settlement he had been brought to was a desolate shantytown that had seemingly thrived at the height of some long gone golden era, but subsequently exhausted, been left to the mercy of the extremities of desert climate. Following Monk's lead they moved towards the larger buildings at the rear of the settlement. To his left Josh saw Jonah jump out of the RV to remove the big, corroded chain from the lockup's door, the large flimsy doors wavering as he opened them to allow the Solarian into its sanctuary that, from the gas pumps he spotted inside, was the source of the unexpected odour.

A draft of warm desert air stirred the dust at their feet, creating dramatic wisps and breathing life into the desolate setting that would look right at home in any classic western. Feeling like Henry Fonda walking into town at high noon, Josh thought he sensed the curious stares of unseen inhabitants watching the group enter their neglected settlement, strangers with no names intruding on a peaceful setting previously cosseted by its isolation. But as he gazed through the dirty window of a nearby building he saw shelves collapsed from their walls, broken furniture, missing floorboards and empty homesteads that hadn't been domesticated since before he was born. The clunk of metal on wood caused him to turn anxiously.

He saw Jonah closing a flimsy door before disappearing inside the lockup. Desolation had found an apt home in whatever place this was. The surrounding terrain that disappeared into the hazy volcanic horizon only emphasised the settlement's desolate gloom, the water tower looming overhead giving the only indication that life had, or continued to exist in the god forsaken spot. Josh's sense of paranoia was rewarded when he noticed a man standing at the base of the huge water drum propped thirty metres above them. A weathered sentinel in a wide brimmed Stetson hat was watching the militia's approach through the aid of a high powered scope attached to an assault rifle. Indifferently, Monk flipped the bird to the solitary guard, causing him to lower his aim. Recognising the insult as that of an associate, he granted passage to the four travellers with a raise of his head before they entered the dilapidated building in front of them.

The half open door creaked open ominously to reveal a large interior slumbering in the low light that entered through its crusted windows. Partially shaded by the decaying sun bleached fabric that acted as drapes, the musty room was a pitiful sight. But unlike the other neglected properties, it was seemingly inhabited.

The man's bright eyes pierced the dim recess in which he was sat. As the servants of the light walked into the centre of the predominantly empty room they locked onto Josh, perceiving his apprehension as the floorboards creaked atmospherically beneath their feet. The inhabitant had a broad wrinkled face of leathery skin adorned by a thick mane of greying hair, making the luminous glare of his sunken eyes all the more intense as they shrunk in their scrutiny of the intruders. Sitting alone at an ancient wooden table with a half empty bottle of whisky, he tossed a shot of the fiery liquid down his gullet and watched them from afar with strangely youthful but suspicious eyes.

Nothing was said. Without acknowledging the lonely figure Josh followed his companions across the room. In the corner was a weathered counter of steadfast construction. Behind it the rows of empty spirit bottles covered with the dusts of the time were epitaphs to the building's former use. With the realisation the rundown room had once served as a drinking hole for the secluded community, Josh followed his companions behind its smooth wooden bar under the watchful gaze of its sole remaining patron. Behind it a door led into the back quarters, but instead of taking the obvious passage Monk halted and removed a device from his pocket so small it was concealed completely by his hand. Its purpose was revealed when the worn, dust incrusted floorboards at their feet suddenly sunk several inches. Stepping back from the miraculous mechanism, Josh watched as they slid aside to reveal the shiny metal surface of a modern trapdoor.

Monk pocketed the remote device and stepped aside as Angelica knelt down to place her hand on a sensory interface. Like the cathode scanner of a Xerox machine it began to analyse her palm, Josh watching and waiting with baited breath as he recognised the gates to heaven or hell were about to be opened. Accepting the key-card that was her biometric handprint, the security system announced its recognition with a beep.

"Ladies first, boys." Angelica casually walked onto the silver platform. Registering her weight it then began to slowly descend into the ground, eerily lowering her sleek form along with it into a black tunnel. *An elevator?* As her arms and shoulders cleared the tunnel's edges, Josh watched as her head suddenly plummeted into the unlit void below the floorboards. Looking around for an explanation he found only the steely poker faced features of his companions, before Monk dutifully waved the next rider to take the stand as the silver platform returned empty.

"Your turn, Flyboy," Alpha sneered, glad that Josh had unknowingly wandered into next position. Unable to jostle out of line, he swallowed his nerves and put a nervy foot onto the shiny surface. *What's to lose?* As he placed the second he found it indeed held his weight. Turning to face Monk and Alpha, who both standing a foot or so above him, he waited for the inevitable descent.

"The name's Josh," he sneered back. Suddenly he felt the mechanism's release. Like a released car jack the platform began its second slow depreciation. As the bar and the two leering figures rose above Josh his shoulders mirrored Angelica's descent down to floor level. The smell of petrified wood and dust filled his nose as it passed the tunnel's edge. "Jarhead!" Josh sniped the insult just as the passage swallowed his head. Before expectation could provide some sense of security, the platform slipped out from under his feet like a gallows trapdoor and he was plunged into darkness.

Josh's stomach leapt up into his throat. Desperate hands flayed out to grasp for holds but found only the rush of smooth cold metal as he fell into nothingness. The platform's disappearance had left him in freefall, plummeting down the chute like dirty laundry as gravity's embrace hauled him into the black void, and surely into certain death. A wall of red light rushed to meet his feet. Falling through it, his back suddenly made contact with the chute as it curved horizontally. In the darkness Josh felt something tug at his jeans. The smooth metal surface had been replaced by a rough fabric texture and was gripping his clothes, quickly decreasing his speed before his feet made an abrupt contact with a soft buffer. In a matter of seconds the death ride was over. After momentarily lying in the dark confine, a doorway slid open above him to reveal Angelica's grinning features. It was only as she reached in to aid him out that Josh realised he was standing almost upright. Stumbling out, the recalibration of heightened senses took a few seconds before they relented he was alive and well.

"Enjoy the ride?" she asked, enjoying the look of bemusement on his pale face. "The first time is always a little disorientating, but you get used to it by the second or third go," she assured him.

"You do that all the time?" he asked. He heard a thump as something landed the large pipe adjacent to his. "I thought I was going to hell."

"Not quite," she answered blankly. His first glimpse of the new surroundings was a shark contrast from the world above. Underground the air was cool and the wide open arid space had been replaced with a cramped, murky tunnel hewn into the desert floor. "Follow me." Angelica walked on, expecting him to follow obediently into the claustrophobic subterranean surroundings. The source of the earlier thump was revealed when the Monk appeared in the opening exit of the adjacent chute. Unruffled he stepped out and waited as the pipe resealed and delivered the big soldier in the same undignified manner. "Mind your head," Angelica warned. His reactions blunted by disorientation, Josh bumped his forehead against the top ridge of the low doorway. He was no taller than five foot ten, but still the maritime styled metal portal forced him to bow like a giant and lift his leg to pass by its high bottom edge.

"What is this place?" he asked as he straightened and followed his guide down the metal walled tunnel. The constricted environment seemed industrial in nature, like the bowels of some ancient liner, but he chose not to voice any advance thoughts.

"Just somewhere in the middle of nowhere," she answered enigmatically, her voice resonating before her into the dim passage in front. Josh ducked his head once more to avoid a low corroded pipe and agreed with the irony in her answer. The secret layer beneath the desert sands truly was somewhere in the middle of nowhere, but the maritime theme haunted the surroundings. If it wasn't for the unorthodox elevator's plunge of several storeys into the earth, he could have sworn he was onboard an abandoned vessel. Angelica stepped through a second low lying, high stepping portal and turned to check on his progress. Josh ducked his head through and saw it led onto a much larger, brighter corridor. He lurched onwards.

"So this is where you guys call home?" Shuffling through, he appreciated the new spacious passage. More welcoming than the first, a nearby grill breathed a cool draft of reconditioned air across his face. At the sight of the high ceiling he resigned the fear of bumping his head and righted himself.

"You could say that, but I doubt the heart would agree," she offered before continuing the tour. The second corridor was brightly lit with strip lighting that filled it with a vibrant luminance closely resembling natural light. Usually such fluorescent strips radiated an aberrant glow that irritated Josh's vision, but he found the current environment surprisingly pleasant and hoped the happy vibes she had spoke of before weren't responsible. At the corridor's end two screen doors hid a more brightly lit area, attracting his curiosity.

"This way," Angelica instructed. She walked in the opposite direction towards a more dimly lit doorway. He took a deep breath, swallowed his apprehension, and then cautiously followed the striding woman further onwards into an adjoining corridor of sealed unmarked doors. His footsteps bounced off its plain walls and he wondered if the journey would ever end. He was tired, hungry, disorientated and yearned for a conclusion to the unfolding drama. He wanted to grab her arm, make her stop and answer the mishmash of questions cluttering his mind, but he didn't have the spiritual or physical energy to execute the desire. Hundreds of miles and almost a day behind him, he had left his home and embarked on the strange adventure that now dominated both his waking and sleeping hours. He was a willing captive to the blonde stranger who had brought him to this foreign place beneath the ground where, in reality, he still remained at their mercy.

There had been a chance to escape this place. Back on the sun-baked road out of LA she had clearly given him the choice to part ways or stay amongst them on the journey of discovery. But as the façade of acceptance was eaten away by the prospect of what lay ahead, he wished he could reconsider. His decision to stay in the RV might just have sealed his fate.

"This one is yours," his blonde guide then stated. Angelica had stopped by a door and pushed it open as an invitation for him to enter.

Josh studied her expression briefly, trying to ascertain any hidden agenda, and then cautiously walked into the doorway that revealed a small under furnished room that looked all too much like a cell.

"That's funny, I don't remember owning a broom closet in the middle of the desert," he replied sardonically, putting off the inevitable abandonment in the clean but cramped, soulless room. Sensing his apprehension she waved him in. Reluctantly he walked over the threshold to stand at the foot of the white iron framed bed that looked like it had been lifted from a ward in the fifties. He admired the neatly folded sheets that made up the bedding.

"There are towels, fresh water and a change of clothes," she explained cordially. "Please make yourself at home." He took one look at the small basin and mirror to his immediate right and saw that the offer of hospitality had been conservative in light of the vast array of toiletries carefully placed around the basin's flat areas. From the basic razor and deodorant labelled *For Men*, he wondered if they had been placed with his imminent arrival in mind. More likely the small room had been prepped for any male visitor who'd been ensnared by the Elite and rescued from their nightmares as he had been, or so he hoped. Angelica began to close the door.

"But I've only just got here," he exclaimed. He turned around and caused her to pause in the doorway. After the journey he was tired and bemused, but with a burning desire to know what awaited him in this subterranean layer, it would thwart any urge to sleep.

"This is our rest time, you'll get used to it," she explained, her tone revealing more of the endearment he had hoped to hear. "We all need to recharge after what we've been through. I'll come get you at oh five hundred." Thus reprimanded, she closed the door. The bolt clunked into place, securing the new arrival in the cramped but comfortable cell. *Locked in?* Sure his guide's footsteps had disappeared down the hall; he tried the door handle and found he was right. *Free to go my ass.* Retrieving his cell phone he checked the display. The battery remained low, its signal nonexistent but at least he could find out the time. *8:24.* It had been over optimistic to believe he could secretly communicate with the outside world through the layers of rock above him, but he was reluctant to dismiss the phone's usefulness totally and concealed it under the mattress.

Paranoia insisted he checked for hidden devices his hosts may have employed to study their new guest. After a quick survey of the exposed corners and edges however he decided the bare furnishing left little cover for such intrusions, or that the technology was too minuscule for detection. The shimmering nature of the cell's four walls then drew his attention. They appeared to be made of the same mystery metal sheeting employed in the rest of the compound. Burnished but not reflective, his reflection was more a hazy spectre. In each corner of the room were more of the same mysterious white spheres he had seen in Calisto's, considerably smaller but otherwise identical. It was then that the crystal clear apparition that was Josh Brenin caught his attention. *Is that me?* He stepped forward to examine himself in the mirror. He looked ill. His pale skin highlighted the dark smudges of fatigue under both eyes that lacked their usual lustre, while the skin colour of the bandage on his brow now looked positively alien. In essence he looked like he felt. Seeing his reflection against the backdrop of the small cell finally grounded the reality of the situation. This was not a dream, he was living the nightmare. Disenchanted by the haunting spectacle, he lay on the bed and prayed sleep would free him of reality.

*****

The zebra skin seat covers were ghastly, but he humoured the poor taste and accepted the ride in Sharon's car. Outside the glass barrier of the passenger door window the wide stretch of road simmered in the light of a summer morning sun, the herd of traffic surrounding them moving at a casual pace as the streets woke up to another Los Angeles working day. In contrast the small car's functioning air-com cooled its interior.

A night of unbridled lust had led onto the hitched drive to work, and the inevitable earache about the short-comings of their relationship. Josh's view from the window afforded some freedom from the arduous task of listening to the inane aspirations, revolving around a future he couldn't visualise and had no intention of committing to with someone he didn't truly love. Their relationship was merely a diversion from the drudgery of his life, but that was no future and he hadn't the heart to do the honourable thing. After all, some company was better than none. But on that morning as she drove him downtown, the thread of apathy snapped.

"Sharon I can't..." He had turned to yell, but what met his disbelieving eyes cut the outburst short. She had been wearing the heavy make up from the night before, the garish pink hoop earrings he hated so swaying from her ears, but as he looked at the woman in the driving seat, an all the more natural beauty had replaced the excess of cosmetics and pink plastic. The baggy necked eighties throwback that had been Sharon's black and white striped jumper was now a feminine white blouse his wife had worn on the fatal morning. He blinked at the unexpected vision.

"Josh what's wrong?" Sarah asked with a smile. "You look like you've seen a ghost." Josh looked around at the street. Recognising the route downtown he knew they were on the way to the ill-fated crossroad.

"Sarah!" he exclaimed. There was little time to act. He had wasted so much precious time listening to Sharon's drivel that the benign realisation would be wasted unless he acted quickly. "Stop the car!" She looked back through the windshield at the slow moving traffic.

"Why?" she asked wistfully, "What's wrong hun?"

"Sarah, stop the car. You've got to trust me; something bad is going to happen." He saw the traffic lights that guarded the crossroads loom before them.

"I think someone needs a nicotine fix!" she teased carelessly.

"We're going to crash! Please, stop the car!" He gripped the wheel, hoping to force her to brake.

"Josh what's gotten into you? Let go!" She smacked his wrist and scowled at her manic partner as though he was mad.

"Sarah if you don't stop the car we're going to crash!" He stared forward dumbfounded as their car lane continued to flow through the halted cross section of traffic waiting to be released by a green light. Josh tightened his grip and readied to yank the steering wheel towards him.

"You will if you don't let go." The placidity in Sarah's reply pierced his tension. *You will?* She was looking directly at him now, enforcing her message with her bright hazel eyes. It was then Josh sensed the world around them begin to slow like a faltering film reel. As though the earth's spinning orbit was decelerating to a standstill, it compelled him to listen.

"Just…" she said softly as they passed the traffic light, "let…" and lumbered to a halt at the centre of the intersection, "…go!" With the final word spoken he saw the killer brown sedan posed to jump the lights over her shoulder and understood what she asking him to do. Fate could not bend to the will of one man's desire to hold onto the past. Staring into his wife's doleful eyes, he let his hand slide away from her slender wrist. Like a released piece of taut rubber the world suddenly caught up with itself in a flashing instant, the sedan crashed into the driver's side and Sarah was stolen from him again.

****

The fatal collision railroaded Josh back to reality. Stunned and disorientated, he felt the warm satin comfort of another slender hand slide away from his forehead and gazed up into the crystal blue eyes hovering above him. He blinked away the awkwardness from his blurry vision. Against his expectations he had fallen asleep in the strange bed, and for the first time in weeks not found himself face to face with the demon Galda Vey. A little startled by his brusque awakening, Angelica straightened and smiled assuredly.

"It's time Josh," she announced. "I'll wait for you outside." With the brief welcome over she walked out, leaving the door ajar behind her as Josh shook the sense into his dazed reflexes by rising quickly from the bed. *This is it.* Swinging his legs onto the concrete floor he took a moment to palm his face in his hands, Sarah's hazel eyes and sweet smile still haunting his inner vision. *Later.* He looked up at the small room and recalled he was not at home. By sharing the refuge of his subconscious with the one person who had ever made him full completely alive, he'd briefly been freed of the cold reality of captivity. But in the strange cell that was to be his new home for an unknown duration, the irony Sarah was dead only made facing the new reality all the more disheartening. Not wanting to keep his new tutor waiting, he stood up to the basin and made use of the generous selection of toiletries at his disposal. Not wanting to face the ghosts of his past he made sure to avert his eyes from the mirror.

After a hasty facial wash he opened his cell door to be led to his future, their footsteps echoing in unison as she led him back into the larger brightly lit corridor Josh guessed to be the backbone of subterranean compound.

"Did you manage to get much rest?" she asked cordially as they passed the nautical style access door to the laundry chutes that had brought him into their cool underworld.

"I wouldn't call dreaming about car crashes particularly restful," he replied dryly, squinting as his eyes adjusted to the all-encompassing light. "But yeah I caught a few." He wondered if by the placing of her hand on his head she had somehow been able to see into his dreams. As her obvious curiosity proved otherwise, he dismissed the paranoia as folly.

"Let's hope you're not psychic," she joked. He was glad that she wasn't also, or so he thought. As they walked on her golden hair swayed gently aside her head with a fresh radiance that came after grooming, its slightly curled ends brushing the white, close fitting, short sleeved top she wore. Revealing the athletic form he had admired in the RV, the unexpected sensuality it provoked caused him to mask his thoughts.

"So is sleep on ration here?"

"Why? You not a morning person, Josh?"

"As far as I'm concerned the only things worth getting up early for are Christmas and taking a wiz. And seeing as I don't believe in Santa Claus anymore that kind of narrows it down." Thankfully his answer raised a smile from his blonde guide.

"You'll get used to it, I promise." Reaching the screen doors at the opposite end of the corridor she pushed them aside and he followed her blindly through into the room which had intrigued him on his arrival. He didn't like the sound of *get used to it. Get used to it* suggested captivity was likely to be long, but thoughts of uncertainty melted away as he found himself the centre of attention for a table of strangers.

Cutlery clanked against plates as the group abruptly stopped eating to study his entrance with a keen interest. He had walked into a wall of awkwardness. The equally brightly lit room had turned out to be a communal dining area, and he had just interrupted the first meal of the day. Sat around a large triangular table that dominated the centre of the room, the assembly of men and women looked on at the unknown recruit standing in the doorway, their blank faces revealing nothing of their thoughts. *Breakfast underground.*

"Wait here," Angelica instructed, breaking the silence. He looked at her, hoping he hadn't heard her correctly, but then realised his day would begin with a baptism of fire. "I'm guessing you're hungry?" Not wanting to look like an idiot, he nodded then watched her disappear through another set of screen doors to their left. Josh had been left right where he didn't like to be; in the spotlight. For a second he couldn't bare to take his eyes from the swinging door through which Angelica had abandoned him, but his angst was lessened by the sound of a familiar voice.

"Don't just stand there, take a seat." Gazing to the table, Josh spotted Jonah's olive features beaming back at him. "We don't bite!" he added jovially, waving him over. The old adage was a good ice-breaker and enabled Josh to approach the table of strangers with a forced smirk.

"Not unless you want us to," a female voice added. He caught a glance of a woman grinning over shoulder, weighing him up with big dark eyes as he made the short walk to where Jonah had pulled out a spare seat at his side. Across the table Josh recognised Monk and Alpha sitting amongst the group. He guessed the cheery looking man on Jonah's other side was Dex, but the others he didn't recognise. The Solarian's mystery driver had a thick mane of fair hair combed back from his chiselled face that gave him the appearance of a lion. As Josh sat down next Jonah, he welcomed Josh with a tip of the head and a reassuring smile of perfect teeth.

"Help yourself buddy," Jonah explained, gesturing towards the bounty of food before him that consisted of bread rolls, fruit, waffles and cereals.

"Thank you," Josh replied politely. As he stared hungrily at the generous choice of foods he felt his stomach rumble. It had been over twenty four hours since he'd had anything to eat and the sight of fried eggs on the plate of a scrawny man across from him made his appetite explode.

"Here," Jonah picked a clean plate and laid it before him. "I saved you some croissants," he declared, then offered a small pile of sticky coated buns on a serving plate. The sight of the French style pastries in the underground desert layer was both unusual and disappointing. Though preferring the scrawny stranger's choice, he took the top croissant and raised his line of sight to quickly encompass the gathering of curious faces sat around the three-sided table. Already acquainted with the latest arrival, Monk, Alpha and Dex impassively continued their breakfast. In between bites, as of yet unknown comrades simply snatched curious glimpses of Josh as they returned to their breakfast, with the exception of the brown-eyed woman who continued to unashamedly stare like a child at a puppy. "Butter? Jelly?" Jonah asked, pointing towards the selection on offer.

"I'll take some of that jelly," Josh replied. He took a knife and cut the flaky croissant in two. *Real enough.* "Croissants in the desert; it's a new one on me."

"Only the best for the best," Jonah explained with another vivacious grin.

"In that case I better take that!" Dex reached over and snatched the roll from Jonah's hand and rammed it greedily into his own mouth. "If anyone deserves the best around here," he mumbled with a full mouth, "it's me!" The getaway driver grinned so that the half chewed roll was exposed for his friend to admire. The childish stunt caused chuckles from the others, though motivated another croissant to be tossed at his forehead from across the table. Jonah's amiable persona had won their guest over, Dex it seemed was just as endearing.

"You see this guy?" Jonah asked Josh. "You ever seen a head that big before? Solid bone my friend, solid bone," he teased as he pushed away his plate in mock disgust. "Nothing in between those ears except bone and engine grease." Dex half choked on the croissant. "See what I mean? Bone and grease." He repeated as Dex turned away to release the croissant onto the floor.

"So are you going to introduce us to your new boyfriend?" the brown-eyed woman then bellowed rudely across the table. "I don't blame you for keeping him to yourself, he's cute. But the question is has he got a name?" Unable to determine he was being goaded or not, Josh waited for Jonah to stop patting Dex on the back before an answer was delivered on his behalf.

"You're right, where are my manners?" Jonah apologised haughtily, "I've been hanging around with this clown too long that's for sure." He sat back against his chair and righted himself to publicly introduce Josh to the group who had impatiently abandoned their breakfasts in anticipation of the formality. "Everybody, Josh!" he began in a booming voice, "He may be the new meat amongst us but I want you to treat him as you would one of our own." Jonah placed a warm hand on the small of his back and darted a wink his way. "Already he's cut his teeth in service against the enemy, and has shown himself to be of some use to our merry little cause. Ain't that right, Alpha?" Josh caught no sign of sarcasm in his benefactor's face, though doubted from Alpha's cold glance he shared Jonah's enthusiasm. "So after tailing his sorry ass for the past week, he's come to stay with brothers and sisters of the light and continue the good work. Josh, meet everybody." Reaching to take his pick of the fresh fruit on offer, Jonah then shook his head as Dex sat up and wiped his mouth.

"Is that it?" the scrawny man opposite asked, hands turned upwards in a gesture of disappointment. "What kind of intro was that?" His inability to pronounce the letter T gave away a broad English accent. "I dunno about you guys but I'm feeling a little deflated by Mr Jonah's rather uninformative, and may I say, shit description of his esteemed friends and colleagues." Josh was immediately intrigued by the man's presence amongst the group. The skin of his face was taut over its prominent bone structure, giving him the appearance of being emaciated. His short mousy brown hair was dishevelled, while his close knitted droopy eyes were separated by an unfortunate large nose, whose bridge curved precariously away from his face like a parrot's beak.

"What do you want a biography?" Jonah replied sarcastically. Whilst peeling the banana he had chosen, the master or ceremony then gave a relenting sigh and took a bite. "Josh, meet Cozmo. He's a Limey," he added between chewing, as if to justify the Englishman's outburst.

"Nice to meet you Josh," Cozmo said as he got up to offer his veiny hand to Josh. "A pleasure." After giving the new meat's hand a firm shake he sat back down looking pleased with himself.

"Do you want to kiss his ass while you're at it?" the man next to Cozmo abruptly asked with a smirk. The tire of extra skin that hung from below the man's chin suggested the huge bulk he hid under the large hooded sports top was not muscle.

"Up yours Tubby!" Cozmo retorted playfully. "And yes I am a Limey as you Yanks so charmingly put it. Born, bred and proud."

"God save the Queen," the rotund man announced mockingly as he raised his glass of cola before draining it.

"And that big beautiful man next to Cozmo is Maestro," Jonah continued his introductions. "Don't let the size of him fool you, somewhere under that impressive bulk is a thin man just waiting to get out."

"Yeah," Cozmo confirmed, his veiny arms crossed over his chest, "'cause he fucking ate him!" More chuckles erupted around the table as the vexed Maestro lowered his glass. He wore a baseball cap backwards over his head of long curly dark brown hair that reached his shoulders and sported a short clipped chinstrap beard in a vain attempt to highlight his jaw line. His beady grey eyes were deep set into his bloated face, though glistened with a keen intellect as he eyeballed his Limey colleague.

"And next to Maestro is the lovely Saffy," Jonah then announced, continuing around the triangular table. The way she'd been watching Josh intently with a quiet detachment suggested a wilful character he found a little intimidating. Like the rest of the women in the dreamscape militia of increasing ranks she was strikingly attractive. At the aired introduction she gave a brief smile and a nod, reflecting her cool reserve, marble white skin contrasting with the raven black hair combed back into a long ponytail to fully expose her almond shaped eyes. "She doesn't say much," Jonah teased. "Seeing as she's a woman we take that as a blessing," Saffy flipped Jonah the bird and quickly he moved on.

"You won't get such blessing from me!" the brown-eyed woman proudly announced from across the table, leaning provocatively forward on her elbows so that the bead-wear around her neck dangled into the half finished breakfast of waffles.

"He'll get to you soon enough lunatic," the red-bearded man opposite chided her. "I'm next."

"The freak worried he'll be left out?" she teased back, but the ill tempered man chose not to dignify the jibe with a response. He had a shaved head and intense blue eyes that reminded Josh of a coke-head he'd befriended at one of the many rock concerts Matty and he had attended during college.

"On the end there," Jonah continued, "the scaring cracker looking guy with the tatts is Merlin." The man's fiery coloured facial hair was long, thick and tapered into a point that fittingly resembled a wizard's beard, but to Josh he had the appearance of a cold hearted Hell's Angel. His exposed arms were muscular and, has his guide had pointed out, covered with tribal tattoos that enclosed the arm from wrist to shoulder. As Merlin's cool predatory eyes studied him, Josh was glad to be opposite ends of the table.

"Josh," he acknowledged sternly, then broke his gaze to finish a bowl of cereal. Josh found the formalities a progressing ordeal; secretly he wished the embarrassing social necessity would end. With his croissant still untouched, his stomach voice its objection with a curdling rumble as Jonah's attention then shifted to the intense brown eyed woman next on his tour.

"And without further ado we get to another fine lady in our gang, Luna." The effervescent young woman straightened at the gracious introduction, then flashed Josh a wink that was more suggestive than endearing.

"Hi, hot stuff," she greeted him. From her loud manner Josh decided a hyperactive mind lay behind and inability to prevent itself from saying what it thought. He simply smiled politely in response, but the young dark woman was determined to exploit her turn in the proceedings. "So where you from?" she asked bluntly, gazing wildly over the half consumed feast before them. "Or more exactly, where did the Latronis lost souls recruitment squad abduct you?" The combination of her dark skin and thick wavy hair, that bounced about her face as she fidgeted like a child, made her the most exotic looking of the group as well as the most animated in her reception of the new recruit.

"Let him eat," Monk instructed suddenly. He looked up from the orange he was methodically peeling, plainly irritated by Luna's vivacious nature. The intervention was enough to curb the dark woman's curiosity.

"No harm in asking." She gave the austere Monk next to her a submissive glance, then retreated to picking at the remains of her breakfast of waffles, her questions left unanswered.

"Did you hear that?" Cozmo suddenly asked, feigning disbelief. "He spoke! I think that deserves a round of applause don't you people?" The gaunt Englishman looked around the table for takers to the unpredicted mockery, but was isolated in his insolence. "Monkey boy actually opened his mouth and said something. And here I was thinking he was a bloody mute!" Though the comments were meant to tease, the sullen mood that abruptly gripped the table relayed Monk's icy glare was for real. Unused to such disrespect he raised a finger, the invisible force it released pushing a half finished bowl of cereal into Cozmo's lap. The Englishman jumped up from his seat as it crashed loudly onto the bare floor and splintered into a mess of white porcelain shards. The sight of the sodden mess in his lap triggered a vengeful scowl, though wary of the latent power Monk's adept raised finger could unleash again, Cozmo bit his tongue, walked off from the table and disappeared through the first set of screen doors to clean up. With the breach in protocol, reprimanded Monk returned to the meticulous stripping of the orange peel.

"And of course Monk, Dex, Alpha and myself need no introduction," Jonah concluded affably, oblivious to the sultry mood of the others. To Monk's right Alpha ignored his introduction. He'd wanted to exploit such an occasion to insist on the use of his real name. Mom and Dad had christened their one and only son Benjamin Wheeler. To friends and family he'd always been Ben. Alpha was the highly trained Delta Force killing machine, a military tag he'd only planned on allowing the Latronis militia to employ as a temporary device. But in light of his tutor's fragile pride, he swallowed his own and returned to pick at his plate with a fork. "Welcome to the club!" Jonah added and gave Josh a raised look, implying he was part of something that required a sense of humour.

He gazed back around the triangular table to the mismatch of characters that made up the mysterious dreamscape brigade known as Latronis. The induction ceremony that had began as a light hearted exercise had ended on a much sombre note. It was as his ravenous stomach's curdling growl interrupted the dejection incurred by his arrival that Josh realised just how formal the impromptu inauguration had really been. From appearances sake he too was now one of them, a servant of the light, whether he liked it or not.

*****

The Principal's footsteps echoed loudly down the corridor as he paced towards the elevator doors at its end. His senses were still reeling from the encounter that had ended only moments before. For once he was daunted by the prospect of failure and its dire consequences. As he passed doorway after doorway in an assertive stride, his mind flashed with images of the secret masters, imprinted upon his very soul by the inter-dimensional confrontation. Such infinite beings were beyond the rational comprehension of the common man, powerful disembodied intelligences that had existed before the dawn of mankind and had watched its evolution with great interest. As Galda Vey admired his black-attired reflection approaching in the chrome finish of the doors, he imagined himself standing at the side of such immortal beings.

Entering the large elevator he selected the button for level four. Shuddering gently it then began the short descent deeper into the bedrock of the Sierra Nevada, its sealed confinement giving him time to collect his emblazoned thoughts. He was determined not to give credence to the notion the secret masters hadn't destroyed him because of his earthly use, and thus proving he was merely an expendable puppet. Galda had wanted to assure them he was worthy of the great accolade, and that he alone held the keys to success for their great work. Yes in essence he was betraying his oath of allegiance, his country, even his race, but when the time came to step up and be counted, there would only be him and the path to immortality, and none of that would matter.

The elevator came to an unexpected halt at an intermediate level. As the doors parted silently they revealed a subordinate agent waiting in an identical corridor. At the sight of the Principal the agent flinched, a reflection of the awe and fear Galda Vey's presence commanded from his younger agents. He entered nervously, made his selection and stood silently at a respectful distance. The agent's novice status within the Elite was relayed by his lack of protective eyewear. Only after serving the project for at least a decade did the mortal body's ocular resistance to light gradually begin to falter.

For Galda his ascension into the highest ranks had been a rapid one. As an especially gifted Nothos, he had passed each ascending grade with cunning foresight and, over the past two and a half decades of service, helped convert what was an experimental black book project into the most powerful and undervalued instrument in Uncle Sam's clandestine arsenal. Sensing the novice's apprehension, he recollected his first years with the Elite.

The Elite, as they eventually branded themselves, had originally been the honorary title for the most gifted Nothos, or naturals, acquired by the small, secured community of Project Olympia; an NSA funded black book operation concealed in the underground fortress of the abandoned military nuclear bunker carved out of the bedrock of the Californian desert. As a splinter organisation rooted in the remote viewing projects of the forties and fifties, its creation had been an act of providence, initiated by the discovery of the Ketron complex; a synthetic psychotropic drug originally designed to improve the capabilities of remote viewers. Its potential for unlocking the parameters of the unconscious, slumbering mind however quickly outweighed its remote viewing origins when first contact was made in May 1979. Unlike the first contacts portrayed by Hollywood, the inter-dimensional entities the early Olympia Nothos encountered were merely disembodied entities, whose ancient intelligence offered the keys to a universal science that was literally out of this world. But the full appreciation of such a breakthrough had been slow in coming.

By the time Galda had joined Project Olympia in the early eighties, its aspirations for acquiring new alien science had faltered. The race of disembodied entities, now calling themselves the Deros, had grown disinterested with the desires of men and had began to make their own demands. The covenant was born. Galda had proved himself the most dexterous Nothos to negotiate with the stubborn entities, who teased the project leaders with snippets of half complete technology, only offering to reveal the full potential of their science to their projecting dreamscape emissaries if they made sacrifices, unthinkable sacrifices that involved relinquishing power over the ruling classes of the world. The disembodied race's price for complicity was an unprecedented surrender of control over the world of man, and the project leaders had declined.

That had been where Galda's foresight had allowed him to understand what his superiors did not; the Deros envied the world of men. The drive for material technology was pointless to such creatures and so they had given it freely to the short-sighted mortals, concealing their true agenda, baiting their pride, and waiting for the opportunity and for a Nothos such as Galda Vey. He alone had seen that the immortality of the higher self was the ultimate prize on offer, not vain, self defeating military objectives that would corrode and expire in the dusts of time. And he had wanted that prize, even at the grave price it came with. The Deros needed the Elite's help to attain their great work of ages. It was then that John Raymer became Galda Vey, the Elite Nothos took control of Project Olympia, and the Deros became the secret masters.

The elevator came to a slow gentle halt and opened its doors onto level four. The novice agent bowed his head submissively and waited eagerly for the doors to reseal as Galda strode confidently into the short corridor terminated by a large blast door. The barrier of thick, chrome finished alloy reflected the prominent agent's arrival. Waiting for the departure of the novice agent he proceeded to enter the clandestine level unauthorised to lower grades.

The simple touch of his pale fingers to the bio-print interface caused the blast door to slid open, allowing the head agent into the dimly lit world of the highest echelons of the black book agency's real world operations. Behind the regimented arrangement of row after row of transparent desks, sat the army of the Elite, sporting their shades in the neon blue light that infused the high vaulted room with an eerie radiance. As the Principal strode into centre stage the ghoulish ranks looked up from their holographic displays, sensing his uncommon presence was one of great importance. Assured that he had his minion's full attention, Galda Vey made his ominous announcement.

"My brothers, the time has come," he declared. "The time has come to finally rid the world of the servants of the light and implement the great work." There was a silence in the great hall of attentive agents, who were duty bound to whatever task enabled the agency to fulfil its primary role. Though insignificant in numbers, the Latronis militia had proved to be a thorn in the side of that duty for far too long. Now that the Elite's global ambitions were on the verge of fruition, the thorn needed to be permanently removed. "Gather yourselves and prepare for war." After conveying all that was needed, Galda turned and exited.

Knowing the only thing that stood in the way of the great accolade was soon to be destroyed, he buried his last pang of humanity deep inside his trampled conscience. Latronis would soon cease to be and the freedom of billions of pawns across the world would be sacrificed in his honour by the very means his secret army would soon unleash. Safe in the knowledge he would never be accountable to the world of men, Galda prepared for the preliminary battle with a sense of pride and conviction. The ace up his sleeve was about to prove he'd been worth every ounce of disruption to the Low Grade recruitment programme. The Principal's personal intervention in the cuckoo's tutelage was about be vindicated, for the seemingly lost Nothos was now about to unwittingly help secure the great work for the secret masters, and with it an eternity of glory for Galda Vey.

Chapter 13

Minimalism was definitely the common aesthetic for the subterranean head quarters. Using the quiet time following the ruckus between Monk and Cozmo, Josh studied his surroundings though concluded they were disappointing, unlike the French pastry he'd devoured which had been the best he'd ever had. The brightly lit subterranean canteen in which he'd found himself eating the continental breakfast contained no other furnishings except those that his current companions sat on or ate off. Under his feet the ground was a simple treated concrete floor hemmed in by similarly bare walls of sheet metal bolted into what could only be the surrounding bedrock. The source of the room's brilliant illumination seeped from the translucent ceiling above their heads, creating an omnipresent, near heavenly light that cleansed any niches of shadow. Quite fitting Josh thought, for it was the shadows that concealed the real dangers in this new clandestine world.

Angelica had been gone for what Josh guessed must have been twenty minutes. Wondering what new mysteries lay behind the screen doors he found his imagination running away with paranoia. Irritably he returned to his new associates. Monk had long finished eating the orange and was enjoying the tranquillity afforded behind his closed eyes as he rested his chin on his clasped hands. The others continued to pick at the remains of the food, swapping tepid glances that hid frustrated conversations. It was the fidgety Luna who caught Josh's inquisitive glance first.

"So you ready to face the light at the end of the tunnel Josh?" she asked, her tone less animated out of respect for the prickly Monk to her right. The dramatic question conjured wild speculation he was to face some new precarious trial. Suddenly he felt uneasy.

"Come again," he replied warily.

"Forever the drama queen eh, Luna?" Dex interceded, changing positions from the bored twisting of the ring on his finger to slouching back into the uncomfortable chrome framed chair. "She means Kristos," he explained with a tilt of the head, but the significance was wasted on Josh as it was only the second time he'd heard the name. From the adolescent sparkle in Luna's big dark eyes however he sensed the reverence attached to it.

"Kristos?" Josh asked anxiously.

"He's the sun we all evolve around," Jonah confirmed dryly. He joined Dex in a slouched pose. "He's the organiser of this little social club.

He's the man with the master plan." As Josh thought himself the victim of some cruel tease, Monk returned from his inner thoughts and turned to bolster the melodramatic comments with his own.

"He'll show you what it means to be alive!" he declared, emphasising his sincerity with his stern blue eyes. The penny dropped in Josh's mind. If the reason he'd been brought to the mysterious surroundings far from home was to meet with the militia's general, it gave his hope of returning home credibility.

"Then I guess so," Josh replied hesitantly to Luna. As the screen doors suddenly swung open he swallowed his doubts.

"I trust you made our guest feel at home?" Angelica asked her comrades as she re-entered, the blank delivery relaying its insignificance.

"Yeah we had a riot," Dex replied sardonically. Josh looked up and sensed her civility hid some hidden agenda. It was then that the brooding rebellion began to rekindle inside him. He didn't ask to be a servant of the light. He didn't want to live in some glorified rabbit warren in the desert. But the drawback of defiance was that these servants were the only ones who could save him from his nightmares.

"Fancy a walk?" she asked Josh directly. Keen to escape the awkward conference, he stood and pushed his chair back under the table, the wretched screech it made heralding his departure for what had to be the light at the end of the tunnel.

"Thanks for the croissants," he thanked no one in particular. Jonah acknowledged him with a nod and a wide eyed look that intimated he was leaving for some momentous engagement. As he turned to leave Angelica was already standing back by a half opened screen door, her thawing persona now seemingly aloof once more as she waved him on through it before following behind. The unexplored corridor was identical to the rest. "Interesting group," he stated openly, trying not to reveal his anxious curiosity over what lay ahead. Walking on, they passed what at first appeared to be a fire alarm protected by a sheet of glass, but an uncanny instinct warned him it most likely held some security function instead.

"A motley crew I know, but they are all good people," Angelica answered without eye contact. Though she paced down the corridor to their unspecified destination beside him, she felt a world away.

"And Kristos?" he asked inquisitively.

"See for yourself," Angelica stopped and waved her hand towards a non-descript door. Without further explanation her unreadable features suggested he continued without her. Relenting to fate, Josh pushed open the unlocked door and entered. As he edged through the doorway and peeked in Josh sensed his blonde guide waiting where she stood, no doubt to make sure he didn't double back. But there was no chance of that. Here at last he was coming to the end of a long journey of questions, to come face to face with the mysterious leader of Latronis, a small militia, who like monastic priests, had seemingly abandoned the outside world to dedicate their lives to a clandestine order of light, responsible for the eradication of their mutual enemies.

With a faint creak of hinges the shutting door announced his presence in the new spacious room. From a quick, nervous glance around Josh found that apart from a selection of mounted sculptures and a water feature that gushed serenely at the room's centre, it was as bare and unfurnished as the others. *No one here.* The only exceptional was the high-backed period brown leather chair that looked like it had been lifted from a Dickensian film set. The room's cooler air suddenly emphasised its barren ambience. Josh shivered, and then noticed a second sealed door at the furthest corner away to his right. Deliberating whether he was to sit and wait for his mysterious host, the raised hairs on the back of his neck abruptly urged him to leave the unoccupied surroundings. *Something's not right.*

Another creak then drew his attention back to the chair. As it swivelled around to face Josh he saw the old man from the dilapidated bar was sat casually in its polished leather moulding. Locking a luminous gaze with the intruder, the man scrutinised again with cool, beady eyes. *You weren't there a second ago.*

"I'm here to see Kristos," Josh announced expectantly. The man then rose with an unpredicted agility and walked over to greet him.

"Something to wet your whistle?" Josh looked down and saw he was holding out a glass of clear water. Graciously Josh accepted the offer from the outstretched hand of tanned leathery skin. Close up he noted the same dark tanned skin on his broad features was the product of a lifetime of living in the desert sun, contrasting quite radically with the long mane of grey hair that he brushed away from its wrinkled forehead. Estimating the man to be in his mid fifties, Josh hoped he'd still have a full head of hair when, and if, he reached an equivalent age.

"I'm Josh," he introduced himself doggedly, the ice cold glass beginning to bite at his palm.

"I know who you are," the man admitted offhandedly. He turned his back on Josh to return to the leather chair, exposing the golden eagle patch sown onto the back of the dog-eared black leather waistcoat he wore. "I'll be with you in a second." Josh contemplated further whether the grungy looking man had been a biker in his youth, or perhaps still was. *What is he doing here?* The chair's leather upholstery creaked as the man retook his seat. While Josh took an edgy sip of the water, his sombre host simply stared on blankly.

"Are we waiting for someone?" Josh asked, intimidated by the by the eccentric's silent study of him. The icy water made his tooth ache, but the flickering light coming from behind the chair quickly distracted him from the complaint. The man acknowledged the question remotely with a nod, but Josh's attention had been drawn to the small log fire, that as a sidestep revealed, now burned away cosily in the period hearth of wrought iron behind him. *Was that there a second ago?* The reticent stranger he could have initially missed due to the chair's position, perhaps even the glass of water he hadn't seen him carry, but the fire? Josh would have bet his bottom dollar it hadn't been there on his arrival.

"And here I am," the man suddenly announced and pointed casually towards the second entrance across the room. As its plain metal door slid open, the aged biker turned away in the creaky leather chair to face the roaring fire. But the rude gesture was quickly forgotten as Josh watched the second man manoeuvre his wheelchair into the room. As this second man brought himself to an abrupt stop in front of Josh he looked up from the mobility seat with a broad grin and beady blue eyes that relayed his guilty pleasure. For a second Josh thought he was suffering a hallucination. He looked back to the high backed chair facing him once more, but like the once roaring fireplace, the original old biker had disappeared.

"What's the matter son you never seen a ghost before?" the second man asked as he wheeled himself past his bemused guest towards the now vacant leather chair. "But of course you have, if it wasn't for seeing ghosts you wouldn't be here," the man continued as he parked opposite it. "Or to use a more suitable term, a person's Ka. That's K A not C A R by the way. Take a seat." The glass of water almost slipped from Josh's hand, though he managed to right it just in time to make the monumental realisation that the two men had been one and the same, except now he was seemingly wheelchair bound.

"Kristos?" Josh dared to ask. His hand trembled as it tried to retain the icy glass. *I'm dreaming.*

"Who else would I be son?" he asked in his rich southern accent, "Please." Kristos waved him towards the period leather chair. Unsure if he still slumbered in the hard bed of his new cell, he took up the offer before his nervous stance embarrassed him. "You see the ancient Egyptians believed that we had two souls," his new host continued swiftly as Josh sat down in the groaning leather upholstery. He wanted to investigate the space where the very real fireplace had once been, but found himself mesmerised by Kristos's intense crystal blue eyes as he spoke fluidly. "An immortal one that passed on after mortal death and was reincarnated infinite times, and a mortal soul which they called the Ka, the very life force or shadow body if you will of the flesh and bone shell the immortal soul was inhabiting." As the enigmatic figure in the wheelchair reeled off the spiel Josh found himself forgetting the uncomfortable realisation he might just have seen a ghost.

With a keen eye he now studied the second Kristos. It was the same face, the same hair and the same biker waistcoat over a spotless white t-shirt, even the distinctive spread of UV induced brown spots on the leathery skin were, from as far as he could remember, identical. Apart from the beaten up apparatus the second Kristos used to supplement an apparent loss of natural mobility, Josh knew he was looking at the same man.

"They knew that this life force could be projected by will," the chair bound Kristos continued, oblivious to his guest's astonishment. "As a vehicle for a person's consciousness to manifest outside the KA-park of the flesh." The play on words seemingly amused Kristos, whose beady eyes took their turn to study Josh's face, scrutinizing the stranger's countenance as though he could determine its own unique secrets. "Do you believe in ghosts Joshua?" he then asked, breaking the silent analysis to reach down the side of the wheelchair.

"Are we talking about real ghosts or Kas?" Josh asked.

"That's the point, there is none," Kristos replied brusquely as he unscrewed the lid of a bottle of bourbon whisky he'd retrieved from a pouch. Retrieving a metal beaker from the same adapted pocket, he poured a generous helping of the spirit into it.

Josh felt as though the old man was testing him, but couldn't quite determine how. *Was the fire and the doppelganger supposed to freak me out?* He even began to think the old man was distracting him while he probed his mind with some hidden telepathic power. Josh had always imagined he could sense if someone else's conscious was invading his own, though decided that this mysterious character's powers ended with the ability to auto project while remaining conscious, an astounding ability that made him a more powerful Nothos than even Angelica or Monk. Kristos drained the beaker, eyes fixed on his increasingly confused guest.

"Where are my manners?" he suddenly chided himself, pulling out a second shiny metal beaker from the pouch and filling it with the brown spirit. "After a perilous journey a man is never quick to shy away from a shot of the old fire water to settle his nerves ay Joshua?" Realising he was being offered a second beverage, Josh opened his mouth to refuse, but found he was lost for words when he saw that his hand no longer clasped the glass of water. "Now a man in my position can't be seen to succumbing to such vices," Kristos explained, "hence why I keep this little beauty tucked away over here. But there ain't no harm in a little libation to the senses now and again."

He slipped the half empty bottle back down into its hiding hole and held out the second beaker. Josh was stumped by his host's latest trickery. He had tasted the water, it had been cold and sweet, but it hadn't been real.

"Now I won't tell if you don't," Kristos said with a wayward smile, revealing his unconventional nature that bordered on oddball. Josh was suddenly reminded again of the vagrants that wandered the back streets of LA; strange, hard drinking men who talked insanely to unseen acquaintances. Though from the examples of this particular oddball's ability to deceive his mind, or even manipulate matter itself, this was not someone who could be dismissed as a social outcast; Kristos was clearly a man of great unimaginable power. Josh looked at the tempting libation, though decided he needed to keep his wits clean.

"I'm fine, thanks." The old man's eyes twinkled mischievously at the response.

"I insist," Kristos replied adamantly. He empowered the assertion by once again proving the extent of his powers. At first Josh had thought the disabled man had got up to push the metal beaker into his hand, simply deceiving him with the necessity of the wheelchair to further toy with his mind. But as he took the beaker from the senior figure now standing over him, he saw that Kristos was also remained in the chair behind. The host was projecting himself in front of his stunned guest. Both apparition and mortal body now co-existed in separate space, one in front of the other, and as far as Josh's senses could determine, both appeared to be as bona fide as the other. Only the one that remained in the chair could possibly be the original host, a deduction that was confirmed when Kristos's Ka winked playfully, before stepping back to morph into its mortal shell like the ghost it was. Josh's initial shock was quickly replaced with awe. The now singular Kristos sat opposite was wide awake and hadn't even needed to close his eyes.

"You see, ghosts exist," he announced proudly. His guest was prone to agree. The projection had existed independently of the known laws of nature, as solid and authentic as its host, but subsequently been returned to nothingness like a discarded tool. "Even though I am an invalid in the flesh, my true self is still whole. It is this truth that is the key to all existence Joshua." Kristos had wanted to shock his guest into acceptance and he had succeeded completely. "We are not our carbon based, bio-mechanical vehicles of flesh," Kristos continued, "For our true selves exist at a much higher multi-dimensional level, and as you just saw, a level of reality unhindered by material parameters. Flesh and Ka are two different frequencies of energy, co-existing so that both bodies can assume the same space at the same time. Well, whatever time is; something else created to keep us locked into the material world and away from our true place in the universe." The silver-haired sage concluded the monologue by draining the beaker. "Though sometimes this world does offer tantalising snippets of heaven in its own way," he joked with the beaker raised in salutation to the bourbon.

"And what is our true place in the universe?" Josh found himself asking with a hint of dissension. "To help the Vanir control humanity?" Faced with the preternatural figure holding the keys to existence, Josh relished the opportunity to test his self assured host. The question brought a smirk to the old man's leathery face.

"Is that what They told you?" He gave Josh a condescending look. "That we are betraying mankind to another race that seeks only to stifle humanity by keeping it in a spiritual cage?" Stroking the smooth tan skin of his freshly shaved chin he let the judgement's irony settle onto Josh's conscience. "Tell me son, what do you think is going on here?" Kristos was aware of Josh's exposure to the political agenda forced upon their enemy's brain washed subjects, though hoped the embers of truth would enlighten his stubborn ego. But his guest was reluctant to face up to the dilemma. By accepting what lay in his heart like a smouldering hot coal, Josh knew he would be committed to a destiny he didn't want. What he wanted was to kick off his shoes and slip back into his own bed, feel the weight of Samson's purring bulk across his chest and dream about Sarah.

"I wish I knew," Josh replied sincerely. Suddenly it felt as though the weight of the world was residing on his weary shoulders.

"Then you must decide," Kristos instructed forebodingly. Suddenly hoping Matty had gotten his message, Josh sensed reality was about to clash with fate, and his sanity about to become its broken victim.

*****

The true power behind auto projection lay with the acceptance that time and space were irrelevant. When a Nothos achieved the absolute centring of his conscious mind, a quantum state produced from the neutralisation of physical and spiritual perception within the brain, he or she was then able to ascend like an un-caged dove from the constraints of the material world and traverse the higher plains of existence at will. Psychologists had referred to it as the Hypnagogic state, a transformation akin to the hazy border which the psyche crossed as a person fell to sleep. But what orthodox medicine mundanely considered the side affect of bio-chemical change within the brain, the members of Project Olympia knew to be a gateway to an alternative reality. In that proto dreamscape, before the world of biological slumber stole true consciousness away, the trained mind of an Ascended One was able to gain control and manipulate existence. For the Principal of the Elite this meant he could appear to his subordinates on the east coast of America without the aid of live feeds, Satellite relays or any other communicative technology. For now the inter-dimensional covenant agenda was close to fruition, he wanted to be sure all would run to plan.

It had been some time since Galda Vey had visited the subterranean base in Maryland. Like its west coast counterpart it too was a decommissioned government nuclear bunker, a throw back from the Cold War that had been repossessed as an Elite sanctuary on the eastern seaboard. Its operations centre lay several stories below ground, carved from the ancient bedrock that had been meant to shield human lives from nuclear megaton payloads. The freedom of projection however meant Galda's form was able to bypass its security installations, and take the liberty of walking through its clandestine halls into the heart of the Elite's global aspirations.

A black clad agent was sat at a network terminal running diagnostics, though as the Principal's form passed through the alternating molecular portal into the operations room, he jumped up and stood to attention. The agent was an Ascended One, trained up from the Low Grades and, due to his computer engineering background, assigned the task of monitoring the giant communications server hub that sat like a giant black monolith at the centre of the secret underground chamber. He bowed his head submissively and waited for Galda to approach.

"All is ready," the agent announced as he raised his head to gaze into the Principal's broad, ghoulish face. Though dressed identically in the black attire cherished by the Elite, the lesser agent had opted to not wear the protective eyewear in the dim environment illuminated only by under-floor lighting and a myriad of computer display units. But as he looked at his pallid reflection in Galda's sunglasses he wished he had, if for nothing else than to hide the anxiety in his own grey eyes. Galda said nothing in response. After a brief study of the agent's nervous countenance, he walked confidently to the monolithic hub that towered over both men and up to where it met the vaulted ceiling, supported by steel frames and a spider web of arches. He gazed at the schematics on one of its many VDU displays and looked impressed by the sophisticated technology that would bring the great work of ages to its long awaited completion. Enthused by the Principal's pleased look, the agent waved the other awe struck agents in attendance back to their workstations, while he walked over to play off their merits. The Principal's presence was more than an honour; for the lesser agents it was a glimpse at true power, perhaps even of their own shadowy future.

"The global relays are complete my Lord," he stated respectfully, hoping flattery would endear him towards his powerful superior. "Giving us complete remote access to every network on the planet. From this very terminal we can gain a backdoor into any other mainframe regardless of local security policy, and accordingly override its primary controls and applications." The prolific claim made no dent on Galda's blank facade. He turned away to stride around the chamber at leisure, taking no notice of the other black dressed agents who busied themselves at an agitated pace on the outer walls of the circular room that housed the instrument of Elite destiny.

Making no sound as his projection's feet strode across the metal grills that made up the chamber's floor and covered the lighting beneath, the Principal finally stood at the entrance to the separate antechamber to the rear of the monolithic computer hub. As another agent scurried respectfully away from his work there, Galda admired the single reclining chair enthroned within it.

"And this?" Galda asked. He turned to the eager agent.

"All is ready," he replied with less certainty. The strange technology was something alien to the inferior agent. A separate team of Elite Nothos agents had installed the apparatus then left without answering his queries. Watching the Principal's entranced study of the unknown device from afar, the agent suddenly became aware of a niggling sensation of insignificance. Galda then drew himself away from the unknown marvel and walked back to the agent.

"When your work here today is complete, leave," he instructed forcefully, and then strode back towards the chamber's only entrance. Before passing through the random molecular portal he was halted by the subordinate's curiosity.

"My lord!" the agent called after him. "Who will man the operation?" He had hoped to exploit his current position to ascend the final grades within the Elite. "I have received no orders regarding functional procedure."

"All is taken care of," Galda replied ominously. As the Principal exited, the agent watched the portal swallow his shadow body, and any aspirations along with it.

*****

Josh had been driven hundreds of miles for the private audience with destiny, but instead of the fulfilment that came from answers; his heart was full of the emptiness of indecision. Paranoia was twisting the knife of doubt in his brain. As the charismatic leader now urged him to confront that doubt, it twisted the blade closer to his fear; was he using his bag of mind tricks to befuddle and derail his already confused sense of reason?

"Look into your heart son," Kristos insisted with southern cordiality. "The answers are plain to see once you choose to discover them." The magnitude of the decision, Josh thought, could very well condemn the very soul he was hoping to redeem.

"How do I know the very people who say they are trying to help me aren't really the bad guys here?" he petitioned. "The Elite were just as insistent to free mankind from the yoke of some inter-dimensional slave mongers as you are. All I want is my life back." Irritably Kristos shuffled in his wheelchair.

"Your higher self is screaming at you right now, and all you want to do is sit on your ass and twiddle your thumbs while the world leaves you behind?" he retaliated with conviction. "This is exactly what the Deros want humanity to do. By blinding us with confusion and contradiction, they want us to forget who we really are!"

"And who the hell are the Deros?"

"The true orchestrators of this mess my friend," Kristos stated as he sat forward in the chair. "And the legion of black Nothoi, the so called Elite, are simply their bastard sons, expendable pawns in an inter-dimensional cosmic war! And humanity, well we're the no-man's-land they are fighting over." The old man was deadly serious and Josh looked into the small sparkling eyes and realised Kristos and the rest of the servants of the light were foot soldiers in a much larger conflict.

"So what, these *Deros* and the Vanir are at war?" Josh exclaimed. He found himself humouring the insane notion that two alien races, of which neither was perceptible to the real world, were fighting a clandestine war over the rights to an unsuspecting mankind. He didn't care who or what the Deros were, all he needed to know was that the enigmatic old man sitting in front of him believed every word he was saying, and that no other possibility made any sense.

"It's time to choose a side," Kristos stated solemnly. His hand twitched towards the pouch, but he terminated the desire by clearing his throat. "There is no middle ground here, only Good and evil, light and dark."

"Angel and Demon!" Josh added.

"If Christianity is your perspective, then yes," he confirmed. "And as our ecclesiastical brothers would also describe it, the ensuing battle of ages will climax in an earthly Apocalypse." Kristos paused as he saw the look of trepidation the prediction caused. He deferred from pushing religious archetypes. "The Deros campaign for the enslavement of human minds and souls is near to its completion, hell it could happen tomorrow, today or it might already have started. The only thing standing in the way of their earthly collaborators is us. Without the Elite, they have no foothold in this world."

"What about the Vanir?" Josh asked expectantly. "If the Elite are the puppets of these Deros, then surely their enemy is our enemy right?"

"They *are* creatures of the light," Kristos confirmed solemnly, "but even so, why should they help the likes of an insignificant race as ours?" he asked rhetorically. Josh looked shocked. "Do we deserve their help? A race whose notion of evolution results in the butchering its own and exploiting and destroying everything creation has given it! Since the fall of man humanity has shown no concrete desire to return to its higher state. You have only to look around, watch CNN, we're happy to revel in apathy while somebody else picks up the pieces. For a race to be embraced by the light it must first openly seek it!" Concerned his zeal would divert from the core message, Kristos slumped back into the wheelchair. "Why should the Vanir help those who won't help themselves?" he then asked calmly.

At first the cynical view of the state of mankind didn't fit into Josh's conservative views, but then he remembered his reluctance to watch the likes of CNN in recent years was due to its depressive content.

"We can expose what's going on, reveal to the world what you know," Josh suggested optimistically. "With your, power, we can get the attention of the press, government, whoever, and get this thing out into the open where it should be. It seems to me the only reason this war is able continue is because no one out there, in the real world, knows what the hell is going on!"

"Son, I think you over estimate your fellow man." Josh sensed the hope-crushing pessimism in the voice of experience once more. "After a millennia of gradual social programming by the likes of the Deros's earthly followers, a manipulation of our race that goes back centuries before the Elite existed; humanity has reached an all time low in its spiritual evolution. It would simply be like explaining quantum physics to a baby."

"Babies grow into children and all children learn things in time," Josh countermined him. But the grey haired chief remained adamant.

"But time has run out! As I said the Deros have been manipulating us through religion and ignorance for millennia. The black agents outnumber us at least five to one in the states alone, and the Vanir, though they sustain us as much as they are willing to, they will not intervene." He raised a hand to itch at the baby smooth chin, then propped his head up by resting an elbow on an armrest. "We are at the mercy of fate," he concluded.

Drawn by his addiction, Kristos lowered the same arm to reach back into the pouch. For the first time Josh sensed a sense of fatigue in the enigmatic old man. Imagining the many years the senior Nothos had to have been an insurgent in the inter-dimensional war; Josh could see as his mortal life approached its twilight years, he didn't relish fighting it in the crippled body for much longer. For the Latronis leader the end-time included his own existence as well as a war that had to be won. As Kristos returned his attention to the bottle's lid Josh tore his attention away from his host's intense glare to study a framed wall mounted photo behind him. Under a thin layer of dust it showed a proud young man with a mane of black hair standing in the desert next to a tall sign. On its opposite side stood an older broad-chested man in a dirty t-shit and Stetson hat, both had beaming smiles on their sun kissed faces. The bold black letters on the white wood between them proudly announced;

C.Fisher & Son
Mining Corp.
White Rock. Nevada.

Nevada! It was then Josh realised he'd crossed the state line out of California. He recognised the broad face of the young man as that of Kristos in his formative years. It was a pictorial record of Kristos and father in what must have been a profound moment in the early seventies. In the background the past glory of the shanty-town could be seen, except its now dilapidated condition was now also reflected in the old crippled man sitting before him. The insight into the past explained their presence in the underground layer. It also drew to light the origins of the disability for the young Kristos in the photo stood unaided. Josh sensed a melancholy nostalgia in the photo's presence. Musing that some mining accident lay behind the disability, he watched Kristos down his latest libation.

"A man must never forget his past," Kristos stated sullenly. "The past is the foundation upon which we build the temple to house our future." He slid the bottle of bourbon back in its pouch as his guest locked gazes once more. "A future we create with the blocks of wisdom and cement with faith."

"Faith?" Josh thought of how his depression had drained the vitality from his own life, leaving a welcome void of disparity that he'd hoped would consume and free him from the emptiness of loss.

"Faith in ourselves and what we are."

"You people keep saying that the key to existence and reality is truth! Then that is what the world needs, truth. That's the key to its future *and* freedom." The realisation that he could have coped with his own bad luck with more dignity suddenly hit home. Drawing strength from the fact Sarah hadn't suffered, Josh realised he had been living a wasted life. The old man smiled a wily grin.

"Spoken like a true Tekton," Kristos announced. "Angelica was right."

"Right about what?" Josh queried cautiously. "I've been called a few things in my life; most in recent years haven't been good. But a Tekton? That's a new one."

"It's an ancient word that roughly translates as someone who creates, like a builder or architect, or from our perspective, a divine architect. You see son all matter is energy. And he who can control energy controls matter and therefore the world around them, both material and divine." Josh was amused that if he couldn't be an architect in reality, he could still be one in his dreams. He considered the explanation for a moment. *What did Angelica tell him?*

"You mean the Leviscape?" he asked.

"Forgive me, yes. I'm trying to avoid the religious mumbo jumbo, but to my old Pentecostal heart this *is* religion, unorthodox as it is," he admitted. A waft of bourbon reminded Josh he still held the untouched beaker. "All Nothoi draw their energy from a universal source that lies within, a sacred heart, just as all things animate and inanimate do to varying degrees. This source of energy, the inner sun, we call the Godhead. But unlike its name suggests, it is a genderless personification of perfection. A Tekton also draws their power from this Godhead, but with a more direct connection, kind of like having cable instead of terrestrial TV! And our friends the Vanir are the quintessence of this, of us." As he listened to the old man's words he became aware of an indescribable change in his appearance, as though being drawn into a dream. "You see the key is the truth, the truth is wisdom and wisdom is enlightenment and power." At first it looked as though Kristos had risen from his seat, but Josh quickly realised the grey haired figure rising up from the crippled body to stand over his guest was in fact the man's Ka.

"The fate of the world rests on those with the power," the double announced as it raised its hand to place a warm thumb on Josh's creased forehead. "And how they use it." A surge of warm energy suddenly radiated into Josh's skull, filling his mind with a utopian serenity. For a few seconds it continued then was gone. As he opened his eyes he saw Kristos smiling back at him from the wheelchair, his double returned to ground. Josh touched the skin above his eyes, reeling from a sense of elation that some great burden had been lifted from his soul.

"This gift of power should also be used in accordance with your own free will," Kristos stated solemnly. "The choice is now yours to decide how you use it." Josh replied by raising the beaker and downing the whisky in one.

To his surprise the blonde haired tour guide was still waiting for him in the corridor. As Josh pulled the door closed behind him she continued to lean against the shimmering wall like a wayward teenager. His look of shock was mirrored in Angelica's own curious expression, revealing his own face now showed some radical change.

"So are you ready?" she asked critically, implying his answer was of the greatest importance.

"He…" Josh started, but found his awe struck mind prevented an immediate answer. Angelica recognised the bemused look. Her assumption was confirmed when Josh rubbed his forehead, still lost in the depths of his thoughts. Angelica pushed herself away from wall with a nimble writhe of her torso. Hands still crossed behind her back, she stood and looked into Josh's elated face for confirmation.

"He removed the Tsadeh," she explained. "The black mark the Elite use to brand their acolytes, their branding of their will over your own." To the blonde Nothos it meant only one thing. She raised a suggestive look meant to prompt an answer.

"I'm ready for anything." The declaration stumbled out of Josh's mouth, but he meant every word. The enthused reply made the pretty blonde reveal her enthralling smile.

"This way." She offered him the lead back down the corridor of echoing footsteps. As her charge accepted the implications of his decision, she secretly replaced the weapon from her hand back into her pocket. The whiff of bourbon she caught on his breath relayed Kristos had succumbed to weakness, but also confirmed her beliefs about Josh Brenin, for the wily leader never wasted a drop. Kristos had valued his soul. As a jeweller might distinguish the quality of an uncut precious stone, he had deliberated what integrity lay beneath the uneven surface of Josh's personality and seen the gem within. The thrower had been a precautionary measure. She had been sure he would follow the path of light, but protocol meant she had had to prepare for the worst. As she led them towards an unknown future, it was with relief she had not had to terminate his life.

*****

The fat cat's love was easy to buy. The feast of tuna steak, fresh cream and cat biscuits pilled in and around his steel bowls meant Samson wouldn't die of starvation after all, even if his master had seemingly abandoned him. As a slender hand wearing faux gold rings and garish bracelets ran itself through his thick fur, it induced the trademark loud purring and revealed how overjoyed he was to be filling his belly once more. Sharon was unable to keep pets in own her apartment, as result she loved to spoil her boyfriend's. She had hoped to make such offerings on a daily basis, if only Josh had asked her to move in as she had suggested. But as she watched the huge feline greedily devour the last of the tuna she knew that particular dream was dead.

Matty had relinquished Josh's request to feed the cat to his latest concubine, hoping a post coital bliss was enough to warrant the passing on of obligation. He had formulated a quick excuse for not being able to help out due to work. At first she had shrugged it off as none of her concern, but knowing Matty's self-centred persona, she couldn't bring herself to let an innocent starve.

With a half eaten bag of chips she'd swiped from the breakfast bar in hand, Sharon decided to take a look around. Instantly the untidy lounge brought back vivid memories of the heated argument. A journal underfoot then drew her attention to a sun drenched glass building located in more exotic climes and she imagined Josh enjoying his sordid few days away at such a place with some mystery bimbo. For a second her female scorn suggested poisoning his beloved cat, but bunny boiler tactics were out of her league and so resigned to spearing her high heel into the glossy journal. She didn't expect Matty to remain interested in her for long, but at least his apartment made her feel like a princess, and not a deadbeat's floozy.

"Time to say goodbye to Mommy," she declared. Spitefully she tipped the chip bag, pouring the salty fragments onto the couch before dropping the crumpled bag after them. Her nostalgia exhausted it was time to say goodbye to her furry charge.

A sudden hellish screech made her flinch like a startled deer. Something had scared the hell out of the cat. Likewise her flinching reflexes span her round to face the intruder in the doorway. Without a chance to react, a powerful blow to the chest shoved Sharon backwards. She landed safely on the couch. For a second she lay there amongst the shards of potato chips while she caught her breath. *The son of a bitch hit me.* There'd been no time to see the face behind the sunglasses, but the slim build in the black suite could have been Josh. As the blow's constricting effect on her breathing alleviated she raised her head, only to see her pale attacker's face peer eerily over the back of the couch. As he surveyed his handiwork with blank astuteness, she immediately returned it to the cushion.

"Don't get up on our account," the ghoulish intruder suggested. The use of the plural was quickly explained as three other similarly black attired strangers surrounded the couch by her head, feet and side.

"Who…" Sharon managed to ask. An uncontrollable fear quickly replaced agony, her mouth twitching involuntarily as she stared up at the eerie intruders surrounding her like some darted animal specimen.

"The real question is *why*, Sharon," the first intruder replied. He lowered his face slowly towards hers, his scowling countenance near pinning her to the couch. Normally a fiery nature would have made her reach out to scratch, punch or slap at such insolence, but the unexpected blow, combined with the inhuman aura of her inquisitor and his associates, left her helpless.

"Why?" she found herself asking the macabre stranger, her scared face reflecting in the dark lenses hovering above her.

"We're looking for Daddy," he replied. "And something tells me *Mommy* might just know."

"He's not here!" she managed to reply. The ghoulish face descended upon hers to with inches. "Get out before I call the cops!" The threat was in vain and she knew it. The next thing Sharon knew her head had been clamped between the intruder's hands. Initially she believed the cold vice sought to inflict pain, instead it drained her of consciousness. As though his face had continued to descend onto hers, it now appeared in her mind's eye as she sensed it forcing its way into her psyche. Sharon tried to fight the intruder off, but no mental defence could stop the blackened Nothos as he seeped into the quantum inner sanctum. As their minds were conjoined in an unholy union she saw what he saw, felt what he felt, his invasive psyche seizing upon her own existence with a zealous negligence.

Writhing like some parasitic worm into her very being he was now journeying at leisure through the chambers of her own mind. *Where's Joshua?* She heard Galda's snarling thoughts in her own. He was in her head and she could do nothing but submit.

Through the normal course of Low Grade recruitment, an ethereal bond between tutor and apprentice was created. Via this psychic lifeline across time and space the tutor could reel in this mystical tether back to its source, tracking its student to anywhere on the astral or material world. But for Galda Vey that bond had been severed, an unfortunate occurrence that happened when Low Grades were consumed by the protective light of the enemy. But this was no mere Low Grade he sought. His former student now resided amongst the unwitting enemy like a tracking beacon. His loss to the light had been unfortunate, but his hidden strength would recompense them as it led the Elite to victory. As a member of the Elite Galda and his colleagues were shunned by the light, but for one close to the Nothos in question, such as the garishly dressed young woman in his power, her emotional bond offered a backdoor, one that could be hijacked.

"Well?" Kladar asked eagerly as his superior straightened in the neglected lounge. On the couch Sharon remained unconscious and drained, though as Galda's devilish smile now announced, his psychic probe had been successful. The time for war had been set and now, so it seemed, was the place of battle.

*****

Aware of its impact on her companion's psyche, Angelica led Josh away from the fateful meeting in silence. She had heard others liken their first engagements with the enigmatic chief akin to being reborn. In essence they had been right. The old subjective life of doubt and ego had to be razed to the ground in order to make way for the new, though for her the unexpected re-evaluation of self-awareness glossed over a more mundane interpretation. Confronting destiny was traumatic for those who disagreed with fate's cruelty, but Kristos knew the power of persuading reluctant destiny-dodgers lay in the wonderment his other-world gifts created on a magic starved race, and how he represented unlimited possibilities in the face of adversity. Stopping in the middle of the corridor she caught the whiff of bourbon once more and decided her own life had not been reborn but saved.

"You got any more room in there for another miracle?" she suddenly asked. Taken aback, Josh halted and looked confused.

"Guess it depends how you define miracle," he replied a little cautiously. He had decided her striking beauty hid a mischievous nature, but which was inevitably alluring all the same. "Sure, why the hell not," he added. Enjoying his perplexed expression, Angelica backed up to another undisclosed door and pushed it open.

"After you," she offered with an exaggerated wave of the hand. With the notion the new room couldn't offer anything more bizarre than a crippled man walking with the aid of a doppelganger, Josh accepted the proposition and walked into a small unlit partition room. Immediately ahead was a frosted glass door, the vivid light seeping in from behind making the bold, black words embossed upon its clouded surface all the more forbidding. *Keep This Door Shut.* Angelica's close proximity behind suggested he boldly walked on.

As he pushed the frosted glass forward he felt as though he were piercing some protective seal that offered safety from the outside to whatever lay within, or worse, protection of the outside from something contagious. But as a warm, humid mist settled on his face, Josh found his unbelieving gaze fall upon a natural wonder. There before him, under the bedrock that separated the subterranean compound from the arid desert high above, was a haven of plant life.

He blinked then looked again at the leafy environment that seemingly flourished around him, only to gaze back to his smirking guide for authorisation to proceed. Angelica nodded him onwards. A large subtle leave brushed against his face as he took the first amazed steps forward into the unexpected world. Looking up into the misted air that rose to the roof, he saw the interior was a storey taller than any other he'd seen.

"Welcome to Eden," Angelica announced. She brushed past to guide him towards the centre of the leafy oasis. "Not very original I know, but when you consider nothing grows up there," she pointed upwards, "except lizards and the odd cactus, then I think you can cut us some slack."

"It's amazing," Josh said sincerely. He followed her through the overgrown pathway that picked its way through the magnificent, thriving flora. Once as a kid he'd visited a man made rain forest in Florida. However an immense dome of thick glass had graciously covered that one, which made finding anything similar under the desert more of a surprise. He followed her towards some more domestic looking species of plant life. "You did this all yourselves?"

"As much as I'd like to take the credit for it, this was all here long before I joined up." Reaching the open plan heart of the leafy sanctuary, Josh recognised a fruit bearing plant that Angelica began to fumble with.

"Fancy a fresh one?" she asked, offering the large rosy tomato she had just plucked.

More curiosity than politeness he took up the offer, though before sinking his teeth into the juicy morsel he wanted to be sure of one thing.

"It's okay," Angelica stated as she noticed his concern. "There's no Frankenstein food here. The UV lights and the self-regulated climate control keep this place alive and the plant stocks are taken from the most potent strains in the world. In addition each bed is individually regulated with the stats fed into a centralised computer from soil and air sensors, just to be sure." Josh spied the tiny network of wires and sensors leading out from each bed by his feet, though as Angelica reached backwards to pluck something else from another abundant source, her white top rode up to expose her navel and distract him.

"So you got any monkeys hidden away in here? This place is a veritable jungle." He darted his attention back to the larger shrubs towering around them.

"Only Jonah and Dex," she joked and took a bite of the apple in her hand. "But they think this place is too girly for big boys so it's usually Saffy, Monk and I keeping this place running." Josh ignored the chance to tease about Monk's feminine side.

"So when did Angelica *join up*?" he asked, "You been growing tomatoes and fighting assholes in bad suits for long?" He walked around a raised bed of nurtured bean pods. Finishing the tomato he hoped to hide his growing interest from the attractive subject.

"Would you believe it if I told you heroine brought me here?" Josh swallowed the last of the juicy fruit and realised his trail of questioning had already taken a wrong turn. "I was a user for five years before Kristos found me. After losing our parents my brother and I split the meagre inheritance they left us and went our separate ways. I ended up wasting what I had in a downward spiral of drink and heroine; while my brother got shot by a dealer he owed money."

She took a despondent bite into the apple, leaving Josh to deliberate on the unexpected tragedy that had shaped the seemingly healthy and balanced young woman before him. He tried to imagine her withered and eaten away by the addiction she spoke of, but apart from her slim physique, the person she spoke of seemed a world away.

"I'm sorry," he said, not knowing how else to console the otherwise formidable woman.

"Don't be, it's life," she replied bluntly. "Some of us are born without direction and purpose. I was a twenty-four hour party girl before it happened. Drink, drugs, uppers, downers you name it, just trying to fill the hole inside of me. But it took three deaths and a heroine overdose before I was able to see the light, literally." Angelica locked gazes for the first time since they'd begun speaking about the past. "I owe that old cripple my life", she stated endearingly. "First I thought my O.D. had permanently fried my brain. Of all the men I could have wanted to dream about relentlessly, a flaky old biker guy in a wheelchair wasn't high on a girl's list." She knelt down and buried the half eaten apple into the moist bed of soil at the foot of a tall exotic shrub.

"So could you do all that, stuff before he found you?" Josh asked, deferring from the negative. "If not maybe there's hope for me." She got up and leant against the framework supporting a raised plant bed, brushing the soil from her slender hands.

"Do you know what your problem is?" she asked back.

"If I did maybe I wouldn't be in this mess."

"This *mess* isn't your problem, only your lack of faith, in yourself and your, forgive the melodrama, destiny." She was standing close to him now and her scent was filling his senses with amorous potential. Alone in the underground Eden, they could have been a world away from the subterranean compound and the ensuing battle. "If a heroine addict from Frisco can do it, so can you. All you've got to do is let go of that bag of bricks you are carrying around with you." *What is it you know that I don't?*

"Bag of bricks?" Josh asked. "I'm an architect not a builder." A deep whoosh was followed by a low hum from somewhere up in the misty expanse; the climate control was adjusting the environment, temporarily upsetting the tranquil setting.

"For some of us the gift reveals itself early and develops slowly with the passing of time, but for others it takes tragedy or some other trauma for our brain to unlock its potential" She was talking about Sarah, he didn't know the ins and outs of how she knew but he guessed the accident was no secret to those who it mattered to. Remembering his dead wife made him feel uncomfortable. He wondered if after years of being deprived of a truly wholesome relationship his body was trying to transfer its needs onto the sincere, intoxicating woman before him. As though picking up on the underlying conflict, Angelica stood back. "As some smart ass once said hundreds of years ago, the path to happiness lies within. You just gotta clear away the deadwood you know?"

"Like a gardener," he stated.

"Like a gardener," she confirmed, appreciating the irony. Her smile diffused the previous awkwardness. Again Josh felt the warm marshmallow feeling in his stomach. *Any other time...*It was then, as they stood in that place, he realised how precious the oasis was to this choice band of exceptional combatants. Not only did it supply them with all the fresh produce they needed, it represented the core of their responsibility. Just as the veritable Garden of Eden would be left to wither and die without their attention, so too would the human race decline and expire under the plans of the Elite and their inter-dimensional masters. It was up to Latronis to step in and clear away the deadwood.

A sudden look of surprise on Angelica's face interrupted his thoughts. Her glazed look over his shoulder made him turn in like to see what had caught her attention by the tall plants guarding the entrance to Eden, but amongst the abundant, languid foliage he saw nothing discernible.

"What's wrong?" he asked. Angelica turned to share the distant expression with him.

"It's time," she replied portentously. Though dispersed before Josh had noticed, Kristos's Ka had entered and summoned them to war.

Chapter 14

There was no time for formalities. By the time he and Angelica had returned to the brightly lit canteen the rest of the small army had already left its triangular dining table to filter into the primary corridor, leaving behind their half eaten feast. As Josh spotted Alpha lurking by its screen doors he spurned a notion the overindulgent banquet of fresh fruit, pastries and cereals may have been the equivalent of a last supper, a last meal for the condemned men and women of Latronis. All their comrades had moved on to some communal rendezvous, except for the bulky doorman who courteously still held the entrance ajar. As he allowed Angelica to pass with a half smile Josh noted it betrayed an uncommon sense of anxiety as he too approached the intimidating soldier. Believing he had removed his hand to shut the door in his face, Josh found Alpha now offered it in friendship.

"I never did thank you for saving my life." The soldier held out the big hand. The *Campaign for Nuclear Disarmament* T-shirt he now sported was obviously borrowed attire, making him look slightly ridiculous to the newest recruit who accepted the cordial gesture with a sense of relief.

"Anytime. Maybe you can do the same for me some day," Josh replied amicably. He noticed the hand shaped bruising beginning to form on Alpha's thick neck.

"Let's just hope the opportunity never arises."

"Let's," Josh agreed. They loosed hands. Alpha returned to his courteous role of doorman by holding back the screen once more. "After you Josh."

"Thanks jar-head."

In the compound's primary corridor Angelica had waited for the new recruits at the entrance to a secondary passage. Seeing the two compliant men walking towards her, she motioned Alpha into it and winked at Josh who followed suite. Like its counterparts the walls of the disorientating second passage were lined with sheet metal bolted onto a core framework; a burnished alloy that created a blurry reflective prism that ushered the stragglers to the blast door terminating its opposite end.

Angelica paused in front of the ominous blast door, Alpha and Josh reciprocating either side of her. The temporary halt was explained when three beams of white light projected from a black eyepiece at the door's centre, releasing an inquisitive energy onto the solar plexus' of the three Nothoi, which content they offered no threat, then retracted back into the black orb with equal blunt efficiency. Stunned but enthused, Josh watched the blast door slide nimbly to the right to reveal a chamber of light. At first its chrome furnishings appeared to be suspended in an infinite catacomb, but as they followed Angelica inside, the new recruits recognised the disorientating illusion of mirrors reflecting mirrors into infinity. The rest of the servants of the light had congregated at the chamber's centre, waiting like lost souls outside the pearly gates of some technological heaven. Instantly Josh was reminded of Calisto's bedroom, but as the three giant white spheres at the corners of the interior proved, on a much grander scale.

"What is this place?" Josh asked mesmerised, trying to unravel the conundrum the chamber posed. Its perplexing parameters confused Josh's logical architectural mind. At first glance it looked to be spherical in shape, but where the triad of white sentinels stood its interior's perimeter appeared to converse into three corners.

"This is where the magic happens," Jonah announced as he took his place between Cozmo and Angelica. At the sight of the final three, the rest of the dreamscape militia had adopted a circular formation, leaving vacancies for the stragglers. Josh checked his surroundings again, but against his better judgement he found the conundrum persisted. *This room shouldn't exist.* Beneath his feet the mirrored floor was flat and firm. From deeper scrutiny he saw it also appeared to curve down into the bottom half of a sphere. As he joined the group, he decided to ignore the optical illusion and focus on the real people suspended inside it.

"You're right it *is* a triangle," a familiar voice suddenly offered dramatically. Josh looked between the bodies to the enigmatic old man sat in his wheelchair amongst them. He studied Josh's bemusement with small sparkly eyes that radiated in the cool, clinical environment of the mysterious chamber. "Strongest primal shape in creation and strength is what keeps us together."

"But it's a sphere," he contradicted. His own voice resonated inside his head, the odd acoustics proving the room's unnatural properties.

"A triangular manifestation within a circle," Kristos corrected matter-of-factly. "The circle being the most sacred shape in the universe represents the singular and the divine, and the protection of the divine is its purpose. Take a seat." Alpha had joined the circle by taking a vacant place between Monk and Maestro while Josh, ignoring his miasma of confusion, crossed to the final vacancy that lay between Angelica and Dex to complete the circle around Kristos.

"Seat?" he secretly asked his blonde neighbour. She smiled shrewdly, and then gestured for him to look behind at the chrome block rising mysteriously from the floor.

"Follow my lead and relax," Angelica coached him. Josh put the radiance of her features down to the luminous surroundings and took a seat on the mirrored stool, the rest of Latronis joining in to complete the circle so that all sat at eye level to their enigmatic leader. His gaze drawn to the floor, Josh became aware of the geometric shapes imbedded under their feet that, like them, were seemingly suspended above the illusionary lower half of the sphere across its axis. From each of the twelve occupied positions an elongated triangle linked them to the centre as if to draw their energies towards Kristos, who occupied the prominent central position in his wheelchair. For some unexpected reason Josh was reminded of the round table of King Arthur. As a child he'd always wanted to be a knight of the chivalrous order, and now, so it appeared, he was.

"Brothers and sisters, this is it," Kristos officially began the proceedings. "Twelve servants of the light against a blackened foe of hundreds of times that number. A foe that exists like a cancer on the soul of humanity, the very soul in fact they aim to enslave and destroy." He began to slowly turn his wheelchair around so that his address was focused on all, captive and loyal to the last. "Though as dark as the even the blackest night can be, It can never extinguish the light of one single flame," he declared dramatically, "And now we are joined by two new such inextinguishable flames." Alpha took the compliment by smiling agreeably with the rotund Maestro at his side.

Kristos was painfully aware of the group's loss. The passing of Calisto, as well as the others who had been lost in the line of duty over the decades, was a burden on the group's singular morale, but he wanted to reassure them the duty they performed for their fellow man was worthy of the ultimate sacrifice.

"You are Nothoi, chosen by the Godhead for this very task. But it is a task we must face and win alone. Because without us, the Deros's plan to enslave the minds and spirits of every living person on this planet will find fruition" The implications struck a chord with everyone in the chamber. Kristos's intense gaze made it to Josh. "It is the war mankind has been fighting inadvertently in his heart for thousands of years. A war that can only end in freedom, or enslavement."

Josh felt his eyelids becoming heavy. An escalating feeling he was slowly coming under some subtle enchantment now began to take hold of his senses. His eyes closed briefly once more as an involuntary snippet of some past event flashed before them; a large crowd gathered outside the front of a temple. He opened his eyes and the vision was gone. Considering the tension in the air, Josh felt unusually relaxed. Though a possible sign of budding confidence, he concluded the mirrored chamber was in fact emanating its own unseen influence much like the blue room used by their enemies. *It's a projection room.* Safe in the knowledge his new colleagues were not manipulating his brain to further the enslavement of mankind; he gave into the lulling urge.

"By following on in our charge we honour the immortal memory of those who have fallen," Kristos continued to his tranquil audience. "Without Calisto and the others, we may never have unravelled the extent of the black agent's control over this world. In fact little has changed over the millennia. In the ancient past a superstitious world was easily fooled into committing atrocities against his brothers and sisters, religion and politics the primary instruments of the hidden agenda for control of mind and body, channelled and applied by the Elites who have always served Them."

The old man's words floated into Josh's head, narrating the visions that were appearing in his mind's eye as if he'd lived them first hand. As the though the gates to the past had been unpicked, he saw the ancient cities and forgotten landscapes buried in the mists of humanity's common soul. A woman was holding his hand, calming him as they watched a holy man preach his zealous sermon, urging the sword wielding men about him into a religious furore of blood thirsty, *divine* inspired vengeance. He was a child and the place was ancient Greece. *I can see the past.*

"But we live in a godless, scientific world now," Kristos's proud southern voice stated. "And as mankind reaches its technological peak, the Deros seek to use that very technology against us." Josh's conscious jumped through time to the present, offered free rein of the modern world with an unrestricted omnipotence that encompassed towers of steel and space age advances in civilisation. "In exchange for other-world technology, the so called Elite are helping the Deros to cage the world in a lower state of existence, by using our own satellites, radio transmitters and communication networks to release low frequency microwaves that play hell with our emotional and physical equilibrium."

In his mind's eye Josh saw for himself how the world's population was existing in the malicious barrage, and how the body's natural electro-magnetic fields were slowly being distorted by the hi-tech spectre that interfered with their minds via their metaphysical stability. Just as the *happy vibes* that had been directed at Josh via Halberstram's hypodermic implant, the people of the world were being smothered by a global net of abused technologies that malfunctioned the inherent rhythms of fragile cerebral-spinal bio-systems. From the disembodied viewpoint he suddenly understood the futility of humanity's modern existence. An executive boardroom meeting, car factory workers, shoppers in a mall, gang members hanging out…Watching their lives, hearing their thoughts and feeling their desires, the sea of discontent was revealed to be more than just cultural; the Elite were fuelling it to further the Deros's plan. *Spiritual enslavement?*

"When I first made contact with the Vanir all those years ago," their crippled leader continued, "they ignited the light of truth in my heart, as result I knew I had to take up the fight. A father's legacy became its stronghold; a small mining colony that became an underground base to begin the retaliation. As I grew stronger I sought out other light-walkers, Nothoi such as you my friends, and together we began the fight against the encroachment on humanity's true destiny." It was then Josh's heightened voyeurism saw the iniquitous fog that clung to this universal humanity, an unseen malicious stain that overshadowed the visions of mundane existence and threatened to swallow it all.

"It was then those black hearted sons of bitches began to pressgang unsuspecting civilians into their ranks. Hijacking them in their dreams and exploiting their minds and spirits to do their dirty work in the Leviscape to undermine the Vanir." The events of the past played back once more for Josh in flashbacks like cinematic show-reels. He saw Galda as a younger man, assuming control of the Elite and coordinating its agenda to swallow the soul of mankind. The visions appeared at a frenetic rate before his eyes, too fast for mortal eyes to analyse, but in the trance-like state, his mind assimilated the images with ease. *What's happing to me?* "As a race of the light, the Vanir welcomed the ascended human souls into Hyperborea as kinfolk. Little did they know these Trojan horses were sent to weaken their power and make way for Derosian control of their world. A control of which extends to ours."

Josh was suddenly aware of a feeling of disembodiment. Lost in the deep communal trance that had descended upon them, the circle of Nothoi had begun to project from their slumbering bodies into the alternate reality, the chamber's resonance neutralising their perceptions of physical and ethereal worlds, unlocking spirit from flesh. Their leader's voice continued to echo around them, guiding them towards the astral rendezvous between time and space.

"And so finally after an eternity of waiting, The Deros are ready to *switch on* the end of the free world by *switching off* mankind's link to his higher self. You are all free men and women, though even *we* might not survive this second fall of man."

A definite sense of outer body experience had taken hold of Josh. In the past his conscious mind had made the leap from Sleepeze induced sleep to projecting into the dreamscape as a subtle change of environment, leaving an unsuspecting mind in the dark as to his true level of awareness. But this time it was different. Akin to floating under water he could feel himself ascending from his shiny seat into a weightless existence. Instead of the clinical confines of the mirrored chamber his Ka's eyes saw a luminous celestial vortex existing outside the physical realms, a bridge between the material and immaterial. It was in this world between worlds that he saw Angelica beside him. Though his mortal eyes were shut, she was visible again, ethereal and free-floating. *This is a dream?* Gazing around he saw the projected forms of Monk, Jonah, Luna and the rest of the ascended squad in their protective circle.

"So I ask you now, are you my brothers and sisters ready to risk all for the good of the many?" Kristos asked as he joined the eleven in the heightened plain of existence. No longer bound by his crippled body, Kristos appeared amongst them as a potent and able being of light. He turned to look at each of his comrade's faces suspended in the fraternal circle around him like some ethereal general. The future was uncertain; this was reflected in their leader's brilliant blue eyes as he waited for each man and women in turn to nod their final acceptance of their enormous charge. As powerful as they were, they were vulnerable in the face of over whelming odds.

Kristos's discerning gaze ended with Josh. The old man's broad tanned features looked refined in this other world. His skin was firmer, unblemished by age, though the long grey hair was now white as driven snow. His Ka had taken a rejuvenated appearance, that of a Tekton, a divine architect of the light. Momentarily his intense sparkling gaze lingered on Josh. Sensing the novice's anxiety in the unnatural arena, he offered a reassuring grin across the void, his words reverberating telepathically in his head. *Not even the darkest of nights can extinguish the light of a single flame.*

Josh's own nod of acceptance completed the circle of conviction, though gazing around like an awe struck tourist he realised he'd enlisted in a war he had no idea how to fight. Beneath the Californian desert their earthly bodies of flesh and blood were to remain behind in the protective chamber, slumbering in silent vigil deep while their projected Kas took flight to do battle with the enemy on the Leviscape. For Josh there was no time to test the sincerity of his valour. Suspended amongst the new disembodied comrades that comprised the intangible militia, the hand of destiny no longer seemed like a bad dream. It was about to become one.

*****

Black Light

The feeling of liberation was indescribable. Josh could only liken it to swimming underwater, but without the draw of gravity or need to break its surface to breath. In this astral ocean all one needed to maintain buoyancy was a simple thought. *Think and it shall be*, Kristos voice had instructed. As part of the disembodied circle he was reminded of childhood space walking fantasies. But in the Leviscape, where the will was the instigator of this heightened existence, the flesh's necessity for oxygen and warmth were irrelevant. He raised his hands before his face. Though they lacked the familiar intricacies and imperfections that defined them as human, he recognised them as his own, embellished as they were by the ethereal purity of a Ka. Clenching them tight he found the sensation of flesh against flesh was as bona fide as it was in the *real* world.

"This is unreal," Josh exclaimed to himself. The alternate reality existed beyond the constraints of bodily needs; as a result the true plain of existence was beyond any mortal comprehension. The comment's irony was not wasted on Angelica who reached out and touched his face, the gesture setting alight the nerves of his skin, if indeed they existed at all. In the new world where the mind and the spirit were conjoined in liberation, it only exemplified the fumbling, wearisome existence of the material world as the ball and chain that it was.

"Joshua you will go with Angelica," Kristos instructed. Interrupting the time-out from which he'd gathered his wits; Josh looked over to see the leader's appearance had changed. Instead of the old jeans, white t-shirt and tattered biker waistcoat, Kristos was now clad in white ceremonial robes that combined the martial attire of the east with a classical divinity. "Dex, Jonah, Alpha and Saffy, you will join them," he added solemnly, "The rest of you are to come with me." At the decree's issue the members of Latronis joined their leader in assuming the appropriate attire, a simple thought manipulating their Ka's appearance in the blink of an eye. Like a master illusionist, Josh imitated his colleagues. In an instant he found his clothes also obeyed the telepathic order to morph into identical outlandish attire. *Eat your heart out Galda.* The circle of now white clad Nothoi then began to form ranks, their small numbers splitting into the two teams that would make a two tier assault on an unsuspecting enemy. Jonah and the other selected three crossed the circle to join Josh and Angelica, their forms manoeuvring with an effortless motion.

"The Elite," Kristos added, "have centred their operations in an underground bunker in the bowels of a disused air force base in Maryland. It is from there they will coordinate the global strategy to switch off humanity. I want you to infiltrate it and reach the network core that exists on the sixth level." As he relayed his instructions the second squad, including a now bald headed Monk and much sleeker Maestro, broke away from the circle to close in behind their white haired general who had adopted the look of a modern day Zeus. To Josh the division of ranks looked uneven. As he measured the collective might of the powerful Nothoi such as Monk and Kristos opposite, his confidence was tainted by the notion he would be entering the arena of dream warfare without them. Not forgetting Angelica was a powerful Nothos, their task however didn't sound like a stroll in the park.

"The rest of us will strike them on their own astral turf; lighten up their miserable lives with a little payback!" As Kristos delivered the final aim of the plan the void around them began to split into two separate celestial vortexes. Destiny was dividing into two clear paths, splitting their numbers across the astral plains. "By chopping off the chicken's head, we aim to keep those bastards busy while you accomplish what has to be done! Godspeed people!"

The latter blessing was lost in the void as Kristos turned and soared towards one of the tunnels. As his white form was swallowed by the spiralling wormhole he was quickly followed by the rest of his chosen companions who chased him down the passage of whirling light. With a reciprocating manoeuvre Angelica then led her own team into the second celestial portal. Entering its mouth Josh was suddenly aware of being propelled forward like a perpetual cannonball as the vortex ensnared their Kas and sucked them forward into its belly. For a second he was aware of travelling at infinite speed, hurtling forward, powerless to stop, before a black nothing beyond the confines of the Leviscape halted its momentum in a millisecond.

The cold air bit into his skin. Like a slap to the face it woke his senses from the disorientated shock of being blasted into oblivion. At first Josh thought himself lost at the edges of the universe, all he could see was black, but through the brisk night air he then recognised the definite signs of life below. Roads, traffic and buildings were soaring under feet, until they disappeared and were replaced by a moonlit landscape of fields and trees. It was then that he realised what was happening. *I'm flying!* Perhaps not in the literal sense of the word, but his realisation was confirmed as he saw Angelica's familiar blonde hair wavering before him, her white garments fluttering as she and the others soared in formation over the silver landscape of trees. Instead of projecting into the Leviscape, Josh and the rest were back in the material world. No sooner did his mind assimilate the wondrous event, the six avenging angels went to ground.

For the novice combatant the landing was unexpectedly easy. As master of his existence he willed himself to follow the others lead, to descend from the night sky and to slow down as though carried on outstretched wings. Like a rebel angel fallen from the heavens Josh was now stood with the others on terra firma and joined their survey of the quiet nocturnal surroundings. *Not a dream*, he instructed his sceptical fears. The crystal clarity of his heightened senses quickly established the very real nature of the damp air around them and the fragile grass underfoot. As he took a deep breath of the foreign atmosphere, infused with a rich earthy odour released by a recent rain, he recognised they had reached the cooler climate of the east coast. *Maryland.*

Certain they had projected to their target location, Angelica led them onwards in silence, the choice of travel now decidedly on foot. Josh had always planned to return to Maryland, but hadn't counted on doing so as a spectre of his own mind. Saffy, Jonah and Dex were on point with their appointed lieutenant Angelica, while Josh and Alpha made up the rear guard. It wasn't long until a tall security fence loomed before them like a giant spider web shimmering in the soulless light of a waxing moon. A lack of a thumping heartbeat in Josh's chest suddenly grounded his perception of the operation. His pulse should be blasting around his adrenalised body like the double bass drum pedal of a thrash metal band, but no such intense biological reaction was taking its toll that night. The reality check was going to take sometime to get used to. For all intensive purposes he was a ghost, a spectre seeking to influence the real world that existed thousands of miles away from his own sleeping body.

Just below the corroded curls of razor wire that ran along its top edge, a metal plate was bolted to the high perimeter fence. On it were the words most civilians feared. *Property of United States Government. Non authorised persons will be subject to the discharge of lethal force.* The stark warning did nothing to dissuade Angelica and the others. Stepping forward they simply passed through the steel wires like water through a net and appeared whole again on its opposite side. But as Josh walked forward to duplicate the feat, his unsuspecting face was met with a cold mesh of impenetrable steel. The rattle of the wavering fence caused his comrades to look back at a perplexed Josh.

"Focus," Angelica instructed. Her stern eyes were trained on his. It had looked so easy for the others. Josh couldn't understand why it hadn't worked for him; surely he was like the others? "You are no longer bound by the laws of this world," she added, walking back to the fence. "For you that fence does not exist, but your mind is allowing your eyes to deceive it." He understood her despondent logic, but the chill of the cold steel inches from his face suggested otherwise. "Think like a Ka!"

Josh watched Jonah, Dex and Saffy's white Kas shoot off into the unauthorised blackness, leaving Angelica and Alpha to sort out the rookie. He studied Angelica's moonlit face for guidance. There was a look of trepidation in the blonde woman's milk-white features, as though she feared her initial analysis of his potential had been grossly over estimated. Shamed by failure, Josh took a step back, imagined the fence was shorter than it was and leap over its barbed summit to land without fault beside her.

"There's more than one way to skin a cat," he announced, enjoying his supernatural accomplishment.

"There's also more than one way to be caught," she chided back. The unexpected retort was followed by a tilt of the head that gestured towards what looked like a small satellite dish perched on top of a pole. Josh squinted his heightened night vision and realised it was some form of motion detector. "This is an air force base, anything flying higher than two meters directly above this place is lit up like the fourth of July." Josh suddenly felt a fool; his swaggering bravado may have just cost them the upper hand. "I guess it's lucky that relic is as decrepit as the rest of this place," she added, letting him off the hook before turning to follow Jonah and the rest into the shadows. Even ghosts it seemed could trigger alarms.

"Let's go Flyboy," Alpha added with blatant irony. His broad macho frame looked out of place in the loose fitting, white attire of a Latronis dream warrior. For a crack team of flying commandos the choice of garments was conspicuous to say the least, but if the burly soldier was comfortable, who was he to argue. The two stragglers hurried after Angelica's distant form, the lack of sirens and searchlights a good sign their detection remained postponed.

Across the base a military guard plucked a rolled up magazine from his belt and lit up a fresh cigarette. He had been on the same guard duty for a month and felt like a glorified babysitter. The base had lain abandoned since operations were transferred to the next county ten years previous, meaning his current duty was nothing more than that of an armed watchdog. As he flipped through the glossy pages the gentle flaps they created echoed gently throughout the empty hangar. In the lofty, enclosed space the plastic moulded seat he had scavenged from the mess hall looked like a grey crumb in a cookie jar, but gave his legs periodic rest until relief arrived at oh seven hundred. Leaning his M-16 Armalite assault rifle against the large sealed doorway at the hangar's rear, he slouched into the hard seat, nudged the camouflaged peak of his military cap up from his brow and thumbed his way to the lesbian twins feature.

"You know you'll go blind don't you." The woman's voice made the guard jump out of his seat, the adult magazine falling to the floor as he grabbed his rifle and trained it at empty space. The instinctual reaction was then faced with a notion of madness, for when he searched around the well-lit surroundings for the source of the interruption; his startled eyes saw no one. Beyond the limits of the empty hangar's huge gaping entrance there was only a wall of night. Inside the hangar's garishly lit interior he was still very much alone.

"Does this really turn you on?" the female voice asked. Swinging the rifle around, he saw the pretty blonde was sitting in his chair, holding up the magazine between finger and thumb like a filthy rag. "You soldier boys really need to get out more." The shocked soldier took a protective step back. He fumbled the assault rifle into his shoulder and glared with disbelief at the unexpected intruder. There was no way he could have missed her approach.

"Don't move or I'll shoot!" he barked with military bluster, unsure if he was suffering some sleep deprived hallucination. Whoever the strange woman was she had managed to totally circumvent his peripheral vision.

"You mean like this?" Before his eyes the blonde apparition disappeared in a whirlwind that gushed around him like a mini tornado, evading any attempt to pin the blurry target in the sights of his rifle. Within a second the intruder was standing back before him, holding his weapon's banana clip magazine in her hand. "Somehow I don't think you'll be doing much shooting without this!" The soldier gazed at the M16's empty magazine slot and panicked. Still his primed military instinct acted quickly. He dropped the useless rifle and swapped it for the Smith & Wesson sidearm he wrenched from its belt holster.

"Stay where you are miss!" He pointed the backup weapon at the pretty face, "Or I will shoot!" His training was telling him to fire and ask questions later. The intruder had breached a secure military instillation and proven to be a threat. But goddamn it, he couldn't bring himself to shoot the unarmed beauty.

"Now the question is," Angelica pondered as she turned her attention to the huge sealed door that was in his charge, "do you know how to open this?" She reached out to touch the foreboding surface.

"Step back from the door, get down on your knees and place your hands on top of your head!" the guard ordered loudly. The crazy woman was running amok on the base, and he would take the fall.

"Or what? You'll shoot?" she goaded him. As though planning to move it by force, Angelica placed both palms against the formidable barrier. For the bemused onlooker the strange action confirmed the intruder was indeed mad. The guard tensed his finger on the trigger, lowering his aim for a leg shot. Military protocol demanded she was disabled immediately. But before he could squeeze off a round a sudden blow to the torso wrenched him from the spot and slammed him up against the door.

The impact dazed the soldier. After gathering his stunned reflexes, he found he was now pinned two foot above the concrete floor like a swatted fly.

"At ease, soldier," Jonah hissed, keeping his raised hand focused on the shocked guard. As the constrained captive looked down he saw the gathering of similarly white-attired intruders approach from the shadows. Next he felt the same invisible force crushing his chest now prise his fingers from around the side arm's grips. "And you won't be needing that!" The freed revolver then flew out of his hand and was caught by his captor, who then released the dishevelled guard. Landing awkwardly, the soldier watched in awe as his M-16 was also spirited away by the same unseen hands and caught by another of the strange intruders.

"Take a seat," Dex ordered as he trained the soldier's impotent rifle on its owner.

"Who are you people?" he asked, backing up against the door. Alpha walked over, petrifying the guard where he stood.

"Just a bad dream," Alpha replied coyly. His lightning-fast strike to the soldier's temple then rendered him unconscious. Catching the falling body, he effortlessly dragged the camouflaged rag doll off to one side and carefully laid it out on the concrete out of harm's way.

"Can we open it?" Dex asked. Parading the useless gun against his shoulder he joined Angelica by the door.

"Watch and learn petrol-head," she replied. With her hands remaining diligently placed upon the metallic obstruction, she bowed her head between the raised arms. After seemingly studying the barrier's surface with outstretched palms, she began to exploit her deductions to thwart it. The immense blast door was a third of the width of the hangar, three times as high as an average man and provided access to the fortified layer that lay underneath the mound of protective earth that backed onto the hangar.

"Why don't we just go through?" Josh asked. He'd noticed no obvious security panel for operating the door, but there was also no obvious reason why they shouldn't just pass through it like the ghosts they were.

"Because it's not real." Dex's abrupt comment suggested a feeling of frustration. It was then as Josh studied Angelica's reflective pose, he realised what they were up against.

"It's an alternating molecular portal," he proclaimed. He walked up to touch the cold, stubborn surface of the blast door for himself. "We need a key card or something that emits the relevant frequency to get through this."

"How the hell do you know that?" Alpha asked in amazement. To Josh the door felt as solid and dense as any foot thick sheet of metal should do, but he knew its solidity hid a paradox of being penetrable. "I've had the pleasure of going through one before," he admitted, remembering his first meeting with the Elite in the flesh.

"He's right," Jonah piped up. "The door's molecules indiscriminately vibrate at hundreds of different frequencies a second, which makes no obvious difference in the real world, but keeps us unwanted types out because we can't adapt our astral bodies quick enough to compensate."

"How rude," Alpha grunted sardonically. But the negative explanation meant nothing to Angelica. At first the door's surface only appeared to dent inwards under the pressure she applied with her hands, though after a few seconds its surface was reluctantly breached. As slender hands disappeared into the metal she continued to push her arms further and further into the failing obstruction.

"Then how hell is she doing that?" Alpha exclaimed as they watched Angelica's slow, agonising progression. As though forcing her way through solidifying tar she eventually managed to force her body into the pliable metal. The others watched in awe as it then swallowed her whole as she walked on through.

"More than just a pretty face," Jonah said with a perceptive grin.

"And what about me?" Saffy asked teasingly.

"You're just a pretty face," he replied. The underhand complement was overshadowed by the sight of the blast door warping and faltering like a degrading mirage. Before their eyes it then disappeared completely to reveal Angelica standing in the large gaping entrance holding a handful of vandalised electrics.

"Care to join me?" she asked. She tossed the wires at their feet, her face betraying signs of fatigue. "We don't have all day."

"What did I tell yeah?" Jonah whispered. Her impressed colleagues strode into the restricted area.

"Good job," Josh offered their blonde lieutenant lamely.

"You haven't seen the worst of it yet," Angelica replied unfavourably. He turned from her flustered features to study the well-lit clinical stairway that descended at their feet. Its modern appearance contrasted with the rest of the dilapidated base in which it resided, implying the seemingly abandoned facility was a façade for what lay underneath. The solitary guard had been part of the smokescreen, enough to keep away prying eyes, though too little to entice curiosity.

Josh gazed into the passageway. An initial assessment failed to see any further signs or security personnel or technology, only the semi reflective surface of shimmering alloy that adorned its walls. All was quiet, but something had Angelica spooked. He tried again, ignoring paranoia's distraction. Then there it was. The place, innocuous in nature, suddenly emanated an aura of unseen hazards. He focused on the latent energy that was suddenly saturating the forbidden place. Like the eerie ambiance of a morgue, death lingered in the air. Whatever it was Josh knew they would have to face it or admit defeat. Knowing defeat was not on the agenda, he knew there was little option but to confront death head on.

*****

The mire of saturated mud created a wretched shallow grave as it overflowed the milk white limbs of a child's discarded corpse. Feet scrambled in the slurry of desolate earth around it, struggling to evade the deafening eruptions of heavy artillery bombardment that exploded around them with random destructive cruelty. Outside a ruined house, set under a sky of dark angry clouds, two weathered soldiers dragged a screaming woman from her home. Her husband put up a brief resistance, but was shot twice in the head for his trouble. The images were of war at its worst and designed to incite emotion, notably revulsion. Viewing the grotesque imagery, that transferred to an Asian village decimated by a huge violent hurricane, was an attentive audience of mirrored eyed voyeurs.

The catatonic spectators were sat in an arc of silver reclining chairs, sucking up the images while their black clad hosts oversaw their handiwork, pale hands gripping their unsuspecting shoulders to insure by some wicked influence the students were subjected to the full rigours of human misery in glorious technicolour. A new batch of Low Grades were being vetted as new recruits, the tutors themselves administered by a hierarchy of identically looking agents who kept close watch on the proceedings. War was at hand, and for fear of unwanted infiltrators masquerading as civilians, the Elite's Nothos ranks had been ordered to enforce security for the Ascended Ones in the dreamscape admissions portal.

Instead of the sparsely manned greeting post for the induction of the projecting minds of unsuspecting insomniacs, the blue room looked like a rallying point for the accumulated forces of the Elite. As confident as the agents were in their combined strength, the Principal had still ordered an almost total lockdown of their secret world of dreams.

For its creators the holographic display had no effect. Having seen the graphic imagery infinite times before its hidden purpose was becoming laborious, but the secret agenda of the inter-dimensional covenant had to continue. The rebellious militia calling themselves Latronis, the so called servants of the light, would soon cease to hamper their earthly plans, but the secret masters still insisted on human infiltration of Hyperbora, and so the recruiting process continued. As Low Grades were either *lost* to the light or destabilised by the psychological trauma their tutelage instilled, the requirement for a constant stream of replacements was as necessary as ever.

Amongst the congregation of Elite Nothoi, unspoken feelings existed that their Principal over estimated the enemy. The Latronis ranks were far fewer in number, worked alone from their allies the Vanir, surely victory was assured. It was in that moment of doubt that the holographic display suddenly recaptured their attention.

The lurid images of an angry mob butchering a township in rural Africa were suddenly replaced by a sunny meadow of long grass and wild flowers. Two children, their cherub faces smiling, chased their playful dog through a happy landscape of childhood nostalgia, destroying the mantra of the previous doom-laden imagery. As a cartoon image of a fairy landscape was replaced with a happy mob celebrating new-year with hugs and kisses, the row of confused tutors let go their grips and turned to the their superiors for an explanation. As the smiles on the mirrored eyed recruits revealed, something was going terribly wrong. The legion of bemused blackened ghouls began to close in on the traitorous display, the blissful images of an earthly utopia reflecting on the lenses of their sunglasses as the head of a patriarchal figure now appeared on a horizon of sun bathed poppies. As he walked towards the screen, his long white hair and white ceremonial garments fluttering in the breeze, the broad, tanned face wore a beaming smile.

Several Elite Nothos began to focus their powers against the unwanted vision, but were unable to change the channel. The white haired stranger continued forward. He raised his hand as a ball of light began to take form within his palm like a burning coal. The bemused agents were taken by surprise as the stranger then unleashed the flaming projectile, sending it crashing out of the screen to explode into one of their colleagues. As the dumbfounded agents watched their colleague's Ka disappear in a flash of blinding light and screams, the beaming face thrust itself out of the disembodied screen.

"Boo!" Kristos jumped through the portal into the world of the Elite. At first the agents panicked. Those that didn't came under a hail of deadly blinding balls of light as Monk, Luna, Cozmo and the rest of the Latronis raiding party breached the portal and brought the war to the Elite.

At first the surprise attack was a slaughter. Kristos and his team surged into the neon blue layer like avenging angels bringing mayhem and death to the scattering Elite ranks. Throwing projectile after projectile in a merciless strategy of extermination, the seven white clad Nothos began to decimate the Elite ranks like fish in a barrel. But as losses converted fear into wrath, the blackened foes closed ranks and returned fire, casting their own destructive projectiles in a zealous counterattack that checked the initial blitzkrieg brought upon them.

A lucky shot caught Merlin in the chest. As he shouted in agony his Ka faltered from the draining effect of the contrasting energy blast, negative neutralising positive. But after returning the strike with a reprimanding bolt of his own that obliterated his attacker's Ka in an impressive blast of light, he gave a concerned Maestro a reassuring wink and continued the brawl.

The ranks of the Ascended Ones were easy to destroy. One direct hit from one of the Latronis fiery hand-cast light bolts was enough to terminate their Ka in one wondrous strike, but the Nothos amongst them were a tougher breed. Due to their greater strength it took several hits before they could be sufficiently weakened. Each hit neutralised the essence of its victim, a grim consequence that the Latronis commandos quickly began to realise for themselves. Like a battle between oppositely charged electrons, the opposing sides effectively sought to cancel each other out in a fervent display of swiping arms and destructive hails of energy. Positive struck negative, black struck white.

Within minutes Kristos and the others had all but eradicated the Ascended agents, their lightening fast arms sending the balls of destructive light to despatch the lesser agents into the nothingness of extinction. Enraged by the audacity and fuelled by hatred, the remaining Elite Nothos continued to return the deadly bolts of energy in a reformed counter attack. Though still outnumbering the intruders, they were unable to match the speed and accuracy in which their enemy could deliver the blinding strikes.

Five Elite Nothos quickly surrounded Kristos. As the spearhead of the attack their survival depended on his death. In such close quarters there was no longer room for castings projectiles, undeterred Kristos speared his outstretched hands into the shadow bodies around him. Forcing a lethal surge of white light down each arm and into the ghoulish recipients, his victims howled like dying animals before they were obliterated before his eyes. Ghoulish assailants quickly encroached upon the rest of Latronis. Forced to adopt the close quarter martial style, they dished out blow after blow in a haze of deadly swiping limbs as they brawled with Elite assailants face to ghoulish face. But greater proximity came with greater risk.

Monk's agonising howl caught Luna's attention. Up to ten black figures were vying for position to spear their lethal blows into his body, attempting to weaken his resilience as he sustained more and more successful strikes from his bestial attackers. Casting fireballs from each hand, Luna exterminated one of her own; in a flash and a scream it was gone. Before their cohorts could fill its vacancy she soared upwards and brought a similar hail of light grenades down on the heads of Monk's assailants. The aerial attack dispersed the agents for only a few seconds, but as they reeled back in agony, some near fading completely and clasping their blinded eyes, Monk was able to finish the job in a blur of jabs and punches that concluded with a huge gap gouged out the Elite's ranks.

In one last push, the swarm of brutish black assailants attempted to surround the servants of the light, hounding them with the insane fury akin to their blackened souls. The assault produced a furious barrage of positive and negative bolts of destructive lights to be cast from Ka to Ka, an impressive hail that weakened its victims until the balance was finally tipped. In the astral theatre of war some shadow bodies defied gravity, taking flight like winged demons in a desperate bid to gain the upper hand. But as the Elite ghouls encroached upon the Latronis militia like a blood hungry wolves, their white attired enemies unleashed emblazoned strike after strike in a frenzy of destruction. Lethal proficiency was limited only by the mind and will of each projection. After a matter of minutes the battle was over.

The Ka of the final Elite Nothos was dispatched into eternity by a thrust of Kristos's mighty arm. As the screams accompanied the projection into death it left behind an empty room. Maestro, Merlin, Luna and the rest of the small band looked on the face of victory. Weakened by the assault they also found to their amazement that their small ranks had remained intact. Cozmo saw his comrade's astonishment and broke the silence with a contagious post-traumatic laugh. Their greatest ambition had been fulfilled. Though outnumbered, they had dealt the Elite a devastating blow. Luna put her arms around Merlin and Maestro. The two white clad Kas reciprocated the act of kinship with a kiss on both her cheeks; even the austere Monk was tempted to place his hands onto their shoulders in congratulations. Their leader's stern features however cut short the festivities, forcing Cozmo into an abrupt return to silence.

Kristos stood in front of the silver row of reclined chairs. The catatonic Low Grades had been released, their mirrored eyes become human once more as their tutors had been otherwise occupied in the fight for survival. Released from entrapment the unwitting projections had returned in peace to their waiting bodies. With a wave of his hand Kristos reduced the instruments of their indoctrination into ashes.

"A job well done, eh Boss?" Cozmo stated after he watched the silver chairs dissolve into the nothingness they had originated from. Kristos turned to the others. Studying the faces of his fellow servants of the light he saw the six expectant Nothoi looked fatigued, making his announcement all the more harder.

"It's not over yet boys and girls," he replied gloomily. The ominous statement was accompanied with a glazed look over the heads of Maestro and Merlin. "Light disperses dark," he stated, "but in the blackest places, also attracts it." In the background the blue walls were revealing signs that something else was coming. Victory it seemed was far from complete.

*****

"Wish me luck," Jonah instructed gravely. Making the cautious descent, all eyes watched as he traversed the thirty or so steps to the meshed lined floor of the adjoining subterranean tunnel. The descending staircase offered access to their target, but a feeling of menace had hampered any temptation to take it willingly. A silent deliberation of exchanged looks had concluded in Jonah going on point. Angelica was the most powerful Nothos amongst them, but after forcing her Ka through the Elite's security portal their blonde lieutenant had been left sufficiently drained.

Seconds felt like hours until cautiously Jonah reached the final step and hovered a reluctant foot above the tunnel's mesh floor. His keen sense navigated the substructure now in view. Testing his will against a growing trepidation, he brought his foot down to step forward and out of sight. From the top step the others waited nervously, but at the sound of Jonah's beckoning whistle their fears dispersed. Josh followed Dex, Alpha and Saffy down the steps, though made sure he kept close to Angelica who he sensed was masking fatigue behind a mask of tenacity. Reaching the ground they came to halt behind Jonah, who stood rigidly to the spot.

"What are we waiting for?" Josh asked impatiently. He shuffled into position around his colleagues and took a look at the ominous passage that continued to descend into the earth at a subtle angle. At its far end he saw it was terminated by another blast door. As they all stared into the clinical tunnel its iridescent alloyed surfaces beckoned them vindictively to continue into the lion's den.

"'Tis the night before Christmas and all was still," Jonah muttered, searching the plain aesthetics for the reason his instincts burned with caution.

"Too still," Dex confirmed. His glance to Josh hinted at some grave danger. Jonah too gazed back for his superior's insight, but her silence denoted its absence. Though Angelica clearly sensed the latent hazard, a loss of verve left her unable to rely one hundred percent on her own heightened abilities. Alpha took the bull by he horns and bent down to rip up a sheet of the mesh flooring. As he threw it into the tunnel the hazard's nature was revealed as the crosswire bombardment of high-density lasers tracked the trellis's flight and reduced it into mangled, twisted scrap. A scornful chorus of metal against metal echoed down the tunnel as they watched the blackened remains come to a depressing halt, several feet short of the opposite blast door.

"Sneaky little bastards," Alpha cursed. A simple walk through the tunnel was out of the question.

"So who's good at limbo?" Saffy asked with a cocky grin. Josh found impatience urging to ask the obvious.

"Can't we just pass through the beams?" In his early encounters with Galda and Angelica Josh had seen the awesome unworldly power a Nothos possessed. As a result he couldn't comprehend how the earthly technology presented a problem for a team of projections. "Surely this security system is only meant to keep out people of flesh and blood."

"Are you willing to find out why not?" Jonah turned and asked the assertive novice, "Because if you are, be my guest." The comment hid a new resentment that made Josh feel stupid and naive.

"There are some things even us Nothoi cannot pass through," Angelica explained, coming out of her weary silence.

"Beams of high density light being one of them," Dex confirmed. Josh looked into Angelica's blue eyes and saw her depreciated state had allowed her Ka to recharge.

"Well, step aside people," Saffy then instructed. She pushed her way to the front, "Looks like it's do or die time."

"Yeah, watch and learn," Dex piped in. Before their brash female comrade could intercede he soared into the tunnel.

Dex's projection flew with the speed and agility of ball lightening. As with the mesh grid, the tunnel's security censors activated the crisscross of lethal lasers in an attempt to track and destroy the zigzagging spectre that eluded them with uncanny foresight. After a few impressive seconds of flashing green lights and perilous aerial acrobatics, Dex's smiling face beamed back at them as he stood intact by the blast door. "Piece of cake!" he hollered down the tunnel, "What are you waiting for?"

With renewed conviction Saffy jumped next into line. Within seconds of accomplishing a similar death defying feat of cat and mouse she landed at Dex's side and waved Jonah onwards with mocking impatience. Proving to be more courageous in the face of Saffy's taunt, Jonah's projection soared into the tunnel and out did the previous attempts with an unnecessary loop-the-loop, toying with the lasers inability to track him before landing safely next to Saffy. After watching the aerobatic display Alpha made his best effort to hide his lack of faith.

In the visceral arena of military warfare he knew he could out perform, out gun and out kill any one of his new colleagues, but in this new battlefield the rules had changed dramatically. Now only his finely tuned instinct, not his physical training, would see him safely through the lethal assault course. Swallowing his apprehension, he bit the bullet and took flight.

His bulky projection mimicked the previous attempts convincingly, but was Alpha no Jonah or Saffy. Through the striking blasts he lumbered clumsily, inexperience unravelling instinct as his bulky spectre faltered and fumbled the split second manoeuvres. An inability to anticipate the swiping beams quickly progressed, costing him more and more of his head start, until within a heartbeat luck ran out. Alpha yelled in agony as beam of high density light struck home. As he had lurched for the blast door the final laser had caught his right arm in a flash of painful sparks. A second beam threatened to finish the job, until Dex dragged Alpha's Ka forward in the nick of time.

Before his and Jonah's eyes the soldier's wounded shadow body began to shimmer. The laser strike had weakened Alpha's projecting psyche, his shocked face now a blank death mask stare as his Ka threatened to falter altogether.

"Alpha?" Angelica hollered down the tunnel. Impulsively Jonah thrust his hand into the soldier's chest and focused his own strength into Alpha's failing Ka, the surge of light he injected halting any further deterioration. As Jonah watched the ebbing form slowly return to its previous density, re-energised by the influx of rejuvenating life force, he breathed a communal sigh of relief. From down the tunnel Josh watched the big soldier shrug off the intimate gesture as Dex gave the two waiting Nothoi a reassuring thumbs up. Relieved, Angelica turned to Josh.

"Guess who's next?" She gestured for the rookie to take his turn on the roller coaster. Jonah's flawless display had left Josh filled with confidence, but after witnessing Alpha's short-comings, a feeling of impending doom descended on his shoulders. He could feel Angelica's eyes upon him, judging him, but with an endearment that came from kinship. The tunnel of shimmering alloy looked peaceful again, its hazards retracted and lying in wait for its next foolish prey. If he backed out he would be left behind, but if he made a mistake he risked losing a lot more than companionship.

"So what's the deal with the mirrored eyes?" he suddenly asked, delaying the inevitable. He turned in search of reassurance. "You know how freaky that looks right?"

"Purely a physical manifestation of the mind," she answered dryly, appreciating his anxiety. "Think of it as war paint."

"What are you waiting for he's fine?" Dex hollered impatiently down the tunnel, waving them on as Jonah and Alpha now studied an interface mounted in the wall. Josh couldn't stall any further.

"Wish me luck," he said quietly, realising destiny, like time, waited for no man.

"We make our own remember?" she replied. With this final assertion, Josh lurched forward. The freedom of being able to soar through the air was a revelation, but now his life depended on his superhuman skills it no longer seemed like fun. The motion sensors tracked the new form, unleashing the lethal green beams in an attempt to dispel the latest intruder. Josh's mind went blank. Though he moved at a heightened velocity he found his mind suddenly switched time frames. Like experiencing a traumatic accident, the world began to slow around him. In the period of flight that appropriated a matter of seconds, the adapted perception made the hazardous feat felt like minutes.

At first the lagging laser's fired into the empty space he'd already passed, but with a malicious cunning it began to predict his path and fire ahead of him. But somehow in the blur of outwitting the bright flashes his Ka ducked and leapt the intuitive last few strikes, until abruptly as it had begun, it was over. Jonah thumped his hand on Josh's shoulder, dragging him closer to the blast door for his safety. *I made it?* It wasn't until he looked into Jonah's beaming face that Josh realised his heightened intuition had seen him threw the ordeal. With inhuman speed and agility he'd outwitted the frantic barrage of beams. The flash and sparks created as the lasers discharged one last time drew his attention back to the tunnel. Before realising she'd even began her attempt, Angelica's form then appeared at his side.

"Well?" she asked as the final failed beam struck into the wall behind her.

"Piece of cake," Josh replied, a surge of euphoria filling his Ka with renewed vigour. Though it sounded like bravado, results had secured a new faith. Standing amongst his comrades once more, he understood that in his current higher state of existence mind and will could outwit even the most sophisticated technology, and it felt good. Another explosion of sparks suddenly erupted by the blast door. Though expecting another destructive beam, Josh found Alpha had resentfully smashed a big hand into the interface. The shorted electrics caused the blast door to retract into its frame and Dex leaned back to taunt the deactivated motion sensors with a hearty wave of his arm.

"Yep that'll do it," he confirmed. He gave Alpha a nod of well done and Angelica smiled at Josh.

"Why didn't we wait for him to do that?" she aired Josh's thoughts; a couple of minutes wait would have spared him the precarious laser assault course. "Just because there's an easy way," she explained, "doesn't mean you should take it!"

"He who dares wins, right?" he inferred. Though flustered by the deception, his resentment was quelled by her mischievous smile and his new found sense of worth. *She knew all the time I could do it.* "Then what are we waiting for?" Out manoeuvring Saffy and Jonah, Josh darted through the breached doorway into the large elevator it had concealed. As the others joined him inside its clinical metal confine Josh ran a finger down the vertical row of Latin numbered buttons and pressed the one marked *VI*. "Going down," he stated. The elevator shuddered gently, and then began the descent into the bowls of fate.

*****

The Latronis strike team turned to find the source of their leader's desolation. Recognising the reconstitution of astral conception they shared the sudden loss of heart. The neon blue shell that housed the Elite's dreamscape layer had begun to falter and lose its cohesion. As it now twisted and warped into an ominous wormhole their ill fortune began to seal itself with the developing cataclysm it portended. The portal through space and time formed into a menacing tubular perfection, releasing a macabre energy into the secret place like the noxious breath of some foul creature. As the only projections remaining, they closed ranks and braced their wits against the impending presence that now hurried to meet them down the celestial corridor. Suddenly they heard the first distant howls, a devilish resonation that descended on its prey like a school of sharks chasing the scent of blood.

"Stay together," Kristos instructed, his voiced rose against the increasingly loud pandemonium that followed the waves of malevolent energy filling the astral chamber. Its stifling presence forced the six Nothos ever closer together. "Whatever happens they can't defeat us if we stand as one." Kristos stood at the front of the small squad now, his paternal presence and vitality assuring his anxious comrades they could face the oncoming assault and survive, if not win. As the surge of unholy energy spurted from the mouth of the portal the Latronis militia staved off its sullying effect by focusing their communal energies into creating a cocoon of light about them. Empowered by a benign resilience and singular belief, the protective sphere sealed its shielding power just as the first Elite projections appeared in the distance.

Like a torrent of struck oil the army of ghouls flooded into the blue chamber. Targeting their enemies they swarmed around the benign opposites like a nest of furious hornets, their eerie howls an ear splitting chorus of the damned that chilled their enemy's souls. Kristos and the others held fast as they watched the horde of angry black clad agents soar around them. Defiantly they gazed out at the seething white faces whirling past in a sea of black forms. Sporting their protective eyewear the Elite swarm leered back with the distorted, bestial features of the insane. The cocoon of light appeared to hold them at bay, but as the tail of the Elite cavalry left the portal to complete the enemy cavalry, the Latronis Nothoi knew they were now exposed to the full strength of the Elite forces.

"There's hundreds of them!" Cozmo exclaimed, his wide-eyed features betraying a repulsive awe of the devilish swarm encircling them like a tornado of blackened souls.

"Don't break the circle!" Kristos ordered, fearing a contagious anxiety might weaken their resilience. "The only way we can destroy them is if we combine our strength, move closer." At the second order the six Nothoi turned back to back and faced outwards to the blurring swarm that grimaced hatefully at the white uniformed intruders. They had trained for such a predicament. As though in communal prayer they instinctively closed eyes and raised their palms upwards. Combining their strength into a cabal of divine power increased their individual powers threefold. Positive now charged positive in an amplified channelling of energy, creating an impenetrable shield that could be felt but not seen by their enemy. *Don't stop.* They heard Kristos's words resonate in their minds. *Focus!* Slowly they began to concentrate the combined power outwards, like a freshly lit lantern struggling for life in the blackest of cellars it began to expand towards the encroaching ghouls.

At first the Elite projections jeered the feeble attempt. Like vultures waiting for a weakened victim to inevitably falter and be devoured they cackled demonically, their vile words penetrating the invisible shield, taunting the Latronis with hissed threats of murderous vengeance. Black agents spurred cohorts to kill the intruders, but none was powerful enough to pierce the benign barrier that separated them from annihilating the small faction. Then abruptly the threats ceased. The invisible barrier was replaced by a brilliant light that now seethed outwards like a giant burning coal, forcing the legion of ghouls to recoil in alarm.

"Its working," Luna announced. Opening her eyes she saw the swarm of white faces blurring in the wall of light.

"Don't look at them!" Monk ordered, "Keep focusing your power!" His own eyes remained closed. He knew the barrage of Elite faces were capable of exerting their own manipulative energy towards them. He continued to imagine the light intensifying with the fiery power of a sun. The others also resisted the temptation, more for fear of the losing the celestial shield than for fear of Monk's stern wrath. But Kristos sensed something was wrong. The black horde's retreat had halted; their howls returning with an increased blood-curdling furore. There was a weakness within the circle. Something was draining their strength. Against his better judgement he opened his eyes. To his horror Kristos saw Maestro's blank face, his open eyes staring into the abyss of leering faces.

"Maestro no!" he yelled. "Don't look at their faces!" But already it was too late. The Elite had found their Achilles heel and had exploited it vindictively. A familiar voice had stolen Maestro from his duty, weakening his resolve with the counterfeit pleading of his dead son. The lost infant had called out to him, begging his father to save him from the Elite agents tormenting him with their vindictive grips, spitefully squeezing and tussling his pathetic form in a malicious attempt to gain his attention. The screams of *Daddy save me* had proved too much for Maestro. In the instant he had opened his tormented eyes to see the dead infant morph into a ghoulish spectre his will had already succumbed to theirs. Much too late for Kristos's intervention, the devious Elite projection pierced the rift and soared into Maestro's Ka. The circle had been breached. Within a flashing second the sphere of light imploded.

The force of the degrading power propelled the Latronis projections apart and into the black swarm. His defence completely compromised by the Elite Ka that had soared into his own, Maestro was unable to fend off the dozen or so black agents that now swarmed around him in a feeding frenzy that resulted in his total annihilation. Torn from their comrades, each servant of the light was now forced to fend for him or herself, fumbling in the sea of raging ghouls that soared forward and clawed at the illuminated forms that acted as homing beacons for Elite wrath. White arms struck out in a frenzied attempt to fend off the unrelenting assault. In close combat there was no room to use their destructive projectiles, only a furious brawl that meandered from pulverising a fist into whatever Elite body parts came into contact, and soaring upwards and away from the hideous assailants. But the swarm's number seemed unlimited. As soon as a black agent was sent reeling away in howling agony another would instantly take its place.

Kristos exploited every opening in the assault, soaring away to momentarily gather his failing strength while thrashing out at his persistent assailants. On one such strategic manoeuvre he caught a glimpse of his comrade's celestial forms amongst the black swarm. Each fought for their own survival against overwhelming odds, escaping briefly only to be consumed by a relentless sea of lethal spectres that stuck to them like living tar. He saw Monk and Luna releasing their own brand of counter attack. They had regrouped; now back-to-back they thrashed out a fearsome display of martial handiwork, dispatching agent after agent with each frantic punch and kick they appeared unstoppable. But like him, their strength was fading quickly. In the split seconds afforded Kristos he caught a glimpse of Cozmo, but saw no sign of Merlin or Maestro. As he lashed down at a ghoulish face, gouging away its forehead with a blazing fist, he knew they must be dead.

He managed to cast down a thunderbolt of light into the faces of two agents. To his dismay it didn't destroy them. Once again they surrounded him in a frenzied attempt to consume the light that empowered his Ka. Desperately he fought back to prevent himself drowning in the sea of black. He punched another ghoul in the face, sent another fist into the torso of another and then crushed two heads together between his blazing hands, but his powers continued to weaken. He could feel his Ka slowly being drained of its essence, each strike and grapple with the Elite soldiers appropriating his power as it was neutralised against the insurmountable numbers vying for a piece of him. One against three, four or five he could have easily destroyed the despicable ghouls, but after dispatching a hundred or so of the Elite projections into eternity, Kristos still faced the prospect of his own extinction. It was then salvation suddenly appeared in an unexpected form.

A final strike into an agent's chest sent it reeling away but its place was not filled. As the deadly swarm began to retreat from the powerful servant of the light, he gazed with unbelieving eyes at the widening circle around him. *They're backing off?*

"What are you waiting for?" Kristos howled vengefully, unsure if the move was part of some new stratagem. "You afraid to die? You miserable sons of bitches!" Anger fuelled the urge to exterminate the loathsome spectres swarming just out of reach, their white faces twisting and contorting as they grimaced at their formidable enemy. Realising the negative feelings only weakened his illuminated form, Kristos called time out, using the break in the assault to determine his next move.

He studied the waiting horde. The attack had halted but they refused to disperse. If he tried to evade them he knew they would follow, possibly renew their attack, and so he remained suspended in the blue astral void and gathered his dwindling strength. *They're toying with me.* He looked again for any sign of his comrades. All he could see was the writhing sea of leering Elite soldiers. In the present calm he should have been able to locate Monk and the others easily. Instead he was struck dumb by the obvious explanation for their absence. The others were dead.

Chapter 15

Josh had never liked elevators. The sensation of movement without visual confirmation always made him feel nauseous. Being a projection seemed to make little difference to the curse. Descending into the heart of the Elite's global network, heading to an unknown fate in a metal box, there was an obvious apprehension as the button marked *VI* lit up to announce their arrival. The entrance slid open.

Another corridor waited before them. It seemed their journey would be a never-ending trek through a labyrinth of subterranean passageways, but didn't deter Dex and Saffy, who pushed carelessly onwards.

"It's show-time," Saffy announced, her dark eyes sparkling with a childish enthusiasm.

"Looks like everyone's out to lunch," Dex added with a trademark grin. Emergency strip lights partially lit the dim corridor, shedding a bleak aura over the plain walls and allowing Dex's heightened night vision to pick out that the surroundings were free of unfriendly inhabitants. "Maybe they heard we were coming?"

"Or maybe they're just playing dead," Josh supplemented. He had shared his comrade's paranoia about the previous passage. Its hidden dangers had resonated from its walls like a bad smell. The dark passage in front of them now however offered no such lingering danger. Instead Josh's astute senses urged him forward. Something lay at the end of corridor. A low frequency emanated from it, making its presence known by the unusual nature of its palpitations.

"What is it?" Angelica asked. She had mistaken his distraction for trepidation, but quickly realised the hesitant stare was the result of something more profound.

"There's something behind that wall," he replied vacantly. Dex, Saffy and Alpha had combed the corridor, studying the closed doors that ran along its length. Josh's foreboding comment however caused them to pause and stare back at him and Angelica in the elevator's doorway. "Can't you feel it?" he asked openly, amazed his comrades were oblivious to the sinister vibrations. Angelica looked down towards the blank wall that terminated the dark corridor. Without confirmation she walked past Alpha and the others towards it with a raised arm. An arc of intense light burst from her palm and fell upon the wall, allowing her to study its seemingly trivial surface.

"The doors?" Dex exclaimed, referring Angelica's attention back to the sealed rooms they hid. He knew her powers were greater than his or any other Nothos present, but he saw no significance in her present interest, especially as it was at the behest of a novice's paranoia.

"He's right," she said suddenly. "There's something here." She pressed her ear against the cold surface and felt the low frequency energy that radiated covertly through the wall, contrasting with the rest of the surroundings. Everything animate and inanimate resonated a vibration but the ominous strength of whatever lay behind was too strong to ignore. "This is it," she proclaimed. Angelica stood back to brush her hands over the smooth surface. Admitting defeat Dex joined the others around her and searched for discrepancies in the wall.

"There was a molecular portal here," Josh declared as he walked up behind, "but they removed it and bricked up the entrance to seal it forever."

"And just how in the hell do you know that Flyboy?" Saffy asked, unsure of the new boy's sudden ability to out perform them. Josh didn't know how he knew. Staring at the wall he found its past was reverberating from its very constitution like an open book. Saffy's comment redirected his attention to her sceptical face.

"I just do."

"In that case," Alpha said as he used his bulk to usher his comrades aside, "I say we make our own." Before Jonah could word a warning Alpha had hurled his massive fist into the obstacle.

The first strike had little effect on the thick wall. He followed it up with a second mighty strike, then a third; fourth, increasing in speed until the soldier's arms became a destructive blur that hammered into the brick wall like a human jackhammer. Within seconds the first cracks appeared. Quickly they spread into jagged fractures that eventually gave way further to Alpha's relentless pounding. After less than twenty seconds he had punched a hole big enough for a Nothos to slip through.

"Nice job soldier boy," Jonah congratulated Alpha, who stood back to admire his handiwork. A harsh blue tinged light funnelled out of the gaping hole to illuminate the dim corridor. Angelica was the first to inspect what lay beyond the breach and see they had stumbled onto the secret heart of the subterranean base.

"What do you see?" Josh asked apprehensively. As though a levee had burst the rest of the group now felt the unnerving wave of low frequency energy emanating out.

"Terrible things," Angelica replied grimly. Lifting her leg she slithered through the foot thick remains of the wall and entered the new chamber. The rest followed their lieutenant one by one through Alpha's doorway and found themselves bathed in the cold light. Though it had little or no effect on their projections, the chamber's temperature was equally bitter. Had they breathed with human breath it would have condensed into a chilled vapour.

"Someone forgot to switch on the thermostat," Dex commented. The frosted vents above their heads relayed the chamber was being purposely cooled, further bemusing the small team to its purpose. Jonah looked to Angelica for instruction. She was scouring the unwelcoming layer for Elite sentinels, but her rejuvenated senses suggested they were alone. The waves of negative energy seeping from the very walls threatened to befuddle her judgement, but did little to interfere with her conviction.

"Let's clean house." She ushered them forward. The chamber was oval in shape. Its vaulted ceiling arched high above their heads, supported by beams of shimmering alloy that convened over the central pillar dominating the mysterious room. Jonah and Dex crossed the mesh grill floor lighted from beneath to tackle the flashing displays placed at equal intervals around the torso of the central pillar. Kicking aside the flimsy chairs the two techno wizards began hacking into the mainframe of what was simply a monumental computer. Saffy and Alpha decided to split up and study the strange inward facing black obelisks that lined the chamber's curved walls, their spectral reflections appearing ethereal as they passed the polished onyx surfaces.

"Why so cold?" Saffy asked. She waved her hand frustratingly before her vacant breath, but there was no moisture to chill. "You could hang meat in here!" As she lowered the hand her own ghostly reflection caught her attention on a black obelisk. She couldn't explain it, but the plain polished surfaces chilled her Ka where the biting temperature failed to. "Is it me or do these black panels seem kind of creepy?" she asked, and then reached out to touch the raven black surface.

"They're the source of the energy," Angelica explained as she followed Josh around the pillar. He had been acting strange since they had entered level six and she was increasingly intrigued by his distant perceptions. "They must be some kind of sustainable localised power source for this place," she offered walking up behind the preoccupied novice, "Whatever this place is. How we doing Jonah?"

"Just a minute, I'm still by-passing security," Jonah replied as he and Dex competed for entry into the pillar's mainframe. With the spare seconds offered her, Angelica joined Josh as he stood before the separate alcove carved out of the bedrock at the apex of the egg shaped chamber. The reclined chair housed at its centre on the raised platform was identical to the chrome plated chairs Josh had seen in the Elite's projection room. Its sparkling form was enshrined in the niche like some sacred artefact and suspended above the mesh floor by some unseen gravity defying force. Taking one unappreciative look at the mysterious technology, Angelica's patience began to wear thin.

"You kicked that security's ass yet?" she hollered impatiently over her shoulder, unable to take her eyes from the enigmatic chair that imparted some new as of yet unspecified threat.

"I'm in!" Dex suddenly declared. He gave Jonah a playful wink then returned to the schematics on the display unit. "Are you seeing what I'm seeing?" he then asked his competitor. His ominous tone forced his dread-locked colleague to abandon his own attempt.

"No, enlighten me," Jonah replied as he swapped screens to study the window into the Elite's global network. Overhearing their progress, Angelica dragged herself away from Josh as he continued his own detached study of the chair by ascending its platform.

Apart from the gaping hole they had forced through the thick defensive wall, the chamber was without any other entrance. Until their arrival the secret room had been prepped for some portentous purpose, sealed for posterity and then left to its seemingly automated agenda. Parallel to Saffy's continued interest in the onyx monoliths, the soulless place constructed of the skeletal alloy framework deep within the earth made Angelica nervous. The dark energy it exuded both intrigued and disconcerted her. As Angelica joined Dex and Jonah at the pillar's terminal she gestured to Saffy and Alpha to remain on alert.

"What you got?" she asked. She could read the flashing imagery on screen for herself, but relied on the two technological wizards to decipher the computer jargon and schematic readouts.

"It's patched into everything," Jonah announced matter-of-factly. "Servers, mainframes, networks, satellites, they're all accessible on a global scale. It's plugged into everything." His keen eyes darted over the screen as his mind processed the torrent of information. The headset he'd clasped over his temples was translating his thoughts into a telepathic pointing device, allowing him to navigate the workstation with super human speed.

"So what the hell is it? What's it for?" Angelica asked.

"It's a primary server that can access and over ride any other networked system," Dex answered. "In other words it can bypass any firewall, invade anything with a central processing unit and hijack its primary functions," he explained with an air of awe, "I've never seen anything like this in my life. Take a look." The screen paused its relentless cyber exploration to display the familiar logo of the Federal Reserve.

"Anyone fancy clearing out Uncle Sam?" he asked with a grin, before continuing his love affair with the computer's abilities. "It's like a tumour; it's got a back door into everything. FBI, CIA, DoD!"

Dex reeled off the prestigious list of classified acronyms as their mainframes flashed up on the screen. "Want to know who killed Marilyn?" he then asked excitedly. Unrestricted access to the secret mandates and databases at the National Security Agency were now at his fingertips. "You could run the world from here and never have to leave this seat." The barefaced comment left them in no doubt over the power the Elite held in its grasp. The deduction also confirmed their greatest fear; the black book agency was poised to unleash an apocalyptic agenda on behalf of the Deros.

"You mentioned overriding primary functions, what's *its* primary function?" Angelica queried. "Something tells me this is more than a glorified hacking toy." Her take on the situation set Dex on a new exploration of the server's directories, while her own attention drifted back to the detached rookie.

"Josh?" She called his name though he seemed not to hear. In the alcove the shiny seat held sway over his senses. An unexplainable magnetism had drawn him to stand over the mysterious technology, his blank face hiding the miasma of perceptions as he disengaged from the preoccupations of his comrades. *This is not of this world.* As if making some sacrilegious reach for a sacred icon, she watched on as he reverently placed his hand on its headrest.

"You're in," Jonah suddenly exclaimed, recognising Dex had disabled the server's security policy.

"Not quite, ol' buddy, this son of a bitch is wrapped tighter than a nun's corset."

"Nun's don't wear corsets, dumb ass," Jonah chided.

"And neither does this baby anymore," Dex boasted as the server's unsecured command prompt window appeared before the hacker's eyes. As their colleagues scrutinised the chamber's external components around them the two Nothoi began to scour the operating system kernels and directories.

Alpha's attention had been drawn to the network of pipes and cables spread under the illuminated mesh flooring. Like the roots of so many blackened trees one such set of optical cables appeared to link each of the wall mounted monoliths to the central pillar Dex and Jonah were busy infiltrating. He double checked the fact with each onyx panel, walking around the outer wall until he had come full circle to where Saffy stood mesmerised by one such slab. Amongst the entanglement underfoot the centralised network did extend to each one. The big Nothos stood beside her, snapping Saffy out of the bemused analysis.

"You figured it out?" she asked. Waking from his own studious daze, Alpha realised he was not alone in his concern.

"Well they ain't here to make the place pretty that's for sure," he grunted back. His distracted eyes drew her attention to the network underfoot. "So energy cells?" she asked sceptically. The brooding low frequency energy radiating from the burnished onyx monoliths that stood as tall as her military comrade didn't seem to tally with the theory. The soldier's face suggested he concurred.

"Evil begets evil," Alpha added philosophically, "Who the hell knows." As the secret heart of their enemy's organisation its malevolent aura didn't surprise him and he hoped the lack of interest by the more powerful members of the Latronis platoon was proof enough they posed no real threat.

"Josh?" Angelica called once more. She had watched him steer his way slowly around the suspended chair, his one hand gliding over its shiny exterior. But now as he lowered himself into it, placing his head instinctively into the headrest, eyes shut and deep in his other world deliberation, she realised its magnetism had overwhelmed his better judgement. "What are you doing?" She walked back over.

"This chair is a portal into their world," he replied, seemingly noticing her for the first time since entering the chamber. He appeared calm and rational, but his preoccupied state made her fear for the novice's sanity. "We can use it."

"We came to destroy their world, not become a part of it." She preferred to leave the underground hub inoperable to its creators; tampering with the mysterious device could only draw attention their way.

"It can't be!" Jonah suddenly exclaimed from behind.

"What have you found?" Angelica queried as she reluctantly left Josh. The look of alarm on the broad olive skinned face as she returned to the terminal didn't bode well.

"Take a look at this." He pointed a finger at the screen. His anxious manner meant the hundreds of lines of unintelligible text scrolling down the left hand side of the screen were not a positive sight. "This code was hidden in the registry of a roaming profile."

"Roaming profile?"

"It's a virtual environment accessible via the local network. The code is an operational kernel, but it's using an encrypted alphabet see?" he explained. The rolling credits of incomprehensible digits meant nothing to her, but she sensed Jonah's explanation was about to get depressing. "At first we didn't think anything of it, but Brainiac here ran a decryption tool and found this." Another window popped up on screen, showing the strange language converting into something more discernable.

"Gimme a break here guys, what does it mean?"

"It's a virus," Dex said solemnly. "The profile is acting as a holding tank. One click of a finger and it can be unleashed into every global security mainframe this thing's tapped into."

The gloomy revelation bypassed Saffy's ears. For the duration of their trespass she had studied the same monolith, enslaved to the niggling sensation there was more to the cold onyx slab than first appeared. While Angelica assimilated the shock find a few feet away Saffy swiped away the veil of icy crust produced by the chilled environment to reveal more of its burnished surface.

"So the Elite are planning to shut down the world? Then what?" Angelica asked.

"They're probably hoping to disable any opposition to the Covenant before consolidating global control to this one server," Jonah speculated.

"Kill the king, long live the king," Alpha added sardonically as he came and glanced over Dex's shoulder.

"Close but no cigar people," Dex interceded. Window after window flashed on and off screen like the pages of some electronic manual as he dug deeper into the fine trail left by the Elite programmers.

"Then what?" Angelica asked, perplexed. "If they release the virus it will shut down the world's mainframes and everything they control. The world will effectively be shut down."

"I'm afraid it's not that simple," Dex announced. Via the telepathic headset he continued to scroll through the unknown codex. "The malware has a specified application. It's only designed for a particular grid, but I don't recognise it yet." Frustrated at the unexpected twist Angelica cast her gaze away from the console. A solitary Josh was still reclining in the silver chair. Suddenly sensing some encroaching doom, she knew time, the concept Kristos had assured them was created as one of many bars to imprison the world's consciousness, was quickly running out.

*****

The Latronis elimination of hundreds of Elite projections now seemed a futile achievement. Though the sizable swarm that survived kept their distance from the weary but powerful servant of the light, it served as a malevolent reminder of the precious brothers and sisters they'd overwhelmed and killed. Kristos found it hard to contain his rage. The very thought of their lethal handiwork invited an all-consuming anger that threatened to infuse his own suspended Ka with an effervescent influx of dark energy. Before it neutralised his shadow body like a self-administered toxin, he centred his emotions, channelling the negative energy away.

Sensing the turmoil in the powerful Nothos the Elite mob slowly began to retreat. As they made the unexpected withdrawal Kristos hoped the circumspect horde were resigning their assault, but as he saw a second inter-dimensional portal forming on the far side of the blue arena, he realised they had merely been containing him. As the vortex fashioned itself into a spiralling tunnel that stretched into a black infinity, he watched its passengers depart and enter the blue arena to join the impending fray. Instead of uniting forces the swarm parted ways to allow the new contingent of Elite projections to surge through and survey the astral battlefield. After making a keen reconnaissance of the trapped Latronis leader they soared back to report to whatever lingered in the portal. Kristos then saw as they beckoned the Elite Ka from its swirling mouth and escorted him through his spectral army to meet the trapped survivor.

The new arrival soared around the trapped light walker in an excitable flight, its broad ghoulish face clearly anticipating some long sought victory. The black attire, deathly countenance and protective eyewear were identical to its cohorts. But from its acidic voice Kristos recognised the Machiavellian psyche of his arch nemesis.

"Kristos! The very name is like an ulcer on my tongue," he declared venomously. "Though I welcome the opportunity of tasting it for the last time!"

"The pleasure is all mine Galda Vey," he retorted as the Elite Principal came to a halt before him. "And I look forward to removing that necrotic tongue of yours!" The threat was boastful enough not to reveal his battle fatigue. Galda's sneering white face grinned back.

"Look around you! Surely even a cripple can see when he's lost. I'm afraid it will be me deciding which astral body parts to detach, not you." His enemy's spiteful assertion did nothing to dissuade Kristos. "Your devotees are now but a memory, and in a few moments you too will simply cease to exist. Leaving me and my associates unhindered in our great task." Kristos cast a glance back to the unstable inter-dimensional tunnel. The secret masters were there, their gaseous amorphous forms watching and waiting on their human puppets to remove the troublesome obstacle. He had seen their dark shape shifting forms only once before. The sight of their empty, menacing energy had chilled his soul then, and did so again.

"Are you really so blind?" Kristos propounded, tearing his gaze from the fiendish presence beyond. "You are a pawn, you are expendable! You are a puppet of darkness, blinded with sugary sweet promises that will lead to your own destruction along with millions of innocent people." Galda's hovering form laughed wickedly.

"Don't let these shades fool you," he replied as he removed them to expose the gold, shining orbs. "My eyes are wide open, while in a few moments yours will be permanently shut!" A chorus of devilish cackles erupted from the jeering swarm surrounding them. "This is a great opportunity for our race, to take its true place in the universe. And you, and the weaklings like you, want to throw it away?" Kristos doubted his nemesis was stupid enough to believe such nonsense. More likely he was maintaining a façade for his devoted onlookers and his own hidden agenda. Either way the fate of an entire world was now balancing on the shoulders of the Elite spectre. "The destiny of the human race is evolution; I'm simply giving it a helping hand."

"This is not our destiny!" Kristos shouted. "To be the mindless slaves of a malicious race such as the Deros!" The black vaporous forms contorted and twisted in the portal, their shapes shifting from vaguely humanoid to an unidentifiable cloud that seethed at the portal's gaping entrance, reluctant or unable to pass through. "Look at them, what sort of future do you think they offer us?" Galda's face momentarily revealed a moment of uncertainty.

"On first contact I, myself, was unsure the path they offered was the right one," he replied, "but then I came to realise this was about something greater than myself!" Kristos sensed the whitewash was for his adherent's ears. Their blackened forms had been indoctrinated into the Elite agenda, fed lies that ignited base emotions and allowed darkness to assume control. They were an army of fools and were following their pied piper into the abyss. "Mankind has dreamed of such contact, of a chance to take the reins of his own destiny. It was then I realised that I should put aside foolish notions of emotion in favour of logic."

"The logic of self obsession!" Kristos condemned him. "You have sold soul and race for empty promises of immortality. Light is the creative force in this universe. Without it even the darkness you have embraced would not even exist." The accusation stretched the Principal's patience. Like an incensed cobra he lunged forward at his enemy, only to be repelled by the invisible shell that cocooned him.

"And what of the light?" he roared at Kristos. He kept his distance, waiting for another chance. "What of the Vanir?" At the mention of their natural foe the Deros twisted and writhed in the portal's entrance once more. "What have they ever offered mankind? Even as their enemies stand to ally themselves with mankind they are content to take a back seat and watch it happen. What possible loyalty could you hold for a race who passively allows such, a tragedy to happen?" The mocking tone that ended the tirade induced yet more cackling from their black audience. Kristos realised he was preaching to the damned.

"Without the very thing you have willingly squandered you will never know," he reproached his leering adversary.

"My soul?" Galda asked, again conceitedly. "What need have I of that! There is more than one way to achieve immortality my friend."

"You, me, them," Kristos pointed to the members of the black swarm, "we are all part of the eternal light, while your masters are without its grace. Humanity and the Deros are not meant to co-exist. The only way we will is in death, and I'll be damned before I let that happen." Kristos had once hoped for such an opportunity, to face the insanity of the Elite and reveal its perversion to itself. But as he looked upon the jeering mob of projections containing him in the neon blue void he understand that what ever spark of humanity may have once existed had now been completely extinguished. Perhaps pity rather than fury would have been appropriate, but as Galda's malevolent laugh echoed around him he knew pity would not save him from destruction.

"And who are you to decide what is right or wrong for the rest of our human brothers and sisters?" Galda propositioned. He slowly manoeuvred around the solitary Nothos, gauging his opponent's weakness with a predator's cunning. "You servants of the light are all the same, self-righteous fools! Before long humanity will be too relaxed to fear an inter-dimensional alliance."

"If you're referring to your little nest in Maryland, think again." Kristos followed his enemy's progress around him, channelling his precious energy into rejuvenating his invisible shield. Galda paused to glare into Kristos keen eyes.

"What is there of interest in Maryland to me?"

"By the time I finish this sentence my remaining brothers and sisters of the light will have infiltrated the sixth level of the abandoned air force fallout shelter and shut down your ace in the hole with a little fire in the hole, and all this," Kristos gestured to their secret world, "will cease to exist!" His nemesis's face showed the signs of panic he'd hoped for. "Our mutual friend, your prodigal son is with them right now. You know what he is capable of even if he doesn't, that's why you went to so much trouble to secure his favour. But by toying with me you have simply wasted what little chance you had of stopping him."

Galda's conviction suddenly terminated. The Principal span around to search the white faces of his swarming army, looking for a contradiction to the enemy's claim. Bar from their now solitary leader, Galda had assumed his competent cohorts had destroyed the Latronis militia completely, but to his shock their macabre features only returned a bemused child like panic that signified incompetence.

"You lose." Kristos announced.

"You lie!" he snarled back. His shadow body twitched as his rage consumed him.

"Didn't mommy tell you that the good guys always win?" Covertly retracting the invisible cocoon around him, Kristos thought of the friends he had lost. Monk had been with him from the start, the others like Luna, Maestro, Merlin and Cozmo he had only known a relative short amount of time, but their common cause had bonded them as kin, and now those kin were no more. With the knowledge he would see his extended family again; he hurled the deadly energy bolt at the unsuspecting traitor.

*****

Visual schematics of the Elite server's core programming flashed up on the console's screen, but the answers remained elusive. As Dex navigated his way through the technological labyrinth via the headset, window after window of unintelligible electronic language appeared, was analysed and disappeared at impossible speeds. Over his shoulder Jonah studied the screen with a similar impatient eye.

"There's got to be some way around its security ratings!" he stated, regaining Angelica's fleeting interest. The rookie was still sat in the mysterious seat as though relaxing at some health spa. His secluded outlook on the mysterious chamber continued to trouble their blonde leader, and her lack of interest in the primary objective worried Jonah. Dex's shortened tether didn't appreciate impatience.

"There's security protocol protecting security protocol over here. Back off!"

"Put it back in your pants boys," Angelica intervened. "We need to know what Kristos meant by switching off humanity. Any takers?"

"The viral code is the answer," Jonah replied. "When Dexter pulls is head out of his ass we'll have your answer." Dex swallowed the quip. As he finally contained the viral kernel its decipherment overruled his dented ego.

In a macabre unison, Saffy and Alpha made their own grim discovery. Her increasing curiosity had made light work of the frosted layer. As Alpha had helped to swipe away the remnants of the chilled crust from the surface of the black monolith, they had found it to be synthetic in composition, a crystalline poly resin. Thumping their hands against its onyx body now revealed it to be hollow. Without the icy coating, its faceplate also appeared partially translucent. Cupping her hands onto the highly polished surface, Saffy leant forward to peer in.

"Microwaves!" Dex suddenly blurted out. "The grid it's targeting is the global telecommunications network. Look." Jonah leaned forward and studied the unravelled codex on screen.

"You're right," he confirmed. "Its satellites, transmitters, cell phone networks, but why?" Dragged out of her stupor, Angelica watched Dex bring up a schematic map of the Earth's global telecommunications network.

"It's patched into all that? For what reason?" she asked impatiently.

"It looks like the server overrides local security policy and injects the virus, which in turn takes over the host's central processing unit." Dex's awe had converted into revulsion. "It then converts the host's primary applications into transmitting low frequency waves at a specified range on a global scale."

"Find the frequency range," Jonah instructed. As Dex locked down the desired information the global schematic was bombarded with an ominous red. Jonah stood back in obvious shock.

"What is it?" Angelica asked.

"They're going to lobotomise us." Angelica stared into Jonah's disturbed features and saw his monotone declaration was sincere.

"Explain."

"You see this," Jonah pointed to a wavering graphic signature that represented the altered signal in question. "It's a high density microwave that will encase the earth's atmosphere. The satellites in orbit at present can cover eighty percent of the globe's surface at one time, which means the ultra low frequency signal will blanket civilisation at the touch of a button." She saw the projection of the Elite's plans come to life on screen in horrendous simplicity. "Localised transmitters and cell networks will cover the short fall and complete the global prison. At that moment no human who isn't more than six feet underground will be exposed."

"Then what?" Angelica reluctantly asked. Her conscience cringed at the betrayal awaiting an unsuspecting mankind.

"Remember the happy vibes? When low frequency microwaves are directed at a human they're capable of influencing emotion. Anger, joy, suicidal depression, intolerable pain, even physical ailments can all be induced depending on the frequency. But at that range," he pointed once more at the sinister, wavering representation on screen, "a person's brain will turn to play-dough!"

"They want a race of mindless slaves," Dex predicted gloomily.

"How better to push a new world order spearheaded by the Deros?" Jonah added grimly.

Saffy's raised voice suddenly broke the spell of despondency.

"Get back, they're here!" Locking gazes with the startled Nothos, her colleague's comprehension was stunted by shock. "There's something inside!" she exclaimed and backed away from the black monolith. Needing confirmation, Alpha peered in through the semi translucent onyx front. Behind it he saw the face of the white skinned occupant. As he gazed on its deathly, androgynous features its slumbering eyelids flicked open.

"She's right!" Alpha yelled, reeling back. Urging Saffy aside with a defensive arm he realised they were far from alone in the underground chamber. An army of unknown sentinels had them surrounded. "Get back, they're waking up!" The malevolence of the black balled eyes that had met his melted the soldier's reserve, exaggerating his warning that was quickly verified as the monolith was illuminated from within. Behind the transparent façade the humanoid form became visible inside its protective hollow. Contagiously the adjacent black slab lit up. In turn it roused the next, initiating a domino effect that saw each of the black slabs illuminate its waking resident one by one in a blue neon light.

"I'm losing access to the system," Dex suddenly exclaimed. As the last roused monolith completed the ominous perimeter the source of the dark energy now made itself painfully clear. *Here the whole time!* Angelica stared around her at the motionless figures that had waited unseen in their onyx coffins. The slabs had indeed held a source of power, but not one she had envisaged. There naked humanoid forms stared inwards, resonating their brooding presence via cold, unfeeling black eyes. "They're taking over the hub!"

"Stop them," Angelica ordered, "Stop them now!" Next she called out to Josh. The rookie was still in the silver chair, the only Latronis outside the malevolent circle. But his distant eyes were closed, his face expressionless; Josh Brenin was oblivious to the danger. Next to her, Jonah's attention was drawn to the steel grills at his feet. The sentinel's arousal had activated the network of optic cabling beneath, linking the monoliths to the central hub. Quickly he realised their stealthy counterattack.

"Destroy it!" Jonah ordered Alpha, "You've got to break the circle!" Linked by some diabolical bond of biology and technology, the confined ghouls were locking the server down. A security force in their own right, they now threatened to dominate the incursion. Without hesitation Alpha raised his hand back, fashioned a bolt of light in his palm and then hurled the projectile into the first monolith.

In a destructive flash the energy bolt smashed the polished façade, shattering it instantly into a myriad of shards. A hellish scream followed the explosion. Its sanctuary breached, the exposed creature had wrenched open its toothless mouth and issued a hideous shriek that filled the chamber with a soul freezing resonance. As if breathing a toxic gas, its naked body then twisted and convulsed in its sarcophagus, its black soulless eyes sinking back into the shaking head before the death throes finally twisted its body free.

The living corpse fell out onto the mesh floor with hideous thud. Alpha urged Saffy aside and watched the morbid body twitch for a few seconds more, its pained screams now a diminishing wale as it finally expired and became still, seemingly dead.

"Now what the hell was that?" Saffy exclaimed unapologetically. The creature was apparently genderless, its white skin now turning into a putrid grey before them as it shrank around the metal interfaces implanted into the back of its head. Vaguely human its hairless body resembled no living creature they had seen before. Angelica walked across and kneeled over the cadaver to inspect the cybernetic ports that had once coupled the inhuman creature with its chamber.

"It's some kind of hybrid," she announced. She watched the skin continue to deteriorate rapidly before her eyes. "It's not human."

"Whatever it is, it's dead now," Alpha added coldly. He gave the cadaver a reassuring kick. He hadn't felt the pleasure of the kill in a long time, but looking at the rapidly decomposing body he was glad he hadn't lost his touch.

"I'm back in, everything's back on line!" Dex exclaimed as he regained control of the server's console. In all the excitement Jonah hadn't noticed his instruction had caused the desired effect. The optics below his feet were now lifeless once more; the kill had thwarted the sentinel's attempt to regain control.

"Can you destroy it?" Angelica stood up from the blackening remains of the creature. From a quick survey she saw the other monoliths were now also drained of light, and hopefully a collective, dependant life.

"Does a bear crap in the woods?" Dex boasted casually.

"Then do it." The fact the Elite's diabolical plan included the manufacture of such unholy creatures only made it imperative they acted quickly. While Saffy and Angelica witnessed the final deterioration of the creature's remains into the cold mesh floor Jonah and Dex made good the boast.

"Why would they create such, things?" Saffy asked, disconcerted at the results of her curiosity.

"Nothing is sacred in the eyes of the Elite," Angelica declared hollowly. "Humankind, morality, life, these are things to be exploited for their, great work. We did it a favour."

"What about the rest?" Alpha enquired as he glared for any recurring signs of life from the other monoliths. His instinct told him to despatch their occupants in the same callous manner, though was reluctant to act without authorisation. Angelica darted one last glance around.

"If they give the slightest hint of waking up, put them back to sleep," she instructed coldly.

"They won't be the only ones, look." Alpha directed their gaze back to the alcove and the evidence time was running short; the solitary Ka in the silver seat had begun to fade.

Before reclining into the mysterious chair Josh had found himself entranced by a higher impulse. Instinctively he had followed its pretext of enlightenment, allowing it to stimulate the petition that urged him onto a separate path from his dreamscape colleagues. Latronis had been the means by which he had been brought to this place, and he had accepted the hand of fate with a willing clasp.

His human eyes were closed, but his vision remained intact. A new disembodied voyeurism tied him into every sight, sound and feeling, an omnipotent extension of his projecting Ka empowered by the Elite technology in which he resided. The chair was some form of astral amplification device. Its mysterious gravity defying frame was artificially attuning to its occupant's unique vibrational frequency, like attracting like before amalgamating the two to create a super-conscious state that excelled the heightened existence of any other projecting Nothos. The voluble screams of the not so far away hybrid had been comprehensible, but were now only one tiny part of the vast universe at his fingertips. He had sensed Angelica's growing concern, Alpha's militant strength, Saffy's tenacious spirit and Jonah and Dex's frustrated attempts to terminate the Elite's global plans. All currently played out before his eyes, all accessible, but irrelevant in the grand scale of his own personal fate.

The dark energy that had led them to the sealed chamber suddenly pulsed alive again. *Something's coming.* A sense of danger crept over his ever-disintegrating perception of the immediate world. Josh tried to revive his failing conscious, but was unable to free himself of the deepening trance that was assimilating his projection into another plain. *I can't stop this.* Like falling into some deep sleep the real world and his friends was being stolen from him. On the fringes of an ultra-dimensional existence he sensed Angelica's fear ignite from the real world, urging her to rush to his aid and prevent his projection from waning any further. *This has to be.* But through the clouded veil of some netherworld perception he envisioned her thwarted by the dark energy that now surged in front of her. *Angelica watch out!*

The golden eyes of the dark humanoid spectre flashed vengefully from the featureless face barricading her way. Its vaporous form was comprised of a dense swirl of black gas that appeared to surge with a blackened rage. Without warning it struck out with a swipe of its elongated arm, the blow flying safely past Angelica's head as she ducked the attack with feline agility.

"They're waking up!" Saffy warned wildly. A new enemy had surged from the black monoliths to confront the intruders. Angelica had heard Kristos talk of such creatures, but had hoped never to confront one. The first malevolent projection swiped once more, forcing her to counter attack with a high roundhouse kick. To her shock it merely passed through its vaporous body. Correcting her balance from the failed strike, she saw Alpha's Ka flying backwards. A powerful blow from another dark projection had struck him full in the chest, sending his bulky form to unceremoniously crash into the opposite wall of the chamber. Realising her attacker was one of many; Saffy's question of 'why' had been answered.

The Elite's creation of genetic hybrids was more abominable than first assumed. More than grotesque products of bio-tech insanity, they were earthly hosts for the inter-dimensional Deros. Forced to protect their sanctuary and their hold on the world of man, there numbers now equalled that of the monolithic chambers from which they'd projected. *Thirteen Deros against six Latronis.* Angelica looked to Josh again for help. To her horror the silver throne was empty. It was thirteen against five. Time had just run out.

*****

Kristos had hurled the light bolt without fear of consequence. Galda Vey, the Principal of the treacherous cabal, had been its target, but the desperate act had been in haste. As planned the cunning strike had collided in a destructive flash of benign energy with the black clad projection, causing it to howl in agony as its malicious form was obliterated. But as its life was extinguished in the void, the target's infuriated black-balled eyes glared back from amongst the swarm, of which there was now one less.

With lightening reaction Galda had dragged the unfortunate minion into the path of the strike, an involuntarily sacrifice of life for its superior. Galda's retaliation was equally as swift. Realising the servant of the light no longer hid behind the impenetrable cocoon, he released his pent up fury by launching himself at Kristos. The collision thrust the Latronis leader soaring backward into the waiting mob. But ready to embrace the conflict Kristos countermanded with an equally maddened effort. In a clash of titans the two opposing projections quickly became a blurred, frantic haze of striking limbs as each attempted to bludgeon the other into a weakened state. Such close combat negated any successful use of energy projectiles. But in the ensuing brawl of light and dark, bolts of destructive light erupted from the palms of both combatants, discharged without focus as a result of the intensity of the unparalleled rivalry, shooting wildly outwards like sparks emitted by the collision of two heated and opposed elements.

The horde of Elite projections watched from a distance, daring not intervene. In their golden eyes their master was the ultimate Nothos in creation. His elimination of the insolent, weakened intruder was inevitable. And so they swarmed around the brawling Nothoi, containing the combatants like a dark sea rising in a tide of contempt.

Fighting the minions had been easy in comparison. The Elite shadow bodies had been compromised to the point of destruction by each and every strike, but in the case of their Principal, his unsullied shadow body soaked them up like a brick wall. The Latronis leader was forced to block and punch in equal measure, berserker fighting berserker as each powerful strike and counter strike contributed to weaken his opponent. But likewise the relentless attack of the snarling ghoul was taking its toll, sapping his vital energy as dark neutralised light in an inevitable battle to the death.

Galda had hoped to find his white clad opponent sufficiently weakened. He had wanted an easy but glorious removal of the final obstacle to eternal glory, but now he decided to focus the dark energy at his disposal into coercing his adversary towards a much crueller fate. Unleashing a barrage of lightening fast strikes into Kristos's unprotected torso, he sent the servant of the light soaring backwards towards it. The white Nothos retaliated by hurling another light bolt at Galda, but finding its target induced nothing more than a malevolent sneer. Bracing for a counter-attack, Kristos found his assailant now kept his distance.

"Had enough?" he hollered defiantly. The swarm of Elite projections manoeuvred to a respectful proximity behind their hovering master, their white faces ogling the remaining servant of the light as their collective presence blackened the astral world around him. "What are you waiting for? Come and get me you bastard!" The longer he held them in the Leviscape, the more time he bought Angelica and Josh. But by the time Kristos recognised their Principal's sneer was in truth a grin of elation, it was too late. Galda Vey's back up plan had surged up behind the white Nothos to destroy him.

At first Kristos thought the assault had come from a rearguard of Elite projections, an attempt to overpower him and aid their Principal's final strike. But the black limbs now grasping at his Ka were too formidable to be those of meagre agents. As they hauled him backwards like a landed catch the neon blue of the astral void began to disappear from around him. Powerless to shake the fanatical clutches dragging him to some uncertain fate, he turned to face his captors, only to see the reason for Galda's caution.

The gold, venomous eyes glowered back from the featureless black faces of the three attackers. As they heaved him further back into the vortex with howls of devilish delight, he realised he was now a captive of those that deserved fear. Too weakened to break free of the powerful spectres he could do nothing to prevent the spiralling barrel of the celestial tunnel from consuming him. At its degenerating entrance he saw his jeering nemesis turn away from the doomed Nothos, taking his legion of Ascended Elite soldiers to bring war to the remaining brothers and sisters of the light. By proxy of his secret masters, Galda Vey had secured his victory. *Not like this.*

A thrash of his constricted limbs suddenly released Kristos from the malicious embrace. Correcting himself in the black void into which he'd been abducted, his assailants shrieked and snarled before regrouping to create an aggressive boundary around him. A quick glance to the way he'd come found the portal entrance intact, but as his captors manoeuvred to prevent his escape, the light walker saw his greatest fear become grim reality. Through its decaying cylindrical walls he had been transported to the lowest plains of the universe, the abyss of myth. But as its entrance suddenly collapsed and vanished into the nothingness into which he'd been brought, it swallowed the neon blue light of the Leviscape, and any chance of freedom along with it. Kristos was now trapped.

Excited by their prize the Deros spectres began to circle him, delighting in his alarm, for no creature of the light ventured to the lower vibrational plains intentionally and for good reason. The abyss was forsaken by creation and all that was divine, nothing more than a breeding ground for malevolent entities such as the Deros. Suspended in the infinite blackness that comprised it, its malicious natives now studied him with the relish of starved wolves gazing upon a stray lamb.

The circling pairs of dull golden eyes peered out eerily from the darkness. Unintelligible voices snarled and hissed their demonic chatter as they toyed with their prey. In their world the servant of light was a fish out of water. Like a lighthouse in an endless black night his weakened Ka now projected a luminous aura, enabling him to see beyond the immediate threat and to the hundreds of the soulless eyes now emerging from the sea of darkness with a hatred of all things benign. Like moths to a flame they came in their droves, drawn by the unanticipated chance of an easy kill. The invisible shield he could manifest at will could only stave off the inevitable; the abyss offered nothing but death for creatures of the light. With nothing but honour to uphold, he cast the first strike.

The first bolt of light caused a malicious black creature to shriek in agony. Its fiendish companions reeled away from the blinding flash it produced, but only to regroup once more and seize upon Kristos with the brutal ferocity of rabid beasts seeking to rip him limb from limb. In a desperate defence he sent his blazing fist into the black forms, keeping them at bay with a sheer will to survive, but each thwarted spectre was quickly replaced by another snarling set of golden eyes that sent its swiping claws to ravage his Ka of its lingering power. As he thrashed his limbs out in a futile whirlwind assault they continued to hit their mark though failed to diminish the attack. The Deros were overwhelming him, their sheer numbers drowning him in never ending waves of hatred. He couldn't last much longer, certain death was seconds away, but then in the distance he saw a light.

Over the rabid legion of Deros vying for a piece of Kristos the approaching radiance appeared like a guiding star, but instead of the tunnel of eternal light coming to claim him he sensed a more mundane deliverance.

The newcomer had found himself transported to the black world via the medium of his newfound supremacy over existence. His Ka had been projected from one point in time and inter-dimensional space to another. At first he had not realised why. Something had called him from the silver throne in the enemy's secret layer where his friends currently fought for their lives, his conscious seemingly abandoning them to answer some higher power he couldn't comprehend. In the black plain of the abyss Josh saw the horde of fiendish spectres swarming around the being of light. It was fighting them off with the desperate fervour of a cornered lion, but its attackers were quickly overpowering its waning aura.

"Get out of here!" The instruction boomed across the void, eerily calm and benevolent. At first he didn't recognise it, but quickly registered its source. "Get back to the others," it instructed peacefully, the tranquil tone at odds with the thrashing source fighting for its life in the far distance. "Find your way back, the Elite must be stopped."

"Kristos!" Josh found himself calling across the void. On the fringes of the attacking horde several snarling forms suddenly turned their golden eyes to its origin.

"Go back! return to the others," Kristos urged as his failing Ka was now almost smothered completely. A contingent of the Deros horde now left the fray to surge towards the brave but imprudent newcomer. "Forget about me!" the Latronis leader continued, his benign voice faltering, "The others need you, stop Galda Vey!" Josh watched on aghast as the remnant of Kristos's aura was then snuffed out by the swarm of manic creatures. "Go back! this is how it must be." The final instruction resonated across the black sea just as his light was extinguished. The enigmatic Kristos had finally succumbed, Josh too late to intervene.

"No!" The breakaway contingent surged towards Josh's Ka with continued relish, their golden eyes piercing the darkness as their fevered shrieks echoed before them. And then a sun exploded.

The blinding flash from behind halted the Deros attack. As if a nuclear payload had detonated in deep space an immense ball of molten light now suddenly flooded the abyss, scattering the horde around it like shrapnel from an exploding canister. The immense explosion seared the darkness and all in its path, scattering the Deros and causing Josh to turn away as the blinding shockwave enveloped him along with the horde. Kristos was gone, his final words now finding meaning in Josh's stunned mind. *Even the darkest night cannot extinguish a single flame.*

*****

The gaseous fiends shrieked in agony. Though outnumbering the intruders the collective agony now stunted their attack of the Latronis militia. The blood curdling sounded pierced chamber and souls alike. Not caring for an explanation, Angelica hurled a bolt of light into her assailant. The impact sent the distracted Deros projection reeling backwards into its monolith, its flaying form disappearing through the onyx front of its sarcophagus and back into its hybrid body of ghoulish flesh. It hadn't taken long before Angelica and the others realised the only way to fight fire was with fire. Simple punching and kicking had only resulted in ineffective swipes through thin air, the vaporous assailants seemingly comprised of some primal dark energy that could only succumb to the power of destructive astral light.

The sudden collective howls of distress signified some undetected cataclysm had befallen them, but after their gaseous forms momentarily warped and faltered, the relent in their defence of the chamber was short lived. Alpha had used the deafening reprieve to dispatch an attacker with a light bolt directly to its dark torso and was rewarded with the satisfactory dissolution of the target in the impressive explosion of light. But the expulsion of the lethal projectile had left him drained. Taking all of his furious strength to project it, he suddenly feared the three remaining Deros edging back towards him might not so easily be dispatched back to hell. Again their elongated claws swiped at his Ka. This time they passed through his projection, the intrusions draining the life force from within as their dark energy polluted and negated his own. Arching away evasively, he saw Saffy leap above her attacker's heads in an attempt to dodge their vicious strikes. Grasping one of the ceiling's support struts to check her descent, she then rained several light bolts down into their snarling faces. From her lofty sanctuary she caught sight of the soldier's plight. Not liking the odds she descended on two of his attackers, her hands blazing with the destructive light that ripped into their torsos like a molten knife through butter. Before her feet touched the mesh floor her two victims had reeled back howling. The third backed off as she swiped for its face.

"Whatever happened to the brave knight saving the damsel in distress?" she asked a disbelieving Alpha.

"Show me a damsel and I'll save it!" he retorted before pulling her towards him. "Look out." His attackers had quickly regrouped to surround the two Nothoi; the soldier's lightening reaction saving his rescuer from a deadly swipe to her back. "See what I mean?"

"Alpha keep them busy!" Dex's strained voice suddenly instructed over the ensuing brawl. The assailants who'd been hounding his and Jonah's attempts on the server console had left to avenge their dispatched cohorts. Drawn to rebuking the male female duo, it gave him and Jonah the break they needed to continue sabotaging the Covenant agenda.

"Finish it now, I'll cover you," Jonah stated. Swapping hacking for defence, he urged Dex back to the console. Behind the central pillar Angelica was struggling to keep her own assailants at bay, though a powerful Nothos, the Deros proved to be formidable and unrelenting enemies. Her rabid hurling of light bolts into the manic spectres kept their thrashing claws at bay, but the juggling act was slowly draining her of the vital strength she needed to remain in the chamber. Behind her the silver chair remained empty. An extra servant of the light in their ranks could have made all the difference, so as she was forced back into the alcove and away from her comrades, she cursed Josh's desertion.

"Dex you gotta destroy it now!" Her command surged above the snarls of her Deros attackers. Behind them she could see Jonah was fending off two more of their devilish cohorts. Cornered and unable to reach them she prayed his fervent defence was enough to secure the window they needed to destroy the malicious technology, before it fulfilled its treacherous destiny. "Dex!"

"I need more time!" Dex's panicking reply filtered across the chamber, freezing Angelica's hope. The window opened and shut with equal promptness as a renewed attack forced him to abandon the interface and defend his exposed Ka once more. But the persistent attack proved Jonah was a man of his word. Ducking as a black claw lunged for his head, he raised his arm to block another and projected a mighty light bolt that send both their assailants reeling back towards their onyx sarcophagi.

"There is no time, it's now or never!" he shouted. Using his shadow body as a human shield, Jonah cornered Dex back behind him, protecting both colleague and console. Thankful for Jonah's power, Dex channelled his own waning energy into maintaining a protective cocoon while he worked his own devilry. His strategy was simple. Masquerading as a diagnostic tool he would activate his own malicious programming within the server core, leaving it free to check and erase the virus without alerting its security policy. He pressed *Enter* and prayed, but immediately something went wrong. Within seconds the diagnostic was cancelled. A desperate effort to reactivate was frustrated again and again. After the fourth attempt to eradicate the malware failed with an ominous *Access Denied* on screen, he realised the reanimated optics below their feet were to blame.

"They're overriding me!" Dex yelled, "They're still tapped into the system. As soon as I bypass one protocol another takes its place. I can't reach the virus!" The gloomy update was suddenly confirmed as the schematic showed the malevolent software being released into the global network like a toxin into a defenceless bloodstream. "Oh my God, It's out!"

"Have you done it?" Jonah exclaimed. Mishearing he forced his attackers to step back with the desperate creation of a blinding ball of light.

"They've released the virus; it's too late!" The attack had merely been a ruse to distract the intruders. Though the Deros had appeared to be focused on their vicious defence, they had also remained omnipotent in their control of the central hub. As the two Nothoi looked at the display, the free flowing progress of the malware into the schematic of the world's global telecommunications grid signified they were watching the beginning of the end. "We're too late," he admitted.

A blow to Dex's head abruptly sent him spinning away to crash into a black monolith. The melancholy realisation had weakened his invisible shield, the painful blow the consequence of his neglect. Seeing the breach in Jonah's defence a Deros spectre broke past to lash out at the fallen Latronis soldier, knocking Jonah aside in the mix. Dazed but determined, Dex jumped to his feet and faced his snarling opponent. He was down but was far from out. Across the chamber Alpha was flourishing with a rejuvenated battle high. Swinging a terrific blow at another Deros he sent it soaring across the secret chamber it called home. As its infuriated gaseous form faltered from vapour to humanoid over and over he caught sight of its cohort strangling a toppled Jonah. Realising the Elite agenda was unravelling to fruition unhindered; he grasped another by the throat and slam-dunked it back into its monolithic cell. With a subsequent rush attack that would level a defensive wall of NFL stars, he thrust his fiery palm deep into the gaseous body lurching over his toppled comrade. With a hellish shriek and a flash of light the spectre dissolved and died.

"Why the hell haven't you stopped this thing?" Alpha shouted at Jonah. The flashing bombardment and snarls from behind the central pillar denoted their leader still fought and lived.

"It's too late, they've released the virus," he replied painfully. Jonah had taken one too many direct strikes and was paying the price. The words *it's over* were on the end of his tongue, but the soldier was unrelenting.

"Get your ass on that console soldier!" he ordered, before being forced to defend against a surprise attack. As the soldier's animated projection began another relentless pounding of the raging Deros, Jonah crawled back to the server interface. To his left Dex fought his own relentless battle against two more of the black spectres. His friend's dazzling display of martial prowess was keeping the fiends at bay, but also far away from help.

"Jonah hurry!" Saffy's directive concentrated the grim reality. *It's up to me.* With the headset gone he tapped desperate commands onto the keyboard and took his turn to begin the weary assessment of the schematics. The entire global network had been infected. It was now host to a devious malware that was clawing its way past firewalls and security protocols to mutate benign technology into broadcasting the debilitating barrage of low frequency microwaves upon an unsuspecting world. It was too late to stop it, but an option remained. From the schematic relays he saw the numerous satellites circling the earth were being hijacked one by one, their pre ordained orbits now slowly realigning to fit into the Elite's grand design. Control centres around the world were no doubt in uproar as they realised they had no control over the spiralling catastrophe and the increasing volume of detrimental waves produced by their own space age technology. Now instruments for further deploying the self-perpetuating virus, the satellites were now the linchpins on which the global coordination began to take root.

More detailed analysis revealed infected domestic communication grids were now relaying the malicious signal within their media broadcasts. The virus had hijacked cell phone pylons and domestic radios, further releasing the debilitating signal until the prison wall began to gradually envelope the entire globe, increasing in potency with every passing second.

A Deros's hellish scream shook Jonah from the shock induced daydream as Saffy sent it back into the abyss from which it came. The viral progression was unprecedented. Quickly he changed his attention to the crux of the invasion. As the complex viral DNA of computer language scrolled across the screen he stumbled upon a dent in its armour. *That's it.* But before he could act on the revelation the pair of hideous golden eyes reflecting in the screen's surface froze his soul.

The intensity of the pain in his back made him fall to his knees. The sucker punch had done more than just stun. Reaching the core of his Ka it had damaged his sacred heart, the inner sun that gave every Nothos its power. There had been no time to prevent the black claw from gouging its way through his exposed projection, and now as he looked up helplessly from the foot of the pillar where he'd fallen he saw the attacker raise its arm to strike again. Staring vacantly into the malevolent golden slits Jonah heard the battle rage on around him. His plight unseen by his comrades, he realised that Alpha, Angelica or Dex could not save him from what was to be. As the Deros swung the claw down to deliver the coup-de-grace a flash of intense light forced him to close his eyes. But as a hellish shriek dispersed into eternity he opened them to find the Deros had been replaced by a white clad saviour.

"You heard him," the novice said. "Get your ass on that console and stop this thing!" As he aided a stunned Jonah to his feet he surveyed the battlefield to which he'd returned. The hand of fate had caused him to desert his comrades, but he had returned a seasoned Nothos and was ready to redeem himself. He just prayed he was not too late.

Chapter 16

The temperate breeze was a welcome respite to the baking heat of the Nevada desert. Wasting away his days on top of the water tower that overlooked the neglected shanty settlement of White Rock was not the sentinel's idea of fulfilling a life's dream, but at least he got to work on his tan, unlike the rest of Latronis who hid themselves away beneath him like veritable gophers. The arid landscape had been particularly afflicted by the sun's ferocity that day, which was why the sudden lapse in the breeze roused him from his slumber. Flicking his Stetson peak up out of his face, he grabbed the hot metal barrel of the scoped assault rifle propped at his side. Raising its stock hard into his shoulder, he rose from the old chair perched at the base of the immense water tank and scoured the weather beaten settlement below.

The high powered scope mounted on the Heckler & Koch G3 made it a formidable weapon, which combined with his elevated position, meant any intruder could easily be tracked and, if necessary, terminated with a single shot. As he swung the telescopic sights over the abandoned surroundings he saw nothing out of the ordinary, except for a tumbleweed that had rolled its way into the compound and now lay motionless at its abandoned centre. A bead of sweat ran into the corner of his eye making it sting. He pawed his brow with the back of his hand then returned his gaze to the scope's magnified viewpoint. Something then caught his attention.

As the crosshairs passed over the makeshift garage that housed the RV, the guard thought he saw a dark figure back out of sight. Returning them to the same building corner he saw nothing but the same sun-baked dirt, until it stepped back into shot. *Madre Mia.* His instinct told him the trespasser was not alone. Swinging the rifle from building to building he found he was right. The next, dressed identically to the first in the non-descript black clothes, stood casually in a porch which moments before had been empty. Another stood on top of a nearby roof, while another came into view in front of the old bar. Through the sunglasses perched upon their pale faces the trespassers reciprocated the insolent scrutiny. *They're here!* In blatant disregard for the weapon trained upon them the ghoulish trespassers then walked into the open. The Elite were everywhere.

"Didn't Mommy tell you it was rude to point?" The frosty question came from behind. The guard swung the rifle to meet the trespasser, but before he knew its scope was struck backwards with such force it buried itself deep into his eye socket, killing him instantly. The cold blooded action didn't faze Galda Vey. Callously he kicked the heavy corpse so that it fell from its lofty perch onto the desert floor several storeys below. As it landed with a heavy crumpled thump he leapt off the tower to soar like a hawk into the old bar below, its tired saloon doors braking off their rusted hinges as the army of Elite invaders now surged into its airy interior.

The dilapidated building complained in a chorus of creaking wood as the intrusive force filled it with their volatile presence. The insight into the location of the Latronis headquarters had been relayed from the depth of the woman's terrified mind. The prolonged, intimate bond of the Brenin Nothos and his lover had created a quantum connection, a connection that had led the Principal fresh from his victory in the Leviscape, across dimensional barriers and to the deserted compound back in the real world. Without knowing, his reluctant apprentice had served a much greater use. Though lost to the light, the astral signature of his Ka had been traced via an alternative path back to its mortal body, which Galda knew would reside amongst the slumbering enemy. Now as he and his legion of ghouls flooded the forsaken wooden building, he sensed the attuned signature emanating from its walls had gotten stronger.

"It's here! Find it!" He snarled the order to his swarming black horde, his anticipation and fury combining into a zealous euphoria. The remaining Latronis were somewhere close by; he could sense them now, further enthusing his rage. Though their Kas were projecting across time and space to thwart the covenant agenda in the secret Maryland base, their mortal bodies slumbered helplessly somewhere beneath the ground at his feet. Instead of heading off the threat across the country, he had decided to root it out at its source. By destroying the light walkers mortal shells he would condemn their Kas to oblivion, leaving nothing to stand in his way.

While Galda mused about how his Washington superiors were welcome to the clumsy world of man, the Elite projections now clawed away at the saloon's walls and floor in an orgy of systematic destruction, prising petrified wood from rusted nails to expose the building's infrastructure. He could taste immortality now, and cared for nothing else.

A sudden howl of excitement came from behind the disused bar. Eagerly he surged over through the spectral swarm to find his rival Kladar crouched on the dusty wooden floor. Ushering the subordinate aside, he gazed upon the flashing security interface exposed in the cavity at their feet. With superhuman strength he ripped the final floorboards aside to reveal the silver panel it protected. They had found the gateway to victory. Now the end could begin.

*****

The hellish assailant shrieked and died pitifully before her eyes. One second the snarling Deros had been swiping its clawed hands at her face, seeking to further neutralise her sacred heart as it faltered like a flame starved of oxygen, the next it had vanished into oblivion, its wide golden eyes revealing the depth of its agony before death claimed its unholy essence forever. Suddenly she was pleased to see the deserter had returned, a simple nod signifying her thanks for his timely help.

"I'm back," Josh announced, somewhat obviously.

"So I see," Angelica retorted. "Now help us stop this thing!" Somehow he'd changed. His eyes now sparkled with a new intensity. As if the excursion into the unknown had ignited some hidden power, his Ka now resonated with some new ethereal potency, a potency that reminded her of someone else, someone close to them all. But time had joined the enemy; the marvel would have to wait. Unlocking gazes she leapt from the alcove back into the fray. *She doesn't know.*

Unknown to his blonde lieutenant the death of Kristos had fashioned new life. Rather than allow the enemy to ravenously feed off his power, he had consolidated and released it to destroy them. As the shockwave of blinding light had destroyed the black minions in its path it had also infused Josh with its rejuvenating radiation, both blinding and empowering him as it conducted from Tekton to Nothos. One brilliant life had been sacrificed so that millions could still be saved. *They need you.* From a distance Josh had watched the eye of the explosion drown into an ember, before being swallowed entirely by the black nothing of the void. Kristos was gone but not dead. Energy could not be destroyed, only passed from one form to the next.

With a single thought Josh had found himself transported back to the underground chamber and the mysterious chair. A new found power was surging through his Ka, energising him with a newfound invincibility that made him feel more alive than ever before. With a forward movement and a focus of strength Josh dispatched a would-be killer wrestling with Jonah. Channelling another burst of destructive light, its deafening screams filled the chamber as the projectile impacted with the vile spectre. But the assault attracted unwanted attention. Like rabid dogs two infuriated Deros forms now turned and pounced onto him. In the surprise attack he struggled to shake them free. As vicious claws and shrieks of murderous glee threatened to tear their way through his soul he flayed his arms desperately about him, only to find they passed uselessly through the dark, vaporous bodies of the Deros clinging to them.

"Use the light!" Angelica's voice called over the mayhem, reminding him to focus. "It's the only way to stop them." She, Dex and

Saffy had joined forces to take on an equal number of Deros. Though several had been killed the remaining defenders remained arduous. The desperate Nothoi tried to shake the fanatical spectres that hindered them from reaching Alpha who, pinned against a black monolith, was now being strangled by one of the creatures.

"Keep them off me, I've almost got it!" Jonah yelled as he remained just out of reach at the server console. Fervently Dex stood in the path of the Deros clawing for Jonah's back. By unleashing a desperate onslaught that kept it inches away from Jonah he sought to destroy its earthly existence. But his energy was failing. The Deros was a formidable creature empowered by its own fury, black emotion fuelling black energy and Dex's projection was fading as the Deros's spiralling power negated his own.

Josh sealed himself in a shield of light, causing his attackers to snarl and retreat. An attempt to pierce the luminous cocoon by one of the infuriated Deros resulted in more shrieks of agony, again forcing it into retreat. *It's the only way to stop them.* Angelica's instruction then detonated in his mind. Suddenly everything became clear. Though he couldn't physically see the Elite's plan unfolding on the computer screen, he sensed its progress through an omnipotent vision implanted in his mind's eye, his higher conscious all seeing and all knowing, alerting him to the imminent doom as Jonah made it back to the server and frantically input the killer commands via its keyboard. Josh closed his eyes and channelled the new found power. As the cocoon's walls thickened around him the snarling apparitions were blocked from view, the perpetual energy rising from within to surge from his out faced palms. *Use the light.*

"Dex!" Jonah called out somewhere in the distance. His friend had been knocked to the ground and was fighting off the Deros he'd diverted from Jonah. Sensing a quick kill another spectre joined it to finish off the vulnerable Nothos. Inside his mind Josh could see his comrades fighting for their lives, but he couldn't abandon his task in their aid. Kristos had destroyed himself to show him the way. He had to succeed for all their sake. Reluctantly he continued to focus.

"Jonah, nooo!" Angelica's voice screamed over the spiralling brawl. Unable to watch his friend be destroyed he had deserted the console to thrust a desperate bolt of light into the back of Dex's attackers. A creature screamed and was destroyed in an impressive flash of light, but exhausted by the potent expulsion Jonah fell back to his knees. He had risked the lives of millions to save his friend. But staring dejectedly at the cold mesh flooring where Dex had fallen, his friend's Ka was nowhere to be seen. The desperate act had been in vain. His friend was dead.

"Jonah get back to the console!" Angelica's instruction flew over the crumpled Jonah, his anger drowned by wretchedness as he saw Dex's killer turn to finish him. Trapped against a black monolith Angelica could only watch on helplessly as the second gaseous Deros pounced onto a weak Jonah. As its grasping claws sought his throat he buckled beneath it. He was too late, it was all too late. Angelica gave out a desperate strike into the face of the Deros snarling to her right, causing the creature to shriek in agony, but remain intact. It was a forlorn release of despair and she knew it. They couldn't stop the viral codex from completing its agenda, but she would be damned before letting herself meet with the same tragic end. Her spirit broken by the realisation of failure, she accepted the Elite's global treachery was now unstoppable. All that was left was to survive.

Another dying shriek filled the chamber. Instantly she feared it was Jonah's. From behind the central pillar a brilliant light was now flooding the icy interior, threatening to sear them all in an all-consuming inferno, though Angelica quickly realised the dying howl had belonged to the enemy. She saw Jonah was pinned against the precious server console, still fighting for his life as the mystery light continued its rapid expanse, growing in intensity like a birthing sun. In the distance she saw two Deros backing away from the dreaded sight. Josh it seemed had deserted his comrades once more, but this time so he could save them.

The energy within the rookie seemed boundless. His out faced palms were channelling the perpetuating sphere of bright light that gushed from within to cocoon its source from sight with a blinding, burning luminosity. As the blazing sphere spread ever outward throughout the cold chamber it forced the Deros creatures to reel further away, its essence scolding and lethal to their touch, it seared their golden eyes and forced them to cower pathetically. All eyes, golden and human were focused on it now. One fanatic Deros threw itself forward in a desperate attempt to kill its creator, but on contact its black form was instantly obliterated. Still the astral sun grew, its blazing energy threatening to consume the entire chamber. From within it, Josh could now sense the enemy's fury had been replaced by fear. Dex's death echoed in his soul. He could sense Kristos was with him, his essence now combined with his in a symbiotic duality that fed the sacred heart of his power. But around him the sphere began to destabilise. The concentration of astral light had reached its threshold. The levee of Josh's mind could no longer contain the torrent it had unleashed. Like gas expanding a balloon he felt it about to burst. As the exertion threatened to tear his Ka apart, Josh let go.

The detonating sphere propelled a shockwave throughout the chamber. For the Deros there was no time to scream, nowhere to hide. Its payload was instant and deadly, the blinding discharge filling every inch of darkness to cleanse the sanctuary of its malevolent residents in one decisive strike of pure ethereal light. Caught in its wake, each of the secret masters was sent back to hell in an instant of agony, their screams in unison as they echoed into oblivion.

Josh fell to his knees on the cold mesh floor. With his energy spent he dared not to open his eyes. The ecstatic sensation of the final release had left him stunned with a euphoric miasma of relief and fatigue. He could sense the surviving Latronis were staring at him, their own stunned eyes quickly returning their sight. *I did it.* Within the blink of a blinded eye the rookie had destroyed every last one of them. Feeling a reassuring hand touch his shoulder, he turned to see none was there.

"What did you do?" Saffy asked. As she walked over she saw Josh's features reflected his own incredulity.

"It was Kristos," he explained enigmatically. Clambering back onto his feet he stared at his hands. They still tingled with the remnants of the immense energy.

"Did it work?" Jonah asked weakly from where he still lay on the floor. His Ka had been badly compromised, but still he lived, the astral payload going somewhere to reenergizing him. At first the question had seemed obvious, but the finger he pointed towards the console screen meant he referred to some unknown handiwork of his own. "The viral code itself was unprotected, so I fought fire with fire," Jonah explained as Angelica helped him up from the floor. Too weak to stand on his own, she supported his eager movements back to the server's screen. "The Deros must have thought they'd won," he continued weakly. "At the last moment they diverted all their attention way from the server, letting me get a clear shot." He stared at the screen only to have hope turn to dismay. The red prison of debilitating microwaves remained global and intact.

*****

The entrance to the secret layer at White rock had been fortified with an energy shield that prevented the blackened Elite projections from entering. Several of Galda's minions had sacrificed themselves for their Principal's piece of mind, their dark forms unable to breach the quantum entanglement shield designed to keep out projecting intruders from breaching the now gaping silver shaft entrance at their feet. He had not anticipated such tactics and snarled irritably as their shrieks of agony confirmed its existence for a third time. The astral defence system was an impervious barrier of super high frequency waves passable only by a Ka encased in its host's flesh. The ambitious Kladar then derided his superior's attack plan with an underhand comment that made an uncomfortable bedfellow with the Principal's pride. Galda stared down the black mouth of the exposed chute that stood between him and his great destiny. For once his subordinate was right.

The one thing he needed to pass through the protective shield slumbered hundreds of miles away in the Elite stronghold. But then the dilemma it posed struck home. The projected Latronis obviously planned to return their own Kas to their slumbering bodies below. This meant that on their return the shield had to be deactivated by an insider or by a non-projecting accomplice on the outside, most likely the sentinel he had just dispatched. The realisation suddenly implanted an unorthodox solution into the Principal's devious mind.

"Bring me the guard," he snarled. The order produced shrills of excitement from the swarm of black projections writhing about the dusty saloon. Two Elite soldiers soared outside to collect the corpse. Galda sneered back at Kladar, who edged obediently away as the lifeless body was brought forward and held upright in front of their leader like some gruesome trophy of war. He had only performed such a rite once before and with mixed results. The blending of a foreign Ka into a living body required the skills of a powerful Nothos, but to attempt it on the recently deceased was considered a dangerous abomination. The very insinuation of the profane act was enough to incite a silence from the horde of onlookers. Kladar kept a respectful distance, however quietly hoping a potential disaster would result in an immediate promotion. Galda was aware of the obstacle he faced, but dismissed the fears as weakness.

He ripped the displaced scope from the guard's eye socket, the grisly act releasing a torrent of fresh blood onto the parched floorboards. Making the realisation he would have only one eye to see with, he wished he had treated the specimen with more care. The popped right arm protruded forward grotesquely from its shoulder socket while the twisted forearm hung at an unnatural angle from the broken elbow. The fall had no doubt created multiple internal injuries that would hamper his progress, but the mangled corpse was all he had. He would only be able to retain its services for a short time, but guessed it would be enough. Galda surged forward and disappeared into the meat puppet.

The human suit he now wore was physically cumbersome, a literal dead weight of reanimated flesh, though the agony created by the injuries as he took control of its tormented senses only made him more determined to shuffle its heavy feet forward to the shaft entrance. The blood continued to pour out of the gaping tunnel that had been the guard's eye socket. The agony was intolerable. Galda felt his hold of the corpse beginning to falter, but with a few burdensome steps he sent it plummeting into the dark tunnel. As the guard's lopsided head abruptly disappeared below ground Kladar and the Elite horde closed in around the opening and listened. They sensed their Principal's swift plunge into the lion's den would be the dramatic break they had been hoping for. In the following seconds of silence their anticipation grew to fever pitch. A minute of silence followed, before their master's snarl bayed for them to follow.

Echoing from the bowels of the earth it funnelled up into the dusty saloon from the tunnel's mouth. The ruse had worked. The rest of the Elite projections swarmed into the breach to join Galda in the depths of the enemy's hidden layer, their seething forms forcing their way into and down the dark passage that would lead them to an easy slaughter. When Kladar surged out of the exit he found the guard's corpse crumpled on the floor of the cramped subterranean corridor it led to. No longer needing the expired disguise his superior had discarded it, disabled the barrier and then gone to find the quarry.

"Find them!" Kladar heard his master bark the order in the distance as he spearheaded the assault in a merciless release of fury. "Kill them all!" The torrent army of invaders now split their assault in an attempt to canvass the entirety of the unknown labyrinth, Galda's minions now flooding into the hallowed corridors like a plague of black locusts on a mission of devour and destroy. Galda hoped to find the remnant thorns in his side helpless and unprotected, their human bodies lying limp and pathetic in some sacred place. It was going to be an easy kill and he relished the notion as he soared from room to room to find his unsuspecting prey. The victory was his, and the immortality it secured, guaranteed.

*****

Before the death of his friend Jonah had injected an antiviral concoction of his own into the global network. Standing once more over the server's console he'd hoped to see its debilitating affect on the Elite's treacherous plans, but the red blanket smothering the global schematic on screen told him otherwise. The global prison of low frequency waves was eighty six percent complete. Near the entirety of the world's surface was being bombarded by the hazardous invisible barrage, humanity's own technology its source and the debilitating effects slowly increasing with each passing moment.

"Isn't something supposed to be happening?" Josh asked expectantly. He was tired, they were all tired, but there was still more to do.

"Give it time!" Jonah snapped, standing unaided as he leaned over to analyse the data schematics.

"We don't have any more time. In a few minutes they'll have a hundred percent coverage and the world will be populated by race of vegetables!" He hadn't heard Dex and Jonah's briefing of the server's purpose, yet somehow everything that had transpired in his absence was etched upon his psyche. Unfortunately the omnipotent insight didn't include a resolution.

"It took minutes for the virus to infect the thousands of networks worldwide, it's going to take just as long to cure it," Jonah explained uneasily. "I reprogrammed the viral kernel to hunt and neutralise their original viral signature and reintroduced it to the network. We have to wait until it's destroyed every trace, but even then that won't kill the transmission. I have to deploy a separate kill command for that from here."

Josh thought about the trauma the stealthy bombardment was inflicting on the millions of people around the planet. At the current rate of increase he estimated the intensity of the waves would reach a critical volume in less than a minute. At its current concentration the low frequency waves were not high enough to cause permanent harm to those exposed, he hoped, but unless Jonah could stop their swift progression his dramatic forecast would quickly become reality. Suddenly distracted by Saffy's absence he turned to see she had joined Angelica. Their leader's silence became more ominous when he saw her kneeling over Alpha's fading Ka.

The soldier's stocky projection lay limp on the cold metal floor, his waning form transparent enough for the mesh grids to be visible underneath. Angelica was holding his hand, nourishing his Ka with what she could spare from her own. Her look of despair foretold a lack of faith in its effectiveness and that the Deros onslaught had sapped his vital essence to the brink of destruction. After his blonde confessor heard his last muttered words she removed her grasp. In front of their eyes Alpha's projection slowly thinned before vanishing completely, taking the soldier's life with it into eternity. Angelica stood up from the vacant floor, leaving Saffy to stare despondently at the empty mesh grills where he'd lain. *Alpha dead.*

"How long have we got?" Angelica asked bluntly, Alpha's death prompting an awareness of their mortality. Josh sensed the profound dejection she hid behind her seemingly cool façade, but as the console beeped a signal it drew them from the emptiness of loss. This time Jonah's analytical interpretation was not required; the screen's projection of events was obvious to all. Coverage had reached one hundred percent. Josh gazed at the crystal blues eyes that, tinted with a new sadness, turned to meet his.

"The others are dead aren't they?" she asked Josh.

"They died fighting," he confirmed. Jonah, too engrossed in acts of sabotage, had not felt the desolation taking hold of Angelica. But suddenly it rained on him as the futility of their hopes wakened him to the unimaginable.

"And Kristos?" he asked, shaken by the unexpected horror.

"The Deros overpowered him, dragged him through a vortex to their world." Jonah turned his disbelieving eyes back to the console. "He destroyed himself, taking Them with him." Angelica's pale face showed a glimmer of endearment. To Josh she was no longer seemed the strong woman, but a child who had lost her father. Disparaging emotions aside it seemed their own Kas were slowly recharging. The detonation of Josh's solar blast had transferred some of its regenerative power into his colleagues, just as Kristos had done for him but too late for Alpha. In the post battle calm the four remaining members of Latronis were rekindling their strength, but confronted by an encroaching sense of doom and bereavement, were powerless to do anything more than watch and wait.

Out in the earth's surface millions of people went about their daily and nightly business, unaware a group of four were the only ones standing in the way of their impending enslavement. As the afternoon light faded on London its historic streets were grid-locked with a workforce of thousands making their way home for dinner. Across Africa armies of warring tribes continued their bloody campaigns, whilst in Beijing a subdued people were obediently asleep in preparation for the next working day. Back in Los Angeles an early Californian sun was warming the asphalt streets as its inhabitants worked, played, hustled and relaxed in the American dream. Yet one common denominator united then all; with every passing second their wills and minds were slowly and unwittingly being fried together.

*****

The frantic search had yielded no results. The underground layer of converted mineshafts was a maze of dead ends, empty storage rooms and empty bunks. Like an abandoned ship it revealed the recent presence of the enemy, but one that remained illusive. *They have to be here.* Each empty cell, room and passage was laid to waste as the army of Elite projections surged their way through every door to discover what lay behind. Tables and chairs were hurled aside in the excess of the fixated hunt that was nothing more than a rancorous campaign of search and destroy.

Galda passed the same quiet passageway adjoining the main corridor for a second time. With raging golden eyes he stared at the blast door at its far end. His fury was fuelling his ghoulish form, allowing him to forego the shades that protected his usual sensitivity. As they now locked onto the massive shield door he could see it was designed for only one thing, and that was to keep the likes of him out.

"They're here!" he snarled. He surged towards the impressive barrier. On hearing their master's call the Elite horde abandoned their own searches and swarmed into the passage in an immense concentration of dark power. Galda's assumption was correct. The heavy blast door was made of an alloy known to have a high frequency composition. Much like their alternating molecular portals it meant passing through without clearance was going to be an ordeal, but its existence meant the targets were close. Placing an ear to its thick shielding he could sense the benign presence of his enemies, their light energy resonating from behind, alluring like some sweet prize he would take pleasure in crushing vindictively between his hands. Victory it seemed was now only feet away.

To his side Kladar flipped open the security panel. Deciding he might save them the tribulation of breaching the door, the subordinate placed a cold white hand on the interface it revealed. As if roused from a slumber the black orb located at the centre of the door lit up and projected an analytical laser scan over the intruders. Before its suspicion was further roused Galda destroyed it with a powerful punch to its eye-like sensor. Reproaching Kladar with a devilish snarl he applied his hand to the blast door's alloy surface. Invoking his fearsome strength with images of unleashing it on the fragile bodies behind, Galda then began the difficult process of penetrating the formidable defence. Eagerly the Elite horde joined their Principal in placing their white intrusive hands upon the blast door, now combining their immense strength to weaken the alloy's composition like chocolate melting in a clammy grasp. As Galda felt his own hands begin to sink slowly into the cool metal he knew it wouldn't be long before he was through.

*****

Jonah's plan wasn't working. Saffy had joined him and Angelica to stare at the console screen, which continued to reveal the debilitating bombardment of microwaves was intact and showing no signs of disengaging. The red cocoon encompassing the global schematic remained complete and propagating to the point of no return. Frustrated by helplessness, Josh paced around the central pillar that housed the console, the monolithic black server now seemingly a veritable monument to their failure. As he came full circle and saw Angelica's anxious face he wished he could channel his new powers to destroy the morbid place, but it was already too late for that, its primary purpose had been served.

Angelica's sad glance checked his strides and then quickly returned to the console. In the low light she looked pale and haunted, like the diabolical hybrid corpses that still lay behind the onyx façades of each monolith. The parasitic spectres that had inhabited them had been destroyed, leaving behind the cadaverous mortal shells as hollow and inhuman testaments to the unholy agenda that was about to reach fruition. An irrational urge to see Angelica's striking features in the sun took hold, except within minutes even something so ordinary as a walk in the daylight was about to become futile. Back at the mirrored projection room of the Latronis layer he was sure their bodies would be safe from the destructive microwaves, but the idea of survival without ever surfacing to see another Californian dawn was now a daunting reality.

"It should have destroyed it by now," Jonah exclaimed. His eyes were glued to the screen, looking for the faintest sign of success. "But I can't be sure."

"This red barrier is the microwaves?" Saffy asked, touching the screen. "It's still complete, whatever you did isn't working!"

"The red only shows the extent of the low frequency torrent, not the presence of the virus," Jonah explained. "For all I know the antiviral code could have wiped the sucker out by now."

"So if it has you can stop this?" Angelica asked expectantly.

"That's my point. The global net has obviously been infected because the satellites and transmitters are blasting the crap out, but if I release a kill command to end all transmissions before the virus is wiped out, it will only spread again and we'll be back to square one!"

"So how the hell do you know when to send this kill command?" Josh asked, frustrated by the inert strategy.

"We don't," Jonah admitted, his desperate glance saying it all.

"You mean we wait until we can't no longer, then try it and hope for the best!" he exclaimed. At first Josh thought his abruptness a product of a brooding sense of doom, though quickly became aware of the niggling feeling that something else was escaping him. Without warning the cold blue illumination underfoot suddenly went out. For a moment they were drowned in a black void, before a low voltage back up was tripped to replace it.

"What just happened?" Angelica asked.

"That's impossible!" Jonah exclaimed as he busied himself once more at the server's interface. "It's locking me out!" His hands desperately punched commands into the Elite computer, but found they were thwarted at every turn. "The network is being locked down, I can't stop it!" Angelica watched as the spider web schematic of the server's global infiltration began to be systematically shutdown. One by one its parasitic strands were blocked in succession, its ties with the outside world cut like so many strings that would leave the server a lifeless puppet. Defensively Josh span around to scour the monoliths. But after projecting his heightened senses into each he discovered no lingering signs of dark energy, the Deros were dead and gone, leaving only one explanation for the latest stumbling block.

"It knows what you're doing!" Josh declared. "You've got to send the command!"

"Coverage is one hundred percent but the frequency hasn't reached its full intensity. We have to wait. We need to give my code all the time we can to disinfect the network!" Jonah explained frantically. He couldn't risk losing their final chance by jumping the gun. Josh rushed over to the console.

"It's shutting the net down! In a few seconds all the ports will be locked out and there won't be any way to relay the command."

"There's still time!" Jonah insisted. He watched on as the tentacles of the server's reach were being systematically severed. The Asia and the Far East nets were now totally inaccessible, their ports methodically disabled by the server's back up security protocol. As Josh had affirmed the server had been designed to act autonomously if it detected any momentous security breach, reverting to cutting off its own limbs to spite any attempt. Armageddon, it seemed, was to exist with or without its remaining in play.

A sudden explosion above their heads resulted in a large silver support arm falling from the vaulted ceiling. As it crashed harmlessly onto the mesh floor with an almighty cacophony of metal colliding with metal, they realised the entire chamber was suffering from the same cataclysmic protocol. Saffy ducked some displaced rubble that fell from the rock ceiling.

"Something tells me we've outstayed our welcome. Any chance we could get the hell out of here while we still can?" she quipped.

"If the Elite's virus isn't destroyed then there won't be an *out of here* to go back to!" Jonah exclaimed, his knuckles whitening as they clasped the interface. His eyes watched the read out showing the intensity of the microwave signature across the globe, pitting its lethal volume against the rapid loss of open ports through which to issue its destruction. The Europe and Africa grids were now lost, and the remaining ports across the Americas were quickly being locked down state by state.

Another explosion from above displaced two more metal ceiling supports and sent them crashing around them in a deafening clamour.

"Jonah we're out of time," Angelica yelled over the pandemonium. "Pretty soon there won't be any in here either!" A monolith, displaced by another falling support beam, crashed forward to mangle the mesh floor behind her. Josh looked from its tangle of life support tubes and fibre optics that sparked and dangled from its back like some upturned spider then, to the gaping entrance, Alpha had pummelled through the wall. Sparks rained across it from an overhead power cable that had been severed by another falling strut. Even if their superhuman abilities allowed them to dodge the falling debris indefinitely, it wouldn't be long before it filled every space and crevice to leave no sanctuary at all.

Josh remembered Alpha's death and Angelica's accompanying look of despair. He didn't know what would happen when his Ka was compromised by a fatal lump of rock or metalwork, perhaps it might explode dramatically like a dying star just as Kristos had done, or maybe it would fade pathetically into oblivion. Either way he guessed his body of flesh and blood back in the desert could not exist without it. He had watched Jonah's finger hover uneasily above the *Enter* key for the past couple of minutes. As a support beam shattered another monolith behind him, he decided to trust his instincts again.

"What did you just do?" Jonah cried out as he pushed Josh's hand away from the keyboard. The question was more disbelief than curiosity. He had just watched Josh punch the key that executed the command. Within less than a minute the satellites and transmitters of the deadly barrage would be disabled, but as the proverbial arrow shot wide into cyber space, Angelica joined Jonah in a look of mortification. Impatience might just have was a wasted last shot at victory.

"The virus is dead!" Josh yelled confidently.

Above their heads a deafening explosion stole away any reprimand. Though surrounded by a destructive chaos the latest explosion drew everybody's attention. The apex of the chamber's central pillar had erupted in a searing blast that was quickly followed by another more destructive secondary that showered it in a scorching rain of cauterised electrodes. As they backed away they watched it sever the life from the screen. The console was dead.

Jonah stared at the blank screen. The question of had they waited long enough had been answered. If he'd hung back for the final remaining ports fate would have stolen any chance to send the kill command. As it stood, Josh's shot in the dark was their only hope.

"We've done all we can," Angelica confirmed bluntly. A fresh hail of rubble and sparks caused her to duck, "We're leaving!" Jonah gave Josh a nod of appreciation, but there was no time for cordialities. A sequential barrage of potent blasts dislodged the central pillar's apex from the chamber's ceiling, opening up a fissure as its primary support was snatched away. As the destabilised pillar wavered under a fresh hail of spluttering wires and circuits the unsupported ceiling of rock began to fracture and disintegrate at an escalating rate.

Through a heavy rain of exploding electrodes and debris Angelica led the escape towards the gaping exit. Following Jonah and Saffy, Josh thought he heard a muffled laugh taunting the fleeing Nothoi. It was distant, perhaps a figment of the mind, but ended abruptly when a colossal piece of dislodged bedrock crushed a remaining black monolith.

The collision exposed the mangled remains of the hybrid's torso. As he turned his back on the abomination, the rest of the vaulted chamber suddenly collapsed in a horrendous avalanche of tonnes of bedrock, filling the chamber, crushing the treacherous technology and any hope of a Deros controlled world. Perhaps one of the gaseous creatures had survived long enough to instigate the final meltdown, but it no longer mattered. Death had reaped its final life in the God forsaken place. As the crushing dark replaced the blue light, sealing the chamber forever, the Elite's work of ages was destroyed along with it, or so they prayed.

*****

The blast door was now a malleable, writhing wall of outstretched hands and arms. Under the concentrated energy of Elite ghouls forcing their way into the formidable metallic barricade, its protective stability had been compromised quickly as they eagerly sought entry into the mirrored projection room. Feeling his fingers suddenly rip through the pliable, rubbery constitution of the one foot thick alloy, Galda Vey realised his prediction had been overrated. The sanctuary had been ruptured quicker than he'd anticipated.

A spear of light jettisoned through the breach, forcing Galda to shut his eyes. A moment's concentration caused the shades to return to his white face. Cursing his negligence he focused his strength into widening the aperture with a final push of his hand. Sensing their master's success, his surrounding minions jeered a devilish chorus of snarls and further enthused pushed onwards to emulate his success. Empowered by his own confidence in a swift victory, Galda now relinquished his humanoid form. Mimicking the pliable nature of the once stubborn blast door, he contorted his form to exploit the insecure entrance he had created. As though his Ka was comprised of living mercury he coerced its black form through the small breech, first one arm, then a shoulder, his head, followed by his fluid torso until his body slid through in a sinuous, serpentine motion that would make any human contortionist blush. As he planted his feet on the mirrored floor that lay on the opposite side his Ka reclaimed its previous humanoid glory. The light burnt his eyes, but the pain would not impede Galda Vey. Before long the light and the rest of his enemies would be no more, and the notion spurred him onwards into the furnace.

At first the mirrored floor caught him off guard. Galda thought himself suspended by some unexpected trickery, but upon seeing the inversed bodies that reflected directly below their fleshy counterparts, he recognised the visual illusion was part of the light refracting properties of the chamber. Behind him his army of rabid soldiers vied for second place. It had taken decades to create such a force, but finally its greatest accomplishment had been realised. The eerie canvas of writhing heads, hands and arms desperately sought to join their master, but none was strong enough to breech the stubborn barrier. *All mine.* When he stood at the right hand side of the secret masters as an equal, the legion of Elite Nothoi and Ascended Ones would have served the term of their usefulness and so to would join the rest of the world in oblivion.

As expected the Latronis members were still in their self induced slumber. Like a ritual gathering their bodies of flesh and blood comprised a sacred circle of defiance. But now they were at his mercy Galda smiled lasciviously. Only four Latronis members still lived. Seven men and a woman had collapsed from their seats onto the reflective floor. These he recognised as those whose Kas had been vanquished on the Leviscape, while the remaining few sat like deified statues on their silver stools at the circles perimeter, eyes shut and in the deepest trance-like state of a projecting Nothos. At the centre of the circle of conspirators the enigmatic leader's body remained in the wheelchair. Galda recognised the senior, long haired man as his nemesis and walked into the circle, savouring the precious sensation of power and destiny over which he was master.

He leant over to peer into the vacant blue eyes. Kristos's lifeless head was slumped back, his mouth gaping as he stared upward toward the domed ceiling. Galda picked up a lifeless arm and let it drop so that it made an assuredly dull thump against the chair's wheel. The Deros had taken their prize. *I win old man.*

Galda turned to gaze around at the various blank features of the fallen. He recognised some as those who had previously escaped his grasp and snarled with delight as he enjoyed the sight of their cold, dead bodies. His powerful army of blackened Nothoi, created by his own will, dedication and foresight had vanquished their benign Kas and he took pride in his handiwork. *Who is nothing now?* The remaining members of Latronis still upright and alive however were an enigma. Galda now rushed over to inspect their blank, entranced faces. Two he had never laid eyes on before and were unknown to him. The blonde woman he recognised as the thorn in his side called Angelica, he would enjoy her death, but it was the face of the last that drew his full attention.

Standing over Josh, Galda felt a renewed shard of hatred strike his black heart. His was the face Galda had hoped would spearhead the campaign to rid him of the Latronis curse, but now the traitor had fallen foul of his own weakness. Unsuspectingly the insecure Berkley graduate was a powerful Nothos. Moulded in the Principal's hands he would have been a high ranking Elite soldier. But neither he nor his black army were relevant now. With the death of the final four, Galda would have fulfilled his diabolical covenant.

He placed his white hands both side of Josh's slumbering head and raised it till it faced his own. Studying the blank, innocent features he imagined the unsuspecting Ka fighting its way into the Maryland base, believing itself a just victor, but with no idea its life was literally in the hands of the enemy. The inherently vindictive nature of murder urged Galda to destroy the servant of light. With a sadistic release of fury he would crush the fragile skull at his fingertips like a chocolate egg, bursting the soft eyeballs in the process by forcing his thumbs into the sockets and through to the frontal lobes of the brain.

"No single flame burns forever," he jeered at his mute victim. "Only the darkness that replaces its destruction is truly immortal." His two white thumbs hovered above the shut eyelids. "I could have taught you that Joshua if you'd let me. I could have given you the keys to creation itself! Instead, you will join the others in their understanding of death!"

To his shock Josh opened his eyelids, releasing an outburst of light that both stunned and blinded his would-be killer. As the brilliant flash erupted from the novice's eyes, Galda was caught in its defiant torrent of pure energy that enveloped him in a beam of divine judgement. *What is this?*

Grounded once more in his earthly body Josh had returned with the retributive power of light. Traversing the astral plain in flight from Maryland, he had sensed the cold hands of death about his Ka like a vice of icy steel. With a single thought he'd soared back to the subterranean projection room ahead of the others, leaving them behind in the Leviscape as his heightened consciousness brought him forth to release a destructive counter-strike.

Fury and fear rooting him to the spot, Galda forced his thumbs down to plug the two infernos below them. But instead of soft flesh they were checked by a scorching white heat that forced him to relent. The pain made him snarl furiously as the blinding astral light surged from Josh's eyes and threatened to obliterate the intruder's enraged countenance. Desperately Galda forced his hands together. The Brenin Nothos had to die; he had to crush the fragile features in his grasp. But like a Chinese finger trap the more pressure Galda applied, the more he failed. Dark was being neutralised by light, vanquishing the heart of his black strength to the point of oblivion.

"No!" Galda roared. The primal energy was flooding out from the mortal body, its serene features now a scorching coal between his hands. The discharge was filling the sanctuary, radiating from the two eyes, ever outwards like the birth of two new suns to sear his golden eyes and ghoulish skin. It was then the Elite Principal realised his mistake. Josh Brenin was no Nothos; he was the hidden light, pure, unadulterated, eternal, everything he had ever feared. He tried once more to drive his thumbs down, but it was already too late. "This cannot be!" As the words escaped his cruel lips the molten sun in his grasp exploded.

In a blinding instant dimensions were united across Creation. As the celestial torrent flooded the chamber, quantum parameters of real and unreal, physical and astral were eradicated as the eruption ripped the howl of terror from Galda Vey's gaping mouth. Josh felt it flowing from his sacred heart like an uncapped volcano, an unyielding ecstasy that now threatened to consume him body and soul. Through some disembodied vision he saw its shockwave rupture the blast door. Like a nuclear warhead it flooded the subterranean labyrinth, cleansing the shimmering corridors of the invasive Elite projections that shrieked in terrified unison as they were vaporised in its wake. Focusing his resolve he began to stem the torrent. If he didn't stop it then he feared he never would. Drawing it back to its source he screwed his eyes shut, sealing it within, dampening the coals of redemption that had ignited the divine inferno. When he opened them again, the demon Galda Vey was gone.

Back in the outside world the Principal's legacy lived. Angelica was staring up at a clear blue sky. As the sun warmed the fair skin of her face she wondered if a similar airborne radiation would soon affect her mind. Around her the decrepit shanty remains of White Rock mining community stood as an eerie monument to their dead leader, its once important utilization now a distant memory in its sun bleached panels. Jonah and Saffy joined her in the morning sun. Their projections had soared home to the deserted homestead through the astral vortex to rejoin their bodies on the west coast, but had remained above ground to witness the end of the world. The astral entanglement field that protected their underground layer would obstruct their entry anyhow. With the guard's absence suggesting he too was dead, their options had been limited.

No one spoke. The three Nothoi raised their faces to the morning sky and waited for the first signs of the debilitating low frequency bombardment. It would have no detrimental effect on their Kas. As long as their bodies remained safely below ground they were safe, and so they stood and waited morbidly on the parched ground outside the deserted bar. Angelica sensed Jonah's doubt. Everything relied on the success of his hacked anti-viral code, but without verification he feared the Elite malware would propagate faster than it could be exterminated. At first his melancholy manner seemed a lingering homage to the loss of his closest friend, instead she now recognised the same hollow feeling of failure within herself. Jonah's head suddenly twitched apprehensively towards her.

"What is it?" she asked nervously. He looked terrible, they all looked terrible. Weak. Fatigued. Ghosts. Their Kas were drained from the prolonged period of projection and battle, but they had to hold on. Jonah looked back to the sky, eyes closed.

"We should be able to feel something by now," he explained.

"Feel what exactly?" Saffy asked.

"Like your head's been put inside a microwave!" He opened his eyes to the skies again. There was no cloud insight, only blue perfection. He judged the time from the position of the blaring sun. "From the rate of the acceleration the torrent should have reached critical volume, we should be able to feel it."

"But if our Kas are immune to the microwaves then maybe we can't?" Saffy suggested impatiently. Angelica looked to Jonah for confirmation. Though their projecting forms were not comprised of flesh and blood, they were still receptive to anything detectible by the human senses and more.

"Maybe we can't!" he stated resentfully. Angelica shared his fear. For a moment she thought of the millions of people across the globe that were being lobotomised by the effects of the invisible bombardment that would slowly turn them into a race of slaves. The idea of projecting to the nearest city to witness the effects first hand turned her stomach. Failure it seemed was complete. Humanity would become a race of mindless robots and the world fall into darkness after all.

"Maybe it's already too late," Saffy exclaimed, confusing the sun's powerful rays as a parallel for the invisible barrage. "Maybe it's all over!" A voice from behind them suddenly affirmed her exclamation.

"It is!" it confirmed. They turned around to the bar's doorway to find Josh standing in its gaping entrance. No longer wearing the white attire of a projecting Latronis Nothos, he stood exposed to the air in a body of flesh and blood. "Looks like you did it, *Flyboy*," he congratulated a stunned Jonah. As he walked out into the morning sun, unimpeded by any low frequency microwaves they realised he confirmed their greatest hopes.

"We did it?" Saffy asked, hoping the cute guy in the T-shirt and jeans was not some cruel hallucination.

"Either that or the new boy had shit for brains before we started!" Jonah joked good naturedly. Angelica gazed with disbelief on Josh's earthly face. She expected him to suddenly curdle at any moment with a delayed reaction, but as they locked grateful eyes she tossed the fear away and wrapped her arms around him.

"We did it," she confirmed affectionately. Before Josh could enjoy the sweet embrace her Ka disappeared in his arms. With the entanglement field deactivated Jonah and Saffy quickly joined her. He knew all too well the relief they would feel as their bodies welcomed them back like long lost lovers, but the sight of their fallen comrades, lifeless on the floor of the mirrored chamber, would quickly dispel any appreciation. Josh closed his eyes and raised his face to receive the warm bath of solar rays. He was usually averted to such reckless sun worship, but that morning its heat rejuvenated his weary body and reminded him how good it felt to be alive. He thought it best to wait a respectful period before retracing his steps back onto the silver platform behind the dusty bar that would take him back down into the cool earth; they would need time to assimilate the overwhelming grief of their loss. But the battle had been won and the huge sacrifice had not been in vain. After so much darkness, he took the opportunity to appreciate the light in all its earthly glory.

*****

It took twenty three hours before the fevered control centres figured out how to reverse the black out. In a desperate rush the data and telecom networks had been reconfigured in round the clock shifts to make sure the world was united once more in an unseen global net, while miles above ground the puppet army of neutralised satellites orbiting the planet were reanimated to serve their rightful masters, who were now only just coming to terms with the extent of the tragedy that had been miraculously averted at the very last second. Across the planet media networks had been down for the duration, televisions and radios had hissed in the void of signals from parent transmitters. The technological lifeline that was the internet had also not been spared, while cell phones worldwide had simply reported a *network failure* to their millions of frustrated users. Jonah's kill command had worked perfectly. While the planet had punched monitors, televisions and fantasised about throwing their cells into brick walls, a small group of four hidden under the American desert had secretly rejoiced. Without adequate time Jonah's handiwork hadn't been specific, as result he had taken the liberty of depriving the world of every networked device to save the millions of lives of its end users.

Reactivated television networks reported the unexplained occurrence as akin to unfulfilled prophecies of the Millennium Bug, creating a media storm that swamped every newsreel for days. Conspiracy theorists and end-timers alike believed it the work of much more fiendish culprits, while behind the scenes the world's military intelligences recognised the hand of their assumed enemies and subsequently heightened security protocols. For once they were all right and wrong and the world remained in ignorant bliss.

The black book agency that held the enigmatic mantle of Project Olympia continued to receive funding for several months before a similar blackout of intelligence prompted investigation. The self contained cell had been so isolated from even the highest ranks of the security agencies that its existence was dismissed as folly. Only when a NSA liaison team despatched to safeguard its multi million dollar slush fund infiltrated the hidden base under the Sierra Nevada Mountains, were the hundreds of black clad agents found dead in the clandestine labyrinth; cause of death unknown.

In the following weeks where blame was passed from one spectre to another, no trace of the Elite virus ever reared its malicious head again. As a result the world and its unaware population was able to carry on where it had left off, with the exception of the world's legal systems, which now enjoyed a fruitful influx of lawsuits from beleaguered consumers and professionals suing for losses. Though humanity had been exposed to microwave frequencies on an unprecedented scale the duration had been insufficient to inflict long term trauma. Those academics that did record the extraordinary bombardment were told it had been a by-product of a hiccup and that safeguards had prevented any serious harm. The lie was met with scepticism, only helping to spur the gold rush of possibilities on internet conspiracy chat rooms. Like all immediate tragedies, the confusion and intrigue was destined to drown in the passage of time, just as the secret Maryland origins now lay buried under a kilometre of unstable bedrock. The human race would live on. The light had prevailed, though the darkness of apathy would continue to hold sway for some time.

Josh switched off the portable television set in his hand and dumped it into the crate at his feet. He had studied the media babble for days with a mixture of curiosity and amusement, but had finally grown tired of the obtuse speculations. If anything, it highlighted the futility of the media. For no one would believe his version of events, and his was the truth.

"Is that everything?" he called over to Angelica. Her footsteps thumped heavily across the dusty wood planks of the porch as she walked out of the bar carrying a bulging military hold all. Josh had helped her with the melancholy task of salvaging anything of worth from the Latronis layer and then to pack it into the back of the RV. Now concluding with her own possessions, she pushed the cumbersome holdall through the open rear of the large silver vehicle they'd nicknamed the Solarian, the sun chariot.

From the shelter afforded by the porch's incomplete overhang Josh watched while she and Saffy packed the past few years of their lives into the defunct mobile task vehicle. Half in half out the side door the vivacious Saffy finished packing a large parcel of food supplies from their ample stocks. Reluctantly they'd had to leave a considerable amount behind. Before ascending with the final load she and Angelica had tended the underground oasis for the last time. There was no intention of returning to White Rock in the foreseeable future and the idea of leaving the subterranean sanctuary to fend for itself had been disheartening but necessary.

Jonah meanwhile busied himself under the hood. His bronzed skin soaked up the hot sun as he tested the oil and topped up water and gas from the onsite pumps. The wear and tear of evasion and warfare had taken its toll on the bulky RV and he wanted to be sure it wouldn't falter on their return to the city. He had spent many hours fine-tuning the magnificent ten cylinder engine with Dex and he tried to honour his dead friend's memory as best he could. Sensing the end was near; Josh stood and picked up the crate at his feet to join them in the sun.

"Everything I own is in there," Angelica stated as she straightened to brush back the blonde hair from her face. Though renewed with rest, Josh sensed the emptiness that hung over soul. "I never realised how little that was until now." Josh slid the crate of miscellaneous electronic items inside and leaned into the shade of the interior.

"So what now?" he asked.

"Head back to the city, pick up a few things then catch a ride to Seattle," she replied matter-of-factly. After reaching in to retrieve a wad of fifty dollar bills from a coffee tin she caught his curious glance. "My family are still there," she explained. Counting off several hundred dollars she then returned the remainder to the jar, "A good a time as any to rebuild those bridges." She tucked the bills into her jeans and reopened a bottle of water. "Haven't seen them since mom and dad died, they're all I got now." While she swallowed thirsty gulps from the bottle Josh felt an emotional shortfall.

"And me? What happens now?"

"That's for you to decide," she replied, offering the remaining contents of the bottle. "The path ahead should seem a little clearer now." Raising the bottle to his lips he used the moments it took to drain it to figure out how to inject his feelings into the practical conversation. He liked her. He liked her a lot.

"And where will your path lead you?" Josh asked enigmatically, "After Seattle I mean." He hoped to hinder her agenda by invigorating any latent feelings. The RV shuddered as Saffy pulled the side door shut and returned to the bar.

"I'm just taking it a step at a time," Angelica explained with a chiding smile that insinuated his tone of disapproval had been noted. "One thing for sure we can't stay here. The Deros will find another way to manipulate this world, they always have. With any luck our kind will be waiting for them." The reminder of the hideous spectres grounded Josh's emotions. He had seen Kristos destroy the Deros in the black void. Hundreds if not thousands had been obliterated in the wake of his exploding Ka. But maybe Angelica was right. There was no way to be sure he saw every last one die in the searing shockwave of light. For the foreseeable future, he prayed, humanity was safe.

"I can't just go home after this," he grumbled, "Not after everything we've been through. All this," he gestured to the real world around them, "seems like the dream now. The only thing that remains real is what's left inside."

"Dreams exist in the place where light and dark meet. They link the material with the ethereal, they act as a bridge between this world and that which is yet to be." Josh gazed into the blue eyes and wanted to act on a growing impulse. "Don't you see? After this you can go anywhere and be anything! You are in charge of your own life; destiny is now a piece of cookie dough in your hand. Go back and bake some cookies!" Josh laughed at the metaphor.

"So I should become a housewife is that what you're saying?" he joked. The heavy thump of the closing hood boomed through the RV. "She's looking good," Jonah called out from the front of the vehicle. "Be on the road in the next ten minutes!" he hollered, and then walked off to lock up the large shack that served as the onsite garage.

"Who was it that said distance and ideology may divide us, but our dreams bring us together?" Josh asked with a renewed seriousness.

"I dunno," Angelica replied lately, "but it's true." She broke the awkward gaze by turning to rummage through the holdall. "You never did explain how you managed to kill that son of a bitch Galda Vey." Josh reeled at the name of his past tormentor. "Not that it matters," she added, feigning trivial interest. Though the subject had been avoided in the aftermath of the surprise victory, Josh had given it considerable thought and come to the conclusion it was best not to look a gift horse in the mouth. After all he was unsure what to make of the miraculous outcome himself.

"Luck?" he offered dismissively.

"Something tells me it was a little more than that," Angelica finished kneaded her clothes into the tight fit of the large green bag and gazed back. "One of these days you're going to realise just how special you really are Josh Brenin. *Luck*, as you put it, is simply fate without the assurances. I could see it. Kristos could see it. When you brush aside the veil of doubt you'll be able to see it also."

A large bird circled overhead. Josh couldn't make out what kind, but its flight path drew his gaze to the small derelict playground that been re-commissioned as a graveyard, its low white picket fence now enclosing the eight mounds of newly disturbed earth. Helping to bury their dead colleagues in the arid surroundings had been the hardest thing Josh had had to do. Working in the relative cool of dusk, it had taken several days for the remaining Latronis members to dig the deep holes in the barren earth. *Dust to dust.* Josh had tried to focus his attention on the job in hand, but it had been fraught with morbid thoughts of Sarah. Death it seemed haunted the living, only relenting, he thought, once you had joined the club. Angelica followed his gaze to the distant enclosure that shimmered in the desert sun. In time the desert would consume the humble memorials of makeshift plaques and claim the surrounding shantytown to leave no physical remainder of what had transpired. But the names of the fallen would be remembered, they would see to that. Her heartfelt eulogy had convinced him of the impending necessity of death as a doorway through which their true selves were set free. The chrysalis metaphor of escaping to emerge as something greater had seemed most appropriate. *There is no need to mourn the dead, only a life without faith in what we truly are.*

"I couldn't have done it without Kristos," Josh suddenly admitted. He watched the bird's dark silhouette drift off into the scorched distance. "I could feel him there with us." Josh remembered the powerful benign energy that had flowed through him at the critical moment. It had burst forth from his Ka like a breeched Levee, uncontrollable, but the force so divine in nature he had abandoned himself completely. He imagined it was something similar to what the Orthodox Church called Rapture, though doubted the term was ever meant to explain such an experience. It had been Kristos's power. The flaming torch had been passed onto him and he had wielded it and won. Josh placed a hand on Angelica's face and found her eyes revealed welcoming thoughts. "I couldn't have done it with you," he added, then leaned forward to kiss her. He found her soft lips accepted his upon them, though their reciprocating motion was brief. Josh leant back and gazed at the down turned eyes that suggested he had imagined her acceptance. "I'm sorry, I shouldn't have done that."

"Don't be," she replied sheepishly, before retaining her coolness with her raised blue eyes. "If there's something this world needs more of its love." She took his hand from her face and held it tenderly. "Love is the message of this crazy thing we call life, without love there is only death. Along with purity and truth, they're the only holy trinity worth living for."

"Maybe you're right. And maybe the world needs to hear more about it from us."

"I reckon so," she concurred. "But right now there's not room enough in your heart for me while it still belongs so absolutely to another." For a second he thought she was referring to Sharon, though before refuting her claim he remembered how he'd caught Angelica studying his brooding features while performing the duty of gravedigger. *It had been that obvious.* Josh smiled a bittersweet acceptance.

"Then sometime in the not too distant future, when the past has been laid to rest, maybe I could buy you a drink? As long as you promise not to follow me into the men's room and kick my ass!" Angelica smiled at the jibe.

"I'd like that," she admitted, "I'd like that a lot."

"Kicking my ass or the drink?"

"The drink, for now," she joked back.

"Five minutes people!" Jonah hollered abruptly across from the garage. He tugged the big corrugated iron doors noisily into place to pass the padlock through the rusted latch. Josh let Angelica's hand slip discreetly out of hers.

"Looks like it's time to hit the road," he said optimistically.

"For us yes, but for you there is a more important journey to make first." Angelica followed the strange statement by placing her arms around his neck and leaning forward to kiss him once more. The unexpected embrace was quickly reciprocated, but Josh soon realised the act of passion concealed a secret purpose.

The familiar head rush of excitement was accompanied by a disjointed feeling that separated the two lovers from the outside world. As the ecstatic sensation spiralled he realised they were leaving the desert surroundings behind as their Kas joined in an otherworldly existence. Before he knew it they were apart and he was staring again at Angelica as she stood a couple of feet away in the busy street, a mischievous smile on her lips.

"You see?" she asked loudly over the din of the passing traffic, "All you gotta do is use your imagination." The sudden change of environment left him stunned, but he recognised the downtown skyline across the way. The morning sun was rising over the downtown LA street and its streams of traffic to embellish the familiar ambience, though he knew it couldn't be real.

"Why have you brought me here?" he quizzed Angelica. She replied simply with a flick of the head, suggesting he look behind. He gazed back at the approaching traffic, and then recognised the silver car that pulled up to the curb beside him. The young attractive driver leaned over to call up through the open passenger window.

"Sorry I'm late hon, the server died and we lost last months accounts." Josh stared into the woman's face in disbelief, then grinned as he realised where he really was. He turned to thank his blonde guide, but she had already left to continue her own journey. "You okay?" Sarah asked, a little confused by her husband's strange behaviour.

"Yeah, I'm fine," Josh said. He opened the door and got in.

"You sure? You look kinda spooked."

"I missed you." Her face was warm to the touch; she smiled sweetly at the tender gesture.

"I dunno what's got into you, but I like it." Her hazel eyes sparkled with life and he realised she would always be there when he needed her. She would always be alive in his dreams, dreams he could now create and control like the cookie dough he had been promised. "So Cantonese or Thai?" she asked sheepishly.

"I tell you what," he suggested as he reached over to turn off the ignition. "Let's walk."

"You're crazy. It's over three blocks!"

"The walk will do us good. Trust me."

As they walked from the car hand in hand he still couldn't decide Thai or Cantonese, but it didn't matter he thought, he was hungry enough to have both.

Lightning Source UK Ltd.
Milton Keynes UK
01 December 2009

146960UK00001B/279/P

9 781907 203022